I0460548

Kenzi

Lee McQueen

1ˢᵗ Edition

McQueen♟Press
Chicago, Illinois

Kenzi

By Lee McQueen
Published by McQueen Press
info@mcqueenpress.com
www.mcqueenpress.com

About the Author
Lee McQueen has been both a librarian and bookstore owner. With a Master of Library & Information Science from SUNY-Buffalo, she indexes and abstracts, works with databases, and takes on research and writing assignments. She writes short stories, poems, novels, and screenplays.

This is a work of fiction. The names, characters, incidents, and locations are the products of the author's imagination or used fictitiously and are not to be construed as real. No character in the book is based on an actual person. Any resemblance to persons living or dead is entirely coincidental and unintentional. Rollins, TX is a fictional town.

Interior design and typesetting by Lee McQueen.

Logo registered mark of McQueen Press.

Copyright © 2007 Lee McQueen
1st Edition, 1st Printing
Printed in the United States of America

McQueen, Lee
Kenzi/Lee McQueen – 1st Edition

ISBN 978-0-9798515-2-0 (pbk)

Works by Lee McQueen

Short Story Collection

Imaginarium

The Dark Fantastic

Poetry

Things I Forgot to Tell You

Novel

Jeannie East then West

Screenplay

The Angel and the Lion

Kindred

Non-Fiction

Writer in the Library! (editor)

We didn't always have what we wanted.
But we had what we needed.

For Emily and Lula

Chapter 1

Kenzi

If Kenzi only knew where the joy and pain of her new life would take her, she would hold her head up high and throw her shoulders back. She would look that life directly in the eye and say, "Bring it!" And when life brought it, she would gladly take it and live it. But until that time, her today was just like her yesterday. But the change *would* come. And thank God for His mercy.

Thin, silver wires twisted, winding around blown glass shaped into three separate spheres of green, blue, and violet hanging from a larger chain. Late September afternoon sunlight shone through the plate glass window. As the sculpture turned from invisible drafts of air, the walls and the floor danced with jeweled color.

Kenzi looked down from the top of the bookstore's ladder. "This is the last one, Stacy."

"For now. Once my fellow artists get a feel for the place, you won't have room to hold it all."

Kenzi ran her hand through fourteen inches of cottony soft, dark brown curly afro. "I hope you're right." She flashed a wide, dimpled smile between prominent cheekbones and glanced down at Stacy. "Thanks so much for being the first to give Kinfolk Books a try. These watercolors are beautiful!"

"Gallery space is so expensive in Rollins, you know. I'll give everyone else a chance, but after a week, I'll bring some more pieces if it's okay."

"Stacy, you know your work always has a place here."

Kenzi first met Stacy when she stopped into the local graphic art studio and print shop to create a poster for Kinfolk Books about six months ago. Back then, Kenzi felt uncertain and somewhat uneasy about her very first business. As the sole proprietor, responsibility for Kinfolk's image fell squarely on her shoulders.

Thankfully, Stacy created simple, sleek designs that reflected Kenzi's own personal style. And now, while they finished going through the other art submissions, Stacy's bubbly, extroverted personality provided a necessary complement to Kenzi's quiet reserve.

"Someday, I want to open my own. It's just a matter of scraping the money together. But I'm making my plans."

But with the store's grand opening less than sixteen hours away, Kenzi barely listened as she tested the sculpture's hook with a slight tug.

"You know, I've been hearing a lot of good feedback about your classes. People are really excited about you introducing art and culture to their children."

Stacy reluctantly put her dream of the future aside to focus on the present.

"I know. I've been getting a lot of phone calls and emails myself. Who knew?"

"Think you can give all those new-fangled electronic gadgets a run for the money?"

"We'll soon see." Stacy tightened her hold on the ladder. "How is it?"

"Just a second." Kenzi got a better grip on the sculpture's chain. "They're starved. We're all starved. These children are passive receivers of corporate advertising disguised as entertainment. Time to turn it off, girl! All the radio, television, and computers… at least for a little while."

Still high up the ladder, Kenzi noticed a flatbed truck pulling up to the curb across the street out of the corner of her eye.

"All that high energy going to waste. But still, you're gonna have to step into the newer age, Kenzi. Try the hook again."

"Are you still on me about coding HTML?" She laughed as she fiddled with the hook. "Back to the kids! Instead of celebrating the next Varnette Honeywood or Frida Kahlo, we're erasing graffiti and repairing vandalism at the public schools. Our precious little darlings tattoo and pierce themselves trying to say something to whoever's listening. And if no one listens then they create a new and improved Heaven out of chocolate-flavored ecstasy. A whole new world." She paused and looked over her shoulder. "Do you have the label?"

"Okay. In other words, go kids!" Stacy's laughter rose as she bent down and scrounged through a box full of scrap paper.

"Oh yes, indeed!" Kenzi's gaze drifted again towards the truck parked in front of Organic Soul. Large plants filled the flatbed. "I already set up the room and I've got extra supplies in case one of the children can't afford them or they forget to bring them."

Those plants are beautiful. She sighed. Kinfolk's storefront appeared plain in comparison.

"Still, I'm going to ask each child to maintain their own supply kits and to keep a portfolio of all their drawings together. It's one way to teach responsibility and pride in the creative process."

"Maybe I can hang a few pieces of their work along side the local artists. Did you find the label? I know it should be in there." Kenzi stared out the window.

A huge man, not fat, but just *large* hopped light as a feather into the back of the flatbed and unloaded the plants. He had to be over six feet tall with an enormous trunk, big arms and big legs that filled out his t-shirt and jeans. Even through the worn denim, she could see his muscles stretch long whenever he bent down and then bunch together as he pushed himself upright holding a plant. His smooth skin reflected the sunlight. But he did not perspire from the exertion. He gleamed. Kenzi's stomach began a hum that traveled down both legs and then up to both arms.

"You sure you made one?" Stacy looked up shaking reddish-brown, curly hair from her face.

"Made one?" Kenzi quickly glanced down frowning to remember what she and Stacy talked about. "Yeah. I made it this morning."

Stacy shook the box and searched again. Kenzi noted with approval that the man lifted with his giant legs and not his wide-shouldered back.

It would be a complete shame to damage that body. He walked off the edge of the flat trailer hitch, took a quick step, and then bent to place the plant to the left of the door in line with the other five. Just one more plant remained to make three on each side.

What on Earth was Stacy talking about? Kenzi frowned not wanting to miss the last plant!

"Um, I'm looking for it. Wait, what is…" Stacy sighed with exasperation as she held up the label. "It was right here in front of me."

Kenzi turned back to her friend with a guilty start. She'd kept the symmetrical, well-built eye candy to herself. A black band at the nape of his neck tied back the locs that hung down to his shoulders.

"This guy is really good." Stacy prattled on as Kenzi attached the label. "We attended art school together."

Another quick glance through the window showed the big guy stroking a broom back and forth on the sidewalk. Kenzi knew her business neighbors only slightly. The preparations for the launch kept her busy with a whirlwind of painting walls, vacuuming the carpet, unpacking books and supplies, and supervising contractors. On the left of Kinfolk sat Baby Things, a shop that sold accessories for infants and toddlers, run by a plain-spoken, middle aged widow. To the right, sat Oliver Drugstore. And across the street, where Big Guy finished his work, sat Organic Soul.

She and Stacy finally finished. Kenzi cleaned up the hammers, nails, screws, hooks, and other accessories while Stacy called back over her shoulder carrying the stepladder to the back room.

"So is your aunt driving down from Dallas with Miss Betty?"

Miss Betty, Kenzi's mother, repeatedly told Stacy to just call her Betty. Stacy told her she couldn't do that because she was always taught to respect people…

"Older than you, huh?" Betty baited her.

"Nope. Wiser."

"Ah, good one, Stacy." Betty laughed. "I see you know how to handle yours."

"Yes, ma'am!"

Kenzi took advantage of Stacy's trip to the back of the store to check outside the window again. He stood with his back facing her studying his work. *Nice job.* She stood a little straighter to study him as she finally replied, "Ahh. Nope. My aunt won't make it. We're not close, remember? It's just my mother coming down. She should be on the road right now. Hopefully she's not running into too much traffic. Dallas highways are ridiculous on Friday afternoons. Everybody trying to escape the madness."

"That's cool you're gonna have some extra help." Stacy bounced back to the front with a smile.

Kenzi forced herself to look away from the window. "Oh, I know. Tell me about it. I was so glad she offered to help out because I hated to ask. She's spending the night tonight and we're gonna come to the store early tomorrow to get set up. She'll probably stay Saturday night too because I'm sure we'll both be exhausted after it's all over."

"Sooo," Stacy drawled significantly. "Has your mother met Franklin yet?"

Kenzi shook her head. "Girl, please. I don't need for her to get excited about something I'm not even sure about myself."

"What are you talking about?" Stacy said, puzzled. "You guys go out and spend time, right? You're saying it's not serious?"

Kenzi sighed. "I'm saying I show up and, basically, so does he."

"Girl, stop!" Stacy laughed and leaned against a shelf.

"Do I know where I'm going to?" Kenzi's laugh ended in a gasp. "Careful! You break it, you bought it!"

Stacy set the vase she almost knocked over further back on the bookcase closest to the check-out counter. Kenzi chanced another quick look across the street. She felt a pang of disappointment as if someone had just snatched away her favorite toy and returned it to the toy box. Both the man and the truck were gone. *Oh well.*

"Well, girl. Let me go and get my-own-self organized. Good luck, okay? And get something to eat. You always get involved in something and forget. I do not need you to fall out in a faint here all by yourself. Get something to eat!"

"Good idea. I better. I'm actually feeling a little light-headed now." *But not totally from hunger.* While Stacy gathered their purses, Kenzi walked around the store shutting off lights and equipment.

"I'm gonna try Organic Soul," she said casually. "I haven't had a chance to eat there yet since I've been so busy here. I heard good things about them from Miss Lydia next door at Baby Things. I met the owner. They'll bring snacks in the morning and the afternoon for the opening."

From Miss Lydia, Kenzi learned in one sitting that Organic Soul evolved as an independently-owned and family-operated restaurant that served traditional Southern cuisine, better known as soul food, and Sri Lankan dishes for nearly four years. She remembered hearing about the restaurant vaguely around the university campus where she used to work, but it didn't lie on her path home or on any of the paths she usually crossed in her day-to-day life so she missed out until she found the bookstore's location.

Finally done fiddling around, Kenzi set the store's alarm. "My understanding is it's got kind of a high energy vibe. International students and faculty. Cowboys and truckers. You know the usual around here. I guess good food has a way of bringing people together."

She picked up her purse and looked back at her first small business with a sigh of accomplishment. "After all that research and surveying, I'm glad Tex helped me to locate the bookstore across the street from them."

Kenzi glanced around the store vaguely.

"Kenzi." Stacy stood with her hand on her hip.

"What?"

"Kenzi! I'm gonna stand right here and make sure you actually go over there and get something."

"Okay, okay. I'm coming!" Kenzi laughed and wiped her hands on her jeans. "I just love looking at the store. I almost can't believe it's really happening." They stepped outside into the golden haze of late afternoon sun together.

"See you tomorrow then. Ten o'clock?"

"Ten o'clock!"

Inside Organic Soul, Ray glanced across the street to the new bookstore and saw two women, one fair and plump, the other brown and medium-sized... but curvy, he noticed looking a little more closely. They hugged and the fair woman walked away while Brown Curves locked the door.

The space across the street next to Miss Lydia's Baby Things stood vacant for as long as he could remember. If Brown Curves was with... Kinfolk, he read the sign to himself, then that might raise more than the quality of life.

She stopped at the edge of the curb to check traffic. He automatically looked both ways too. She bounced off the curb with a toss of dark brown hair that rose like a cloud to frame her warm, brown face. Her hair pointed in every direction. It reached for the sun that made it sheen and waved to the wind that caused the curls to beckon. Her coils pointed at the trees, the birds, and people passing by. Her hair pointed at him too and he felt a *zing* of anticipation streak through him.

She turned her face slightly upward with a wide smile. And then he saw her almond-shaped eyes as she approached closer. Whenever the sun touched her eyes, they turned from clear brown chocolate to golden honey and then back to chocolate. Chocolate, honey, then chocolate again.

"Dharma, she's the owner of the new bookstore, right?" Ray didn't turn his head.

"Yeah, we're catering for Kinfolk tomorrow. I met her a couple of days ago when she stopped in here. She's nice. You'll like her, *Raman*." Dharma smiled mischievously.

Kenzi walked into a warm peppery, spicy smell blended with something sweet and citrusy. Voices chattered and plates clattered. The after-work and after-school rush continued in full swing.

Her stomach growled loudly. To the left she saw fried plantains and fried okra sharing a plate with avocado and tomato salad flavored with garlic and onion dressing. To the right, she saw black-eyed peas and the ever-present curried or steamed basmati rice.

She saw rice as the main dish served in a mixture of squash, apples, raisins, onions, ginger, and sunflower seeds. Shock-to-the-system sweet deserts like blackberry cobbler and pecan pie alternated with fresh fruit and sweet potato custard and rice pudding served with exotic teas, coffee, or coconut milk. English, French, and Spanish shouts rose from the steamy kitchen. Low mutterings of Japanese, Chinese, French, Hindu, Arabic, and slow-drawled southern American English punctuated by occasional laughter rose in the dining room.

Kenzi spotted Dharma across the room and waved. Her skin tingled. Her eyes widened and her stomach gave a nervous leap. That strange pulse coursed through her and she felt herself grow warm. He scrutinized her as closely as she scrutinized him earlier. Through a plate glass window from several yards away, he created a strange reaction. Here, in the same room, however, she actually had trouble breathing.

"Hey Kenzi! How you doing?"

"Good, Dharma! Very good. Getting this show on the road."

"Yeah, I've been seeing a lot of coming and going out your front door. I told myself, they're about to set it off across the street! Oh, this is my brother, Ray. Ray, this is Kenzi." No surprise there, Kenzi thought, Dharma and Ray looked nearly identical.

He dominated the room. Even his large hair dominated. Locs coiled and twisted into ropes of long black hair that lent him a regal, kingly appearance. Like Samson. And if he were Samson, then who was his Delilah?

Out of nowhere, a young girl about seven or eight bounded up to Ray and wrapped her arms around his waist. She threw back her head with its two symmetrical curly French braids and giggled as he laughed with her. There didn't seem to be any joke, just happiness to see each other.

Her little pretty face had the same family resemblance. Smooth dark skin and black brows and lashes surrounded her sparkling eyes. She was a bursting ball of energy in a little red sundress. Ray could have given birth to her by himself she looked so much like him.

But Ray's personality radiated stillness and calm. Kenzi wondered if the child's energy existed as a legacy of her mother. *Delilah?* Kenzi tried to not peer around too curiously. Underneath Ray and Santi's excited chatter, Kenzi placed her to-go order with Dharma.

"Daddy! I saw you moving the plants!"

"I thought you were gonna help me lift them, Santi!"

"*Daddy*, they're too big! I'm a little girl."

"But I'm old!"

"You're not old!"

"Yes, I am. I'm an old, old man. And, by the way, I give you all the piggy-back rides. You never give me *any*."

They all laughed at Ray's mock wounded expression. Kenzi liked the way his total attention focused on the child as he waited for her to respond to the banter.

"Daddy, cause you're too BIG!"

"Okay. Then Auntie Dharma can give us both a piggy-back ride. How about it Dharma?"

"Forget it! Don't even try it you big ole bear!" Dharma crossed her arms as she returned from the kitchen.

"I meant one at a time, Dharma. Not together."

"No!"

"You're too BIG, Daddy!"

Charmed by them, Kenzi felt the familiar pang of longing she thought she'd finally buried after accepting her father's total lack of interest in her as a human being. What a lucky little girl! And what an even luckier man. He obviously thought the world of Santi and he smiled down at her whenever she spoke.

As for Santi, she gazed upward to her father in complete adoration as if he had become an action superhero flown in to save their day. *I wish I knew how that felt.* And with a start, she realized she didn't know whether she meant how it felt to have a father look at her that way or for Ray, himself, to look at her with the intense stare and full lips curving into a smile. *Sheez! I obviously have more issues than any magazine rack.*

As if he heard her thoughts, Ray focused his dark gaze on her and Kenzi felt a pulse of excitement. "Santi, this is Ms… Sorry, is it Mrs or Ms? Or Miss?" He seemed slightly mocking. Her stomach made a funny leaping sensation. She felt annoyed with the fact that she felt very relieved to be single.

"Either Ms or Miss is fine."

Kenzi smiled and shrugged. But she didn't miss the speculative gleam in Ray's eyes before he turned again to his daughter.

"Santi, this is Miss Kenzi. She's going to run the bookstore across the street."

Santi stared shyly a moment before she held out her hand still leaning against her father.

"So nice to meet you, Santi."

"Nice to meet you, Miss Kenzi."

"Do you like to read?"

Santi nodded.

Ray's low voice rumbled a baritone, "I read her stories at bedtime and sometimes she reads too."

Santi looked up at her father and smiled as she vigorously nodded her agreement again. Kenzi added her nods of approval as well. They all agreed, then, on reading.

Dharma spoke up. "We also have a brother named Dhan. He attended Prairie View and now he's at Rice working on his MBA. He drives up from Houston once in a while. You'll meet him soon."

"Yeah, you'll meet him when he drives up for a free meal and to do his laundry!" Ray and Dharma laughed.

"Or a free book, Kenzi." Dharma winked.

"Yeah, right!" Ray snorted

Kenzi laughed along. Ray's turned full attention to Kenzi's smile. He didn't miss the slightest nuance of her expression. "So is it just you running the store? No partner?" He caught her off-guard.

Kenzi felt her face grow warm as she replied in a light tone, "Nope. Just me. I'll get help from my family once in a while though." She shifted.

Along with the still personality, Ray had a way of just staring straight into her eyes that made her a little nervous, specifically, because her body reacted to the attention. Kenzi cleared her throat.

Dharma, broke in. "So we're still on for tomorrow?"

"Definitely!" Kenzi appreciated the rescue. They discussed her catered order for the bookstore's opening. Ray and Santi drifted to the side as he asked Santi about her day at school.

"And then what did you…"

Kenzi felt his voice rumble over the chatter of other diners. His voice echoed and resonated inside her. She could almost feel the soft stroking of the air from his mouth on her skin. Which seemed silly since he stood several feet away. Even so, while she spoke with Dharma, she felt his gaze slip over her from top to bottom and then back to the top once in a while.

"Oh! Your food's ready!"

Once again, Dharma rescued her. Kenzi smiled her relief as she held the to-go orders stacked one on top of the other.

"Bye Miss Kenzi!"

"Bye Santi! It was so nice to meet you."

"Bye Kenzi. Good luck tomorrow. And congratulations."

"Thank you so much, Dharma. I am so glad I stepped in here. Your restaurant is just terrific."

And again, the deep voice rumbled across her and the dark gaze stroked her. See you around."

She felt a quick, hot sensation all of a sudden. It sounded like he meant so much more. What was he doing? Why did she feel so strange around him?

"See you." She paused for a brief second. "By the way, you have a lovely daughter." She smiled and looked directly at Santi, "I certainly hope you can stop in sometime. We have a wonderful children's section you might want to look through."

Santi rewarded Kenzi with a beautiful smile again.

"Thank you, Miss Kenzi."

As she took her leave from Organic Soul, all plans for tomorrow confirmed, she felt a strange tingle and buzz crawl up and down her spine. She felt little prickles under her arms.

She knew he still watched her. She felt it. She did a quick half turn swinging her massive hair and twisting her waist. Sure enough, he stood motionless behind the lightly tinted glass, not even pretending to politely look away.

He met her gaze with dark obsidian eyes. He remained still as a beautiful ebony statue. She felt a quick flutter in her stomach. The tingle grew warmer.

She felt… naked.

She clutched at the to-go plate making sure not to drop it or to trip and fall in front of that relentless stare.

Just minutes later, Betty Malton pulled up to Kinfolk Books in her old sedan. Like Kenzi, Betty had cheekbones sharp enough to cut paper. Her African slave ancestors fled to Texas from Louisiana, Mississippi, and Arkansas to live under the freer authority of the Spanish, French, and Mexican rulers of Texas. And those newly freed men and women fled once again to Native American tribes when the war to maintain slavery in Texas jeopardized their uncertain futures. Many marriages and descendants later, the prominent cheekbones remained a stubborn family trait that refused to dilute through the generations.

Betty entered the store with, "Oh my baby's grown up and got her own store now!"

"Ga ga goo goo, Mom," Kenzi hugged her.

Betty laughed.

"Mom, do you think if my father could see me now, he would be proud? Do you think he ever thinks about me? Or about us?"

Betty loved Kenzi but hated these questions about her father. How do you define the indefinable? Betty never had the words to explain her ex-husband to her daughter and so answered as well as she could, with reassuring nothingness. Kenzi stopped asking. Ten years passed since Betty last searched her mind for words of comfort and reassurance regarding the ghost and shadow that had Jonathan become.

But Kenzi grew too old for soothing nothings. Although Kenzi never went into too much detail (thankfully, sparing her from clutching the pearls), Betty sensed that her daughter had already experienced life full of its bright lights and lowlifes.

"Kenzi, what brought this on? You haven't asked about your father in years."

"I know. I preferred to forget about him since he preferred to forget about me. I just… I don't know…"

She gazed wistfully around the store.

"I mean, I was across the street and met the owners of the

restaurant. It's a family restaurant, right? And there was a man with a daughter there who was just beautiful and so happy. When I looked at them together, I could tell they meant the world to each other. They not only loved each other, they actually *liked* each other. And I just wonder why... I just... I just don't know how my father could pretend that I never existed. How could someone do that to a child?

Betty looked pained.

"Oh Mom, I'm sorry! I really am sorry. I didn't mean that you didn't do a good job. I didn't mean it like that! You've been a great mommy. I know you did the best you could. And, of course, if it were not for you, I wouldn't be here right now."

Betty smiled sadly at her daughter.

"Kenzi, you don't have to apologize for how you feel to me. Sometimes, I don't think you realize who you really are and what you mean and the effect you have on people. Look around you. Look at this store. Look at all that you have accomplished in life. Think back. Really think back, Kenzi. I stood there at your graduation and cried my eyes out when you waved to me and smiled from the stage. It was the highlight of that entire decade to see you shake that man's hand and take your diploma."

Kenzi blinked rapidly. "Mom, to tell the truth, sometimes I wondered if you paid any attention."

Back then, Betty worked long hours at a full and part-time job to keep the various roofs over their heads. Kenzi had her own part-time job and school activities that kept her coming and going from sun-up to sundown. They saw each other mostly in passing as she grew into a teen and then wandered off to college.

Betty laughed slyly. "Kenzi, I'll bet you didn't know that I stopped by your school on my lunch break from time to time. I'll also bet you didn't know I kept schedules of your classes and called your teachers to see how you were doing."

"You're kidding. Tell me you didn't do that."

Betty raised her eyebrows.

"When?"

"All through junior high and high school."

"So how was I doing?"

"You showed up for class. You did your work. No problems other than you didn't dress for gym class a few times. The gym teacher told me about that. So yes, baby doll. Mother paid plenty attention."

"Okay, you got me. I couldn't stand gym class."

"You went on to college. You traveled… met people from around the world. Got professional experience. Learned various languages. You've done things that most people only imagine or see in a movie! Now sometimes I did worry about you. Look at these gray hairs, Kenzi.

Mother!" Kenzi groaned.

"I always knew you would be okay because you have a good head on your shoulders. But still a mother does worry!"

"Yes, indeed, a mother does worry. Look, I'm sorry, Mom. I didn't mean to cause stress. I guess I just wanted to find out who I was supposed to be."

"I know, Kenzi. I know. I understand. But do you know now? Do you have it all figured out?"

"Well, I'm still working on it," Kenzi laughed. "I do feel that I'm getting closer to the answer. This store is the hardest thing I've ever done in my life and we're not even open yet. But I do feel that all the paths I've chosen in life led me here. I feel right about this. It feels good to me. It's difficult, but I like the challenge. It means a lot to me and I'm so glad you supported me all the way."

Betty nodded thoughtfully.

"You sound very sure."

"Well, I'm not *exactly* sure, to tell the truth. But I'm sure that I feel good about Kinfolk Books. I can see myself doing this for a long time even if I'm not getting paid. Um… which I'm actually not. I'm forgoing a salary for the next year to reinvest in the store."

"Well, one must do what one must do."

Betty hesitated.

Kenzi, familiar with that hesitation, sighed and braced herself for the transparently casual tone that followed.

"Soooo… Anyone special in your life?"

Kenzi looked away in confusion. Because well-dressed, well-groomed, closely-cropped-hair Franklin did not float through her mind. Instead, she saw a tall large dark man with long flowing black locs that begged to be stroked and enormous arms that...

"Kenzi?"

"Oh sorry! N-Not really. I've gone out a little. But nothing really serious. Work and research for tenure at the university always took up most of my time before. And now, the bookstore's going to require my total focus."

"Ummm."

"Yeah, I know. Me too. Sorry Mom." Kenzi laughed. "I guess I've got it together in some areas more than others."

"Oh, give it time child. Just do what needs to be done. And speaking of that," she gathered up their now-empty plates, "Let's get this party started!"

Betty made a few suggestions. "Put this here." They moved furniture. "Let's put these over here." They stacked up paper. "Now we need to straighten this and this." They fixed a few signs.

"I wanna side order of fries..." They walked amongst bookshelves as Betty pretended to be a customer making hilarious requests. She threw up her hands. "Whaddaya mean you don't have milkshakes? Gimme a milkshake!"

Finally, they called it a night.

"Kenzi, just leave the bike here. I'll drive us to your apartment." So Kenzi left the bike hooked to its cart, her usual mode of transportation. She locked up the store and they left.

While Betty relaxed from the drive down from Dallas, Kenzi washed her hair and blew it dry on low heat. Then she and Betty twisted its fourteen-inch length into long rope coils that just barely touched her shoulders.

"Lina's coming down tomorrow." Betty's tone seemed neutral.

"Lina who?"

"Lina, your cousin. Who else?"

"Oh." Kenzi felt a momentary pang of dislike followed by curiosity. "That's weird. I always thought she didn't like me." She paused. "How did she know about the store anyway? I don't think I've talked to her in years."

Betty responded somewhat defiantly, "She knows about it from me. I saw her at the mall a couple of days ago. You know she's a hairdresser out there. I told her about the store."

"Mother, why would you do that?" Kenzi almost didn't want to know the answer. "By the way, you don't even live close to the mall. You don't like the mall. Why were you there?"

"Kenzi, it's high time that you and Lina find a way to get along with each other. Start acting like cousins. Not enemies."

"Well, what about you and Aunt Jalissa?"

"Kenzi, this is about you and the store and Lina coming down to help. Not me and not Jalissa."

Kenzi gave up. "What did she say?"

"Kenzi, she… said… she's… coming… down… tomorrow." Betty tapped her head lightly with the comb.

"I still can't believe you invited her down here without asking me first. Is she coming down to help or to hate?" *God, I can't stand her.*

"Kenzi, stop!" Betty laughed. "We'll see. At least, give her a chance to do something right."

"Well, I guess I can use all the help I can get." Kenzi sighed.

"True. Lean back a little." Betty gave a slight tug.

Kenzi felt like a little kid. Her mother parted and twisted her hair. But soon her thoughts gave way to the very adult vision of a man with well-shaped, muscular arms that looked like steel covered by black velvet. She wondered how those arms would feel wrapped around her, the hands clutching her hair, pulling her head back.

Chapter 2

Ray

Santi chattered all the way home as their rusty, dusty, trusty pick-up rattled down the long, dirt drive leading up to their house.

"Daddy, did you hear her say I could look at the children's books?" Santi asked him this three times already.

"Yep, I sure did, sweetheart." Ray remained patient.

"Can I?"

"Can you what?"

"Can I go over and look at the books?" Santi unbuckled her seatbelt as the truck rolled to a stop.

"Oh yeah." Ray opened his door.

"When?"

He heard Santi's question as he walked around to help her down.

"Well, it's gonna be open tomorrow."

"Can we go tomorrow?" Her voice piped insistently. Santi liked to have things spelled out and confirmed.

"I'm going to be working hard tomorrow, sweetheart. Lots of deliveries at the restaurant. But I'll bring you with me later in the afternoon once the work slows down. Okay?"

"Yay!" Santi danced a little jig holding his hands. "Can I take Miss Kenzi some flowers, Daddy?" She beamed up at him hopefully.

Ray smiled down at her. He had the most difficult time with Santi sometimes. He never liked to tell her "no" and she knew it. Fortunately, he had his sister, Dharma, and Aunt Tilly to help coach him along whenever "no" had to happen. But he could compromise now.

"Tell you what. Dharma said she would give Miss Kenzi some plants. You can take those over, okay?"

"Okay. I'm gonna bring some plants, plants, plants!" Santi danced a little, pleased with the idea.

Ray thought about Santi's mother and felt the familiar sadness and hurt. *Darlene missed out on this sweet, beautiful girl.*

Raman Grant or Ray, as he preferred, did most of the heavy lifting and equipment installation for Organic Soul. A carpenter by trade, he did contract work around town. While outside work remained seasonal due to heavy winter rain, he managed to stay busy with a full schedule of indoor electrical and plumbing jobs. Fortunately for him, he enjoyed what he did for a living. He loved the satisfaction of completing a task and seeing the result right before him. He had the benefit of many referrals. He also did heavy work on the family home where he, Santi, Aunt Tilly, and the family dog, Jackson lived.

He kept the long coal-black, luxurious, well-groomed locs almost always tied back in a black band. Six feet, three inches tall, his well-built frame revealed tight musculature from the amount of labor he did daily. Intense, dark brown eyes seemed even more so with two dramatic heavy black brows that gave him a mysterious and rather rakish appearance. His looks attracted a lot of female attention. But a hint of sadness and guarded caution shadowed his eyes. Those eyes neither encouraged nor promised long-term commitment. The quiet air and the weight of responsibility combined with the raising of his only child tended to thwart even the most determined of female ambitions.

His soft-spoken baritone might have made him a target for those who mistook quiet for weak. But his large size and intense stare accompanied by a low, measured, deliberate voice served to intimidate whenever circumstances deemed it necessary. Because of his father's discipline, he raised his voice only when provoked to the extreme. And he raised his fists only as a last resort. He loved his family, particularly Santi, intensely.

"Hey Jackson! What've you been doing all your life?"

He got Jackson as a puppy from the local animal shelter for Santi after Darlene's abrupt departure from their lives. Santi had seemed so sad and confused. His heart ached for her. He'd gone to the shelter promising himself that he'd just look at the dogs.

The sight of the orphans made him think of his own beautiful mother who'd died just as he reached twenty-one followed the next year by his father. At least his parents were together now.

He didn't even notice the little black Labrador, at first. Rather than leaping about and wriggling and excitedly barking at the new visitor, this sad little inky black puppy sat still and looked at him as if reading his mind. His little head cocked to the side as if to say, "Ray, I know just how you feel. It hurts sometimes, doesn't it?" He brought the young puppy with the old soul home with him and even Aunt Tilly, after giving it some hard thought, had been captivated by Jackson's friendly, empathetic nature. They loved Jackson and he rewarded the Grants with his total devotion.

Santi held Jackson a little too tightly in her arms when he explained to her that Darlene wouldn't be back – almost as if she were afraid Jackson would leave her as well. She didn't completely understand. And her young eyes begged and pleaded for him to say it wasn't so. Ray wanted to take it all back as soon as the words left his mouth. Instead he hugged his little girl and held her in such a way that she couldn't see the tears in his own eyes. Not necessarily for Darlene, but for Darlene's daughter. This wasn't the plan he had for Santi.

Tonight, after Santi finally wound down from the day's excitement he put her to bed and read her a story.

"Goodnight, sweetheart."

Jackson lay on the rug beside the bed and sighed to himself. He knew he would need a full night's rest in order to keep up with Santi as she ran through the gardens and the fruit trees, past the ant mounds and the pond full of catfish.

Ray looked at bright stars sprinkled across the night sky and fantasized about golden eyes framed by a wild mane of dark brown hair that reached for the sky, reached for the earth, reached in every direction to touch everyone in the world, including him maybe. No harm in fantasies. Fantasies hadn't hurt him much during these alone years.

But he kept seeing those eyes. When she glanced back at him as she crossed the street, a golden laser struck through him. Where had he seen eyes like that? He cast his mind back. Gold flecked by black changed to brown, back to gold, then back to brown as she turned towards and away from the sun.

He remembered suddenly a necklace, bracelets, and earrings all brown, red, and gold - the necklace his mother wore for special occasions. She brought them with her from her homeland. She told him that the stones were tiger's eye and hyacinth. A grandmother he'd never met gifted the jewelry to his mother on unbreakable strands of gold wire.

He frowned as he got up to look for the wooden box that held photographs, mementos, letters, his fathers medals, and other family keepsakes. They still lay there like a pile of cinnamon, chocolate, and butterscotch candy. The last time he looked in the box years ago, he made sure to tell his younger brother, Dhan, what he knew of the family's history. Dhan had been young, just fourteen when their parents died. He didn't want Dhan, or even himself and their sister, Dharma, to ever forget their parents.

Gently, he picked up the photograph of his mother and father. Reginald Grant gazed proudly back at him with dark brown eyes in a midnight black face capped with woolly, precisely-cut dark brown hair. Vasanti's long hair hung in coal-black waves. Her skin, nearly dark as Reginald's glowed smoothly. She smiled beautifully in the picture as if forever in love. His mother's dark, nearly black eyes were her legacy to both Ray and Dharma although Ray's large, powerful build undeniably came from his father as did Dhan's facial features. Reginald leaned protectively over Vasanti's shoulder. She curved towards him. His parents looked as if they'd been born to be together.

Now he held the beautiful necklace in his hands. This is why Kenzi pulled at his memory so. *But what did that really mean?* He stared at the necklace and pushed the bracelets and earrings around the palm of his hand. He put them away. *Probably nothing.* Maybe.

He turned to walk to his bookshelf and looked through encyclopedias printed the same year he arrived to the world. "Hyacinth, a reddish-bronze zircon placer-mined in Sri Lanka (formerly Ceylon), Cambodia, and Thailand, can be found in magmatic, sedimentary, and metamorphosed rocks." Okay... "Tiger's eye glows as a fibrous quartz whose yellow color alternates with brown. Western Australia, India, and California hold large deposits of tiger's eye."

Tiger's Eye. Hyacinth. That described her. Golden eyes and brown curves. Dark brown hair that turned reddish in the sun. His stomach tightened.

Ray stood back and looked over the bookshelf with its decades-old encyclopedia set, car and farm machine repair manuals, out-dated television guides, almanacs from two years ago, and encyclopedia of native Texas plants. He worked with his hands and didn't spend much time reading except the occasional Saturday nights and bed-time stories for Santi. He wondered what Kenzi would think if she could see his shelf right now. She probably wouldn't be impressed. *Maybe time to stock up?*

Bounce and sway when she crossed the street. Bounce and twist as she walked back to her store. More curves. And a clear, steady golden-eyed stare that shot through him like a laser when she glanced back and saw everything he wanted to be. What did she think when she looked back? Did she think of him now? If so, then he could meet her in a dream.

Kenzi riding a motorcycle wearing nothing but shiny black boots, leather gloves with the fingers cut off, and a silver-studded belt that holds a whip. She pulls up in front of him. "Get on!" He hesitates, unsure. This woman is much too wild for him. She narrows her eyes and drops her hand to the whip at her waist menacingly. He gets on and frantically clutches her naked body in order to not fall off as she revs the engine.

Nasty.

Kenzi sitting next to him in the darkness of a movie theatre. He's looking at the screen, but he's not watching the movie. He hears the whispers of the audience, but he's not listening. He feels her hand reaching in the dark and grabs its soft warmth, to guide it to the special place that strains for her touch. Her hand wraps him in a tight embrace. He sucks in his breath sharply.

Oh Kenzi.

Kenzi running to him on a sunny beach with the wind blowing wildly through her hair. Skin like smooth toffee. Long, slender legs like a deer. Golden-eyed. A thin gauzy white dress wraps and clings. The waves crash and roar as she calls to him, "Ray!" She jumps into his arms and wraps her legs around his waist and her arms around his neck.

Warm, soft Kenzi.

Ray closed his eyes with a shudder.

Chapter 3

Kinfolk Books

Five o'clock Saturday morning, just after the alarm sounded, Kenzi remembered to check her phone messages. She depressed the button on the machine and listened to last night's missed calls as she got dressed.

"Hi Kenzi, this is Lina. I see you're not home yet. Out on a heavy date huh? Or just reading all those dry books again? I'm just kidding, girl!" *Hideous cackle.* "See you tomorrow!"

You can't pick your family.

"Kenzi! Hey girl. It's Stacy. I just wanted to wish you well for tomorrow. Everything's going to be great! I'm so excited and really happy about the bookstore opening. We need it so badly in Rollins. The flyers are good to go and I'll get there about ten to help out. See ya!"

Kenzi smiled.

"Kenzi, I told you I was going to call about eight o'clock. Obviously, you aren't there. I hope this isn't how you plan to operate the shop. Anyway, I just wanted to say good luck and get some rest. I'll stop in to see how you're doing on my lunch hour. Bye now."

Kenzi shrugged off Franklin's patronizing tone. She met Franklin, a history professor at the university where she used to work. They attended a few meetings and lectures together. Once in a while, they dated. Good-looking with a gigolo reputation. She'd heard a few stories.

After all, the elusive Good Black Man existed as urban legend. They whispered about him in Rollins churches and kitchens and beauty parlors. Everyone's cousin's sister's friend's mama's coworker had captured one in their claws at some time or another or so the rumors declared. Because a woman would have to be a natural fool to not clutch the Good Black Man tightly with both hands and commence to mate him immediately. Once spotted, you had to move fast to beat off competitors.

Betty overhead Franklin's message. She also didn't miss Kenzi's brief flash of irritation.

Kenzi unwound her twists and ran her hands through them to both fluff her hair and to smooth away pre-opening jitters. She finished getting dressed and grabbed her to-do list and schedule for opening day. Her to-do lists always seemed too long. Betty, a fantastically (or fanatically) faithful early riser, was already set to drive Kenzi to the store. Along the way, she fussed about Kenzi's bike and cart.

"What do you have against cars? You're thirty-one, not thirteen."

"*Mother!* Nothing! It's just that I can't afford payments or maintenance and repairs and the store all at the same time. Besides, if I use the bike cart, then I don't need a gym membership and that's more money saved at the same time. I don't want to pay someone to allow me to exercise when I can do it for free. Best of all, I can eat whatever I want and not worry about working it off. All the biking and walking I do running errands means whatever I eat burns up by the end of the day."

"Well, I see your points. All eight of them. But sometimes a car is good in an emergency."

"Yes, that's true. By the way, I am glad you wanted to come down, Mom," Kenzi smiled at her, "It's helping me out a lot."

"Changing the subject," Betty accused with an answering smile.

The high school student at the drive-thru cash register tossed their breakfasts through the car window. Kenzi rattled the paper sack and crinkled the paper wrappers to avoid listening to Betty's commentary about the perils of fast food eating. They'd done this so many times before. Kenzi made a casual observation about parents who cross the boundaries of their adult children. The trip from Kenzi's apartment to the bookstore seemed much longer than if she'd ridden her bike.

From inside Kinfolk, Kenzi waved to Dharma across street as Dharma unlocked the front entrance to prepare for the daily seven a.m. opening of Organic Soul. Kenzi wondered if she'd see the big guy, *Ray,* today.

But never mind that. She vacuumed, made coffee, and tested equipment. She rearranged some book displays giving little one-inch pulls this direction, that direction, this direction. She watered plants and patted books into place.

"Mom, go ahead and help yourself to some coffee."

"Way ahead of you."

About an hour to go now.

Kenzi answered email which containing queries from publishers and authors and a few artists. She made updates to the website using good ole HTML code. Hyper-Text Markup Language appeared nearly indecipherable to the untrained eye. But Kenzi had worked with the basic code so long as a student, she didn't really bother with software unless the images she needed were too complicated and time-consuming to create manually. Stacy had already commented on her being lost in the 90s.

Under her breath she murmured, "Open close bracket... bold close... open italic... a href..., close a href... mailto..." The sameness of it all relaxed her... like knitting. File Transfer Protocol sent color images of the interior and exterior of the storefront from her computer's hard drive to the website's file storage and she linked it to the homepage. HTML, always consistent, reliable, and universal remained comfortable with no surprises.

"Save!" She clicked the mouse of her six-year-old pretty baby computer with satisfaction.

Half an hour to launch.

She poked her head out of the back room to note passersby slowing down to read the large "OPENING SOON" sign posted last week with a little blurb about Kinfolk Books and what it hoped to accomplish in the community. Some people began to linger and chat amongst themselves. She saw a few come from Organic Soul's entrance to stand outside and join the chatter. Kenzi frantically rattled through a pile of paper.

"What are you doing, Kenzi?"

"I'm just doing a last-minute check of all the paperwork."

Tex, her business attorney had checked off and carefully reviewed the necessary forms one by one. Her first business ever!

As the adrenaline coursed through her, Kenzi took one last deep breath as she unlocked the front door to Kinfolk Books. Betty strategically positioned herself further inside the store to help guide the excited visitors as Rollins, Texas poured into Kinfolk Books in a wave of excited chatter and drawled exclamations.

"¡*Buenos días!*"

"Howdy!"

"Good morning!"

"Heeeey, how you doin'?"

"What's up?"

Texas, as a whole, spread across a land of contrasts. Boundaries touched the swamplands and forests of the American South, the rolling prairies and plains of the Midwest, the beautifully isolated American West, and the brightly colorful regions of Mexico. Canyons, mountains, deserts, bayous, grasslands, and rolling hills rose and fell across the state. An adventurer's paradise. Certainly paradise for the farmers, oil field workers, cowboys, shrimpers, foresters, and everyday lawyers and teachers and doctors who earned their livings and provided for their families under the endless sun and sky.

A small to mid-sized conservative town, Rollins surrounded itself with woods, farms, ranches, a few rivers and two lakes in Central Texas. Pick-up trucks and 4x4s roared up and down paved roads then bounced and bucked along gravel and dirt roads. The excitement generated by the large university peppered the quiet, slower aspects of country life. Economic vitality ebbed and flowed with the university calendar as students arrived, studied, and graduated again and again. All retailers planned their sales schedule around the students with their fresh driver's licenses and loan checks, as well as the faculty who often brought families with them. The university energized the region's economy and fed the stream of customers wandering through the store.

"Do you have books in Spanish?"

"¡*Claro que sí! Son marcados con un punto naranjo como esto.*" Kenzi showed the customer a book with an orange dot on the spine.

"We're trying to find something on snakes?"

"We have some books on snakes in the animal and pet section. Right this way." Kenzi headed to the middle of the store with two young boys.

"Quisiera un libro sobre Estevánico, el Negro o Alvar Nuñez Cabeza de la Vaca." Kenzi remembered this purposeful undergraduate student from the Dominican Republic from her days at the university. *"Ah Luís. ¡Bienvenido! En Texana o Historia, hay,* Los Naufragios.*"*

Kenzi pointed towards the section with books on all aspects of Texas as well as the history section where the books on Spanish conquistadors would likely be, particularly, *The Castaways.* The student wasted no time, seeming to know exactly what he wanted already.

"¿Bueno?" Kenzi checked in with him.

"Ah, sí. Eso sí que es, Señorita Kenzi. ¡Obligado!" He held up the slim volume in triumph and turned to do further exploration of his own.

Despite her adaptable nature, Kenzi still felt slightly overwhelmed by the throng of the crowd that pressed its way into the store – young and old, male and female, from the campus and around the way, in business suits and cut-off shorts. Congratulations and handshakes and goodwill wishes rang from every direction as the book lovers and the curious scattered to various corners to browse. The CD of a local jazz trio mellowed the atmosphere. Being a big believer in the support of local arts, Kenzi quickly agreed to play their music from time to time and to keep a tray of their CDs for sale near the register.

"Congratulations, Kenzi! Tex, her business attorney, shouldered his way past with a quick handshake.

Entering with the second wave, Ray scanned the crowd quickly for Kenzi's large hair while pushing a cart with two large trays of pastries, a tray of sliced peaches and grapes, and a clear glass jug of coconut milk and one of freshly-squeezed orange juice from Organic Soul. The customers swarmed him. He shot Kenzi a surprised look of amusement, but somehow managed to set the trays and jugs down without spilling on the refreshment table that already held coffee and hot water for tea.

Kenzi chuckled, "Are you okay?"

Ray grinned back at her, "No problem. It's like this every morning at Organic Soul. As a matter of fact, I see a few of your patrons that ate at the restaurant decided to follow me over here for a second round."

Kenzi laughed out loud and reached for a pastry herself as Betty walked up to meet the tall man talking to her daughter.

"Didn't you just eat?" Betty looked puzzled.

Oh no, she did not. Kenzi blushed, mortified.

"Mother!"

Ray smiled and held out his hand to greet Betty. In the midst of their chatting, Kenzi could feel his eyes on her, stroking her again. *What was he always looking at?*

Kenzi followed Ray's glance downward and turned away in annoyance to greet an elderly couple who lived near the store. Ray had an even better view. He smiled but shifted his gaze as he handed Betty a package of Darjeeling tea packets from his pocket.

"Courtesy of Organic Soul. My sister, Dharma, thought you might like to experiment."

Betty beamed back at Ray. "Why thank you, Ray! That was so thoughtful of her! Everything looks just wonderful. Would you tell her thanks for us?"

Betty casually knocked the generic brand of tea packets into the trash basket next to the table and put the Darjeeling in place. Perfect!

Various religious, social, and political groups jockeyed for Kenzi's attention and for dominance of the events calendar. They introduced themselves to Kenzi with a knowing smile as if to say, "We know you're on our side."

Local artists with work featured in the store mixed with the crowd. A few local authors sent volumes of their latest works – cookbook, poetry, home schooling guides, historical fiction - for display in the local and regional racks towards the front of the store. She'd even located the memoirs of certain families whose descendants lived in the area while out scouting. You never knew what you might find by looking in dark, dusty corners.

The retirement community chatted in small groups. University students and faculty noted with either pleasure or confusion the widely divergent opinions and subjects grouped together on the shelves.

A natural with people, Betty, helped her work the crowd. Not only did Betty speak French, she also knew how to negotiate the unspoken rules of urban areas heavily populated by lower-income families as well as incense-laden bohemian hangouts and upper-class country clubs with its tennis courts and highly manicured lawns. Kenzi's own wide travels taught the secret to survival when wandering across borders and back again with nothing but a backpack and a passport to sustain her for weeks and months. You just had to be yourself while using courtesy and common sense to work around the hard spots.

Lina, dear cousin Lina, was nowhere in sight.

Thankfully Stacy arrived half an hour early to promote the art classes to parents. The crowed mobbed Stacy as they had Ray earlier.

"Good sign," Kenzi thought.

"Stacy, I'm so glad you made it!"

"Me too, girl. Look at this crowd!"

"I know!"

More people surged up to Stacy. "I'll be back, okay?" Kenzi backed away to work another section of the room.

At noon, Ray returned to clear away breakfast leftovers and to set down a huge plateful of avocado, tomato, spinach, red pepper and red onion sandwiches with spicy hummus spread, chunks of cheese sliced pecan pie and, more tea. This time, ice and mint leaves floated in the tea. Iced tea, a Texan staple, graced almost every gathering. A glass decanter contained something dark purple that Ray explained as an Organic Soul original – blackberry wine – sat next to the iced tea.

Kenzi smothered a laugh when she noticed customers facing the very real dilemma of a choice between iced mint tea and happy juice. She made a little sign that read, "Delicious! Try Both."

At that moment, Stacy pushed through, breathless, for a refill.

"Stacy, this is Ray. His family owns Organic Soul."

"Ray, this is Stacy, one of our featured artists."

"Hi Ray!"

"Hello," Ray smiled and Kenzi was surprised at the twinge she felt to see him share that smile with someone else. Puzzled with herself, she continued, "Stacy's in charge of the children's art program."

"Great! I heard about that! I have a daughter myself."

"Awesome! She might want to join in then."

Kenzi told herself to smile. "Ray, why don't you hang out a minute, if you have time?"

Ray looked pleased by the invitation and finally curved the warm smile her way, immediately drawing her fascinated gaze to his mouth as he replied.

"I want to, but I can't since I have to unload a truck across the street. I'll come back with Santi later this afternoon. She's been asking about the bookstore ever since yesterday."

Franklin, having forgiven her for missing his call last night, strolled up to hear the tail end of the conversation. Without a word to either Ray or Stacy, he pulled Kenzi to the side. Ray frowned though he continued a brief exchange with Stacy.

One by one, Franklin leveled his charges:

"Kenzi, you don't know what you're doing." Why didn't you talk to that one woman? Why don't you have more volunteers? You should have had entertainment. These unpainted shelves make the store look like a lumber yard. This basket of giveaway books is *insulting*! You need to open earlier. You need to stay open later. You need to open on Sundays. You need to get out in the community more. These prices are too high. Those prices are too low."

Kenzi tensed and moved away from Franklin who continued talking as he followed her back to where Ray waited. By then, Stacy had turned back to the crowd to do more promotion.

Franklin spoke in a low voice:

"You obviously haven't done enough research. It's hard to take this store seriously. Do you know what you're doing?"

Kenzi didn't answer him. She caught the slightest flicker in Ray's eyes as he met Franklin's gaze. Some sort of unspoken male tension crackled between Franklin and Ray – a measurement or an assessment. They didn't like each other. She missed something in their exchange, a signal or clue to the shifting testosterone levels. Surely, a man thing. The classic game of masculine one-upmanship, sometimes called the dozens, initiated. And Kenzi's presence raised the stakes from genial challenge to something else entirely.

"So you unload trucks? I'm glad I don't have to lift and tote in the sun."

Casually, Ray put his hands in his pockets, a move that flexed and emphasized his arm muscles.

"Well, there's always a gym membership if you're trying to get back into shape," Ray replied pleasantly with a significant look at Franklin's smaller frame.

With a *whatever* shrug and frown, Franklin turned once again to Kenzi, but found himself still thwarted by the large man who leaned into his space with a sardonic smile.

Incredulous, Franklin eyed Ray up and down. They'd drawn symbolic lines on either side of Kenzi. She wanted to say something or make a joke, but didn't know what exactly would diffuse the encounter.

"Okay, the first one who lifts a leg and decides to mark territory gets maced!" she declared.

Stacy, still standing nearby, with her back turned, snickered as she walked away to circulate amongst the crowd.

"Kenzi," Franklin still eyed Ray as he spoke to her. "I'm gonna check out the English literature section."

Franklin started to ease away. "You know Chaucer, right? Right?"

Kenzi held her breath hoping Ray wouldn't rise to the bait. And a small part of her tried not to wonder whether Ray actually knew Chaucer.

"See ya, Freddie!" Ray gave Franklin a jaunty salute then winked at Kenzi on the sly. "Well, I've got work to do," he announced.

Kenzi didn't miss Franklin's eye roll away from Ray's supposed stupidity.

"I'll be back," Ray smiled and took off.

"Wow," Kenzi shook her head with a small laugh and walked back into the crowd.

Out on the street, Ray wondered why women were attracted to guys with the deep pockets, soft hands, shallow personalities, and diarrhea of the mouth. What did Kenzi see in him? What did that say about her as a person? But even more, w*hy had he even bothered to go head to head with the idiot?* Ray, the oldest child, almost always maintained calm and control over tense situations instead of escalating them.

"Kenziiii!"

Kenzi heard Lina before she saw her and groaned. The tension caused her scalp to itch.

"Kenziiii!"

Dear Cousin Lina had finally arrived fresh from the Dallas salon where she worked as a stylist. Her hair curled into crisp parallel rows at the ends that were then shellacked with hairspray. Lina smoothed her face with orangey foundation that almost matched her hair color. Lipstick and powdered eye shadow and blush decorated the surface and... *what was going on with her eyes?*

She and Lina leaned together and lightly touched each others forearms in a fake hug.

"Look at all this." Lina gazed around in amazement. "How did you get all these people to show up?"

"I didn't get them to do anything. They wanted to. As a matter of fact, I just ran out of business cards."

Lina evaluated the crowd, hand on hip, speaking over Kenzi's shoulder.

"I bet you wish you kept your job at the university."

"What?"

"And what do you mean you ran out of business cards? Kenzi! Never be without business cards!" Lina exclaimed authoritatively.

Kenzi felt her teeth clench together.

"And this is all the food you have? You couldn't afford more?"

Dramatic incredulity shot Lina's eyebrows to her hairline.

"There's no meat here!"

Kenzi tried to not stare at the false lashes as the comments flowed forth punctuated here and there with the occasional giggle and sidelong glance.

"Okay, but what about multicultural children's books?"

Lina gestured around the store with flourishes that showed off her nails painted the same hot pink as her head-to-toe two piece form-fitting tank top and short set, leather-like purse, and platform sandals.

"Okay, but what about children's programs?"

"Talk to Stacy over there," Kenzi cut Lina off quickly, "By the way, thanks for the help, Lina," Kenzi smiled with sarcasm. "Dive right on in, why don't you?"

"Okay, but all I'm saying is what kind of black-owned bookstore doesn't have incense? Where are the candles and the beauty products? Just tell me that and I'm through."

Kenzi cocked her head to the side thoughtfully. "Um, the black-owned bookstore that I opened and you didn't?" Then she shrugged and allowed herself to be carried away by the bookstore's customers.

Lina sauntered around the store on her platforms, shook her stiff hair, and clucked her tongue in dissatisfaction until she bumped into a man whose designer clothing and shoes as well as the value of his glasses and watch tabulated to just the right number.

Lina slid into place. "Excuse me please," she said innocuously searching for and then grabbing a random book to thumb through as well. She could do intellectual. She could also do artsy. She could even do gangsta when the situation dictated that. A few restless shifts of her body, a few persistent throat clearings, and several small smiles initiated conversation.

"I just love Maya Angela."

Franklin turned to Lina and swiftly swept her head to foot with his eyes.

"What's not to love?"

"Oh, I saw that movie! Ike treated Tina so wrong! They should have won an Oscar."

"Ah…"

The conversation moved on to family backgrounds, careers, schools, personal wealth, goals, marital status, parental status, and upward-mobility.

"Yes, Kenzi's my cousin and that's my Aunt Betty over there. I came down to help her keep things on track."

"Nice of you. She could use the help. Do you have a business background yourself?"

"I'm," Lina quickly decided to upgrade, "more into fashion, beauty, and design than books."

"Obviously," Franklin smiled slowly. Lina beamed back.

Franklin enjoyed the wide-eyed approval. And as the conversation of lighthearted but purposeful innuendo progressed, Lina smiled like the cat who finally figured out how to hit the latch to the canary cage at just the right angle.

Oblivious to the new development, Kenzi straightened and tidied the refreshment table and pointed out a few more books. Betty stood at the register totaling purchases.

"Okay, here's your change and your receipt. I'm going to give you a few coupons for your next visit. And if you know of anyone who cares about the community literacy, we're encouraging people to join the mailing list and to sign up as reading volunteers."

The middle-aged woman holding her bag of goodies hurriedly reassured Betty that she, herself, cared about community literacy and signed up. Kenzi moved closer to the register.

"Thank you so much, ma'am," she added her thanks to Betty's.

A half hour later, the crowd thinned slightly and the television crew from the local station captured Kenzi's sound bites for the evening news.

"One guiding principle we decided upon before opening was that all classics should be equally accessible and treated with equal reverence. For instance, Guillermo Cabrera Infante sits just before John Irving on the shelf instead of being split into a separate section based on language and country of origin. Frank Peretti is with Stephen King in the suspense thriller section instead of religion. But Walter Mosley's drama, mystery, and science fiction are separated by genre."

"But what about foreign language books? Where are those?" The reporter looked a little confused.

"German, French, Russian, and Chinese language books are shelved by subject matter regardless of language."

"But isn't that unusual?"

"That's Kinfolk Books." Kenzi laughed. "We place books where we think customers will search for them."

Out of the corner of her eye, she noticed a stocky man with graying hair staring at her. *Must be the afro.* It always attracted attention.

The community radio station called into the store and interviewed her over the air.

"Ms. Malton, so basically, Kinfolk Books is a liberal sort of store."

"No indeed," Kenzi replied firmly. "Kinfolk Books is a social, religious, and politically neutral environment."

"You mean…"

"No favorites. Kinfolk Books symbolizes a place to learn, share, and grow."

"But most people would think that this is a sort of left-wing hangout."

"Definitely not. Each customer and community group is accorded full and equal access to the store and its facilities without regard to a social, political, or religious agenda or affiliation. Everyone is welcome."

"But still, some customers might be excused for having the expectation of a progressive agenda."

"It's a tightrope," Kenzi admitted. "Perception is reality. Kinfolk Books, however, welcomes everyone's money." The unexpected publicity, though a blessing, made her anxious. She tried her best to get the Kinfolk Books mission and message across to the public.

Closer to five o'clock, the crowd dissipated except for stragglers here and there. Kenzi and Betty began to tidy up. At long last, they slumped down together after Kenzi locked the door. Lina had long gone by two o'clock.

A university seminar, an animal rights group, a church youth group, a book club, and children's art filled the activities calendar and meeting room schedule for the next two months. The small rental fee would bring extra income into the store.

"Mom, guess what? We received book donations from five different people!"

"Oh, Kenzi! More blessings. Who donated?"

"Let me think. Two donations were by university professors and two donations were from retirees that live near the store. They were so generous. But the most interesting donations came from someone anonymous."

"Really? Who?

"Anonymous, Mom."

"Hm. I wonder why."

"Gosh, I'm not sure. It's funny. They came from this person's private collection. A graduate student brought them over. I asked him who donated the books because I wanted to know who to thank. He just set down box after box and said the person donated for his own undefined reasons and preferred anonymity. That's all he would say about it."

They walked over to the uncovered boxes, "especially when you consider the subject matter. There looks to be about four hundred books on revolution, Black Power, and social unrest."

Betty laughed as she poked through a few of the volumes. "No wonder he wanted to remain anonymous. Rollins is a pretty conservative place. Actually, I've seen most of these titles before. I read some of them in college, myself."

"Well, these books will either spice up the political science and sociology sections or set them on fire! We needed books like these."

The donated books, approximately six hundred all together, sat in a mountainous pile on one side of the store. Kenzi made a mental note to carefully go through each book next week to sort the pile into keepers and giveaways.

"You know what Mom, the biggest illusion non-booksellers seem to have about the bookselling industry is this romantic notion of the owner sitting around, drinking coffee, and flipping through Victorian romances, and holding genteel conversations about poetry with the mighty literati. I mean, hardly. Every time I hear that I just laugh."

Rather, bookselling was the dirty, dusty, moldy business of lifting, packing, unpacking, sorting, cleaning, pricing, inventorying, and shelving thousands and thousands of volumes of various sizes and flavors. Not to mention daily accounting, bookkeeping, and repairs. And all that usually took place after closing and before opening. Customer service fully occupied open hours.

For each book that sat upon a shelf, on a table, or in a display rack, she would put on a face mask to flip through to make sure nothing strange lay inserted between the pages. One never knew what one would find serving as a bookmark between pages of a valuable first edition or the latest popular suspense-thriller. Since buying bulk inventory and scouting at various garage and estate sales and online auctions, Kenzi found photos, receipts, letters, candy wrappers, and even expired identification cards. Sometimes, she learned more than she wanted about the previous owners and chose to quickly forget after moving on to the next volume. But those were the more ordinary encounters.

On occasion, she cracked open a book or unpacked a box to find living creatures scurrying from the light or smelly mildew creeping silent and relentless through the pages breaking down paper and binding that would otherwise have endured for hundreds of years. These infestations she removed from the store in plastic bags.

For those that passed inspection, she carefully erased pencil marks, unfolded dog-ears, and ironed curled pages flat with a travel iron. She unpeeled obsolete stickers with a razor and smoothed away grimy gummed surfaces with acetone. Her office turned into a laboratory. She always had to strike a careful balance between going far enough to delicately clean a book and stopping just short of damaging it. She did the painstaking work lovingly, as a person who truly loves the work they do so much that it ceases to be a chore and more a fascinating way to pass the afternoon. Some marks of previous use and ownership she could remove. The removal of other marks would further damage the book and lower the value. Those marks, she left alone. Books like that would keep that special lived-in, been-around-the-block, previously-loved used book appeal. Sometimes she wondered who had turned the same pages and how long ago. It lent an air of mystery to used books.

She would check the copyright date, the edition, whether it had an autograph or any other special characteristics that made the book special. Then she used the internet to estimate true value.

"The truth is," Kenzi said a little dreamily, "the finding and discovery and care of the books are the appeal. You have to either love it, or not even bother to do it. And matching the right book to the right buyer at the right time is icing on the cake. You saw that this afternoon, right?"

"It was a fun day, Kenzi," Betty replied wearily.

"The books found a home with someone who loved and appreciated them."

"And… you made a heap of cash."

"Well yeah. That always helps too."

Even the mishaps and slightly awkward situations created by Lina and Franklin seemed to render her dream of bookstore ownership just that more real as opposed to the fantasy she'd created while researching dry factoids for her journal publications and conference papers.

Running the tenure track took all the fun out of being an academic.

Even so, when universities with no tenure requirement offered positions, she'd still felt, so *blah*. Every time she pulled out a job description, "No, no no!" clanged and bumped against the inside of her head.

Betty smiled at her daughter's musings. "Kenzi, I'm proud of what you've accomplished today. I still thank God that even when you wandered the world, you never forgot the importance of your education. My worst nightmare was that you'd drop out of school or give up on yourself."

"Mom, I know you had some scary moments with me. I never told you this, but sometimes I was scared myself."

"Whoa!" Betty laughed. "Now I didn't think I'd ever hear you admit it. I knew you took pride in your grades. You didn't think I scattered books all over the house accidentally, did you?"

"Ah, very clever! I always suspected there was a method to the madness. Well, it worked." Kenzi laughed.

Several times, Betty had tried and failed to put on the brave, nonchalant calm face while Kenzi called her from the four corners of the U.S. and beyond thanks to the various scholarship and travel grants and study abroad internship programs she won. Betty wanted to be the hip and happening mother that her daughter could see as fun and not like all the other mothers who cramped the wild style, but Kenzi made that difficult at times. Betty accepted that she had to be her daughter's mother, not her friend.

"Kenzi, is that gunfire I hear in the background? What's happening? Where are you?"

"Mother! That's just the television."

Right.

"What show is on?" Nothing that sounded remotely like gun-fire showed on any channel coming from her television. Was Kenzi even in the U.S.?

"What station?"

"It's a video, Mom. I have to go. I have to *mumble*."

"What? Wait! Kenzi! Kenzi!"

She'd tried. If only Kenzi's father... She shook her head and told herself to not even bother with that line of thought. What could have been, what would have been, what should have been didn't exist. Because they never happened.

Well what could a mother do but wait for her daughter to figure out who she needed to be and then be that and where she wanted to go and then go there? Just forwarding Kenzi's mail made a career in and of itself. The Texas-Mexico border, Costa Rica, Baja California... To her relief Kenzi finally completed graduate school at twenty-eight and accepted the university position. Three years later, Kinfolk Books!

The vague meandering flights of fancy converged to form this new woman. Kenzi would be all right. Betty wheeled the television out from the meeting room so they could watch the news while they cleaned up from the excitement and totaled the first day's sales.

Just as Kenzi went to lock the front door, Ray returned for the third time with Dharma and Santi to gather Organic Soul's dishes and to take a quick look around the store. Santi carried a large bowl of fragrant plants.

"Look Miss Kenzi! We brought you some plants. You can smell them."

"Hi Santi! I'm so pleased to see you! Thank you so much for bringing these!"

"You can put them out in front of the store."

"What a great idea! Maybe you can help me do that sometime soon."

Kenzi took the bowl and obediently bent for a sniff.

"Smells like, spearmint and lemon balm."

Dharma spoke up, "Very good, Kenzi. That's exactly what they are. They're from our garden and you can use them in tea or just pluck them for a little pick-me-up."

"Thank you so much. Thank you!"

"I figured you and your mother might be hungry after the first day. Here's a couple of to-go plates on the house."

"Oh, you are too kind. As a matter of fact, I'm starving. How about you, Mom?"

"Bless you, Dharma. By the way, I'm Betty, Kenzi's mother."

"Nice to meet you!"

"Well, I've met Ray, but who's this pretty girl?"

"I'm Santi."

"Shake hands, Santi," Ray rumbled.

Santi shook hands with Betty and then made a beeline to the children's area and plopped into a bean bag with a whoosh of air.

"Could we put up some of our flyers on the bulletin board?"

"Oh sure, I've got some tacks."

The newscaster broke in with a brief mention of the store and a split-second flash of Kenzi. They all cheered.

Kenzi and her mother ate wild rice with pecans, mushroom soup with garlic, fried plantains with caramel sauce, and fresh blackberries and sliced fresh peaches drizzled with honey. Dharma and Ray looked around the store. Dharma thumbed through cookbooks and glanced through the family and relationship sections. Ray headed towards business and then on to the gardening and agriculture section. Betty yawned for the third time.

"Mom, you should go home. I can finish up here and ride my bike home."

"I don't like that. I don't like you riding at night by yourself."

"Mother, I do it every night."

"I don't like that," Betty repeated. Kenzi frowned.

Ray spoke up, "I'll take her home after she's done closing."

Dharma noticed Kenzi's hesitation and spoke up quickly, "It's okay, Kenzi. Santi comes to my house for our weekly Saturday night sleep-over. It's our time for girl talk." Dharma gave Santi a conspiratorial wink as Ray laughed.

"And while they're doing that, I talk man to man with Jackson."

"Who's Jackson?" Kenzi asked.

"Jackson's our dog! Daddy talks to our dog!" Santi giggled.

"That's because Jackson tells me everything naughty you did while I wasn't looking," Ray told her.

Santi covered her face and giggled even louder.

Dharma didn't mention that the Saturday night sleep-over gave Ray the opportunity to "go out." Unfortunately, Ray usually ended up staying home watching rented movies or, apparently, talking with Jackson. But not this Saturday night!

Dharma, having managed her two brothers growing up, the staff of Organic Soul, and her own twin boys easily maneuvered this group. "So, it's really not a problem at all," she said quickly. "Santi comes with me and Ray, you'll take Kenzi home after the store's put back to rights." She turned reassuringly to Betty, "Ray will take good care of her."

Kenzi wondered at what point she lost control of the situation. Betty, impressed by Ray's thoughtfulness throughout the day gathered her purse and gaily waved her way towards the door before Kenzi could get a word out.

Dharma sang out loudly, "Goodnight, Kenzi! Congratulations on the first day!"

"Goodnight, Miss Betty!" Ray rumbled his baritone. "See ya, Dharma."

"Goodnight, Daddy! Goodnight, Miss Kenzi!" Santi piped in her child's voice.

"I'll see you tonight, Kenzi," her mother said placidly.

Kenzi still stood looking from Dharma to her mother to Ray to Santi. "Uh, okay? I'll be home soon."

"No rush. Take your time."

Kenzi felt her face flush. And there Ray stood grinning at her while her breasts tingled in response.

As she turned back to Dharma, Dharma rushed out, "Well, Santi, let's go! Get your things!" She nudged Santi towards the front of the store.

Kenzi trailed behind them.

"Dharma," she managed to cut through Dharma's rushed chatter and quick stride to the front door, "Dharma! I just wanted to tell you thanks for the catering and everything else."

"Oh! Okay Kenzi. Bye now!"

"But really…" As the front door slammed behind Dharma, Santi, and her mother, Kenzi locked it once more and looked at Ray with uncertainty. *What just happened?* Ray leaned his large from against a shelf of books laughing silently at Kenzi's confusion.

"That's our Dharma. Gotta love her."

"She's very… efficient." Kenzi shook her head.

"That she is." Ray grinned at her.

All of a sudden, the atmosphere at Kinfolk Books became noticeably more quiet and intimate.

Chapter 4

The Grants and the Maltons

"You've been so nice today, Ray. All the food deliveries and helping me to get things cleaned up. I couldn't have moved all this furniture and the books without you." Ray smiled slowly and Kenzi felt her face heat up.

She quickly added, "Would you give these picture books to your daughter? I saw her reading them earlier and I'd like her to have them if it's okay."

"Sure," Ray's fingers deliberately brushed hers as he eased the books from her hand. "I'll make sure she gets them. Thanks, Kenzi."

Kenzi laughed a little breathlessly. "Yeah, I need the whole world to read."

"Well, there's worse things."

"By the way, I think Santi might enjoy the art classes with the other children. We also got a few volunteers for weekday story times."

"Nice. Very nice, Kenzi. Santi would love it, I know. I could use the help, actually. Even though I read to her almost every night, I usually start dozing off before she does."

Kenzi smiled. Ray's eyes dropped to her mouth accented by a dimple. His eyes shone dark and intense under the heavy brows and Kenzi held her breath. For a moment, neither of them spoke while they held eye contact. And then suddenly they both filled in the strange gap that lingered too long to not matter with conversation.

They dropped the dishes off at the restaurant. On the drive home Ray told her, "You know, Kenzi, I wish you well with Kinfolk. This community definitely needs it. And it sounds as if you're on the right track."

"Thank you so much. You and Dharma and Santi were great to have around on opening day. And thanks for the lift. My mother was very tired and I'm glad she didn't have to wait around while I finished cleaning up. Thanks for everything."

"Of course. Us small businesses have to look out for one another." Ray paused. Tell you what, when do you have your days off?"

Wow! He sure worked fast. "Sunday. Turn left here."

Ray turned the corner parked outside her apartment. "Not this Sunday, but next Sunday, we're gonna pick figs and grapes. The late summer batch is near ripe and we all pitch in to gather them up."

"Oh that sounds like fun! I think next Sunday would be good." Kenzi did a quick mental calculation of her schedule. "Because this Sunday, I plan to collapse!"

"You definitely earned it. Let me get your home phone number." He scrawled it across the back of an envelope from the glove compartment.

"Wait, I'll walk you." She'd already opened her car door, but paused to let him hold on to the handle. Gotta love the southern gentlemanly style. He even gave her a hand as she gathered up her purse. They strolled up the short walk to her door and Kenzi wondered what he would do. *What would she do?* Moments like this were so awkward. *Would he try to kiss her? Would she let him? Should she let him?* Maybe he would hug her. Kenzi felt her stomach leap at the thought of full body contact. Shaking each others hands seemed so silly. *Did he expect her to invite him in?* She cleared her throat after unlocking the door.

"Uh, well… this is it." She stood uncertainly.

"Yep." He looked at the door. That didn't help much.

"Yeah."

"So next Sunday, right?"

"Oh, definitely! I appreciate the invite."

"Okay."

Did this conversation have a plan or a direction? Kenzi shifted her feet. She looked up at the moon.

"It's a clear night."

Ray gazed up as well, "Yeah, it is."

Apparently, it would be up to her to somehow end the evening. She stuffed her keys into the pocket of her jeans drawing Ray's gaze to her hips. He didn't miss much. She tentatively held out her hand which he ignored. Instead, he kissed her hard and fast on the cheek.

"Oh!" Kenzi felt her face and entire body grow warm as a lightning pulse of response startled her.

Ray grinned as he called, "Goodnight!" over his shoulder walking to the pickup quickly. He'd already opened the car door and drove off with a roar of shifting gears before she recovered her thoughts. She felt herself smiling at empty space and shook her head as she stepped inside.

Betty drove back to Dallas the next morning. All the next week, Kenzi focused on the day-to-day of the store. She learned as quickly as she could while drawing up her mailing list, organizing various programs and activities, and sorting out the continuous additions of donated books. Small business ownership involved heaps of paperwork, gallons of flexibility, and tons of multi-tasking. She worked hard to keep the volunteers, artists, community groups, sub-contractors, and authors organized. The business classes she took were useful, but the skills she learned on-the-job were phenomenal. She accomplished tasks she'd never dreamed of doing previously. *She loved it!*

Ray's stolen kiss intruded on her thoughts at the oddest moments. She caught sight of him once or twice and waved in passing receiving his beautiful smile in response. Both Kinfolk Books and Organic Soul buzzed in the midst of the back-to-school rush and there hadn't been much time for conversation. He called her Sunday morning while she lounged around in her pajamas.

"I'll pick you up at one o'clock, okay?"

"Sure, I'll be ready." Kenzi allowed the smile in her voice to pass through the phone line.

Precisely at one, she heard the unmistakable roar of his flatbed truck. She dressed in a white t-shirt and jeans. Over the t-shirt, she wore her favorite over shirt she'd had since high school. Once upon a time, dark bluish green melted into purple paisley swirls. But sixteen years of repeated wearing and washing faded the shirt to a yellowish grass green with dark red swirls and softened the fabric's texture to the point it almost seemed she wore a second skin. Ray dressed in jeans as well and a cotton knit short-sleeved shirt.

Ray towered over her. "Are you ready?"

"Are you?" Kenzi smiled flippantly.

Ray grinned at her.

On the way, she listened to his deep drawled southern baritone recitation of the Grant homestead.

"There's about five acres of land and we try to get the most use of it possible. My grandfather planted orchards when he got back from military duty. He planted peach, pear, apple, pecan, and fig trees. Then my father added blackberry bushes and grapevines. They all grow really well in this climate. The only work is cutting them back or tying them to stakes. There's a grove of cane that's pretty tall and we use those as stakes.

Every year, we have a pretty large vegetable garden. My mother used to tend it and sell vegetables at the farmer's market. Nowadays, Aunt T cans and dries a lot. We have tomatoes, peas, squash, lettuce, spinach, collards, snap beans, shell beans, green peppers, yellow peppers, red hot peppers... let's see... okra, scallions, leeks, garlic, sweet corn, sweet potatoes... some other stuff... let me think... We use some at home and then we also use some at the restaurant. Whatever we don't grow, we buy from the farmer's market and little bodegas around town. Sometimes we buy from Houston."

They bounced from the highway to a dirt road as the surrounding area became more rural in appearance with fields of grass and the occasional cow mooing them along their way.

"There's strawberries. We have chickens and a little catfish pond. I love to fish, by the way. Do you fish?"

"No. I can't say that I do, really."

"Too bad. You like bees?"

"I... don't have anything against them."

"We have honeybees that I take care of. No one else really wants to. The bees are used to me and my father showed me how to work with them."

"I can't help you with the bees, my friend."

"Ah, this close!" Ray snapped his fingers. "Well anyway, we grow hay for the horses and once in a while I can sell a few bales when I have help."

"How many horses do you have?"

"Just the two. I ride them around the homestead to check things out and just for fun. Do you ride?"

"Not really. The riding that I've done was mostly trail riding and I didn't have to guide the horses. They already knew what they needed to do and I let them have their way."

"Well, Bud and Star are very tame. You'll like them."

"I hope they like me."

"What's not to like?" Ray gave her a sidelong glance and Kenzi felt herself flush again.

Suddenly, a large, old-fashioned white wooden house complete with wrap-around porch and porch swing emerged from the trees. A silky black dog ran alongside the truck and barked a welcome.

"That must be your homeboy, Jackson," Kenzi laughed.

"Good ole Jackson. Hey boy!"

Jackson wagged and dashed and darted around Ray as if seeing him for the first time in years.

Ray pointed to her. "That's Miss Kenzi, Jackson." Jackson glanced over and licked her hand. She scratched his head and he wagged for her too then dashed around the back of the house.

"He's on his way to tell Santi I'm home."

Kenzi raised her brows. Sure enough, two enormous puffballs on either side of an excited brown face ran behind Jackson to join them as they started towards the house.

"Hi Miss Kenzi!"

"Hi Santi! It's so good to see you again!"

"We're going to pick figs and grapes today. Are you picking too?"

"I'm going to try my best."

"Aunt T's at church."

"Oh?"

"Aunt T goes to church but we don't."

"Oh."

Ray looked a little embarrassed as if wondering what she thought about that. Children often gave more information about a family's lifestyle than they wanted disclosed. Kenzi shrugged. "I don't go to church either."

Ray looked slightly relieved but didn't say anything.

They gathered gloves and tin pails from the tool shed connected to a small greenhouse. "We use the greenhouse as a nursery for new plants."

Kenzi glanced around and saw dogwoods dotted with pink puffballs sitting on either side of the house. Honeysuckle twisted through trellises made of cane attached to the sides of the house. Aloe vera, cacti, and other succulents grew in rock gardens underneath the windows and either side of the front door. Tall, buttery-yellow sunflowers tied to stakes rose in clumps scattered here and there in the large yard.

Partially shaded by a dogwood in back of the house by the kitchen door grew a mint garden in a circular design. Apple mint, spearmint, peppermint, chocolate mint, lemon mint, lemon balm, bee balm, rosemary, lavender, and chamomile spiced and sweetly scented the air.

"Aunt T prepares these into home remedies and Dharma uses them to make teas for us and for the restaurant. The bees visit here too for the anise and basil. They can't get enough."

Ray, Santi, Kenzi, and Jackson walked past the grove of cane that whispered and rustled in the breeze.

They strolled the orchard.

"The fruit we use in salads. Some we make into likka!"

Kenzi laughed and Ray joined her. "For special occasions, of course."

He continued, "There's several rows of preserved fruit from years ago down in our basement." He pointed upwards. "You can see all of these are pecan trees. We use the pecans in cakes, rice dishes, salads, and pecan pie.

"Oh, I love pecan pie. Apple pie and sweet potato pie have their place. But pecan pie? Now that's the stuff dreams are made of!"

"Good girl!" Ray rumbled out a laugh of approval. "Aunt T uses the blackberry juice for cobbler sweet enough to blind you. She also makes blackberry jam and blackberry wine that's really good." They continued talking while they started picking blackberries amid the brambles.

Kenzi looked impressed with the overall resourcefulness of the homestead. "It seems like you have everything you need right here."

"Almost. We still order tea, rice, and coconut. I don't know. We all seemed to have developed a taste for that from our mother. It's funny. Between my mother's exotic flavor and Aunt T's down home style, Dharma really developed her own thing. No one else here in town does it like she does and I think that's why Organic Soul is so popular. She knows how to combine the best of several worlds."

"Dharma can definitely do the thing. I've had the best meals I've had in a long time from Organic Soul."

"She's coming with her two boys later."

Ray continued his lecture. "So the majority of the plants and trees are self-sustaining. They grow without too much tending since the climate is ideal. They're either self-pollinating or planted near similar plants that would pollinate each other. We have a strategy for the vegetables as well. Radishes and carrots are mixed to help each other grow. Pumpkin and squash are planted with corn to control weeds. And we put down hay between some plants to mulch and control weeds. I plant basil with tomatoes and peppers. And then I rotate peanuts among various sections on a schedule that I plot for every season. Very practical. Keeps costs down. Saves us extra work."

"I heard that."

"Waste not, want not. We try to grow everything naturally and organically. The other plants that require more attention I tend with Aunt T and Santi. We use horse manure and chicken manure to fertilize early in the spring and we keep a compost pile. We dust the plants with sulfur and ash to keep bugs and fungus away. That's always a concern for organic plants. Sometimes I spray with non-detergent soap. And, as you can see here, I painted some tree trunks with hot lime mixed with water to prevent pests. Another trick is to put castor oil on corn tassels to keep bugs away."

"Sounds like a lot of work."

Ray sighed but stood proudly surveying the homestead. "It is. There's always something to be done. But I wouldn't have it any other way. I love this place."

During the discussion, Kenzi's paisley overshirt flapped around and finally ripped on a blackberry thorn. She took it off and laid it on a bush since she felt hot under the mid-afternoon sun. She would pick it up after they finished the blackberries and moved on to the grapes. Ray noted the soft outward curve of her breasts in the t-shirt and the inward curve of her waist where the shirt tucked into her jeans. Once in a while she bent over to pick berries low on the vine.

She had a tight, well-toned body. He wondered if she worked out. Jackson also eyed Kenzi. Or rather, he eyed the shirt that flapped at him in the breeze. As Kenzi moved away to continue picking, he sidled up closer. All of a sudden, Jackson snatched it in his mouth and ran with it streaming behind him as if carrying the torch to open the Olympic Games.

Ray and Kenzi gave chase.

"Jackson, come back here!" Ray called his name over and over and reached out to snatch the shirt, as Jackson danced near. Jackson had the time of his life eluding their clutches. Santi yelled at him and joined in the chase. By then, Kenzi didn't want the shirt back full of dog saliva and paw prints.

"Oh, let him have it." She laughed breathless.

"Bad dog, Jackson!" Ray reprimanded Jackson who trotted away with his prize. "Bad dog! Sorry about that, Kenzi."

"No, no! This has been the most fun I've had in a long time. It was worth it. I'll just have to remember to keep my clothes on."

Too late, she realized the hidden meaning in her words and caught Ray's sidelong glance and sly smile. She flushed and walked away quickly towards the grapevines.

About three o'clock, Dharma drove up with Reggie and Davey in tow. The boys tumbled out of the car and ran towards Santi and Jackson while Dharma called out a greeting. She wore overalls and looked ready to work. As the children ran off with Jackson barking and running circles around them, Dharma and Kenzi started on the blue black grapes that swelled near to bursting from ripeness. They worked quickly to get as many grapes picked before the light faded too much to see and Ray moved off to get started on the green grapes. Everything they picked would be left for processing by Aunt Tilly with Dharma's help.

"Dharma, your boys are so cute."

"Oh my, they're a handful." Dharma smiled ruefully. "You have no idea what it took for me to get them dressed and loaded into the car. But they'll sleep real sound tonight after running around with Jackson and Santi."

"I'm guessing you have help?"

Dharma's face softened to a near reverent expression. "Oh my, yes. David's a great father. And I am so in love. Before we married, Ray and Dhan gave him the once-over. It was kind of funny. They tried to trip him up and find something wrong, but no matter what they put on him, he always came out better than ever. Sometimes they made me mad with the tough-guy games, but Ray told me, a real man doesn't let anyone or anything stand in the way of the woman he loves. They're all pretty tight now. Even Aunt T had to admit David was a good man for me. I can't even imagine my life without him. And, of course, with the boys being so active and high energy, I need him to give me a rest now and then. It's real good."

"You know, it's funny. I know I'm older than you by a few years, but it seems as though you've lived much longer. You're a business owner... married with children... Someday, I'd like to know what that feels like."

Dharma laughed. "Oh Kenzi! You've already got the bookstore, so that's one down and two to go."

"Yeah, and the bookstore's probably the easy part!"

"Probably. How's business?"

"Business is busy. Very, very busy!"

"Hey that's a good thing!" Dharma gave her shoulder a pat.

"Definitely! I'm learning something new everyday."

They moved along the rows of vines filling their pails with *thunks*. Once one pail filled, they got another and another.

Kenzi mused thoughtfully. "I often wonder if I'll ever really settle down."

"Well." Dharma gave her a sidelong glance. "Truthfully, I often wonder what it might have been like to travel as much as you have. Just pick up and pack up and see the world whenever the mood struck. But only once in a while. My life is here and I would never trade my children or my husband for anything in the world." Dharma gave Kenzi another sidelong glance. "I hear the single life is pretty rough on a sister these days."

"You would not believe." Kenzi sighed but decided not to elaborate further. Both of their gazes drifted to Ray. She quickly changed the subject remembering Dharma's tendency to direct the flow of conversation.

"So, out of curiosity, how did you fall into the restaurant business? I mean, what you've done with Organic Soul is simply phenomenal and I'm definitely impressed."

"Let's see. How did it all begin?" Dharma wrinkled her brow. "Well, our parents died when I was eighteen, just after I graduated high school. Ray was already in college, but he dropped out to work. We talked together and decided that I would take business classes at night. During the day, I worked full-time at the soul food restaurant and worked upwards in responsibility every so often. The owners liked me and when they decided to retire, they approached me to buy them out. By that time, I was manager and I knew every position in the restaurant – the floor, the kitchen, and the office. So, I brought it up to Ray and Aunt T and we talked it over. We all put our money together and even Dhan kicked in to invest, and we prepared for the launch. About that same time, I met David. We started talking and he thought it was wonderful that I wanted to own and operate a business. Ray, Dhan, and Aunt T wanted to make sure he wasn't trying to take advantage and that's why he got such a hard time. He proved himself though. He had his own thing going on and wasn't trying to hang on. Once we married, he also invested in the store and now he works in the kitchen or wherever he's needed."

"That's such a beautiful story. Your family sounds very close."

"Reggie and Davey drew everybody even closer together, you know. I think we were all still recovering from the deaths of my parents and it seemed as though Reggie and Davey made the holidays brighter for the whole family. Santi too. My only regret is that my mother and father never got to see my children." Dharma paused briefly as tears came to her eyes.

"I'm sorry, girl." Kenzi stopped working to face Dharma sympathetically.

"No, no it's okay. It is. I know they are watching over all of us and we try our best to keep the family legacy going. I don't know what we would have done without Aunt T, though."

"I wonder when I'll meet her."

"Oh, one of these days. And once you do, you'll surely never forget her!" Dharma laughed.

A short distance away, they saw Santi, Reggie, Davey, and Jackson move their games closer to Ray. They romped around him keeping up chatter while he worked. Kenzi heard deep laughter ring out as Ray nudged Reggie (or Davey?) and rubbed their heads over a joke.

Dharma noticed Kenzi's interest and remarked, "You know, Ray always kids me that Santi bosses Reggie and Davey around the same way I used to boss him and Dhan. Well, actually, he says I still do." Dharma laughed. "I can't help it, though. Sometimes they need my help!" Kenzi laughed with her.

"You do seem to have things organized and in its proper place."

"Ray and Dhan let me do a little pushing and prodding. I've been doing that anyway since we've been little. But David? No, no, no, no, no. He won't stand for it. He let's me know exactly how far to go and where to stop." Dharma sighed. "Oh, I love that man."

They'd picked every grape and blackberry within reach just as dusk fell. In the kitchen, Dharma made sandwiches for everyone while Kenzi and Ray rinsed the fruit in large tubs with small holes punched in the bottom. These they left for Aunt Tilly. Kenzi sat in the midst of the children still excited from the afternoon's romp and talked with Ray and Dharma about the bookstore's first week. They told Dharma about chasing Jackson around for Kenzi's shirt and Dharma added her own, "Bad dog!" to Jackson who responded with a "What?" expression. She'd never known how lonely she had been for a family setting all the years she lived alone until that moment. The atmosphere got a little crazy with Jackson's occasional bark and the children's rolling and jumping and giggling.

Once, she overheard Dharma mention that Santi's smile reminded her of Darlene's. Out of the corner of her eye, she saw Ray's locs swing followed by a long look pointed Dharma's direction. Then a single low-voiced word.

"Don't."

Then the children's voices piped up and covered the silence.

Kenzi felt sorry to leave. She felt recharged and energized for the second week of work. She wore a small smile all the way home as she and Ray listened to a local blues station in comfortable silence. At her door, she paused as she woke a little from her stupor and became aware of Ray's large dark frame filling in the tiny space on her doorstep.

Sure enough, he kissed her. This time, on the mouth. The kiss lingered and she felt her body shake as tiny bolts zinged from one point to another. Even though his mouth pressed hers only for a few seconds, she felt the response all over her body. And again, she froze into place.

"Kenzi, thank you so much for coming out today. I hope you had a good time."

"I had a great time. Your family is terrific."

"Well, you haven't met Dhan yet." Ray had a solemn look of warning.

Kenzi raised her brows.

"I'm teasing! Dhan's a cool bro. And you'll probably get to know my aunt soon enough." Ray laughed.

"I appreciate you sharing the day with me, Ray. It was a nice change of pace from watching television."

He kissed her swift and hard again. He rubbed her cheek and she leaned into his hand. A quick image of her leaning on his hand in bed after a love session made her catch her breath. He smiled at her.

"Goodnight, Kenzi."

"Goodnight, Ray." Her heart fluttered for a good ten minutes after he left.

Monday morning, Lina called from Dallas. "Why did I get voicemail during your work hours, Kenzi? Naughty, naughty." *Cackle.* "I saw from the website you're having a children's sale the day after tomorrow. Sounds like you might need some help down there if you can't even get to the phone. So I'll be down tomorrow. Bye!"

Well, she needed the help. Kenzi sighed. Volunteers didn't fall from the sky or grow on trees. Everyone's own lives kept them so busy. *Do it for the shop, Kenzi.* She told herself to make the most of whatever resources she had available. That included Lina.

And so, late Tuesday morning, Lina sailed into the store and Kenzi handed her a feather duster. After a couple of bored swipes, Lina gave herself a coffee break and thumbed through a few beauty and fashion books while Kenzi vacuumed around her.

"Lina, would you bring us both back a lunch from Organic Soul?" At least if Lina kept out of the way, she could finish cleaning. Lina came back half an hour later with a greasy sack from a fast food restaurant. "It was too crowded in there."

"Any change?" Kenzi asked.

"Nope, I used that for gas." Lina shrugged.

So the dusting and the lunch run didn't work out so well. Kenzi asked Lina to face out the front covers of the children's books on the shelves for higher sales. Lina decided to stack them on tables face-up.

"Better this way." Another shrug. "At my salon, we always try to make the most of the space we have."

Kenzi wanted to hit her with an encyclopedia. The real heavy blue one just inches away from her trembling fingers.

"Okay, take it from the top."

"Mom, some days, I feel as if I'm pushing a loaded cart uphill and that someone's on the other side pushing down. I work ten to twelve hour days to provide service for the store and to keep the hours I posted, but it never seems enough. I'm trying, but there is pressure coming from many directions. I'm feeling a little stressed, to tell the truth."

Kenzi looked stressed as she counted off the complaints.

Betty put on the lecture hat. "I know. Some people are never going to be happy with what you do. If you invited Jesus down from Heaven to do a book signing of the King James Version, someone would have a problem because you served crackers instead of chips. Some advice and criticism, as long as it's constructive, is good. Other times, it has no merit and is spoken just to put you down and make the other person feel justified with their own personal failures and shortcomings. In that respect, the criticism isn't constructive at all. It's destructive. It's very important to know the difference."

"Okay Mom, along those lines, Lina really seems to have either something against me or the store. I think it's me. Even though we're cousins and we're supposed to be family, she makes these snide remarks and then goes out of her way to do the opposite of what I ask her to do. For instance, in organizing these displays, not only did she not help me, she created more work for me since I have to go behind her now and fix them. And I gave her clear instructions. I just couldn't take it anymore, so I gave her the afternoon off. She's probably on her way back to Dallas."

"You know, in some ways, Kenzi, I think Lina looks up to you." Betty hesitated for a moment and then continued. "You've been places and done things that she hasn't and that forces her to look at her own life and what she might want to do but hasn't been able or thinks she hasn't been able to do."

"That makes sense, but still, I'm not her punching bag."

"It's a lifestyle choice, Kenzi. And it's prioritizing what's important in life. Where a person spends their money says a lot about them. You spent yours on education, travel, and now Kinfolk Books. Be proud that you focused on what was important to you and went the one step further of actually *doing* what you said you would do instead of talking about it and making excuses."

"I don't mind that she has different priorities, I'm just tired of her throwing salt and shade over what I'm trying to do. She's made fun of the way I speak, my clothes, my hair. I mean, I'm still not even sure what I did to her to cause this."

"There are people who derive their power and a sense of worth from their ability to build. And then there are those who derive their power from their ability to tear down. And in this way, they try to make their problems your problems. All you can do is just keep focused on making Kinfolk the best it can be and not let yourself be distracted. Keep it moving. Okay?" Betty waited.

"Okay, thanks Mom. Thanks for listening. I do want to stay focused on building the store. I'm ready to get some real work done today! I'll see you soon, okay?"

"Anytime, child. But Kenzi? One last thing."

"Yes?"

"Watch the whining."

Zing.

Betty did know more than she let on how Kenzi felt. Once upon a time, she too rose as a shining star, growing up in a place where bright lights attracted the wrong kind of attention. She came of age in the days of segregation in the South where active thwarting of economic success and educational ambition pressed down the lives of black residents. How far could the Malton family have come without their lives and labor robbed and stolen under the share-cropping system sanctioned by Jim Crow?

Betty remembered those days of intimidation. She remembered her father, Kenzi's grandaddy, devoting sunup-sundown hours growing fields of cotton just to break slightly less than even when the landowner tabulated production at the end of the day and changed the price of doing business to suit himself. She vowed to help Mama Dee and Grandaddy to hold on to their land and even as she worked her way through school, she sent money back home until they paid the very last note. At last her father and mother could rest. They moved to the city to live near Betty and rented the property to tenants in order to keep up the property tax.

When Betty met Kenzi's father, she admired his upward-mobility and ambition. He admired her spirit and strength. They married and seemed to be set for middle-class comfort.

After Kenzi hung up the phone with her mother, a middle-aged gentleman stopped in the store. A regular visitor, but not a customer. Always careful to never spend any money at the store, he drank five cups of complimentary coffee. He stood by the shelves staring at her. Then he crept closer to lean against the counter to stare at her, moving a few inches away only when a customer approached to pay. Generally, the conversation would last two hours and end...

"You know what you need? You need more customers."

"That's a very good point. Kinfolk can always use more customers. I'm going to put these receipts in order, but feel free to browse the store."

"Oh, I don't read," he said, not moving an inch and still not blinking, "Can I have some more coffee?"

"Sure, help yourself." *To the sixth cup.* "I'm gonna shelve some books in the children's area to prepare for our sale tomorrow. If you need anything, just let me know." *You stay there.*

She walked backed to the children's area. He followed her with his coffee. She announced that she would hang a painting near the front. He followed again and hovered closely over her. She announced that she would go to the other side of the store to move some furniture. He decided to head that direction as well. Kenzi had had enough for the day. She took a deep breath and faced him.

"You know what? I'm so sorry I'm unable to visit with you today. Since I'm the only full-time employee, I can't afford to let work pile up too much." She smiled her regret. Inside her head, she screamed hysterically, *Oh, God. Please leave. Leave!*

He left, but not before he asked for and received another cup of coffee for the road.

An hour later, Betty arrived. Kenzi reenacted her encounters with the elderly gentleman. "The guy is really creeping me out and making me nervous like I'm being stalked in my own store."

"Kenzi, it's still a man's world in the South. Since you are young and pretty, he's attracted. From all the time he's spent here and the conversations you've had, he probably knows that you're single. He's not going anywhere until you make it clear there's no chance."

"I'm definitely not attracted to him. But how do I finesse a conversation like that since he's a customer? Sort of. For all I know, he's highly connected in the community. I don't want any trouble."

"Well, he sounds a little dense, to tell the truth, from all the hints you've already dropped. He probably won't get it until you present a large boyfriend, real or otherwise, to talk to him man-to-man. Some old-school men are the types who respect an answer of 'no' only from other men. They would never take the authority of a young woman seriously. They tend to resent that authority and challenge it various ways – you know, push boundaries to see how far you'll let him go. That type."

Sigh! Activate... Franklin?

Or not.

"I'm too busy for those games, Kenzi," he said. "Besides, I carpooled."

Activate, Ray?

Betty stayed overnight. The next day, the children's sale went extremely well. News of the store's existence spread further into the community. Betty helped her to sign up more additions to the children's art class and even got an offer for story time reading. Moments of bookselling like these, Kenzi loved. She hugged her mother.

"Thank you so much for everything yesterday and today. I couldn't have done it without you."

"Hang in there, Kenzi. No one said it would be easy or fair. This is the business world. Chin up, girl."

"You're right. I'm gonna hang in there."

She finally called over to Organic Soul.

"Soooo... Ray finally gets to be Kenzi's man, hunh?" Ray teased her laughingly.

"Well, pretend to," Kenzi muttered.

"Tell you what I'll do." Ray paused dramatically.

"What?" Kenzi laughed.

"When he shows up, call over to Organic Soul and tell me... tell me my book order has arrived... and I'll know to come over right away. How's that?"

"Your book order has arrived," Kenzi repeated carefully. "Okay, sounds good! And Ray?"

"Yeaaaah, boooo?" Ray drawled spectacularly, just for her.

"Please don't call me that. Yuck!"

"I'm just practicing. I thought we were going steady?"

"Pretend steady, Ray," Kenzi laughed.

"Only for you, baby."

"Uh, thanks, okay?"

"You got it, boo!" He hung up on her.

It went without a hitch. Later that week, her shadow showed. Kenzi made the call and then walked back towards the children's area. He followed her and this time, Kenzi took note of the glint in his eyes. He thought it was funny. But not for much longer.

As they returned to the counter, they encountered Ray filling the elderly gentleman's spot with his large frame. Whenever the elderly gentleman attempted to address Kenzi directly or follow her around the store, Ray engaged him in conversation. *The Shadow Meets The Hulk.* Foiled at last! Thwarted by the big man and Kenzi's unresponsiveness, he mumbled something unintelligible under his breath on his way out.

Kenzi felt so relieved and grateful for Ray's being there for her. Without questions, without blame, without pointing fingers, without excuses, he just came.

Kenzi put her hand in his. "Ray, I think it worked."

"Well, anytime you need a man, *a real man* in your life, give me a call." Ray looked directly into her eyes and gave her hand a hard squeeze.

Kenzi sucked in her breath as she felt the now-familiar warm tingle flow from her scalp to her toes.

"I'll... keep that in mind."

Chapter 5

The Interactions

A large color photo of Kenzi standing in front of the children's section appeared in the *Rollins Gazette*. The unexpected write-up on Kinfolk Books boosted traffic at the store.

The young man spoke in earnest. "Radicals in Anarchy Brotherhood usually have very tame meetings. We'd only need the room for three hours to recruit and do a short talk."

"Three hours?"

"Well, usually any talk we give is followed by a pretty intense Q&A."

"I… see. Let me read through your newsletter and check out the website and I'll get back to you as soon as I can."

A university faculty member asked about holding a seminar in the meeting room. Kenzi signed up Sustainable Development in the Urban Arena.

"You know," the woman running seminar casually mentioned, "the university has a grant for small businesses involved in community service programs."

Kenzi glanced up sharply.

"If you write the proposal and have it accepted by the committee, a grant like that could pay for additional help and supplies for your children's art and story time volunteers. Then you could use the savings somewhere else in your budget. I know a few other businesses in Rollins have done that."

"Do you know the deadline?"

"November 15th. That doesn't give you a lot of time, but if you really want it…"

Kenzi decided to send in an application. With Betty's help, she set to work documenting the program.

"Mom, I'm gonna work on the budget and statistics. I'm also tracking expenses. We can do this in time. I know it."

"Well, what else do you need?"

"Pictures. Pictures of everything we do here. And testimonials and letters of support from the children's art participants – everyone involved with the art class."

"Right on, Boss Lady!" Betty saluted.

"Mother, stop!" Kenzi laughed.

It didn't escape Ray's notice that Santi had taken a real liking to both Stacy and Kenzi. Santi imitated Kenzi's hairstyle, fluffing out her curls into an afro. In a slow period between contract jobs, he sat in on the children's art class in fatherly support for Santi's efforts. That day they worked on portraits. Stacy appeared greatly amused when he drew a picture of Kenzi with a great oversize bush of gigantic frizzy, curly afro and deeply golden eyes ringed by black in loving detail.

"So what do you plan to do about that, girl?" Stacy demanded.

"Do about what?"

"What do you think? Look at it!"

Kenzi shrugged looking through her desk drawers searching for something. "He's just having fun."

"Uh-huh. Right, Kenzi." Stacy rolled her eyes with a laugh.

One day, the door to Kinfolk Books buzzed as it swung open. Kenzi recognized the store's visitor from opening day. The man who'd stared at her in a hard kind of way.

"Hi," he greeted her curtly then stalked from section to section of the store.

"Can I help you find anything?"

"No, you don't have anything I want here." The man shook his head and pursed his lips in disgust.

"What are you looking for?"

"You don't have it. As a matter of fact, you don't have a lot. You have a very limited selection here." He stepped closer to her and continued abruptly. "Where do you get your inventory?"

Kenzi felt a little taken aback by his abrupt attitude. She held out her hand. "Hello. I'm Kenzi Malton. How are you doing?"

"I'm Bobby Forrest. You're the owner, right?" He ignored her outstretched hand.

"Yes, I'm the owner." Kenzi frowned and dropped her hand to shuffle various business papers off the counter.

"So answer the question." He spoke to her as if she'd just started kindergarten. "Where do you get your books? How much do you pay for them?"

Slightly confused, Kenzi felt unease prickle through her. "Well, to tell the truth, there are too may sources to name."

"Like where?" He waited expectantly.

"Just all over the place." Kenzi waved dramatically and dismissively.

"Hmm. This is your first business isn't it?"

"Yes. It is."

"I thought so. You need some more science fiction." He pointed to the store's science fiction section. "I have some in the trunk of my car that I can sell to you. No one's going to come here just for what you have on these shelves."

The bell rang and a large, heavyset woman walked in and gave Kenzi a brief wave. Kenzi waved back and smiled.

Bobby Forrest repeated the same questions different ways and impatiently prodded Kenzi for answers. She wondered whether he was an undercover cop on some case. The heavyset woman stood quietly browsing the sports section, but Kenzi sensed she listened to the exchange with Forrest. Forrest ignored the woman completely as if she didn't exist.

After hearing Kenzi politely deflect a question about the mark-up percentage on her inventory for the second time, the woman decided she had no interest in speed-skating after all. *That conversation should have ended sixteen questions ago!* She cleared her throat loudly and authoritatively and walked the slow, measured, regal walk of a woman who hadn't taken mess off anyone in a long time to the check-out counter where Kenzi and Forrest stood.

"He-e-e-y, Miss Kenzi! And how are you today?"

The woman maneuvered her matronly frame to crowd Forrest. When faced with two large bosoms and a prominent back side, he had no choice but to give way or involuntarily feel up a respected member of the community. He gave way.

"I'm fine, thank you. How are you?"

The woman's, "Are you still here and did you have anything left to say?" expression pretty much finished Forrest off. He had no place to go except back out the door. The woman shrugged and shooed him out of her mind the same way she shooed him out the door.

Kenzi managed to keep a straight face to hide both her relief and the urge to laugh out loud. This woman didn't play around. Having seen photos of the family at the Grant homestead, she realized suddenly that this woman had to be no other than Ray's Aunt Tilly. Her words drawled out with a deep, dark, sweet, smooth, slow molasses southern quality that often lulled the unsuspecting into a sense of comfort. Then the tangy aftertaste hit. It caught the overconfident off-guard leaving them dazed, unsure of whether or not she'd just told them off.

"Well, well now Miss Kenzi. Is it Miss or Mrs?" Aunt Tilly already knew Kenzi's state of unmarriagement from Dharma. But if Kenzi revealed this herself, then technically, it didn't count as gossip.

"I guess it would be Miss. But please just call me Kenzi. Are you Miss Tilly?"

"I am. I guess Santi must have told you 'bout ole Miss Tilly, hunh? That chile loves to talk and she's been goin' on and on about all the Kinfolk. So I had to come and see what was goin' on heah."

"Santi is a beautiful child. She told me a lot about living out in the country and I had so much fun when I visited. I'm so sorry I missed you. I did learn that you make quilts. Are those the quilts I saw hanging in Organic Soul? They're wonderful!"

Bless her heart. Aunt Tilly thought as she beamed back. The girl has a little bit of sense about her.

"Oh yes, honey. I been makin' quilts for long as I can remember. My mama showed me, her mama showed her, and her mama showed her. All the aunts and grandmothers and ladies of the church would get together and work on quilts. We told stories and shared recipes. We talked about what was going on in the community. Back then, we didn't all hang in front of the television and the computer so much and have cell phones rangin' all the time. We actually spoke to each other back then. *In person.* Folk just don't do that so much nowadays. Gone out of style. Just like quiltin'. The young people go to factory outlet malls and order quilts out of catalogs and then try to call that country decoratin'." She snorted derisively. "Country decoratin' they call that. No appreciation for the old way."

"Well you know, Miss Tilly, there might be people like yourself who still view quilting as an art and tradition. Sometimes people miss each other in the hustle and bustle of life. I could post a notice on the bulletin board if you want to start a club or a quilting organization. I'd be happy too."

Aunt Tilly looked at her sharply and saw Kenzi gazing back with a smile and an air of wide-eyed inquiry.

"Ummm hmmmm." Aunt Tilly made that long, drawn-out sound characteristic of someone who speculated, considered, and turned over a piece of information and ran it through an internal database of human response analysis before forming an opinion or making a decision.

Aunt Tilly covertly eye-balled Kenzi. The girl didn't seem to have a crazy look about herself. She had an education. She had a "white" way of talking but didn't put on too many airs. So far, she hadn't indicated any criminal tendencies. Because Aunt Tilly wouldn't have any flighty golightly, siddity, wannabe, ghetto thug-lovin, bling-blingin around her nephew and grandniece. *No sir!* Not again, at least.

Santi's mother, Darlene, had caught her off guard and she hadn't acted quickly enough, but now she knew to look sharp. She wouldn't take any mess and neither would Ray or Santi. Besides, she actually did want to see if any quilters out there had appreciation for the way things ought to be done. Still, the girl needed to know Aunt Tilly wasn't easy like Sunday morning.

"Let me think on that for a minute. I don't just rush into somethin' just 'cause it sound like somethin'. Us old folk like to take their time, you know."

Kenzi watched the speculation play across Aunt Tilly's face. She knew that Aunt Tilly not only evaluated her offer, she also evaluated Kenzi. The way Kenzi spoke, the words she used, how she used them, her hair, her clothes, her demeanor, her character, her integrity, all these underwent consideration. She felt Aunt Tilly's eyes rove over her gigantic afro and worn jeans and starchy white cotton shirt from three years ago and leather sandals broken in to fit the shape of her feet. She wondered what she looked like to a woman who wore her silvered hair firmly tucked under a proper straw hat, a green sun dress, matching green slippers, and a straw purse neatly snapped shut.

Like a boho hobo, maybe.

Kenzi took a breath. "Would you like some tea, Miss Tilly?"

Aunt Tilly brightened. "Why yes, thank ya, Kenzi. That is very kind." She cleared her throat gently. "I am a tad thirsty."

Giving Aunt Tilly time to overcome her suspicions and to finish her inspection, Kenzi got up to make them both a cup of spearmint tea. She spoke on the subject she knew they could both agree on.

"It is so easy to see Santi has been raised by people who love her. She's so happy and smart. We have some of her drawings hanging in the children's area. Would you like to see them?"

Well, of course she wants to see her grandniece's drawings! Make sure they were hung correctly. She and Kenzi slowly made their way over to the children's area while Kenzi pointed out various points of interest in the store. Aunt Tilly's response each time remained the long slow, drawn out, "Ummmm hmmmm" noise that could mean everything or nothing at all. After a careful inspection of the children's area, Aunt Tilly seemed pleased. They discussed Santi some more and Aunt Tilly was quite forthcoming.

Kenzi understood that somewhere between the quilt conversation, the tea, and Santi's drawings, Aunt Tilly accepted her.

But she remained aware of Aunt Tilly's unspoken, but clearly indicated assessment of how things stood. *You hurt my family, you hurt me. And when someone hurts me, I git ta body-slammin' first and askin' questions later. I don't want to do that. I don't look to do that. But sure as I'm standin' here, I will do that.*

"Well, the one thing that makes us all human is that we come from families and situations that aren't always ideal. We've all been hurt and experience pain. When I was young, my father left us and my mother struggled to keep a roof over our heads. I used to miss both her and him. I'd miss him because he found other things to do besides be a parent. I'd miss her because she had two jobs and was always working. My mother knew that I was lonely and scared. She kept books around the house for me to read and when I read them, I could use my imagination to pretend that things were better than they were."

Kenzi seemed to be looking at a point far away instead of at Aunt Tilly. Aunt Tilly listened quietly and didn't interrupt.

"At school, my teachers tried to track me into the lower level classes. But my mother insisted they put me in the accelerated classes, the hard ones with all the smart kids. Because I'd read so much, I had quite a large vocabulary so spelling and language and literature came easily to me. So I kept up with the other kids but I still missed my friends. They always seemed to have a lot more fun than I did."

Kenzi came out of her reverie of memory to look at Aunt Tilly.

"Still, you know, that is why I feel it is so important to catch children when they are young and to guide their educations and their talents. There are so many people out there saying so many true and untrue things about the future of children these days based on their own personal prejudices. They crush that creativity down and kill the spirit behind it. They prescribe medication. They standardize tests. Worst of all, they make pretty prejudiced assumptions about intelligence levels.

You know, if my mother hadn't intervened, I do think I might never have really believed in myself. I don't like to think where I might have ended up. Thank God she paid attention and didn't allow it to happen. She sacrificed a lot for me.

Miss Tilly, I don't have children myself, but I care very much what happens to them. I think most children are just looking for someone to believe in them and to provide the means for them to express themselves."

Kenzi had begun to wave her hands in the air to illustrate her points. She always became excited about subjects she truly believed in.

"But back to Santi… Ray is a good father to Santi and he did what no other parent has done. He sat in with the class and drew with them. He looked like he had a good time."

Kenzi decided to leave out the part that Ray's drawing caricatured her.

"He is very supportive and I respect him for that. Actually, he is the type of father I wished I'd had growing up."

Kenzi teared up for a second and turned away slightly to gather her composure by pretending to straighten a couple of the chairs. She felt embarrassed that she'd opened up her feelings like that. She'd never told anyone all of this. Not even her mother or Stacy.

Aunt Tilly stood silent a moment, taken aback both by Kenzi's dedication and her revelations. She didn't expect all that. *High strung,* she decided. Still, as one educator to another, she empathized and gamely helped to smooth out the awkward moment with plenty of drawled molasses.

"Child, I hear ya. We do need to watch out for the children today. Too many people want to use them for ill or just ignore them and walk away like a broken toy. I used to be a schoolteacher myself and I've seen it happen first hand. Some of the ones I tried to reach, nobody cared for them at home and they drifted away not knowing what to do with themselves till the law came and gave 'em some hots an a cot. Sometimes, even your family's like that and you got to make hard decisions to keep the rest safe. Cryin' shame. But we keep our Santi and her little cousins safe. You've got quite a store here and I think you'll do all right. Imma stop in from time to time to check on thangs. I like to know what's goin' on."

Kenzi knew the older woman's casual glance sweeping over her and the store missed no detail.

"But before I go, chile, lemme tell you one thing you need to know. And listen to Miss Tilly good now."

Miss Tilly's stare hardened. "Don't let *nobody* crowd your space or try to make you feel less than what you are. Hear? Don't let *nobody* handle you. You let people know what the boundaries are. It's okay to have rules for people to follow. This *your* store and if you don't make decisions, people will make them for you."

Kenzi nodded her head.

Aunt Tilly didn't really hug people she barely knew. Long ago, she learned that Ray and Dharma and Dhan were touchy-feely when she came to live with them. They got that from their mama. Of course, Aunt Tilly learned to hug them every time they reached for her as well. Not until beautiful Santi came along and broke her heart did Aunt Tilly start handing out her big soft hugs like candy. She loved all those children – beautifully, sensitive Santi who followed her around asking questions and mischievous Reggie and Davey who tumbled around with Jackson in the grass and came to her to get their little cuts and scrapes cleaned up.

This time, she compromised by putting her arm around Kenzi's shoulders for a tight, quick squeeze. Aunt Tilly certainly had a way.

Kenzi had poured out her life to Aunt Tilly without realizing it. And Aunt Tilly hadn't even asked her to do so.

"Thank you so much, Miss Tilly. I'll keep everything you said in mind."

"By the way, how did you get a name like Kenzi? Is that African?"

"No, no," Kenzi laughed. "My full name is Mackenzie which is longer than most people want to say or are able to say. Some of my classmates tried to shorten it to Mac, which I couldn't stand. So I headed everyone off at the pass and decided that Kenzi sounded more like me."

"Ummmm hmmmm." Aunt Tilly made a slow, gracious turn and spoke over her shoulder. "I'll make a flyer and have Santi bring it to the store to post up. Next time you come out to the homestead, make sure I'm there so I can show you around proper."

As the door shut behind her, Kenzi smiled as she shook her head. Everyone needed an Aunt Tilly in their lives.

Kenzi received various propositions.

Bachelor Number One offered to help Kenzi with handy jobs around the shop such as shelf-installations, painting, and heavy lifting. Kenzi could repay him on her back while cheerleading his bizarre (and somewhat sinister) resolution to become a minister.

She shuddered and shuddered again at the pseudo-religious-intellectual babbling intercut by leers and nips from a tiny silver canteen of scotch. The poor, deluded creature. She remained upright and taught herself how to use a drill, how to paint, how to saw, and how to find studs behind the walls through trial and error. She marked several walls with her mistakes. These, she caulked and sanded down. *Oh well. Live and learn.*

Bachelor Number Two assured her of his credentials as a "good catch" and sought to go for the hard sale by requesting Kenzi to please not force him to adopt a "European women-only need apply" policy in his love life. Sheez! Got emotional blackmail? Got manipulation? *Do what you gotta, man!* Kenzi wondered who actually gave birth to these fools and why their mothers thought the pain seemed worth it.

Bachelor Number Three revealed his two divorces and the fact that, "Me and my latest ex-wife still use each other for sex." He had no intention of remarrying and didn't want to be kept on a tight leash.

"I need time to hang with the fellas without a lot of drama, you know." Kenzi stared in amazement as she silently rewarded him points for honesty.

She snatched the points away immediately once he revealed that he absolutely, positively did not want any more children other than the eleven-year-old daughter he already allowed himself the privilege to father. Kenzi considered asking him whether he thought someone like himself would make a good catch for his daughter, but decided she didn't have enough attention span to wait for the response.

This brought Kenzi's thoughts to Bachelor Number Four - Franklin Bellaire - who strolled in from time to time to offer Kenzi advice. Kenzi, herself, quickly learned that talking and doing existed as two entirely different things. A small retail business had more in common with a roller coaster than the more level, heavily regulated and bureaucratic maze that defined the university system. Unfortunately, never having owned a business himself, Franklin didn't know that. Kenzi struggled to remember why she spent time with him. *Oh yeah, because I've watched all my dvds twenty times already and television gets dull after a while.*

Sigh.

Kenzi locked the front door and returned to the backroom to do some late-night repricing in anticipation of the new load from the estate sale she would bid on tomorrow.

Books don't price themselves.

What about Ray? He had issues too. What was the deal with Santi's mother? Some hard feelings remained there. What was that all about? And he scared her. All that staring! He stripped her body and soul naked every time he looked at her. And whenever she looked at him, she felt herself melting away. He made her feel high. He made her feel addicted. Her breasts still tingled at the thought of him. That is too much man for this whole Earth.

Just finish this rack and call it a night.

She wakes up suddenly feeling a heated presence in the room. Ray, darker than the night itself, bending over her nude body. A black curtain of locs hangs down touching her neck and breasts. He grabs her wrists and pins them to the bed over her head and slowly lowers himself down supported on his elbows. He covers her completely with his massive frame and begins to massage her with his body like a heavy, living, undulating blanket. She drowns helplessly in a whirlpool of moans and velvety dark skin.

Twenty-five cents. Fifty-cents. One dollar.

Ray fixes a light in the back room shirtless. His massive muscular arms are lifted over his head. As he picks up various tools to manipulate wires, his muscles flex and undulate, tense and relax. Her gaze is locked onto the tight, rounded firmness of his backside in jeans. He turns, suddenly, and catches her looking before she can look away. His expression is mocking. She stands helplessly embarrassed and unable to look away.

This one has pages ripped out. Toss.

Ray, wearing nothing but velvety dark brown-black skin. He holds a bowl of strawberries swimming in melted chocolate out to her. She loves strawberries. She loves chocolate. Kenzi reaches longingly, pleadingly. Ray sees the desire in her eyes and smiles teasingly, tantalizingly. He overturns the bowl in his naked lap. She can have all the strawberries and chocolate that she wants.

This belongs in rare and collectible.

Ray bending.

Fifty cents.

Ray reaching.

Pages stuck together.

Flexing.

What happened to the cover?

Teasing.

Damn!

Kenzi irritably clutched the price gun and savagely branded innocent books in the discount rack like so much cattle on the nearby Rollins ranches.

Chapter 6

Kenzi and Ray

"Kenzi, you should have called earlier like we agreed. You told me you'd be ready at three. It's four-thirty. I don't have time for this."

A customer tipped Kenzi to the estate sale. Franklin gave her a lift to the edge of town to place bids from the small budget she set aside for new acquisitions.

"Franklin, I'm sorry. I couldn't get away at three. There was still bidding on books I needed for the store and I couldn't stop to call in the middle of the bidding. Then I had to go and do the paperwork to claim them."

Franklin remained silent.

Am I supposed to beg?

"Franklin, I think it's going to rain and its getting dark outside. I need to get these books to the store so they won't get wet. I paid five hundred dollars for this inventory. Can't you pick me up?"

Kenzi. You just don't think. You remember I tried to give you that order and you couldn't handle that either."

"Franklin, you asked me to purchase over one thousand dollars worth of books. Like I already told you before, Kinfolk's start-up costs were too high. It was even more than the money I'd set aside for emergency expenses. There was no way I could have obligated the store to that large a purchase. I told you I could place the order at a discount if Kinfolk received payment in advance."

Franklin was disgusted. "Kenzi, that's just stupid."

Kenzi was firm. "Well, Kinfolk absolutely could not carry more debt. Plus, I needed accountability for the time and expense involved in placing the orders."

"Which is why I went with a chain bookstore. How can you call yourself a bookstore if you don't do special orders? How do you expect to be taken seriously?" Yet, he still sent the students to her to purchase the books forcing her to explain why the store didn't have the books. Kenzi shook her head and told herself that *that* should have been the final straw. Not this.

"And that guy with his dreadful locks and jeans and sandals brings down the atmosphere."

"Franklin, what on earth are you talking about now?"

"What's his name? You know. *Ramen* noodles or whatever foreigner he's supposed to be. He hangs around too much. Your store looks like a homeless shelter."

"He's been helping me out."

"He's simple, Kenzi. How is he helping you? With what? His G.E.D.?"

Kenzi sucked in her breath. "You know what? That is mean, Franklin, even for you. I don't even know his educational background. It never came up in conversation. But he knows what he's doing."

"Scaring away customers."

"Uncalled for, Franklin! And untrue. As a matter of fact, almost everyone who comes into the store knows him and Dharma. The same people who eat at Organic Soul also shop at Kinfolk. We share customers. What's your problem anyway?"

"He has an out-of-wedlock child, doesn't he?" Franklin gave an ugly laugh. "I guess what the world needs now is yet another baby daddy. Or maybe you do."

Kenzi could hear her voice rising. "Franklin! You are just way out of line on this! Way out of line. He is a wonderful father to that child and she is beautiful, intelligent, and talented. More men could learn from his example."

"More men like *who*? You must be joking! Or in heat. Call *him* for a ride since you like him so much."

As the conversation between and Franklin became heated, Kenzi walked further away from the workmen who broke down the booths and packed up unsold merchandise from the estate sale.

"Franklin, why are you acting like such an ass? We worked this out days ago. You said you would drop me off and then pick me up. I wouldn't have come out here if I'd known you wouldn't give me a ride back. You should have said so." He really pissed her off.

Franklin kept his voice annoyingly calm. "Kenzi, number one, you're hysterical. Number two, you're a nag."

Kenzi let out her breath and paused to regain equilibrium. "Wait! Just wait. Look, Franklin. Just what is going on here? What brought all this on?"

"I'm trying to help you to do a better job and be a better person."

"You never have anything good to say, Franklin. Just criticism after criticism. You do know it's possible to offer an opinion or suggestion about something without insulting the person. Don't you like anybody?"

"You are so goddamn sensitive, Kenzi." Franklin's tone was snide.

"And you're unnecessarily negative. About yourself and everyone else."

"Get a job, Kenzi."

"Franklin…"

"Call the Baby Daddy for a ride. I'm busy."

Click.

After he hung up in her face, she cursed for a full five minutes which helped her to clear her mind of a lot of issues. She'd known he had personality flaws. She had to admit that she'd chosen to overlook them because she had flaws of her own. She'd overlooked too much about herself and the men she'd allowed into her life.

But at least Franklin had done her a final favor. He released her. She now knew that there would be no chance of her accepting him back. She would never overlook the hateful remarks he'd made about Santi. What kind of man would talk about a child like that?

Thank you, Franklin for freeing me with your sheer, self-important, egotistical stupidity and assholery. Kenzi reviewed herself for any feelings of fear, regret, or guilt. She felt nothing except profound relief flooding her.

But she was still stuck out here.

She heard the sound of thunder and felt heavy atmosphere pressing down. The workmen seemed close to finishing, having stepped up the pace because of the approaching storm. Kenzi panicked. *Why didn't I ride my bike cart out here?*

"Because its fifteen miles in the countryside," she said aloud. If any of the rare and collectable volumes already in delicate condition got wet, they would be ruined. She dialed Stacy.

"Stacy, look, girl. If you get this message, call me at my cell. I need help, okay? I'm stranded in the boondocks and I need to move these books out the rain."

She couldn't afford to lose this investment. After a desperate pause, she called Lina's cell number.

"What did she say?"

"Oh, you know. The usual. Me, me, me, me. My bookstore, my bookstore, my bookstore. It's always been about her. All she thinks about is herself and nobody else."

"I couldn't take it after a while myself. I always had the feeling she was seeing that guy behind my back. She really needs to get a grip. And that bookstore is a joke. You, however, are very down to earth."

Dark clouds gathered. She watched them move and shift against the sky which had gone from dark blue to gray-black within seconds.

Lina's tone grated more than usual. *What is it with people today? Oh, how did I forget? Lina can't stand me.*

She phoned Ray.

Ten minutes later, his pickup bounced over the grass and pulled up beside her as the first few drops fell.

An ancient tree stood less than two feet away. His large legs, encased in khaki shorts, led downward to feet strapped in brown leather sandals that solidly touched the earth as if to plant themselves firmly wherever he stood. As she gazed upward, her body gave a twinge of recognition, as if it already knew him and her breasts tingled their own greeting.

His powerful trunk grew wider at the top and branched into thick arms that now sat akimbo waiting for her to speak.   Kenzi had a brief flash of him gripping handfuls of her hair. She had a brief flash of herself unwrapping a thick, rich, delicious candy bar. She swallowed and cleared her throat and somehow croaked out what she needed him to do. His intense dark gaze rested on her face, her hair, her breasts, her hips, and then her face again.

He didn't say much as he helped her load the heavy boxes. His hair, free from its usual black band, swung back and forth across his shoulders in a long black curtain as he bent and lifted, bent and lifted. Kenzi wanted to hold his long luxurious locs in her hand. She wanted to run her fingers through them and rub them across her face and body... Suddenly, they swung around again as he turned to her and said simply, "Where to?" And she blinked in surprise, "back to the bookstore."

Once they sat in the truck and back on the road, Ray quietly asked her about the sale and the different books she bought. She happily chattered, relieved he didn't ask her how she came to be stranded in the countryside. She really didn't feel like explaining. The rain no longer sprinkled. It poured down as they unloaded each box at the rear entrance of Kinfolk as quickly as they could. Thankfully the books had remained dry on the ride back into town due to the rain-proof tarp from Ray's truck that covered them. The heavy cardboard boxes protected the books while she and Ray unloaded them.

Back at her apartment, Kenzi offered Ray one of her boxed microwaveable dinners. She handed him a drink and a towel to dry off. Then she tossed him the remote control to play with while she showered. Ray ignored the remote and chose to look around Kenzi's tiny apartment instead. It didn't take long. A screen separated a closet-sized office from the main room. A futon sofa and chair sat in front of the television. Nothing else as far as furniture. Pictures of Kenzi and some of Betty decorated the walls. Pictures of Kenzi hiking alternated with Kenzi standing in front of various buildings and sitting in class, then wearing a cap and gown, then sitting on a conference panel, then standing on a pyramid. She had an eclectic music collection with many cds in Spanish and a few in French. Books lay scattered on various horizontal surfaces built into the walls with dog-eared pages and little colored scraps of paper sticking out here and there. Artwork hung from the ceiling, hid in corners, and sat on shelves. Baskets filled with carvings, colorful rocks tumbled about.

Naked in the shower, Kenzi thought about Ray as she soaped herself clean. *What if he came in here and... stop it!* Stop it! Stop it! She exited the shower and put on a thin robe and moisturized with shea butter. She looked at the reflection of her body in the mirror then slipped the robe partly off for a closer inspection.

She saw herself completely naked every morning and night. But now she really saw herself for the first time in years. Things still seemed to be where they used be. But some things had changed. This section looked a little big here and there. She could tune this up a little over here.

She turned to the side to look at the curve of her back as it dipped smoothly in to her waist and then swelled out and then back to her thighs and legs, toned from biking her cart full of books around town and walking everywhere else. She'd caught Ray looking at her backside more than once.

"Well, if he likes it, then I love it," Kenzi smiled and struck a sexy pose. *Oops! He was waiting!*

"I'll be out in a minute, Ray!"

Kenzi hastily blow dried her hair until it puffed just slightly damp. Taking a peek out of the bathroom door, she saw Ray take their dinner out of the microwave. She changed into faded sweats and a t-shirt. *I hope he's not expecting a black satin negligee. Nope! No, no, no, Mr. Lover Man. Think again!*

Maybe she should put her robe on over this. Overkill. *Just be cool, Kenzi. Damn! Just calm down.* She gathered a container of shea butter and another of aloe vera and returned to the living room with nothing much on her mind.

The longing she saw in his eyes when he looked at her, touched her in places she'd chosen to forget existed. She felt uncomfortable and unsettled. Thrilled. *Did she say thrilled? No. No thrill tonight.*

The guy got to her. *Just relax, Kenzi! Don't start none, won't be none.* Deep breath. *Okay? You got this.*

Ray sat fascinated when she lifted her arms to run her fingers through her hair as she made one-inch square parts, moisturized, and then rapidly wound two strands of hair together. On occasion, she leaned over and took a quick bite of what turned out to be a broccoli, cheese and rice dish.

Kenzi didn't realize her t-shirt clung and revealed the shape of her breasts each time she raised her arms. As she leaned her head to the side to twist fourteen inches of fluffy dark brown hair, her neck curved at the shoulder offering and displaying itself. Ray thought he could sit here all night and enjoy the show. He liked the intimate, vulnerable Kenzi. He tried to focus his mind on the question she just asked him.

"I'm sorry. What did you say?" Ray took a second to refill their plastic champagne glasses with sherry.

Kenzi, meanwhile, felt irritated that her body responded so strongly to the desire in his eyes, the shape of his mouth, the solidness of his large body. She tried and failed to not to think about the huge statue with warm eyes. She wanted to fulfill his every perverted fantasy.

"I, uhm, I," Kenzi lost track of the conversation herself. "Oh yeah, I was wondering about your family."

Ray had long since finished his dinner and watched as Kenzi multitasked snatching a bite here and there while twisting. At this rate, it would take her two hours to finish her hair and her dinner.

"Let me give you a hand with that." Ray smiled.

"With what?" Kenzi contorted to twist the top middle section of her head.

"Those twists." Ray laughed. "You look like you're in pain."

Her arms grew tired. Her stomach growled. Still, she hesitated at the thought of her back being nestled against his front.

"I'm actually feeling a slight twinge in my neck," she admitted. "You can twist?"

"Of course. I do my own hair and Santi's. Those giant ponytails of hers don't just happen by themselves," he laughed. "And I've caught on to the importance of matching the ribbons and barrettes to her clothes. Aunt T or Dharma does the French braids though. That's beyond me."

Kenzi sat surrounded by two large, dark muscled legs while he stroked her hair softly. Weird as the scene came across when she thought about it, it felt good to be pampered.

"So tell me about your family," she repeated.

Ray's baritone rumbled and drawled, "My parents are deceased. I'm the oldest son of Reginald Grant and Vasanti Sankiri Grant. He was a military man. He met my mother on leave in Ceylon in 1970. Sri Lanka. She was a Tamil Hindu. Her family worked on tea plantation outside Colombo. They fell in love. Her family wasn't happy about it. Something like that – a black man with the U.S. military, marrying one of their women. It had never been done before. They couldn't accept it. No one approved. Everyone was uncomfortable and stressed. There were negative reactions within the family and from the community, which I gather, was pretty close-knit and very traditional. There was also tension in the air due to the political uprising in Colombo."

Ray paused, as if deep in thought, seeing something far away and long ago. Kenzi waited.

"The pressure got to them. When my father returned to the States, my mother came with him. By that time, she was already pregnant with me. When I asked her about it, she told me she was excited at the better job, educational, health opportunities that America afforded. But the loss of her family and her homeland meant she had to adapt to Texas culture as well as she could. So they settled at the homestead. There've been Grants in this region for as long as anyone can remember. Aunt T, you met her, took care of things with hired help while my father was away. Once he finished his duty to the government, he fixed up the house and rebuilt some structures that had fallen down. He tended the orchards his own father, Papa Dan, planted." He paused. "You still with me?"

"Yeah, I'm listening," Kenzi murmured sleepily.

"You know, Papa Dan was a rare black man in Jim Crow era Texas. He managed to not only acquire land and successfully cultivate it, but to also hold on to it. And that wasn't always easy with the menaces to society circling around with lynching rope. You know, the good ole boys never meanin' no harm." They meant plenty of harm to blacks striving to uplift themselves through economic means. The family held tight though. Papa Dan carried on and wouldn't let anyone stop his plans. He was practical. He was an optimist with the outlook of a realist. And the orchards still bear fruit. Those trees are a living testament to his skill as an agriculturalist. He didn't even have to go to school to learn all that. He didn't ask anyone's permission. He just did it. I respect him and my father for being forward-thinking. The house, barn, tool shed, greenhouse, and chicken house all of it represents the generations of the family. Fortunately for me, I inherited being skilled with my hands."

"Hmmm, yes you did," Kenzi teased. "My twist-out should be off the hook, hunh?"

"No doubt!" Ray laughed. "Wanna to hear some more? I'm in the homestretch."

"I'm not going anywhere."

"My mother raised us – me, Dharma, and Dhan - and took care of the home, and tended the vegetable and herb gardens. She came from a rural community and so she really didn't have any problem adjusting to life on the homestead. But... adjusting to the Texas lifestyle and its people took a little more time."

"Yeah, and that could happen from someone from New York or Oklahoma, let alone Sri Lanka."

"Right. Although it helped that she'd learned to speak English in a mission school near the tea plantation. She never quite lost the accent though. Often, she'd inject Tamil phrases in her conversations with us. Usually when she couldn't think of the English word. Most people assumed she was from the Caribbean. She just found it easier to let them think that than do a ten-minute explanation each time."

"Oh. Then that explains something."

"What?"

"There was something about your voice that I noticed when we met at Organic Soul, but I couldn't figure it out. Not when you talk to me. But when you talk to Dharma, I notice it. Kind of different."

"Yeah, I've been told."

"It's nice."

"Chicks dig the accent."

Kenzi elbowed Ray in the shin.

"Silly! So what about your hair? I think it's beautiful, you know. When did you start your locs?" *I want to wrap myself in them.*

"Dharma started my locs after... a tough period when Santi's mother died." Ray sat silent a moment. Kenzi nearly apologized for bringing it up when he started speaking again.

"Me and Darlene were never married. But she was the mother of my child. It's still kind of painful when I look at Santi. Santi doesn't remember her."

"What about Darlene's family? Do they spend time with Santi?"

Kenzi felt Ray's tension through his fingers. He actually clenched her hair a little too tightly and Kenzi flinched. Another silence lasted a while longer. Kenzi said a mental, "oops."

"Look, I'm sorry. It's none of my business."

Brusquely, Ray replied, "Just family drama, Kenzi. It happens."

"Yeah, it does."

"You too?"

"Everyone's got things that they'd rather not think about too long."

"Yeah." Ray continued by going back to the previous discussion. "Well, I allowed my little afro to grow longer, to almost two inches. Dharma washed and conditioned it. Once it dried, she sectioned it into small, square blocks just slightly larger than a pencil eraser. And you can see the locs expand as they mature. She applied a small amount of pure aloe vera from our garden to the section. Then she divided the section into two parts and then twisted them together into a coil of rope. Like I'm doing with your hair now. If you didn't take down your twists or comb through, probably in about two months they would start to loc. And in a year, it would be completely loced."

"I'm tempted. Locs are so beautiful. But I'm not ready for that kind of commitment yet. My life has been so unsettled lately. Someday maybe, I'll get my loc on." Kenzi smiled wistfully. "I unwind my twists and fluff them out."

"Yeah, I dig that wild fro. It suits you."

Kenzi felt so gooey and pleased inside from the compliment that she gave herself a mental check. Careful, girl. Don't get in too deep too soon. The soft baritone stroked her.

"After Dharma started my locs, I maintained them myself. I used a tea tree shampoo. But I didn't use a detangling conditioner. That would have softened and loosened the locs. I used olive oil instead. And I would tighten my hair as it grew by winding loose strands around the roots. The sun dries it while I work outside. And I tie it back at the neck with a band. You should give it some thought. Your hair is beautiful."

Kenzi remembered that first afternoon when she saw Ray unloading the plants in front of Organic Soul with his hair tied back. He must have just washed it.

The intimate setting, the rain outside, combined with the sherry made them both drop their defenses. Just like a barber and beautician working on a client, they told each other about themselves, their hair, and their past lives.

Kenzi repeated to Ray most of the information she'd told Aunt Tilly about herself earlier. She told him, "I've been very blessed. All of my studies and adventures have taken me around the world, but I always felt a pull towards Texas. The only problem was something within me wanted more. I mean I was definitely not in love with my job. I had dreams."

"That's some story. But what about the other part?"

"What other part?"

"The part where you fell in love."

"How funny."

"No falling in love? Is that the unsettled part you talked about?"

Kenzi sighed. "Way too many issues. I don't know. I'm not sure I have a lasting relationship in me."

"And Franklin?"

"We're not together."

"Does he know that?"

"As of this afternoon, we both know."

"Really." Ray let his voice drawl the word in a leading way.

"If it was meant to be, it would have been. But thank God it wasn't and won't ever. Oh well."

"You don't seem upset about it." Ray inquired curiously.

"I guess that should tell you something."

"Tells me a lot. A whole lot." He changed the subject. "So I see from the pictures you like to travel. You gonna stick around here a while?"

"That's the plan. You've been here all your life though. What keeps you here?"

"It's just small and kind of quiet. My family is here, and my daughter. I would have thought you'd be in Houston or Austin or back in Dallas."

"I'm a small-town girl in a big-town world."

She relaxed herself into a deeper trance under his strong hands as Ray picked up the conversation.

"Since we're talking about backgrounds, I stopped my education after high school to work and save money for college. I finished three years towards a business degree at the university, but I dropped out to take care of the family after my parents died. This was eleven years ago. The first thing I did was to make sure to settle all debt by paying the property tax and the loan for the farm equipment. I took vocational and trade courses at the community college at night and I hired myself out as a carpenter. I started a yard work business providing care for area lawns and gardens for a couple of years. But after Dharma opened Organic Soul, I became part owner of Organic Soul and now I do much of the heavy lifting, repairs, and deliveries there. Things like that."

"And Santi?" She held her breath wondering if she'd gone too far again.

"Santi is my pride and joy. She was born when I was twenty-four. She's named for Vasanti, my mother."

Ray paused a moment.

"Like I mentioned earlier, Santi's mother died when Santi was pretty young. I think she'd just turned two-years-old. I definitely count myself lucky to have Dharma serving as stand-in mother figure for Santi. Dharma loves Santi and Santi thinks the world of Dharma. They have a good relationship. And Aunt T is always willing to baby-sit Santi whenever I'm on a job. I love them for doing that and I trust them completely. Still, I kind of think Santi would like to have a mother of her own as she grows older."

"So, she has you all and her grandmother?"

"She has us."

"I see."

"Darlene's family, including her mother, Santi's grandmother, did not provide a healthy environment for Santi. And because of that…"

"Because of that…"

"Because of that, she has us," Ray finished flatly. She remembered that tone from her day at their home when he shut Dharma down. Well, if his sister wasn't allowed to address the issue, then probably she wouldn't be allowed either.

"You know what Ray? You are the best example of a father I've ever seen. Including my own, unfortunately. Santi clearly adores you and I can tell you love her to pieces. I think you're doing a great job."

"Thanks for that. I like to think I'm doing a good job with her. She's a beautiful girl and pretty much the best thing I've ever done with my life."

He finished Kenzi's hair. It hung in gleaming coils to her shoulders. They sat in comfortable silence a moment.

"Sometimes I wonder if I'm husband material though. It's been years since Darlene's death and no one really serious since."

The rain, the thunder and lightning, the sounds of rubber tires on wet cement ceased to exist. Only Ray remained.Only Kenzi remained. And waiting quietly with them, not daring to breathe rose the scent of possibility that slowly circled and wound around them.

Ray softly kneaded Kenzi's neck. She sat helpless and limp as a rag doll letting him do it. His hands felt as strong as they looked and obviously, he knew how to use them. As Ray's hands moved to the right side of her neck and shoulder, Kenzi's head listed left onto his thigh, hardened with muscle she could feel through his jeans.

Kenzi whispered hoarsely, "I wouldn't know what sort of husband you'd make either since I don't have an example to go by."

She meant it to come out light-hearted. Arousal changed her voice to a husky invitation, a smoky proposition. Ray's hands stilled momentarily. He tried to get control of himself. Kenzi's soft cheek leaned on his thigh, her mouth so close... The slight pressure began a burn where it met his leg and coursed upward tightening his body. Kenzi felt his leg muscle flex and harden. Ray silently pulled Kenzi from the floor to his lap. The contact of her soft curves against his hardness made both of their breaths quicken.

"Well, if it's an example you want..." Ray said in a low growl.

His arms circled her waist as he kissed her soft smooth neck still buzzed from his massage. Kenzi jerked and shuddered from the soft sensations that sent electric bolts through her body. Ray tightened his hold as he worked his way from her left ear to the right and back again. Kenzi's breathing deepened.

Ray could feel and see every rise and fall of her body. He ran his hands quickly up and down her bare arms creating streaking paths of heat. His hands moved over her thighs then back up to slightly touch the sides of her breasts, then down once more to the thighs he'd looked at with such longing at the bookstore opening.

"Looks like those pastries went right where I hoped they would after all," he chuckled.

Kenzi giggled and then quickly sucked in her breath as Ray used one hand to pull her head back by the hair he twisted. He held her there staring at the smooth butter-soft silky brown of her skin. Her body betrayed her and shut down her mind in a surreal haze of glitter and electrified sparkle swirling, whirling, dizzy. She felt warmth on her skin before his mouth moved to the soft, warm hollow of her throat where her pulse beat faster then even faster. Her nerves tingled from his soft kisses, his breath gentle on her face, and his body warm against her back side. Kenzi, excited by the exquisite domination, melted then oozed. She moaned helplessly and closed her eyes.

Oh, I'm weak.

His arms surrounded her as his legs had minutes before. He maneuvered her to half face him as her side leaned against his front. She looked like a goddess. Her golden honey, chocolate brown, almond eyes glowed in the lamplight. Like a queen. Isis. Sheba. Nefertiti. Her prominent cheekbones gave her a regal, exotic appearance and he imagined her reclining on a throne in a faraway palace.

His eyes shone with intent and purpose. Her eyes answered his in a hazy passion that overwhelmed her senses. Her body responded to his every touch. She clutched his arms to steady herself and ran her hands slowly up and down fascinated by the sight of her soft smooth brown stroking his deep dark chocolate. Hard steel, twisted with muscle, tautly contained within warm dark skin velveted by a light covering of hair.

The center of her body clutched on itself. She felt herself flush as she began to tremble. Waves of sensation radiated from her center. He felt her reaction and wound her twists in his fist. His full mouth no longer explored softly. He dominated her mouth, passionately twisting her head from side to side.

"Oh… ohhhhhh!" She opened her mouth for him with a moan and he rewarded her for her cooperation roughly sighing, "Oh Kenzi. Kenzi."

His tongue stroked her, explored her, and joined her. Now he, too, trembled. The hand holding her waist slipped under her shirt and encountered silky smooth belly. His kiss deepened.

They wound and tightened around each other.

Kenzi felt an inner warning go through her. If she didn't stop now, she never would.

"Ray. Ray, wait. Please."

Ray froze and stilled his hands.

They returned to that same pause. The silence, the wonder, and the possibility. The waiting. Ray held her closely to him as their heartbeats slowed again and their breaths came more regularly.

Kenzi cautiously searched his face for annoyance.

"I didn't mean to lead you on."

"No. No, Kenzi. Don't apologize. Things just got a little out of hand." He stared back at her, his eyes taking in the way her hair framed her warm-toned skin, still slightly flushed. He kissed her cheek.

"Yeah, just a little." Kenzi smiled and Ray's eyes immediately dropped to the mouth he'd just made love to. It swelled soft and tender from his intense exploration. Ray felt the familiar tightening as his body acknowledged Kenzi's rounded hips resting on his legs. Time to get Kenzi off his lap or he'd have to ask her for an extra pair of sweatpants.

"Look, uhm, Ray. I.." Pause. What exactly did one say to the man who made you make funny, panting noises?

He helped her out smiling, "You…?"

They both laughed.

Kenzi diffused the moment further, "Hey well, if those were your examples of what kind of husband you'd be, then put me on the short list, okay?"

"I'll draw you up an application."

"Do you need references?"

"Um. No?"

Though he laughed, the humor didn't quite reach his eyes. A fleeting hint of bitterness disappeared when she gazed at him questioningly. The spell that had captivated them both and shut out the world disappeared under the occasional wet grind of rubber against cement on the street, as designated drivers made their way back from the bars and the clubs to either continue partying or flop fully-clothed, facedown into their beds. Or someone's bed. The rain stopped.

Time to call it a night.

Kenzi suddenly felt the two hours she waited at the estate sale plus the packing and lifting of boxes. Ray noticed her droop and kissed her quickly on the cheek. He just couldn't stop touching her.

"Kenzi, look. If you ever need me to give you a lift or haul something or move something heavy, just let me know. And if anyone bothers you at the store, call me. You don't have to do it all alone." Ray looked her directly in the eye. "And you don't have to rely on a selfish jerk who'll leave you by yourself in the countryside in a thunderstorm. It's okay to call me, you know. Okay? I won't leave you hanging."

Did he want to make her cry?

For so long, just she and her mother tried to make a living together. Kenzi wondered over and over how her father could have just left like that and missed so much of her life. Much better to depend on oneself. That way, you never got your hopes up and you never got hurt. And now here stood Ray, this glorious man, asking her to trust him, to need him. Making her want him.

And she did want him.

And now he knew that. How easy it would be to sink to her knees and beg him to stay and service her all night. He did say he'd be there for her no matter what, right? The imagery dizzied her a little. He waited for an answer.

Her face reddened. "Okay. I'll keep it in mind."

"Kenzi, I mean it."

"I know you do. It means a lot to me that you'd offer. I appreciate everything today."

"Everything?" Ray raised his eyebrows and looked at her intently.

Oh my goodness. Hot-to-death and a sense of humor! She laughed and tapped him on the arm and felt once again solid muscle. She felt a rapid pulse streak through her.

"You know what I mean!"

God, she had to get him out of here! She covered her sharp intake of breath as she pushed against his hard back to shove him slightly to the door.

"Now go home before the rain starts again!"

Go before I throw myself quivering into your arms and beg you do everything you promised me you would with your eyes.

Chapter 7

Trouble

Kenzi always remembered December as the Bad Time. Usually, retail sales increased during the holiday season, but Kinfolk Books still had not established a large enough customer base. She had to work hard to let people know of its existence.

"Stacy, look." Kenzi handed her friend the letter.

Stacy skimmed through quickly. "Oh, I see." She looked disappointed. "So the university rejected your grant proposal for community programming."

"Yeah," Kenzi sucked in her breath and exhaled as she explained. "Because of this, the art class is uncertain for the spring unless I take money from another part of Kinfolk's budget."

"Kenzi, oh no! Those children and parents are counting on me. They're pretty invested in the art program." Stacy stared at her a moment. "There's nothing else you can think of?"

At Kenzi's miserable look, Stacy quickly followed with, "Sorry, girl. Nevermind."

After Stacy left, Kenzi wondered if Stacy blamed her for the difficulties.

In addition, the book signing she scheduled and planned for the past two months canceled in favor of a better offer from the lucrative chain bookstore in town.

"Yeah, I know," she thought, "its business, not personal."

It cost money to both advertise the signing and to announce the cancellation. The budget shrank further. She removed the projected sales from her cash flow estimate. It didn't look good.

Kenzi soon developed additional skills – The Art of the Fiscal Juggle, The Invoice Shuffle, and the Hope for the Best Leap of Faith.

Betty horrified her when she offered her retirement fund. *No way!* Though she loved her little bookstore, she loved her mother more. She felt okay cleaning out her own holdings, but she wouldn't allow her mother to do the same.

Still, Kenzi borrowed from Peter to pay Paul. She left some bills unpaid in order to pay others. Paul thanked her for her kind cooperation. Peter screamed in protest and slammed Kinfolk with late fees and service charges. Kinfolk took hits left and right.

A machine stopped working. The price of various supplies increased. Taxes never stopped. The bills came like clockwork and she ranked them in order of the amount of devastation wrought if they went unpaid past deadline. She cut and slashed through the budget like a madwoman in a chainsaw horror movie.

She entertained herself on the cheap by reading various books at the store rather than renting movies or attending ticketed events. She took the food quality down a notch. She used black marker to fix the scuff marks in her shoes rather than buying new shoes or shoe polish. She took walks in the park and rode her bike for recreation.

Thankfully, she didn't visit hair and nail salons anyway so that was no loss. She made excuses of being tired or busy to cover for the fact she couldn't afford most outings. Her neighbors, Miss Lydia and Mr. Oliver, both small business veterans, gave her the occasional pep talk.

"The first year of any small business is always the hardest and the most difficult," Miss Lydia of Baby Things swore.

"Hang tight, Kenzi," Mr. Oliver said as he gave her a grandfatherly bag of candy from Oliver Pharmacy. "Don't give up!"

On one Sunday afternoon of stress-relief and contemplation in Central Park, Kenzi reflected on what exactly she brought to the table and how she could use that to better serve the store. A decade of travel and language instruction while crossing borders left her the gift of adaptability. But it took more than knowing how to cumbia and use chopsticks to run an independent bookstore.

Word got around that the store struggled to survive. Kenzi received another unsettling visit from Bobby Forrest who left her with the bizarre statement, "Sometimes, I use pens as weapons," as he looked down at the pens held in a coffee mug for customers who wrote checks. After he left, Kenzi moved the coffee mug out of sight. She would just have to remember to offer a pen from that time on when someone wrote a check.

She received a phone message from Franklin.

"This is Franklin. I was just checking on you."

She ignored it. The sound of his pompous voice irritated her. Ray's slow baritone drawl made Franklin sound like a boy. The next day, another phone message from Franklin blinked on her answering machine.

"This is Franklin. I was just checking on you. Trying to see how you're doing."

She ignored that as well. Finally, out of curiosity, she returned his call. To keep things impersonal she called his office. For the first time, a secretary picked up his phone, announced the department, and then asked how to direct the call.

"Franklin Bellaire, please."

"What is your name?"

"Kenzi Malton. I'm returning his phone call."

"Oh… then he's in a meeting."

Kenzi laughed out loud.

The wind blew in a friendly neighborhood bird that chirped news to Kenzi that Franklin and Lina kicked it together at Franklin's condo when Kenzi called them separately for a ride from the estate sale. She wavered between hurt and anger. She felt bad, not because of Franklin, but because her own cousin apparently hated her so much she would do her that kind of dirty behind her back.

After a few days to get her head straight about Lina's betrayal, she called Lina's cell.

"Family don't do each other dirty like this, Lina." Kenzi couldn't keep the hurt out of her voice.

Giggle.

Lina's sheer callousness surprised her. "Why is this funny to you?"

"Oh Kenzi, just calm down. It is not that serious." Lina's patronizing tone accomplished it's intent to provoke.

"Lina! I got rained on! And if the books hadn't been boxed up, they would've gotten rained on too! I just can't believe you sat there with Franklin while I was stranded outside city limits. How could you do that?"

Lina's voice revealed a smug tone. "Well, we weren't actually sitting."

"Lina, you're un-fucking-believable. You know that? Completely un-fucking-believable." Kenzi's speech quickened. "Just listen to yourself. He's not even worth it."

"Oh now wait! Back off, Kenzi. You're talking about *my* man now. He's not yours anymore. You got that? You hear that? Get used to that."

Both of their voices rose.

"You know what? Keep him. He's all yours!"

"Oh, I plan to!"

"Good. Do that! You both deserve each other!"

"Oh, I will!"

"Fine!"

"Fine!"

"Whatever!"

Bitch.

A choked sob of disbelief escaped after Kenzi hung up the phone on the most idiotic conversation she'd ever had in her life. She felt angry that she even wasted tears on the selfish, childish, button-pushing little brat. She'd heard from the same little bird perched on the grapevine that Lina had already moved into Franklin's condominium and started work at a hair salon in Rollins. Figures.

She and Lina had never been close even as children. As young adults, they saw each other only by accident when they lived in Dallas. The conversations never lasted long. Dallas's large size meant that a person, who didn't really want to, could choose not see someone for a long time. Now in tiny Rollins, they gave each other an even wider berth. Thankfully, she and Lina had no accidental meetings despite the town's smaller size. Kenzi's finances limited her social interactions.

But good conversation still came free. Kenzi sought Dharma's company now and then to talk shop.

"Dharma, what made you decide to open the restaurant?"

Dharma smiled serenely. "I didn't want to work for anyone else. I knew I had what it took to own, operate, and manage a restaurant since I'd worked with the previous owners for years. Also, I knew there was a market for the type of food and atmosphere I wanted to bring."

"Were you scared?"

"Oh, of course!" Dharma said thoughtfully. "People are conditioned to find jobs and work for large corporations rather than to strike out on their own. I was conditioned that way as well."

"What made you change your mind?"

Dharma sighed in remembrance. "Well, after our parents died, I saw Ray struggling to make ends meet. I wanted to help him. The only thing was, I didn't know how to operate a jigsaw and I didn't intend to ever know." She laughed. "When he started working as a contractor and doing lawn care, I thought hard about what I liked to do. I worked in a restaurant. I took management courses. I saved. And I wrote down all the recipes that my mother and Aunt T taught me. In the meantime, I met my husband, David, and we had the twins. Everyone was very supportive. Between me, David, Ray, Dhan, and Aunt T, we were able to buy the old restaurant and put our own special stamp on it."

"That's truly awesome."

"Yeah. Definitely. We put our money together. Divided the work. Divided the profits. Reinvested. Paid back the loan. The rest is history."

"Was it pretty hard the first year?"

"The first year is always the hardest. But if you can make through the first year, establish a customer base, and build trust, then you stand a chance to make it the next year and the next and then the next."

"Yeah, I keep hearing that." Kenzi sighed. "It's certainly something to look forward to."

She visited Houston's museum district with Stacy and they went shopping afterwards. Or, rather, she window-shopped while Stacy made various purchases. The Kinfolk budget did not forgive lapses in judgment. Lapses in judgment made the budget very, very angry.

Kenzi pointed to a mannequin wearing a dark, orangey-pink ensemble posed for ultimate sophistication. "Oh Stacy, look! That is such a nice dress! I love that color."

"There's shoes and a purse to match."

Kenzi ruefully noted, "Wow! Only one seventy-five… not including the shoes and purse... Maybe later when I win the lottery." She smiled and shook her head.

"Girl, do *you*!"

They both laughed and strolled away.

"So Stacy, I mean, if you weren't at the print shop, what would you be doing like right now?"

"I'd be in New York. I would free my mind and just let the art flow forth. I would have a studio to rent to other artists and I'd have a gallery. There would be live music, poetry, spoken word, all sorts of self-expression." Stacy's voice trailed away.

"That sounds so exciting! Very glamorous. I would be first in line to visit your studio."

"Someday you will!" Stacy changed the subject. "So how're things with Ray?"

Kenzi sucked in her breath as a bolt went through her at the mention of Ray's name. She covered and replied casually, "I dig him. He digs me. It's all right, I think. I see him now and then."

"His family seems cool."

"They are. They really, really are. I feel less alone down here when I spend time with them."

"You are so damn lucky, Kenzi. And you don't even know it."

"Well," Kenzi smiled, "I like to think, both me *and* Ray are lucky."

Kenzi harvested winter vegetables with Aunt Tilly, Dharma, and Santi, while Ray and David supervised the restaurant. Jackson barked and rolled around in the grass with Reggie and Davey. Everyone else filled basket after basket with turnips and parsnips and radishes and carrots from the huge gardens. After they stored everything, Dharma took a much needed nap while Santi bossed Reggie and Davey's hide and seek adventures. Jackson always helped Santi find Reggie and Davey no matter how carefully they hid.

Aunt Tilly mashed the turnips and parsnips together, chopped in horseradish, carrots, leeks, and garlic then spiced it all with black pepper and a dash of sugar. The dish had no name but it had a lively, hot, sharp, sweet biting flavor. She also cooked turnip greens and black eyed peas and allowed Kenzi to make cornmeal pancakes under close supervision. She slathered these with butter and honey. Kenzi tried to follow directions without messing up Aunt Tilly's kitchen.

"So Kenzi, you cook much?"

"Uhm…"

"Tell the truth, child! Tell the truth and shame the devil."

"I sort of just microwave stuff."

"Uhmmmm hmmmm."

"Uh yeah, you know… You uh poke holes in the top of the plastic and then set it for ten minutes. Usually, I take a shower while it's cooking."

"Nah, I don't know nothing 'bout that."

"Uhm… right." *Cough.* "So it looks like the pecan trees are really producing."

"Yes, and we're trying to keep up with the squirrels. The trees are producing more than usual this year because Ray fertilized them."

"There's nothing better than pecan pie."

"Nope. Nothin' better than that. 'Cept pecan pie with ice cream."

Kenzi gave her mother updates on the store that didn't include the financial struggles.

"So how are thing's going down there, at Kinfolk?"

"I'm hanging in there. Working hard for every dollar."

"Kenzi, are you taking care of yourself?

Not really.

"Yeah, I'm doing all right."

Neither Dharma, nor Stacy, nor Aunt Tilly, and particularly Betty mentioned Lina, a kindness for which Kenzi remained grateful.

Santi's continued visits after school brightened the day. She had a secure lifestyle blessed by baby sitting by Aunt Tilly and Dharma, playing games with her twin cousins, being spoiled and teased by Dhan, and being doted on by her father. She loved her visits with Kenzi, a new adult to add to her circle.

One morning, Ray came to Santi's room to comb her hair before school.

She already stood before the mirror fussing. "I don't want to wear ponytails today, Daddy."

"So what are you going to do?"

Santi fluffed her hair up and out into a wildly curly afro. At Kinfolk Books, she was a constant presence in the children's room of the bookstore reading aloud or drawing.

Kenzi wondered from time to time if Santi felt lonely and did she feel sad about not being allowed around her mother's relatives. After all, Kenzi knew what it felt like to have missing pieces in her life. But she knew better than to ask Santi about it.

Aunt Tilly kept herself busy. She didn't mention that she often felt more tired than usual. She had a harder time getting out of bed most mornings. Older than her brother by ten years, Aunt Tilly enjoyed her role as the family matriarch. She took pride in Reginald. When he returned from military duty with a Tamil wife, she frowned, nonplussed. But the knowledge that Vasanti carried Reginald's son and her nephew ignited Aunt Tilly's protective streak. When the tight-knit, rural community whispered at Vasanti's exotic background, Aunt Tilly set people straight with the quickness. Vasanti's quiet manner, hardworking spirit, and obvious dedication to her home and family resolved the rest. Aunt Tilly had a spirit ready for battle but even she could not conquer full-blown diabetes.

"We got a nurse for her," Ray explained to Kenzi on the phone. "So instead of going home from school, Santi's going to walk the few blocks to Organic Soul from school. What I wanted to know was if it was okay for Santi to sit quietly at Kinfolk Books or maybe help you out until I come get her?"

Kenzi felt a trifle uneasy. Funny that he would want her, someone he'd only known for months, but not a single soul from Darlene's family.

"Kenzi?"

"Oh, of course! Santi's a wonderful child. But I'm so sorry to hear Miss Tilly's unwell."

"Yeah, one of those things, I guess. But thanks. Santi will see you tomorrow, okay?"

"Okay, I'll watch for her. And Ray?"

"Yeah?"

She nearly thanked him for allowing her in, but instead she simply replied, "Santi's always welcome, you know."

Santi held up her end of the agreement. She watered plants, dusted books and shelves, stapled papers, and cleaned windows. She helped to choose books and arrange floor pillows for Tuesday and Thursday's story time. She even helped to bag books at the cash register as Kenzi stacked them for her.

"Thank you for shopping Kinfolk Books!"Santi proudly bagged books as the customers beamed back at her.

"Santi, you are a wonderful, beautiful, talented child!" Kenzi took care to not overstep boundaries as a mother substitute, but as Santi helped her to choose children's books to order from a Joliet Publishing catalogue, Kenzi knew in her heart she would love to have a child just like her.

Stacy sorted through a pile of the children's artwork that accumulated in the back room.

"So are you attending the Kwanzaa celebration at the university?"

"Well, I don't know. I attended that with Franklin last year, but you and I both know the deal on that. I'd rather be kidnapped by aliens than see or speak to him again. But I'm just too stressed and on edge to go by myself." Kenzi didn't mention the money woes and her limited wardrobe dominated by jeans and old but sturdy shoes. No one really knew how precariously the store's finances balanced on the edge. She wished she didn't know.

Stacy glanced over Kenzi's shoulder. "Well, what about Ray?"

Ray, by then, had entered Kinfolk Books to ask Kenzi about something and overheard the discussion about the Kwanzaa. While he waited for Kenzi's reply he echoed Stacy's question. *Yeah, what about Ray?* He smiled expectantly at the back of Kenzi's head.

Kenzi's heart beat faster. There's nothing more she would like than to have Ray hold her in his arms. But money, or lack of it, remained an issue.

"I don't think so."

What? He stepped around the bookshelf and joined the conversation. "So... what about ole Ray-Ray, Kenzi?" Kenzi had the good grace to look embarrassed. Stacy cleared out with a quickly muttered excuse.

"Thanks a lot, Stace!" Kenzi called after her.

"So what about ole Ray? You don't think so? Why don't you think so, Kenzi?"

Kenzi's excuse sounded lame even to her ears, "I'm just tired."

"Tired. Or embarrassed? What is it really, Kenzi? Does the thought of me slopping horse manure around get to you? You still longing for the phony Franklin type who dogs women out? Is that the type of guy you like? Because I'm not that guy. Know that first."

"And I'm not that type of girl! I'm not like that, Ray. And I can't believe you're saying what you're saying! Ray, you know Franklin's with Lina now."

"So what? Are you jealous about that or something?"

"Ray!" Kenzi's shocked disbelief finally swayed the argument.

"Okay, forget them. But just what is going on here with us? I mean, what am I to you really? A security guard? A day laborer who moves your furniture once in a while? What are you even looking for? A booty call?"

"Ray, what is wrong with you?" The accusations both disgusted and hurt Kenzi. Even though the thought of Ray servicing her on-demand definitely had an appeal and her body flinched at the thought, the crudeness had no place.

"How long have you felt that way about me, Ray?" Kenzi had braced herself for the eventual betrayal from Ray and now the betrayal arrived. "How long have you been silently accusing me of being this horrible person?"

Ray stood silent.

Kenzi felt her heart sink. "You keep raising that bar higher and higher so no one's ever good enough and you don't have to take anybody but yourself seriously."

"Excuse me?"

"Goodnight, Ray."

"Kenzi…"

"I said goodnight!" She turned her back on him and fumbled through some papers. "Please leave."

Ray didn't say much when he picked Santi up the next few afternoons.

Kenzi figured if she didn't have anything nice to say, then she wouldn't say anything either. And she didn't have anything nice to say to Ray.

Santi, being an only child and close to her father, sensed the change in the air whenever Ray and Kenzi met face to face, although they acted like their normal selves apart.

Ray stared at the ceiling. "Santi, thank Miss Kenzi for the books."

Santi looked from her father to Miss Kenzi banging the edge of a stack of papers on the counter with determination.

"Now Santi, your father knows for a fact that you're more than welcome to those books for all the great help you give me everyday."

Uncertain, Santi remained silent. Finally, Ray asked Dharma to pick Santi up from Kinfolk Books in the future.

Kenzi knew Ray must truly dislike her if he couldn't stand to be in the same room with her. Well, fine. *Same to ya!* "I'm not a golddigger!" she thought painfully.

Dharma saw the hurt on Kenzi's face before Kenzi could cover and hesitated while Santi gathered her schools supplies into her little backpack. "Kenzi, is something going on with you and Ray?"

Kenzi still a little confused responded, "No, I've just been very tired and not thinking straight lately."

Dharma talked to Ray while she busied herself in her kitchen making the Christmas cake Vasanti used to make for them close to the holiday season. She chopped up raisins, pineapple, ginger, sultanas, candied peel, cherries, almonds, and pecans together.

"Kenzi looked surprised to see me when I picked up Santi this afternoon. You didn't tell her?"

Ray leaned against the counter eating the remaining pecans. He shifted uncomfortably and didn't answer.

"Ray, hel-lo?"

"We're just on the outs a little bit."

"What did you do?"

"What are you talking about, what did I do?"

"Well?"

"Why do you assume its something I did?"

Dharma flashed him a meaningful look then poured the fruit and nut mixture in a large bowl.

Ray exhaled loudly. "You know what? I don't know! I honestly don't, Dharma. We were doing okay. I asked her about attending this banquet thing at the university and then all of a sudden it turns into an argument. We said some things. Now she's freezing me out."

Dharma added honey, brandy, rose water, and vanilla to the bowl then searched in the cabinet.

"I knew something was up. That's too bad. How serious is it? Do you think you guys can make it up? Santi can sense something's wrong, you know."

"I know. Santi does pick up on things quickly." He shook his head. "Look, I want to try with Kenzi, but I'm just not sure what's going on. I'm not even sure how the argument started. And now she won't talk to me."

Dharma located the spices she needed and set them down one by one on the counter.

"So just take a minute to ask her what's on her mind."

"I did. I asked her and she won't talk."

"Ask her again. And Ray?"

"What?"

"Try to ease up."

"What are you talking about now?"

"I'm just saying."

"Saying *what*, Dharma?"

But Dharma simply sprinkled nutmeg, cinnamon, cardamom, and cloves into the bowl and mixed the sweet, spiciness together expertly. She would let the mixture sit for twenty-four hours so the spices would be absorbed into the fruit. Then it would be added to the cake mixture, baked in two greased tins, allowed to cool, and spread with marzipan.

She dwelled happily in her marriage and because of this, she desired the whole world to share in the same sort of happiness. Of course, she and David disagreed from time to time, but that came with the territory of a relationship. And then they always enjoyed the opportunity to make up. Dharma smiled. She loved David and the twins. She often worried about her big brother because he seemed so lonely. He still wore the scars Darlene clawed into him.

"Leave it alone, Dharma," Ray said the few times she broached the subject of finding someone for him.

"Tend to your business, Dharma," David told advised her when she puzzled over Ray's reluctance. "And your business is me."

So, she did what she could. She invited Ray and Santi over for birthday parties, Juneteenth and July 4th celebrations, Memorial Day and Labor Day picnics, Thanksgiving, Kwanzaa, Christmas, and the rest. The family tended to combine the last three into one general December festival. Sometimes, a family friend or a coworker just happened to be invited as well. Nothing really ever panned out.

She liked Kenzi. After Ray finally grumped himself away, she nodded her head to herself decisively while she cleaned the counter. She would make sure to include Kenzi on all the guest lists until Ray figured out what he really needed.

"So take that, Big Bro!" she laughed to herself.

Chapter 8

Orange Silk Sari

Kenzi sleepwalked in the day time. Worry about the store's finances and long hours on her feet wore her down. She also missed Ray. She missed his deep voice rumbling through her. She missed his large frame filling up entire rooms. Those deep, dark eyes of his that held her suspended in motion. She didn't feel that crazy, familiar tingle that crept through her at the sight of him anymore because she didn't see him. *It took me just three months to screw that relationship up. Has to be a record.*

Saturday evening, she counted the register, switched off the lights, set the alarm, and turned off the machinery. While locking up, she noticed Ray staring at her across the street. He stepped aside for a couple entering the restaurant, exchanged brief pleasantries. His eyes remained on Kenzi, warily seeing what her next move would be.

Though Kenzi longed for him, the hurtful words they exchanged still lingered. Kenzi fumbled with the keys as she considered whether to give him a quick wave and smile, a quick wave and no smile, or ignore him completely since he couldn't seem to stand her anyway. She finally decided on the quick wave with no smile option and locked the door as she headed to the bike rack to unlock her bike for the ride home.

Ray made up his mind. This had gone on long enough. Before she lifted her hand, Ray crossed the street with long, purposeful strides. He didn't even bother to check the traffic.

"Kenzi, can we talk?" Ray looked at her anxiously.

"It's dark out here, Ray." Kenzi turned to move away.

"I know, but…"

"Look," she cut him off, "We've probably said enough to each other. I need to get home."

"I'll take you home."

"No!" she almost shouted. Alone and vulnerable with Ray she really didn't want.

Ray raised his eyebrows.

"I mean," she lowered and calmed her voice even as her heart raced, "let's stop in a coffeehouse."

"Whatever," he shrugged as if it really didn't matter. She rolled her eyes to the sky, irritated.

A few blocks away, Kenzi looked at Ray over her hot chocolate and carrot cake and his hot chocolate with biscotti. The steam from their drinks drifted gently in the air between them as Kenzi tried to start a conversation. Any conversation at all.

"Where's Santi?"

"She's visiting Aunt T at the hospital. I'm going to pick her up later."

"Is Miss Tilly getting any better?"

"No." Ray's hesitation broke her heart. "I, we're... we're not sure if she'll make it, Kenzi. But we're surrounding her with love."

"I hope she gets better soon, Ray. I love that woman."

"Me too."

A full minute of silence fell over the table as Kenzi glanced around the coffeehouse not sure what to say next. Ray stared down at his drink, by now, no longer steaming.

"I've missed you Kenzi."

Kenzi gulped and whispered, "I've missed you too."

Ray took her hand and squeezed it.

"Ray, why did you accuse me like that? Of being some kind of shallow snob? You practically called me a gold-digger. Why?"

Ray had the good grace to look ashamed as Kenzi continued.

"I mean, I'm a thirty-one-year-old woman who rides a bike! I'm wearing clothes from three and five years ago and from high school. Help me out here. Where does gold-digger enter the equation? I mean, where do you see that?"

Ray closed his eyes briefly and looked down. Then he sighed.

"Kenzi, you didn't deserve that. I just confused you with someone else."

"Oh really," Kenzi sat back. "Who?" She already knew, but she had to hear him say it. She wanted him to admit it out loud. She wanted him to put it in her face so she could have the opportunity to finally smack it down.

Ray sighed and glanced around the coffeehouse. He returned his gaze to Kenzi and leaned forward slightly. "We spoke about Santi earlier and I told you that her mother, Darlene, died when Santi was too young to remember her."

"Right."

"I didn't tell you everything."

"Okay, tell me."

"Santi was born when I was young and in love. I struggled to provide a home for Darlene and our baby in a small apartment in town. Darlene refused to move out to the homestead. I think she had a problem with country life and Aunt T, as well. Darlene... was dissatisfied. With me and where we lived and how we lived. It wasn't easy. Most of the money I made went towards paying bills and to take care of Santi. I was optimistic. Maybe romantic. So in the middle of all that, I asked Darlene to marry me. She... turned me down."

Ray paused and she could hear the hurt still in his voice.

He wasn't over her.

"I didn't make enough money. Most of my time was spent working on contract jobs and fixing up things at the homestead. I had a hard time just breaking even. It wasn't enough. She left us."

"Darlene left?"

"She left both of us." Ray glanced out the dark window. "Another guy came along and made her a better offer, I guess. He was a drug dealer and had a lot of things I didn't have. She died of a drug overdose less than a year later."

Kenzi began to understand.

"Oh my God," she swallowed. "That must have been so painful for you and Santi." Kenzi unclenched one of Ray's hands from his cup and held it. "But Ray, please understand me when I tell you that I'm not Darlene. I would never do that."

"No, you're not. And I should have known that."

Kenzi rushed on barely hearing him in her desire to make it clear, "I would never do something like that to you. I missed out on having a complete family and I would never subject a child to the same thing. I mean it. The reason why I don't have children now is because I'm not in a relationship and I don't want to raise a baby by myself. That's something too important to half-step."

"I know that now, Kenzi. I know. I believe you. Look, I'm sorry for what I said the other day. I was out of order on that."

"Thank you, Ray."

"But if it wasn't my being blue collar, or whatever, then what was it?"

Kenzi took a deep breath and felt her face grow warm from shame as she stared at the table.

"It wasn't anything like that. It was," she cleared her throat, "I don't have anything to wear appropriate for a formal party. All of my clothes are kind of regular, like me."

Ray looked up at the ceiling as if to ask for strength and exhale a breath of air. He wanted to shake her. "Kenzi, you cannot be serious. You mean to tell me that all the drama we just went through was because you didn't have anything to wear and were too proud to say it? Are you serious? And by the way, you're hardly regular."

"Ray, back off! I mean, thank you. But some of that was your drama too! You know I couldn't go to something like that in jeans and sandals and I can't afford to buy anything new or even used. Money is really tight at the bookstore right now."

"Okay, I'm sorry. I didn't mean to yell. But Kenzi, *come on!* This is a problem we could have solved together. But if you don't talk to me, how can I know what the problem is in order to find a solution? Don't keep it inside. This relationship belongs to both of us and you're not pulling your weight. Please don't do something like this to us again."

Kenzi felt awful and tried not to cry. "I tell you what, Ray." She lifted her chin in challenge. "I won't if you won't."

"Deal." He cleared his throat. "You know, I can buy you something."

"No."

"Kenzi, *look!*" Ray's voice rose to an uncharacteristically loud level. Other patrons in the coffeehouse glanced over.

Kenzi and Ray argued all the way to the hospital about how to get Kenzi something to wear. They left it unresolved as they joined Santi who prattled about her artwork as she held up each piece for Aunt Tilly to consider.

"...and this is me and Jackson. I drew this yesterday with my watercolors."

Aunt Tilly didn't even seem tired. "Oh, that's beautiful, Santi! Wait a minute! What is Jackson eating? Is he chasing the chickens again?"

"No," Santi said anxious to protect the family dog. "I just made that up."

"Okay, 'cause he'll be in big trouble when I get home. Tell him to let them chickens 'lone now."

Kenzi went over to the bed and gave her a hug. "Hey Miss Tilly. I've been missing you!"

"Oh, I'm maintainin.' How're all the kinfolk?"

"The kinfolk are doing all right. Doing just fine."

"Hey, Aunt T," Ray stepped forward and hugged her.

"How's my big boy Ray, hunh?" Aunt Tilly laughed.

"He's just fine, auntie." Ray took Aunt Tilly's hand carefully.

Kenzi turned to Santi, "How about we get some snacks?"

As Ray smiled at Kenzi and, she smiled back, she realized their spat both cleared the air and melted a lot of ice. She walked with Santi to the vending machines down the hall for juice and a snack and then held Santi on her lap more for her own comfort than Santi's. Later, Ray found them both leaned back against the wall dozing together.

Ray decided to take a side trip to Dharma's house. "I called her from the hospital. She's expecting us."

And now Ray and Kenzi stood in his sister's bedroom while Santi played with her cousins, Reggie and Davey, and Uncle David.

Dharma carefully laid two saris wrapped in plastic on her bed. "I only wore them to try them on."

"They're beautiful, Dharma."

"You know, Kenzi, the multiple folds of a sari can be worn various ways. And regardless of a woman's height and weight, the sari can be refashioned to fit. It was very common for women to wear the saris of their grandmothers."

Dharma removed the plastic. "You wear the orange one," she decided.

By the time Kenzi opened her mouth to protest, Dharma, as usual, shoved the conversation right past her with Ray's help. "I agree. Definitely the orange."

Dharma held the fabric next to Kenzi's face, "Because your skin has an orange-yellow undertone. Even your hair tends from dark brown to red-orange at the ends."

"I don't know," Kenzi said uncertainly.

Dharma ignored her. "I'm going to wear the red one. My hair is black and that's a nice contrast."

"Exactly," Ray nodded solemnly.

Both women laughed at him.

"Dharma, are you sure?" Kenzi said reluctantly. "These are heirlooms."

"Kenzi, where have you been?" Dharma laughed. "It's already decided. Pay attention."

"You know you have no chance, Kenzi," Ray added. "Lay back and enjoy it like the rest of us."

"I've been looking for a chance to wear them and now I won't be alone. Come on, Kenzi!"

Kenzi shrugged and gave up. They were both too much in a double team. "Alright, Dharma. You'll help me with it though, right?"

Dharma clapped her hands, delighted. She'd grown up surrounded by men – her brothers, Ray and Dhan. And now she raised three men – the twin boys and her husband. She didn't even realize she missed female company and secret-sharing until Kenzi opened her store across the street and they become friends. Often she'd slip away from Organic Soul for a good girlfriend chat about life and love with Kenzi.

So early Sunday morning, Dharma called Kenzi.

"We're going to be sinfully indulgent and treat ourselves to an afternoon of beautifying while Ray and David take the children out to a movie."

"Sounds good to me. Sounds great, actually."

"You know what Kenzi, I love my restaurant. And I know you love the bookstore, but every once in a while, it's important to take care of yourself and just let the troubles and problems of the world disappear."

"At least for a few hours."

"I'll come get you at about threeish, okay?"

"I'll be standing outside."

In Dharma's huge bathroom, they washed their hair and conditioned it with olive oil and avocado under plastic bags wrapped in towels.

"Okay, next, we exfoliate with sea salt then moisturize with either coconut oil or shea butter. Depends on how you feel."

Kenzi braided Dharma's hair as their clay masks dried. And as Dharma sat under the dryer, she manipulated Kenzi's hair into long twists.

"Okay, I'm dry. Your turn."

Kenzi sat under the dryer while Dharma got them both some lavender tea with honey. "Beautifying is hard work," Dharma declared. "We have to stay hydrated."

They listened to jazz, and talked more about life, business, family, and the future.

"Dharma, I've been wondering something for a while."

"What?"

"Well, the biracial, bicultural upbringing you and Ray and Dhan had. It's kind of fascinating. I wondered if you guys ever feel torn between two cultures. Like you ever had to make a choice?"

"Hmm. Our mother was determined to adapt to American life. But she never completely gave up her identity, at least inside the house. The food, religion, culture, and sometimes even the language. From time to time, she'd speak to us in Tamil. And we could understand her. But we never really spoke it ourselves. We pretty much identify as Black. It was easier, you know? But she definitely made her mark. Some of the lotions and teas we're using I learned from her. It's all natural."

"This tea is no joke. I feel so relaxed. Is there ever an opportunity to interact with other people from Sri Lanka here in Rollins?"

"You wouldn't think in this little town there would be. But there are. Mostly university students from the engineering program who come to Organic Soul. They like the food."

"How can they not!"

"True!" Dharma laughed in agreement. "They know they're getting genuine dishes on the menu, but with a twist of soul. I can understand them a little when they speak. But I stick to English."

"Dharma you know what? I feel better already and the night hasn't even begun yet. It's been a long time since I dressed up for anything."

"Enjoy it. I know I am."

Ray and David dropped the three children they deliberately tired out to David's mother who gave them warm drinks and hustled them off to bed. The adults choreographed the operation smoothly and the children made no protest. It took Ray less than half an hour to get dressed at home in a suit and tie. He captured his long dark hair in a black rubber band which gave him a sleek, sexy appearance. Then he and David returned to the Gardner home so that they could check Kenzi and Dharma's progress while David got dressed.

"You know I always appreciate the way your mother welcomes Santi with Reggie and Davey."

"Ah, naw, man. You know mama always likes when Santi comes to visit. She tells me to bring her all the time. Plus, she needs the extra help to keep Reggie and Davey in line."

Ray laughed aloud, "I believe it."

"Yeah, them two can be a handful if someone's not used to having them around all the time."

"Aw, they're all right."

"Okay, so you'll take 'em next weekend, hunh?"

"Now wait."

"That's what I thought." David chuckled as Ray drove along. After a moment, Ray sighed.

"I kinda wish Santi had the same kind of experience with her mama's mama. You know?

David remained impassive. "I know."

Ray shook his head ruefully.

David glanced out the window briefly. "You know, I see Maya's people around the way now and then. Here and there. Looks like she's trying to get things together in her life."

Ray grunted.

He'd thought about Kenzi all day. In the darkness of the movie theatre his mind drifted from the animated feature to brief flashes of their first meeting and the night of the estate sale.

His eyes widened when Kenzi entered the living room. She looked softened. All bright, shiny, smiley, and relaxed. Her long hair held sheen from its conditioning. It fluffed and waved and gently beckoned for him to stroke its softness. Her brown skin glowed and she looked radiant. Her high cheekbones drew her full soft lips wide into a smile that left him breathless. Her honey eyes shone in the lamplight. She wore kohl around them which emphasized their clearness and almond-shaped slant. Vasanti's hyacinth-tiger's eye necklace and bracelets might come later. Tonight, Kenzi wore amber earrings that dangled and matched her necklace and bracelets.

"You look stunning." Ray couldn't keep his eyes off the silken folds of the sari that draped and gently molded her curves. The deep orange color reflected off her skin and she lit up the entire room.

At the banquet, they circulated the crowd together. Ray with his long, black locs, tall body, and quietly commanding presence complimented Kenzi's brightly exotic coloring and glorious hair.

"I'm trying to be careful, Ray. I don't want to spill or rub this sari on anything."

"Anything other than me, you mean," Ray grinned. His arm moved restlessly from her waist, to her back and shoulders, and back down again.

"Yes, that's exactly what I meant, babe," Kenzi laughed.

Ray didn't let her get too far away. .

"You left one space on your plate uncovered, Ray. You know that's a no, no!" Kenzi looked up laughing and he kissed her swiftly. She smiled like a giddy school girl.

At one point, they ran into Lina and Franklin. Kenzi felt Ray's hand tighten around her waist in warning as her sister and her ex-boyfriend approached. Remembering their first interaction at the bookstore, Kenzi hoped nothing would jump off. She didn't want anything to ruin the evening.

A long, reddish-brown fall decorated Lina's hair. It actually looked nice. Long. But nice. Lina took a lot of pride in the ponytail as well. She swung it back and forth over her shoulders like a new toy as she glanced around the room.

"Are you guys enjoying yourselves?" Ray asked.

Franklin nodded coolly.

"What?" Lina looked at Kenzi's orange silk outfit as if confused. "Oh," she shrugged and smiled.

Kenzi and Ray managed to keep the conversation polite. Still, Kenzi exhaled when, after two minutes, she and Ray disengaged to head back over to the refreshment table. Ray smiled at her in understanding.

"Parties are fun, huh Kenzi?"

"Parties are real fun."

"Are you glad we came?" Ray looked at her.

"I'm glad I came with you." Kenzi let her head fall back as she gazed upward with a smile. She squeezed his arm and didn't miss the look of pleasure in Ray's eyes that met her statement. She meant every word.

She, Ray, Dharma, and David drove back to the Gardner house so Ray could collect his truck and take Kenzi home. Kenzi managed a quick, "Thank you for everything," to Dharma before David pulled Dharma away and grinned back at Ray. David knew Ray wanted to be alone with Kenzi and decided to not let his wife engage in a girlfriend chatter session this late.

Ray and Kenzi walked to her door. She fumbled for the key. He stood so close to her, she could feel him even though their bodies didn't touch. Her response to his body and his breath on space of her neck uncovered by her hair and the silkiness of the sari made her nervous. She invited him in and decided to offer him either coffee or tea. She turned to him feeling so happy at their successful evening and to apologize again for her silliness earlier.

"Ray, I want to thank you for…"

"Take it off." Ray growled at her.

Kenzi froze in place, startled. She stared at him, barely in the door. She knew she'd taken extra good care of his mother's sari.

"What?"

His gaze didn't waver as he stared back at her.

"Take it off, Kenzi."

She blinked. His deep brown eyes signaled deep raw need and hunger. Her skin sizzled in response. The familiar surge of need shot bolts of sensation across her body. She had missed him so. There would be no turning back tonight. She knew this.

And as he looked into her slanted golden-brown eyes, he knew she knew this. He smiled the smile of the victorious.

He shut and locked the door and leaned against it to watch while she slid the silky orange fabric off slowly and carefully. Her hands trembled as she laid each piece one by one on the chair next to her. She reached to her ears to remove her amber-colored earrings with its matching necklace and bracelets.

"No, leave those on." His voice became even huskier.

Kenzi closed her eyes and swallowed. She quivered and her heart beat faster. She stood vulnerable in front of Ray who watched her without speaking. Kenzi wondered if he noticed the marks that life had left her. The left leg with its long scar from a long-ago playground adventure gone wrong. The tiny parallel streaks of stretch marks on her hips where she'd rapidly gained and lost weight in college. The slight bulge of her soft, rounded tummy. She self-consciously moved her hands to cover these from his gaze.

"No." Ray looked hurt and offended. "Don't. Let me see."

He gazed in wonder at the smoothness of her brown skin. The gentle outward curve of her full breasts restrained in the lacy bra. The softness of her shape as it curved in and out and around and down and under excited him. His eyes glazed at the thin straps of her panties that rose high over each hip, leaving not a lot to the imagination. He'd missed her too.

Kenzi steeled herself and raised her chin. She met Ray's gaze. Gave him a good long look at her. Time to equalize the balance of power anyway. If a thing had to be done, then it had to be done right. Because, no doubt, the thing would be done tonight.

Baby, you want to see?

Kenzi moved her right foot back and slowly pivoted so he could see her profile. She ran her hands up and down her arms and then bent to her legs and back up again. She knew she had Ray's full attention and reveled in it with a sly smile. She took a deep breath. Then she pivoted again, deliberately and agonizingly slow, until her back faced his silent, thorough scrutiny. Her legs stood slightly apart. Her hands sat on her hips with one hip deliberately cocked sassily higher. Her wild hair flowed and curled and curved and twisted against her neck and shoulders.

She waited.

Ray looked at the shape before him from top to bottom. She curved in then out then in then out then in. His gaze dropped down to her waist and he imagined his hands circled there gripping and pulling hard. Her skin glowed like smooth dark orange-brown caramel with shades of chocolate here and there. Legs long and silky and… he looked closely… slightly knock-kneed.

Ray smiled slowly. It would be a most interesting evening.

As he stood quietly in contemplation, she heard movement behind her but didn't turn around. She heard cloth rubbing. He undressed. At long last, the movements stopped and she chanced a peek over her shoulder and saw his proud, tall, glorious naked body sculpted and chiseled and dark as if carved out of ebony wood. His body planed in straight parallel lines shaped by the muscles that defined his strength. Her knees trembled. How could any woman have the strength to walk away from this man? She couldn't take a single step if the room caught on fire. She craved him.

He allowed her to look at him for a moment and then whispered hoarsely, "Turn back around. No the other way."

Obediently, she presented her back to him once more and felt him drawing near. She felt his heat radiate from his skin even before he touched her. Her breath quickened with excitement.

"Oh Kenzi," he whispered, "I've waited so long…"

His arms circled around her tightly and he pulled her hard against his large, solid frame and quickly removed her bra and panties. His chin rested on the top of her head that still smelled of coconut oil and they stood in a naked embrace together quietly for half a minute. Then he kissed her shoulders, her neck, behind her ears while whispering softly.

"Don't hide from me. Don't ever hide from me, Kenzi."

He held her breasts in his hands and kneaded them with his strong slightly callused hands. She groaned and shuddered, then closed her eyes as she leaned against the chair for support.

"I'll always find you."

They twisted and wound their limbs together and the various shades of brown blended and swirled. He squeezed and pushed and pulled and showed her ways of pleasure her body had never known possible.

Chapter 9

The Benefactor

Just when he thought he'd made amends with past failures, wrong decisions, and youthful mistakes, they reached out to sock him on the left and then the right and then a final uppercut to the chin. Feelings of self-loathing and guilt that he thought he'd laid to rest assailed him whenever he thought of things left undone.

He slowly took out the unmarked, brown envelope he carried in his briefcase everywhere he went. It held the news article with the colorful photo that introduced Rollins to Kinfolk Books and its owner, the woman with the wild hair and golden-eyed stare.

He looked at the other photos laid out on his desk and thought back to that morning long ago when his world turned upside down and he nearly vomited on himself.

"Miss Jessie, please. Please, oh God. Even if you can't tell me where they went, please just give me a picture of my little girl. Please! I have nothing at all. She took everything with her. Please, Miss Jessie."

He sank down on the steps and began to cry with his head in his hands. He heard footsteps behind him and looked up to see Betty's mother standing wordlessly next to him. She dropped the photos beside him and returned to the house. As she shut and locked the door, he clutched the photos, grateful for even the smallest kindness.

The memory of the worst day of his life played inside his head like an endless nightmare.

He shuffled those same photos now. He didn't know her. He had no idea of her character and personality. All he did know he read in various local weeklies, saw on her website, and heard through others.

In a parallel universe, he circulated through the shelves at Kinfolk Books. He got a cup of coffee or tea and meandered over to the African history section or the international relations section. He imagined it many times. Someone read poetry. Incense floated through the air.

Hello, Ms. Malton.

He shook her hand.

I am Dr. Jonathan Farrell.

No.

I am Professor Farrell.

No.

Please just call me Jonathan.

Then… what?   He could never get past the introduction. What would he say? What would she say?

He thought about that whenever he saw Kinfolk Books listed in the weekly event calendar. He saved every scrap of information on the store and kept his ears open for news. He could have called her, but did not. He could have called her mother, but definitely did not.

He knew from Franklin that Betty drove down from Dallas to help out at the store from time to time. He waited for the right time. He waited for the right words. Which never came. He did nothing. "Because that's what you're good at, Jonathan. Waiting for nothing." his inner voice mocked.

Franklin knew Kenzi. Somewhat.

"She still calls me now and then. So my secretary handles that. I definitely prefer Lina. Kenzi wasn't my speed. Too whiny." The braggadocio in Franklin's voice grated.

Jonathan endured Franklin's commentary with clenched teeth as they walked across campus to a faculty meeting. Franklin didn't even notice Dr. Farrell's silence. The older man didn't seem the talky type. He came to campus, did what he needed to do, then left. In many ways, Franklin looked up to him.

Dr. Farrell's stellar record on teaching, publishing, and community service meant both students and faculty liked him. His presence lent an air of prestige to the department that recruited him heavily less than a year ago from Virginia.

Franklin sought to bond with Jonathan man-to-man over the common subject of women. Had Franklin talked about any other women besides Kenzi and Lina, his intricately-laid plan to stomp with the big dogs might have worked.

"She applied for the grant that the university awards small businesses."

"Who?" Jonathan pretended to lose track of the conversation.

"Kenzi, the owner of Kinfolk."

"Ah yes."

"Yeah, she applied. I happen to be on the committee. Who cares about service though? Really, what does service get you? Nothing. Research is where it's at." Franklin shrugged impatiently. "I told them I had a bad feeling about the shop's management and finances. That woman definitely does not know what she's doing and it really shows. The store is very lacking. It's her first business. Money down the drain. Grandpas reading to the children. Art for the children. I mean, what is that anyway? Finger-paints?"

"Really." Jonathan remained neutral.

"Yeah. Of course, people are interested now since it's so new. But in a few weeks or a few months, they'll move to the next thing."

"You think so."

"You can just look around and see the store is financially unstable. In another two or three months she'll be closing down. Nobody likes to throw good money after bad. I had to recommend another business. The committee pretty much went along with it." With just the right amount of regret, Franklin continued, "I hated to have to do that to a struggling sister, but oh well. It's business. And I have my own reputation to protect. It's like that."

"So it seems."

At the faculty meeting, Jonathan only half-listened to the speaker while his mind went through what Franklin told him. He'd felt some disquiet about the man when he first met him, but never could put his finger on the reason why. He knew why now.

What a glorious asshole.

Completely unlikable. Underneath the charm, the clipped speech, the careful grooming, and name brand clothing lay total self-absorption and ego. No empathy whatsoever for a fellow human being. He sat next to Franklin's obsequious show of thoughtful concentration for the speaker.

"…issues of diversity on campus to be addressed at an upcoming event during which the chancellor…"

Now and then, Franklin nodded his head at regular, practiced intervals. He wrote down a word or two on a notepad.

"…by the end of the next fiscal year, we're going to be obligated to show a narrower margin in order to offset the expected shortfall…"

Jonathan leaned in close despite his distaste to see that Franklin's notepad was a mess of doodled idiocy: "FRESH PRINCE BELLAIRE, FUTURE PRESIDENT OF ALL I SURVEY." This he followed with arrows pointing to dollar signs and "RECOGNIZE."

Suffer the children. Jonathan leaned back and sighed with disgust at the new jacks without any sense of history or community who entered academia and wreaked havoc through their ignorance. The thought of Franklin having the power to frame and shape young minds in the classroom or, perish the thought, at the administrative level depressed him.

The fact that his daughter associated with Franklin, even for a short while, caused him concern regarding her judgment. But he blamed himself.

Thankfully, their relationship ended. But the cousin…

Kenzi spent Christmas in Dallas with Betty. They shopped and saw a couple of movies. They lounged around Betty's apartment.

"Wow, Prince is coming to town soon." Kenzi flipped through the entertainment pages of the newspaper. She still felt the high of her and Ray's magical night together. She floated on air.

"You sure have been smiling a lot," Betty noted. "Ray's acting all right, hunh?"

Kenzi laughed bemusedly. "We still see each other, but between his family obligations and the retail season – you know sales, returns, and inventory markdowns – it's rushed." Kenzi thought of Ray often though. The quick sightings never failed to send tiny quivers radiating through her. "I'm glad I gave myself some days off. I really needed them."

Though she felt happy with the new developments between her and Ray, troubling times still visited the shop. The retail boost passed by Kinfolk Books with not a lot of notice. She sold a few gift certificates. But event cancellations and diminished sales along with the grant application being rejected made things harder. She tightened the budget and her belt. She increased her hours at the shop and racked her brain for solutions. Even if she didn't know her and Ray's future, or if they had a future together, she knew that the carpet needed to be vacuumed, she had to pay sales tax, and she needed to shift inventory. The routine gave her a small bit of comfort.

Back in Rollins, she rarely saw Stacy.

"But can you blame her? How many times can someone listen to the same sad story anyway, Kenzi?" Kenzi let the thoughts run through her head as she rearranged artwork. "Everyone's got their own problems." Still, the unreturned phone calls made her uneasy and a little sad. The art class had been Stacy's baby. The hiatus forced by the lack of funding apparently did not sit well.

One day, two boxes arrived in the mail. She'd implemented a moratorium on spending so she knew she hadn't placed the orders. The return address appeared to be a local post office box. Nothing indicated the contents.

Slightly curious as well as cautious, Kenzi flicked the blade on her box-cutter with the nonchalant ease of frequent use. Inside the first box lay children's books - new and used, English and several other languages. A typed list of the total contents with title and author lay across the top of the books. The word, "GIFT" marched boldly across the top of the list.

Extremely curious, she turned to box number two.

Inside, crayons, watercolors, drawing paper, colored pencils, colored chalk, erasers, etc squeezed together, neatly stacked and tightly packed. Small sticky spots revealed someone had meticulously scraped off all the price tags.

Wow!

Someone took the time and expense to send boxes full of what Kinfolk Books really hurt for. *Who sent this? Ray? Dharma? Betty?* Kenzi rustled through the packages. No information of a personal nature indicated the sender.

She finally found another envelope wedged inside one of the books after flipping through the pages of almost all of them.

She expected to find a letter or another list of contents. Instead, what appeared to be a money order fell out. Kenzi threw the envelope down as if burned.

"It can't be! It cannot be. I didn't see that. I did not see a money order made out to Kinfolk Books for five hundred dollars. Lord, please don't play with me like that. No, no. NO!" Kenzi tentatively reached for the money order without looking directly at it.

The bottom left memo line held the type-written words, "children's art." In the center, "Five hundred" surrounded by dashes jumped out at her. The small box to the right confirmed the zeroes – "$500.00." Who did this? Ray? No, not Ray. He had a daughter to raise and a farm to keep up. She would never allow him to take money away from his daughter to help her store.

She phoned over to Organic Soul.

"Ray, Kinfolk Books received pretty sizeable donations this morning. There were books and art supplies and a money order for five hundred dollars."

Kenzi waited.

"Wow! That's wonderful Kenzi!"

"There was nothing included to tell me who sent it. Someone wanted to remain anonymous."

Kenzi waited.

"How about that?"

"Ray."

"What?"

"Did you do this?"

"Do what? Did I send all that stuff?"

"Did you?"

"Me? No I wish I could have helped you more, but I'm definitely not in the position to donate five hundred dollars. Someone else."

"It's right on time too. By the way, how are you doing today?"

"Good. Definitely good. Thinking about you, of course."

Kenzi felt a warm burst of fizz course through her, but said simply, "Of course." She smiled.

"But hey, look. I've gotta run, babe. We're about to hit the lunch rush in a half hour. Congratulations!"

"Yeah thanks! Bye babe."

His voice sounded so nice in her ear. Electronic translation could never minimize the deep rich rumble of his baritone.

She still had no clue as to the sender. She decided to display the children's books and art supplies in the front window and print up flyers. She could use the pictures they'd digitized for the grant application to create posters. *Waste not, want not.* Even though they rejected the application, it helped her to become more organized and aware of what the program needed.

The money order meant she and Stacy would be able to do a nice exhibit of the children's work like they'd spoken of early on. *Stacy. Could Stacy be the donor?* Maybe that's why Stacy acted so distant lately. That didn't make sense though. Why would Stacy donate to her own program? Besides, she knew that Stacy's income from her own artwork and the graphics/printing job wouldn't allow for such a sizeable contribution. Including the money order, books, and art supplies, the overall value of the contribution approximated eight hundred dollars.

Stacy and Betty would be overjoyed. Kenzi acetoned the gummy residue from the books carefully and arranged them one by one in the window exhibit. She took a picture of the exhibit and digitized it for the website's front page. She wanted the person who made the donation to see her appreciation. If they kept up with the programs, they would probably hit the Kinfolk website as well.

Stacy was right about one thing. Kenzi sighed. She needed to overhaul the website and start using software. It would free up some additional time in her day taken up with coding and make the website look more polished. And she would start by listing the store's complete inventory online to increase the customer base. Fully inspired, she stared herself bug-eyed at the computer screen late into the night.

Aunt Tilly loved church. She loved the Lord. A people person, she enjoyed the social interactions and community togetherness that church attendance guaranteed. Young and old prayed together, sang, listened to the word of God, and took care of one another. God was real. He watched over her and her family. She prayed for the Grants everyday. She had recovered enough under the nurse's care to attend church on Sundays as long as she promised Dharma to take it easy and cut back on other activities.

The Grants had blessings from God. Of course, they had their trials as did every family, but they truly had blessings. Even though she loved the Lord and she loved her neighbor, Aunt Tilly never pretended not to understand the weaknesses of man. A man who loudly proclaimed his love of the Lord in front of the church quietly proclaimed his love of another man's wife behind closed doors. The woman who wore the biggest hat on the front pew and sang the loudest and longest and strongest song gossiped. All God's children remained the mere humans He created.

So when she accidentally overheard a discussion by two elderly deacons on the way back from the bathroom, it came as no surprise. The deacons never seemed to learn that walls have ears. Yet another good ole boy church chat meant nothing to her, until she overheard "Kenzi" and "Kinfolk Books" in the same sentence. She decided to "watch and pray."

"She doesn't belong here, you can tell."

Aunt Tilly recognized the voice. *That's Deacon Waverly.*

"Oh, right? You can tell, hunh?"

That's Deacon Thomas.

"She's very money-centered. It's always about money with her. She has all these rules. And the way she speaks is *different*. She's not one of us. Something about her, I don't like and I don't trust."

"Something about her, huh?"

"Yeah, I wouldn't want to waste my money there."

Deacon Waverly and Deacon Thomas moved away.

God bless us all. How did that happen? She recognized the careful feeding and tending of a rumor mill.

They'd tried that mess with Reginald and Vasanti until Aunt Tilly got into the mix and let the saints know not to trifle with her brother, his wife, and especially not their children. She did not want to have to call the saints out one by one, but sure as she stood there, she would if she heard the slightest word against her family. They knew it too.

Later that evening, Aunt Tilly caught Ray alone.

"Have you seen Deacon Waverly at Kenzi's shop?"

"Actually, Kenzi had a little bit of a problem with him she asked me to help her with. He'd been hanging around kind of messing with her head and not really taking the hint that he was making her nervous and uncomfortable."

"Why was he doing that?"

"I don't know, actually. She called me over a few months ago to get him to leave her alone. She was too polite to tell him and he took advantage of that."

"I see. So what about now?"

"I haven't seen him. I don't think she has either. She hasn't said anything. I guess it worked and he's leaving her alone. I check on her now and then since she's by herself there most of the day."

"Ummmmmm."

Aunt Tilly pieced the story together. *That man, that man!* She'd seen much worse happen in Rollins. Same game played by different names. Shrill voices raised, indignant letters to the editor poison-penned, and hard stares thrown on any subject you could name.

Santi flourished under Stacy's artistic guidance. Many of her signed pieces hung in the children's section interspersed with Stacy's own watercolors. Aunt Tilly slowly walked into the mint garden and found Santi drawing yet another picture of Jackson, her favorite subject.

"Sit!"

Jackson wanted to play.

"Stay!"

He jumped and wriggled and whined.

"Don't move!"

Poor Jackson tried to figure out a way to obey Santi's orders and play with her at the same time. Even so, Santi's picture came out well. Later, it hung on the refrigerator door. Aunt Tilly sighed. She would definitely have a word with Deacon Waverly. She would also have to do damage control at the church next Sunday.

"Kinfolk Books, this is Kenzi."

"Hello Ms. Malton. This Jonathan Farrell calling from the university."

"Oh, hello… is it Mr. or Dr.?"

"Uhm Dr., but… just call me Jonathan."

"Oh no, no! Good morning, Dr. Farrell. How can I help you?"

"I've been reading marvelous things about Kinfolk Books in the paper and I apologize for not making my way there."

"Well thank you for the kind words. We're trying to be everything we can be to the Rollins community."

"Ah… I noticed that you do book signings."

"We love to do signings. We had a cancellation recently, but we're hoping to schedule more soon."

"Oh, very good. That was the reason I called. I happen to have a book in progress. I'm sending it off to the publisher and they're anticipating a fall release."

"Oh how exciting! That's definitely something to look forward to."

"Yes, indeed. I was hoping Kinfolk Books would be available to host the signing."

"Oh thank you so much for considering us! I do appreciate that. Would you be able to send over a synopsis of your book and a short bio of yourself? That way, I would know how to promote it properly."

"Sure, I'll have everything in the mail to you."

"Great! I look forward to it. Thank you so much for calling this morning. Wow! What a great way to start the week!"

"Thank you as well. I look forward to it already."

They hung up.

Kenzi glanced around the store to see if the coast was clear. All clear! She did a surreptitious cabbage patch dance.

Jonathan trembled slightly as he stared at the phone. She sounded the way Betty used to sound when they first met.

The last time he'd seen Betty, however, she'd used her beautiful mouth to call him filthy names both unholy and inhuman in nature. She made it clear that she hated him. Granted, with reason. He wondered whether she hated him still. And what had she told Kenzi about him? Nothing, apparently. Kenzi had no reaction upon hearing his name. Jonathan tightened his mouth. He missed seeing his daughter grow up. Betty made sure of that. But Betty would no longer stand in his way. Someday soon, he and his daughter would meet again.

He assembled a press kit. After a moment of indecision, he inserted the black and white photo that would be used for the book jacket. She may recognize him. She may not. Fate returned them all to Texas for a reason. Time catches up to everyone. He sealed the envelope and mailed it. At last he did something instead of the usual waiting for nothing.

Ms. Malton, may I call you Mackenzie? I am your father, Jonathan Farrell."

Kenzi received Dr. Farrell's press kit the next day and flipped through the synopsis and book chapter he included. Academic, but written as creative non-fiction with accessible vocabulary. Relevant to historical Texan issues. She could promote it statewide. She looked at the photo of a man whose eyes hid behind thick bifocals with salt and pepper hair cut low to the skull. He must be famous. His face seemed somewhat familiar. Quick as a flash, she loaded his information to the homepage.

At last, some good news to tell Betty.

"Mom, it's so wonderful that he went out of his way to choose Kinfolk Books when he could just as easily have chosen a chain bookstore. Things are looking up."

Betty reacted strangely. "Dr. Farrell. Dr. Farrell, you said? I see. That's… wonderful, Kenzi." *So this is how it ends.*

Betty tensed. "So have you met him? Did he stop by the store?"

Kenzi sensed her mother's distraction. "No, we just spoke over the phone. He sounded like an okay kinda dude. Why, do you know him?"

"I, ah, I've heard his name mentioned before." Betty swallowed. *That okay kinda dude? Well, he's your father.* "But yeah, Kenzi. That's wonderful news. I'm happy for you and the store."

"Yeah, I was thinking he must be well known because I feel like I've seen his face before. Mom, are you okay? You sound funny."

"Oh yes, sweetie, I'm fine. I… was just thinking of something I forgot to do. Look, Kenzi…"

"Oh Mom. I gotta go! Some customers just walked in." Kenzi hurriedly hung up the phone to greet a group of women who asked to see the children's books featured in the window.

Meanwhile...

Betty stared at the phone out of the corner of her eye. She called information in Rollins and wrote down the numbers one by one. Her life counted down as she wrote.

She would call him and ask him... what?

Tell him... what?

Say... what?

She picked up the phone again. She hung it up. Waited a moment. She picked up the phone and dialed. It rang once. She hung up.

Betty rubbed her forehead and her neck.

Chapter 10

Aunt Tilly

Fruit trees showed their pink and white blossoms in the spring, filling the air with the sweet scent of new life and new promises. The honeybees grew ever more excited and buzzed and hummed from flower to flower. Butterflies flitted here and there merrily exploring the orchard. Birds danced and circled and chose each other for the sheer fun of furthering the species. They built their nests piece by piece and screamed and swooped at passersby who walked too close and lingered too long. The vegetable garden pushed up slender, pale green shoots through earth not quite as carefully tended as the year before.

Spring was when Aunt Tilly died in her sleep after another return from the hospital from diabetes complications.

Ray found her before the nurse arrived for the morning rituals of the sick. Aunt Tilly frequently told the poor lady, "I left the hospital to get away from nurses!"

Ray always knew this day would come, but pushed it from his mind as impossible. She seemed so peaceful. As if she knew her work on Earth had finished and she'd put forth her best effort.

"You just do your best, and let God do the rest," she said whenever Ray felt uncertain about the answers to the questions in his life.

God allowed Aunt Tilly her rest.

Ray whispered quietly, "Good-bye, Aunt T."

Santi discovered Ray and Aunt Tilly with Jackson, as usual, at her heels. He rocked Santi in his arms and tried to calm her by stroking her hair. Her little brown face turned purple as she cried until she tired herself and he put her back to bed. He hated to see his little girl cry. Jackson whimpered and cried mournfully for the woman who washed and fed him most of the days of his life.

He called Dharma at their restaurant and Dhan at Rice. They sat together talking it over after the ambulance and the coroner had come and gone.

"It was back when all young men search the streets for a purpose… and for manhood and respect. That pressure is real, you know," Dharma and Dhan nodded soberly at Ray as they took a break from making phone calls on the sofa. "Sometimes I saw them try to take it by force but they never got respect that way – the hard way."

Dharma walked to the kitchen to start lunch since their restaurant would be closed that day, "They got fear and that's very different," she answered Ray over her shoulder.

Ray and Dhan trailed behind her and sat at the table.

"I knew my purpose was to keep us all together after *Amma* and *Appa* died. Keep us all out of trouble. I wanted our parents to be proud of us."

Ray spoke directly his younger brother who sat quietly, still somewhat in shock.

"I just looked at *Appa*. That's all I had to do. Manhood meant you took care of home, you took care of business, and you did it how and when it needed to be done. Manhood was doing the right thing even when that meant sacrifice."

Ray leaned back and thought a moment then started again.

"One day, I was just another kid – one of three. Then all of a sudden, I was in charge. I was the authority figure. But let's not try to discuss so-called discipline, Dhan."

"Yeah, let's not, Ray."

"It was scary. Every day it was scary. Aunt T tried her best to fill in the gaps of what I didn't know even though she'd never raised any children of her own. She never hesitated to pull me to the side and ask if I could think of a better way to get something done."

"No, Aunt T wasn't one to hold her tongue," Dharma laughed. "But she was one to help those who tried. We know you tried, Ray."

"You did all right. I mean, look at me!" Dhan's mocking smile turned wistful. "You always knew Aunt T loved you even though she never said it out loud."

"You know what, you're right. I don't think I ever heard her say the actual words 'I love you' out loud. That's funny. I guess I never thought about it. Maybe she thought it was silly to say something so obvious."

"Well, to her, actions spoke louder than any words." Dhan got up to set the table while Ray answered another sympathy call. "You remember all those stories?"

"Of course! She told them over and over. I never tired of listening to them though. The honeybee story is a classic. I tell it to the twins now and then. Reggie and Davey just laugh and laugh."

Ray set the phone to voice mail and came back to join them.

Reginald Grant had a sweet tooth and decided to take on an entire hive of honeybees to satisfy it. "I laugh too every time I think about *Appa* running from bees and jumping in the catfish pond to hide while they buzzed overhead looking for him."

"That's still funny. He was so stern and disciplined, but I can see it happening," Dhan laughed.

"Fortunately, he showed me how to use smoke to scatter and confuse the bees in order to get the honey so I didn't have to go through the same thing."

"You're still the only one who messes around with those hives, Ray. I know I won't," Dharma declared as she spooned up their lunch. "Here, take this to Santi." She handed Ray a small plate to give Santi who napped in her room, tired out from crying earlier. On the way, Ray reflected that Aunt Tilly voiced the sole dissenting opinion about Santi's mother, Darlene. No one else said anything until after Darlene left.

"Whistling girls and crowing hens soon come to no good end," Aunt Tilly intoned ominously after she got a good look at Darlene's overblown, glitter. Ray dismissed Aunt Tilly as slightly crazy and maybe jealous. Aunt Tilly shook her head at him the way that older folks do at the foolishness of younger generation. "There ain't nothin' new under the sun, boy."

After Darlene's death, however, she kept her low opinion of Santi's mother to herself in order to not hurt Santi or deepen Ray's pain. Her only caution, "Boy, don't you never let nobody piss in your face and then tell you it's raining outside. You ever seen yella rain?" And then she simply turned and walked away.

Santi lay on the floor asleep with Jackson. Ray tucked a blanket around them both and set Santi's lunch on top of her dresser where she could reach, but hopefully, Jackson couldn't.

Back in the kitchen, Dharma and Dhan relived a few of the generational arguments they'd had with Aunt Tilly. At one point or another, Ray, Dharma, and Dhan had each sat in silence after a royal screw-up in finances or mishandling of a household responsibility while Aunt Tilly launched into an endless, but meaningful lecture about ingratitude, civil rights, marches and sit-ins, fire hoses and police dogs, intolerance, and Jesus. These two-hour reminders shamed them into shaping up.

Dharma finally sat down to eat. "But even after she scolded one of us for violating decent Southern behavior, she'd throw in a punch line to take the bite out of her words."

I remember 'Lookin' like Whodunit and Why and What For,'" Dhan teased her.

Dharma groaned and rolled her eyes. "Oh my God. Don't remind me about that. I'm still mad." Dharma pouted exactly the same way she did years ago when Aunt Tilly commented on her short-lived experimentation with punk style inspired by *MTV*. Blue-streaked hair looked exciting in a music video, but not so much in real life as Aunt Tilly made clear. "Lookin' just like Whodunit and Why and What For," she cackled. When Dharma tried to toss her hair at Aunt Tilly in response, it bent creakily over, stiffened by an entire can of hair spray. Dhan and Ray joined Aunt Tilly's cackle and collapsed together in laughter.

"I went straight to the bathroom and washed all that crap out of my hair." Dharma laughed with Ray and Dhan had another good laugh.

At Kinfolk Books, Kenzi, thought about her and Aunt Tilly's last conversation together. Aunt Tilly finally asked Kenzi about the enormous, now sixteen-inch dark brown fluffy hair that surrounded and framed her face like a halo.

"We used to wear our hair like that back in the power days."

Kenzi laughed. "I loved looking at photos of everyone's hair in the '60s and '70s. My mother wore her hair in a little afro. I was never allowed to. After every washing, she'd French braid it real tight. I wanted so much to look like the Jackson 5. Everyone did. But I had the

Stevie Wonder braids and beads. That's probably why I let it loose now. I'm making up for lost years."

"I braided mine too. Then I'd undo the braids and fluff it out with a pick. Hair was healthier then. Not a lot of chemicals and strange colors."

"Well, somehow, over the years, African people in America have been conditioned to adapt their hair and their minds to a culture that doesn't see beauty in kinky hair. There's a real lack of acceptance and love of self."

"Well, what we saw comin' up was advertisements for skin lighteners and hair straighteners that used to be marketed by black-owned companies once upon a time. But now, it's these large corporations that make a lot of money telling people with our kind of hair that hair needs to be changed."

"Like dark skin and kinky hair is a genetic defect to fix."

"That's one of the reasons why Reginald and Vasanti made sure Ray and Dharma and Dhan knew that they were absolutely beautiful. Their features were classic no matter what the mainstream said. Vasanti was very dark, you know. Dark as Reginald. Dark as me. Maybe darker. Often people forgot she wasn't African. She looked like a black woman with a wig. I always respected her for the way she raised all three of them. She raised them right."

"Santi is such a beautiful child. I love Santi's hair. It's so thick and healthy. And boy does she have a lot of it!"

Aunt Tilly laughed.

"Yeah, that child does have some hair on her! And we all style it for her. Now she says she wants to twist it like you."

"Twists are fun. I twist in the summer a lot when it's hot. I need the ventilation." Kenzi laughed.

"Yeah, and you got a lot of it too. I think when people are taught to hate their own hair it's almost a killing of their spirit. Our hair is our crown and glory, you know."

"Well, I probably save about seven hundred dollars per year by keeping it in the natural state. That's more money that I can invest into my business. Besides, I like to look different. I don't see hair like mine much around here."

"Yep, just be yourself, darlin'. Let the rest take care of itself."

Kenzi remembered all of her conversations with Aunt Tilly. They'd talk about something mundane or routine and suddenly, in the middle of it all, a pearl of earthy wisdom wound its way innocently through jokes and stories.

"Oh, Ray!" she breathed on the phone. "Just let me know how I can help between now and Saturday. You know I'm always here for you."

At the funeral, Kenzi sat with Ray's daughter and Dharma's twins who appeared as solemn as she'd ever seen them. Reggie and Davey sat still next to their father, David, soberly dressed in their little suits and holding hands.

Ray spoke.

"After our parents died," he indicated Dharma and Dhan sitting next to the podium, "Aunt T made sure the Grant house and homestead remained a home. She babysat Santi while I looked for extra work to pay for doctor visits, clothes, and shoes - all of the extras a child needs." Ray surveyed the room.

"It was Aunt T who Santi followed all around the house and the garden and the blackberry patches and the chicken yard." Ray's eyes found Santi in the audience. "Right Santi?" Santi nodded at him and leaned against Kenzi's arm.

"Santi, Reggie, and Davey helped their Aunt T. She made picking up pecans and snapping beans a game." Ray looked down and laughed ruefully.

"You see, in another life, in another time, in another place, Aunt T would have been the head of a Fortune 500 company. But in Rollins, Texas during the Jim Crow era, she was a schoolteacher, leader, administrator, and community activist. She never married or had children of her own. Being the older sister, she was already working past retirement age when our parents died. She stopped working and took her retirement to care for her brother's family. Us. Our family and our community are so much better for her efforts. We are the lucky ones."

Dharma stood up to hug Ray and picked up the narrative.

"She was a superstar." Dharma smiled through her tears. "Ray, Dhan, and I used to watch in wide-eyed fascination as Aunt T canned fruits and vegetables, made the blackberry and grape wines, and sweet potato pie. We watched her pick through the herb garden for what she needed and then we nipped little mint leaves to chew when she wasn't looking, or pretended not to look."

She turned to Ray and Dhan. "Ya'll remember?" They did.

"She was a magician and a mad scientist. A superhero better than any cartoon or comic book character. If Aunt T suddenly draped herself in a cape and took to the skies in flight while singing one of her gospel tunes," Dharma paused and choked on her words, "I don't think any of us would have been entirely surprised."

Dhan stood up to take his turn. Sounds of weeping and rustling followed the sniffles and blown noses.

"Aunt T believed in tradition and family. She told us stories about our father and the early days when they played together. She told us about the love between our parents, Reginald and Vasanti Grant. And when Ray, Dharma, and I got older, she passed on those same stories to the next generation – Santi, Ray's daughter, and Reginald and Davey, Dharma's twin sons. So my niece and two nephews were able to laugh with all of us."

The audience laughed with Dhan. "For some reason, children love to hear stories about the childhoods of their own parents." Dhan paused thoughtfully. "Perhaps, because knowing one's parents bent the rules and made mistakes humanized them to the children they towered over with demands for good behavior. And Aunt T missed her brother and his wife too. Her stories helped her to remember and care for us at the same time."

Dhan surveyed the room.

"We invite you all to sing Matilda Grant's song and tell her story for always."

The crowd of cousins, neighbors, and church friends exchanged words with Ray, Dharma, and Dhan with steady streams of casserole dishes and hugs and offers of, "If there's anything I can do, just call and let me know."

Weddings and birthdays and funerals reunited families and acknowledged the passing of time. Union, life, and death followed the nature of the universe as surely as the stars formed in a marriage of metals, minerals, and gas. The younger stars clustered and rotated around the older red giants bathed in the light and beauty. The death of the giant pulled and tugged everything near and far to fill the empty space. The way of the world always be like this until the end of time. Except…

Nothing could ever fill Aunt Tilly's space.

Kenzi smiled sadly at Ray who she could tell struggled to provide leadership and a sense of comfort to Dharma and Dhan. He looked back at her, eyes naked and vulnerable, and smiled slightly until another well-wisher walked up and engaged him in conversation.

Deacon Waverly edged his way over and Kenzi smiled cautiously.

"Hello there, Miss Kenzi. This is a sad occasion."

"Yes, it is. It's very sad."

"Miss Tilly was an important member of the community. She was definitely one of us. We know the Grants from way back. We came up together, you know. Me, Miss Tilly, Ray's daddy, Reginald, all of us came up together. Yeah… ole Miss Tilly… when she talked people listened."

"Yes, indeed."

By now, Ray had spotted them and walked over putting his arms around Kenzi's waist.

"People come here and try to change things… try to run things… and they don't know what we're about. Rollins is old school. We know who and what and where. Miss Tilly was old school too."

Ray interrupted firmly, "Kenzi's worked very hard to serve the Rollins community. She makes everyone feel welcome."

"Yeah but…"

"And Aunt T supported her completely. WE support her completely."

The "we" Ray referred to meant the Grants, a family thoroughly ingrained into the fabric of the community. All of them with strong personalities and fierce spirits. Even Santi and Reggie and Davey had that strong love for each other.

Ray tightened his arms around Kenzi's waist. Kenzi leaned back against him. Kenzi could see from Deacon Waverly's expression that he now experienced the classic gaze that Ray leveled whenever he made a point not to be missed. Deacon Waverly had to either give way or disrespect Aunt Tilly, his old friend, as well as the entire Grant family in their own home while he ate and drank from their table. After a slight pause during which Waverly assessed Ray's determination, Waverly chuckled slightly.

"Yeah, I talked to Miss Tilly a while ago. She did say that you're all right. She loved the Kinfolk and the children's classes. I got some grandnieces and nephews of my own that've been asking about the class. They draw and things."

Kenzi spoke finally, "We'd love to have them join the other children. Here's my card. Wait. Let me get your information. We're starting up again."

"Oh... thank you."

Now that communication flowed along the straight and narrow path, Ray told him, "Deacon Waverly, did you get yourself a plate? There's plenty."

"Oh, I will. I definitely will. I'm kinda letting the crowd thin out a little. I brought that plate of catfish over there. Fried it up myself."

Ray smiled. "Thank you, sir. Thank you, indeed. I can see people have been making inroads on it too. People have been very kind to us today."

Deacon Waverly seemed to be working his way up to another point. This being the South, it would be reached in good time. Kenzi and Ray went along with the discussion.

"Yeah, I told everybody to send their children on over. I hear you're having a Juneteenth thing going on too, hunh?"

"Oh yes! Stacy's working with the children on their exhibits. We think it'll be fun for the families."

"Well, hopefully my grandnieces and nephews can get in on that too."

"Definitely! Contact Stacy and she can get them started."

And at this point, Ray kissed her quickly and moved off to circulate amongst other mourners. Deacon Waverly seemed to want to make a new start and Kenzi did as well.

"You know, I do Buffalo Soldier re-enactments. Me and a group of old-time brothers, we dress up in uniform and tell stories about black men on the Texas frontier."

He paused expectantly. Kenzi stepped up to the plate.

"Well, I'm still in the planning stages of the program. I'm trying to fill in a two-hour space between one and three on that Saturday. If it's not an imposition, or too short notice, maybe your group might have interest in talking to the children and their parents about the Buffalo Soldiers. We might even get the children to draw pictures of you all while you're speaking to add to the exhibit."

The moment of decision arrived. Aunt Tilly did her part to win Kenzi support from the community. Ray chimed in. Kenzi presented her case. If they accepted Kenzi, they would support Kinfolk Books. If they did not accept her, the struggle would continue until the store died.

Deacon Waverly thought it over.

"Hmmmm. I'll... I'll let the fellas know to be ready for the children at one o'clock on Saturday. And I'll tell them to be extra careful with the moustaches since they're going to have their portraits done." His eyes twinkled.

"Perfect! I'm looking forward to hearing about the Buffalo Soldiers, myself." Kenzi beamed back at him.

"You know some of the women and young mothers at the church may have interest in helping out at the bookstore. And some of the youth might shelve books and pass out flyers once in a while."

"You think so? That would help me greatly! I've tried to make contact with the churches in town, but I never really got a firm response."

"Well, heh," he chuckled, "They pretty much feel better about things when one of their own tells them about it. You see, Miss Tilly came to me."

"Ah," Kenzi nodded her head. So it worked like that. That explained his strange behavior at the shop. Thank God for Aunt Tilly's insight. If not for her understanding of community culture and social politics, Kinfolk would have remained on the outside looking in.

Along those lines, Kenzi wondered, uncomfortably, if she'd accidentally said something or did something to cause Stacy's cool vibe. She tried to think back carefully even as she replied to Deacon Waverly.

"I'm so glad she did. So see you on Juneteenth?"

"God willing and the creek don't rise, we'll be there."

Ray walked back up to hear the last part of their exchange. He reached out and shook Deacon Waverly's hand. Deacon Waverly offered condolences once more and moved off to explore the tables of food.

"Miss Tilly did a beautiful thing for Kinfolk Books. I miss that lady. And thank you too, for always being there for me, Ray."

"Of course, beautiful." He kissed her.

What Ray didn't mention was that while Kenzi worked things out with Deacon Waverly, he ran into an unexpected mourner – Maya. After the slightest hesitation, Ray's manners, drilled into him by Reginald and Aunt Tilly kicked in.

"Maya," he clasped her hand in two of his. "Thank you for coming by."

She bowed her head, grayer than he remembered. "I… I'm not disrespecting the court order, Ray. I just wanted to pay respects to the family."

"Thank you. I appreciate that." He looked into her eyes that showed ten lifetimes worth of road wear. Maya had been around the block many times and had frequently taken Darlene for the ride with her. She nearly took Santi for a spin after Darlene died, but Aunt Tilly's determination and Ray's quick legal action prevented any harm. Ray neither bent nor bowed to threats and pleading. Years later, here Maya stood.

Her tired eyes, beige instead of white surrounding the brown irises, searched the crowd until she turned to Ray with a look of inquiry.

"Santi?"

"Santi's fine."

"It's been a long time since I seen her."

"Yes." Ray waited.

Maya pursed her lips and looked at the floor. "I just thought that maybe…"

"No."

"Ray, I don't mean no disrespect…"

Ray's voice hardened. "Then don't."

Maya flinched. "Okay," she replied in a low voice. She looked around the crowd once more. "It's just, you know, I got clean. I attended the AA and cleaned up my life and I'm trying to make amends. I know I've made some wrong decisions."

"*Some* wrong decisions?"

She took a deep breath. "Ray, you got to know that I know I did wrong by Darlene. I know I did. I miss her. I really do. But don't blame Darlene anymore, Ray. Please. It was me. It was always me. I want to do right by Santi. I do. And I figure, Santi might need her grandmother."

Ray raised his eyebrows in a "you must surely be joking" way.

"What with Miss Tilly passing away and all and your mother gone."

Ray suddenly reached the end of civility. Too late, Maya saw that she'd lost him.

"Ray, Ray…" She touched his arm.

He shrugged her off.

No spectacle would be allowed today or ever again.

"Help yourself to the food, Maya. You found your way in, so you know the way out."

He turned and walked away. He wasn't worried about Santi. Because as soon as he spotted Maya, he located Dharma across the room and tilted his head indicating Santi's bedroom. Dharma, well aware of the court order and Ray's need to keep things on the level with the other guests, quietly led Santi away without Santi realizing the reason why.

Late that afternoon, Kenzi served each guest a piece of Dharma's *elachi gaja* - a spiced shortbread that included rice flour, rosewater, pistachios, and almond essence - with coffee and the usual iced mint tea. As the shadows under the tall pecan trees deepened and the crowd dissipated, Kenzi and Stacy stored the extra food in the refrigerator and freezer and washed dishes while Dharma looked through a photo album with the children. The guests, though they tried their best, barely put a dent in the huge supply of macaroni and cheese, cornbread, salmon croquettes, potato salad, spaghetti, fried chicken, fried catfish, chicken and dumplings, mushroom casserole, tuna casserole, red beans and rice, fried okra, corn on the cob, candied yams, muffins, cakes, pies, and cookies. The leftovers would last about two months in the deep freezer while the Grants recovered.

Ray, Dhan, and David spoke amongst themselves in low, short sentences as they moved furniture and then walked outside to the gardens. Kenzi guessed they discussed a new division of duties regarding the house and surroundings, and the care of the children. Kenzi watched through the window and felt the pain she could see in Ray's face and in the set of his shoulders.

After they put the house back in order, Dharma and her family, Stacy, and Dhan left amid comforting hugs. She would definitely call Stacy later and hopefully leave a message that would get returned. But right now, Ray needed her, she knew.

Ray put an exhausted Santi to bed and read her a story until her eyes drooped closed and she fell asleep. Even Jackson didn't move though he thumped his tail a few times. The house seemed so empty.

On the sofa, Kenzi leaned against Ray quietly as they watched dusk approach through the windows. The sky turned from dark blue to violet to pitch black. Ray flipped on a lamp and they sat there listening as the owls and cicadas and frogs mourned. Ray drew comfort from Kenzi's presence. She didn't speak much that day, but her presence filled him with warmth.

Kenzi knew she could stay in Ray's arms for the rest of her life and not even miss the whole world. She rested her head on his chest. She knew he didn't sleep. He just lay quiet.

Finally, with a sigh, Ray stirred beneath her and got up. Watching her, he pulled off the black band that held his locs away from his face and they fell down in a black mane past his shoulders. He looked at her a moment as she stared back up at him. He held out his hand which she took. He led her quietly to his room and kissed her mouth hungrily.

"Kenzi," he asked urgently. "I need you. I *need* you. Stay with me tonight."

She met kiss after kiss then pulled away to answer him

"I'll stay."

As if she could ever leave him.

They looked like dancers standing stage right and stage left, waiting for the cue to join together and to move to nature's orchestra of gentle, rhythmic night music. His wide-shouldered body shone darkly in the lamplight like mahogany. His eyes filled with emotion as he held his hand out to her again. He drew her curved, soft, firm shape in a close embrace and they rocked together a moment.

"I'm so glad you were here with me today."

"Ray, I'm always here for you."

He kissed her neck and shoulders as she held him for balance.

"Kenzi, when we make love," he whispered, "I want to see your eyes. I want you to look at me. I don't want you to look away. I need to know that you're there with me."

Kenzi realized the depth of his need then and wanted to please him, to make him feel better.

"I won't look away."

He unhooked her bra gazing steadily into her eyes and she shivered feeling the delicious sensation of his large hands warming her breasts. Then he slid her panties slowly down looking up at her as she held his shoulders. He stood and started to slide down the boxers that outlined the shape of his arousal when she grabbed his hand. Her turn.

She took the waistband in both hands and tugged it gently downward. Her soft hair lightly brushed against him and he made a choked sound in his throat as she smiled. She knelt on the floor in front of him. That the desire in his eyes had grown even more intense and that the pace of his breathing increased pleased her. She rose to her feet slowly, allowing her breasts to stroke his skin upward along the way.

With that, he pulled her under the quilt covering the king-sized bed made for his king-sized body. Kenzi had never made love this way with such a calm sharing of openness. But with Ray, any way was the right way.

No foreplay.

"Now," she breathed.

Ray braced himself on his elbows and pinned her down by her fluffy cottony hair spread across his pillow. He entered slowly watching her watching him.

"Don't look away."

'I won't.''

Her tiger eyes, golden in the lamplight, told him everything she felt as she whimpered and panted from the agony and raised her hips to meet him. Ray's face grimaced from the pleasure as she softly stroked him. She loved the way he gave her everything she needed by allowing her to see his emotion and his need for her. It excited her. She would do this for him forever if he needed her to.

She widened her legs and he sank further into her and drew comfort from her tightness surrounding him, embracing him as her arms and legs embraced him.

"Oh Ray. Deeper, oh God…" she choked out.

The emotion and intense longing rolling in waves over them. Ray gripped her hair harder in his fists and cried out her name again and again. He stared into her eyes insisting that she feel what he felt.

Their bodies surged together for the final descent into a swirl of magic. Wave after wave rocked Kenzi's body where they joined and she made unintelligible moaning sounds as she convulsed from the hard sensations that rendered her helpless under his gaze. He took triumphant satisfaction in the sight of her eyes glowing with an inner fire. Ray poured his life into her and held her tightly clenched to his chest. His eyes shut as he shuddered and then relaxed his hold.

Kenzi stared upward over his shoulder and felt something invisible break away and leave from her. A part of her soul joined with his. And she cried within as she clung to him, because she knew she would never get that part of herself back from him. Gone forever. She loved him. She was his and only his from that night until the end of her days.

Ray's locs spread across her body as he lay with his head resting between her breasts. They lay still in each other's arms, too exhausted and too weary to move. Kenzi closed her eyes with sad acceptance. Tears slipped from her eyelids. She didn't try to fight it. She couldn't. Her spirit would be forever tied to his. No matter where he went in the world, no matter what the future, she would always belong to him.

Night took over again as the old house settled and creaked. The wind blew gently on its way to elsewhere. The trees touched and whispered. Water rippled over the catfish pond. They all said goodbye to Aunt Tilly. They listened to Kenzi silently declare her love for Ray. They creaked and blew and rippled and whispered that news too.

Chapter 11

Aunt Jalissa

Jalissa Malton woke up late for work that afternoon at 2:32 p.m. and cursed as she realized that she forgot to set the alarm again. She worked the second shift last night and every night until 11:00 p.m. At home, she sat back sipping, thinking of nothing in particular, watching cornball late night television from midnight until 3:00 a.m. when she finally dreamed of a blank wall.

She was supposed to get up at 2:00 p.m. Just enough time to arrive to the plant at 3:00 p.m. to do it all again. The grind of it all tired her. Sleep, eat, work, drink, sleep. Rinse. Repeat. And for what? For this? She looked around her shabby apartment. Being late would be something new to do.

Well, maybe not new, but different.

She lay face-down for another five minutes to decide whether she would have to deal with a either a headache or an angry stomach during her shift. She rinsed off in the shower but didn't bother to style her hair or fix her makeup. No time for that. They'd written her up for tardiness twice this month already.

"I hate this job."

She put on the uniform that made her feel hot and the hat that made her feel stupid. However, the hat would hide her uncombed hair. If she didn't work, she didn't eat and she couldn't pay for utilities because the son-of-a-bitch cut off his payments to her. *Well, fuck him too!* Most importantly, if she didn't work, how else could she have paid for the taste she purchased along the way at 2:59 p.m.?

Speaking of taste, the liquor made her tongue feel funny. Probably because she hadn't taken time for a little nicotine pick-me-up. She needed a little something here and there to smooth out the rough edges of her empty life now that her siddity-acting daughter moved to Podunk or Roland, whatever the hell they called it. Everybody always left her. Even after she used all that money to put Lina through beauty school, Lina hoitied-toited her siddity-self on away. This younger generation acted so damn ungrateful. Not like back in her day.

"Shit," she told the rearview mirror resentfully. "I'm still young!"

People used to mistake Jalissa and Lina for sisters. But the melanin in her skin that protected her from the sun did not protect her from the addictions that aged her appearance an additional ten years.

She never drove down to see either Lina or Kenzi. And she hadn't seen Betty in years though they lived in the same city. She really didn't want to see anyone until she could get herself together. She'd fallen so far apart.

Just a little more time and I'll be back on my feet. Just a little more time is all I need.

She took another drink and searched for a cigarette with one hand as she changed lanes to get closer to the exit from Central Expressway.

"The bastard ain't paid me," she told her review mirror. "So I ain't got to be quiet no more. Oh, I'll sang it, honey. I'll sang it to the world!"

She laughed and croaked along loudly to an old Motown classic on the radio.

Dallas highways zoomed off the rails on Friday afternoons. Nobody gave a good goddamn. Other drivers called ahead to their destinations on cell phones, circled awkwardly around construction, cut across each other, tail-gated the slow, cursed the ignorant, searched for the least annoying radio news, reapplied makeup, drank coffee and soda, and chewed greasy mounds of salt and fat from fast food hamburger joints.

At 3:05 p.m., Jalissa heard the blare of a car horn.

She swerved to avoid the pickup truck roaring by on tires taller than the top of her rusted blue compact. Her slowed reflexes made her miss the exit. But she didn't miss the ramp.

The concrete divider raced crazily, jerkily up to the car's lightweight metal frame and scraped it, crushed it, punished it, and made it scream out and cry shards of glass that glinted like tears when they rained down upon her. She screamed too as bright light and pictures flashed through her mind.

Darkness. Night time? *Shouldn't she be on her way home then?* She hoped so. She felt so tired and confused.

She still heard the car horn. Her car horn. She leaned against it. It hurt to move. Tears streaked down her face and joined the life that flowed slowly over newly cut diamonds. Her eyes closed. She didn't see the diamonds become beautiful, shiny rubies that glinted in the sun.

Lina got the call from Betty and arrived to the Dallas hospital later that evening with Franklin. Though Betty's phone number sat in Jalissa's address book under the Malton last name with (SISTER) next to it, Jalissa never used Betty's number. And Betty never used Jalissa's number. It was emergency personnel that decided time had drawn nigh for a family reunion.

"Lina! Oh Lina!" Betty gripped her niece into a hug.

After a moment, Lina pulled away. "Where is she, Aunt Betty?"

Betty shook her head sadly and Lina started to cry. "She's gone, baby. She's gone."

Betty held Lina for a long time while they cried together. Franklin shifted but thankfully chose this moment to follow the adage, "If you don't have anything good to say, don't say anything at all," and, "If you are not part of the solution, then you are part of the problem." So Franklin said nothing. Kenzi and Ray arrived forty-five minutes later.

"Mom!" Kenzi ran to Betty, hugged her, and then turned to Lina. Hesitatingly, the two hugged each other.

"Lina, I'm so sorry."

"I know." Lina shook her head not wanting to continue.

"Hi… Franklin."

Kenzi hoped Franklin would not try to hug her. Thankfully, Ray stuck out a huge arm blocking her to shake Franklin's hand.

"Hey, man."

"Hey."

Kenzi turned back to Lina. "When did you get here?"

"Just minutes after she died." Lina turned back to Franklin who patted her on the back. "I just can't believe this."

Conversation between Lina and Kenzi as well as Franklin and Kenzi remained awkward and strained while Betty spoke with the doctor on duty. Ray silently held Kenzi in his arms, his back solid against her, holding her up.

While the other three spoke short, jerky sentences with long pauses between the words, Ray experienced an epiphany. Occupied with his own remembrances of death too soon, he realized that Lina's brittleness hid a wealth of hurt. She now stood vulnerable, looking years younger than she had when he first met her at the bookstore opening.

At that first meeting, Kenzi's cousin reminded Ray so much of Darlene that he'd recoiled and exercised mostly polite caution around her in the smallest doses possible. Just now, he wondered if he ever really knew the real Darlene. A small niggling at the back of his mind told him that a woman who would leave her own child and her child's father for the streets had a deeper pain than perhaps anyone, including him, could ever have known or understood. And, of course, he remembered the brief exchange with his daughter's grandmother at his own Aunt Tilly's funeral. He frowned to himself uneasily as slight twinges of guilt nagged him. Reminders of mortality really did strange things to one's head.

Betty joined them once more. Lina didn't want to see her mother's body after hearing the description of the accident.

"What's the hotel closest to you, Mom?"

"The Holiday Inn. You can follow behind me. One of you can call ahead to make a reservation."

Over the next several days, Betty, Kenzi, and Lina packed up Jalissa's apartment. Ray stored her belongings in the bed of his truck for the drive back to Rollins. They helped Betty with the details of Jalissa's life as well as they could. Lina cried as she signed various release forms.

Jalissa's funeral didn't take long.

Betty and Kenzi stood on either side of Lina while Ray and Franklin stood behind them. Betty turned to Ray, "I'm so sorry about your aunt. I wish I could have made it down." Betty teared up again and Ray enveloped her into a large hug.

Kenzi noted a familiar figure standing several yards away. Dr. Farrell stood on the outer edge of the group staring, not at them, but into the distance, either preoccupied with his own thoughts, or just not wanting to engage anyone in conversation. *Why was he here?*

Kenzi leaned over to ask Betty.

"Mom, Did Dr. Farrell know Aunt Jalissa?"

Betty had a strained look. "Kenzi, please let it go for now, okay?"

Kenzi stared at Betty in contrite confusion. "I'm sorry, Mom."

Betty clung to her daughter, not looking forward to what she knew she had to do. Who would have thought they would all end up in the same small town of all towns in this great big state, in this great big world, even? Giant Texas seemed very claustrophobic now. The universe required an ending for every beginning. She just wished it didn't have to be the same day her younger sister died.

Betty closed her eyes. She couldn't bear to watch the dirt thrown on Jalissa's coffin. She heard the little clumps fall against the hard surface.

"Lean on me, Mom," her daughter whispered. Betty leaned against Kenzi who held her tightly.

The relatively small crowd at the gravesite included a coworker or two and a few neighbors. Aunt Jalissa's addiction to alcohol, Lina's brittle edge, and Betty's transience had not made for strong community ties for any of the Maltons in Dallas. None of Aunt Jalissa's drinking partners showed.

Lina's horrible crying broke into a screeching wail and Kenzi went to comfort her and to wipe the tears away from her reddened face. "Ray could you bring a glass of water? Franklin, we need a chair." They hovered over Lina the next few minutes.

"Betty."

Betty, lost in thought, looked up and faced her ex-husband for the first time in twenty-nine years. Jonathan's hair had heavy doses of salt sprinkled lightly with pepper. He wore thick glasses that obscured his eyes somewhat. The same hazel, golden-brown eyes she saw in her own daughter's gaze. Though tall as she remembered, he'd grown a little stouter.

Betty stared back at him expressionless. Jonathan looked up at the sky. Then he looked at the ground. Neither the sky nor the ground had anything to say.

"I'm sorry about Jalissa." Wordlessly, he reached out and drew Betty to him. Memories surged back and washed over him. Brief portraits of their love flashed through his mind. Betty still felt the same in his arms. He released her.

"You are beautiful, you know."

Betty smiled sadly.

"So is Mackenzie," he looked a short distance away at the small group still comforting Lina.

"Yes, she is," Betty said with obvious pride.

Jonathan turned back towards Betty. "Does she know?" His voice hardened.

"No."

Jonathan shook his head and reached for Betty once more. He held her in another close embrace. Anyone watching would have thought he offered more comfort. Instead, he whispered coldly and purposefully in her ear.

"Betty. Tell it all." Betty stiffened and stared over his shoulder. "Tell it right." The quiet menace and edge to Jonathan's voice let her know that no excuse would suffice.

"Tell it today."

No doubt, if she did not obey, Jonathan would shed the academic demeanor and wreck havoc left and right. She knew him and his cold heart. Guilt and shame held him back this far. But now, obviously, nothing would. He had paid her price.

"Or I will." Angry and fed up, he paused to let his words sink in. "Where are you going later?"

"You can follow us."

Betty pulled away from him and turned her back to walk towards the group surrounding Lina. Jonathan walked towards his car. Franklin and Lina rode together. As she sat between Kenzi and Ray in his truck, Betty stared straight ahead, not bothering to check the rear view for Jonathan.

Back at Betty's apartment where they ate a late lunch, Kenzi, still puzzled by Dr. Farrell's presence, said nothing and neither did he. All of their own thoughts pretty much substituted for conversation.

Kenzi felt uneasy as the day wound to a close and finally spoke up.

"We checked out of the hotel this morning, Mom."

"Okay," Betty sighed. "I'm just gonna put this food away."

Kenzi shook her head. "I'll do that."

"I'll help," Lina walked past Kenzi's surprised face into the kitchen

And as she and Lina put the food away, Kenzi sadly remembered performing the same task just a couple of weeks ago at the Grant homestead. Ray caught her eye and she knew he understood. He gave her the same supportive smile she'd given him. She smiled back, so glad to have him in her life.

"Well, in that case, I'm gonna go through the remembrances." Betty organized the flowers and cards in order to send notes of thanks.

Even with these tasks, tension within Betty's apartment heightened between the six people. Ray still felt the pain from Aunt Tilly's death just a few weeks ago. Jonathan sat on edge from what he knew Betty would say in the next few moments. Franklin contained his curiosity about Jonathan's role at the funeral. Kenzi felt torn between compassion for Lina and irritation with Franklin's presence.

Ray and Franklin sat on the sofa while Jonathan sat on an overstuffed chair. Cable news blared on television. Franklin, particularly uncomfortable, persisted with a stilted conversation to fill the silence.

"What channel is this?"

Jonathan didn't bother to watch. "Not sure."

Franklin spoke to the wall. "That storm is gonna be bad for Arkansas."

"Yeah." Ray could barely be heard.

"Think the recession'll last much longer?"

"Hope not." Jonathan spoke with finality.

Ray simply grunted.

Betty saw the tight set to Jonathan's jaw. She also recognized the abrupt tone in his voice. She'd seen plenty of that. Betty stood up.

"Kenzi. Lina. I need to speak to you both a moment please. In the bedroom."

"You two are not cousins, you are half-sisters." Betty threw the words into the air and let them fall wherever they decided to land.

Lina and Kenzi sat side-by-side on the bed with identical blank expressions. "Mom, are you feeling…"

"Kenzi, listen to me." Betty held up her hand for quiet. "You two are not cousins. You are half-sisters. Jonathan is your father," she said to Kenzi. "And your father," she said to Lina.

Kenzi and Lina stared at each other to see if the other already knew. Seeing the same confusion in each other's eyes, they turned to stare at Betty again.

Kenzi shook her head, speechless.

"Yes, Kenzi. You are."

Kenzi shook her head again still not speaking. She always felt her and Lina's resemblance appeared uncanny, more than that of most cousins. The knowledge that Betty withheld the truth from her for years made her stare at her mother in disbelief. Years of lies. She finally found the words.

"Mother, how could you do this? How could you do this now? Today?"

With a sob Kenzi crossed her arms in front of herself and paced the room. While Betty told them the bare outline of the story, Kenzi tried to shut it out and leaned against the window that looked down into the pool area of the apartment complex searching for an escape from her mother's madness.

"My father is that man sitting out there? Jonathan?"

"Yes, Lina."

Lina crumpled in on herself like an accordion and cried. Lina's keening wail snaked across the room and raked across Kenzi's scalp and ears. She opened the bedroom door and started blindly for the front door. Jonathan reached for her as she passed his chair.

"Kenzi…"

"No!" She choked out, snatching her hand away. "No!"

Her tears started before she made it completely out of the door. She slowed down as she ran into the guardrail by the stairs. She didn't know where to go to escape her mother's stupidity. Besides, Ray had the truck keys.

Inside, the men sat shocked and worried, both at Kenzi's anger and the sound of Lina's tortured crying from the bedroom. Those highly, intense emotional moments made grown men freeze in fear of not knowing how to make the tears stop and how to make the pain that they couldn't see go away. Ray recovered first and followed Kenzi outside.

"Take me home, Ray. I have to get out of here away from these people. Now."

"Kenzi, you can't leave like this."

"Ray, please!"

Ray folded her into the comfort of his large body. "Kenzi, I'm not sure what just happened, but I don't want to leave without saying good-bye to Miss Betty and Lina."

Kenzi shook her head, still buried in his chest.

"I can see you're upset, Kenzi. Let's try to work it out first, okay? Whatever it is."

"Ray, it's awful. Awful."

"Look, I can see a vending machine near the mailboxes. Let's just get something to drink, cool off, and then we can say our good-byes, okay?"

They walked around the pool not speaking. Kenzi didn't tell him what started the explosion from the bedroom. She could scarcely bring herself to admit that those two people, either of them, had anything to do with the start of her life.

Franklin stood up reluctantly, more from a sense of obligation, than a real desire to offer any comfort. Jonathan shook his head and waved him back down. Both men sat together grimly staring at the stock prices scrolling across the bottom of the television screen. They heard, but tried to not listen to the sounds of sobbing from the bedroom.

"I was conscious of it. The fact that my birth was the result of an affair. My mother didn't tell me who he was. But something in the air always made me feel so... edgy. All those whispers." Lina looked away. "No wonder we never saw each other."

Betty pulled Lina's face back towards her.

"Lina, even though I forgave Jalissa, our relationship had grown understandably distant. We agreed that it best for everyone to not make the affair public knowledge in order to not hurt you or Kenzi. We did what we thought was best for everyone at the time. Unfortunately, Jalissa still felt guilty. None of us recovered completely. And we weren't able to offer any comfort to each other because we were the source of the other's pain. I wasn't there for her when she needed me because... Because I think I truly hadn't forgiven her. Lina. Honey, I'm so sorry for everything."

"Aunt Betty, I asked my mother why we never saw you even though we lived in the same city and she said it was for the best. I thought you'd done something to her and I decided that I shouldn't like you or Kenzi either if you didn't like my mom. I wasn't sure really. She never said. No one really came out and said it."

"I know, sweetheart. Too much left unsaid. Too much pride and shame." Betty sighed, "Look, I know it's a lot to take in, especially today. But Jonathan and I both agreed that you should be told immediately before any more time passed."

"Why did he leave, Aunt Betty? Why did he act like none of us were even alive? Didn't he know my mother suffered and that there were times we struggled just to eat? How could he not care?"

"Lina, you have every right to be upset. You and Kenzi, both. Please, just please give us all a chance to work through this. I'm going to go get Kenzi. But before I do, I need to tell you what your mother told me before you got to the hospital. Before she... before she..."

Lina started sobbing again with her head in her hands as Betty held her tightly.

"Lina, your mother lost a lot of blood from the accident. The doctors told me that they would not be able to save her. She was too far gone." Betty closed her eyes as she remembered the hurried run through the hospital corridors that ended abruptly at her sister's hospital room.

"Oh Jalissa. Oh my God!"

Betty cried to see her little sister, who she used to carry around like a doll and push on a swing, cocooned in bandages with bruises still showing the marks of the steering wheel. Scratches from windshield glass criss-crossed her face.

"Jalissa."

Betty cried and shook her head in disbelief at the horrible sight. It wasn't right. She wanted to wrap her little sister in her arms and carry her away from all of this. Instead she stood there helpless.

"They stopped the bleeding and gave her something weak for the pain although I was told she still had alcohol in her system. I called you and Kenzi, then I was at her bedside for about an hour before she woke up. The medication wore off. I think she was surprised to see me since we hadn't spoke in so long. And…" Betty hesitated, "…I think she knew she was dying."

And here Betty choked back her own tears to continue.

"Jalissa looked at me. She was smiling. I smiled back at her because regardless of anything that happened almost thirty years ago, she was my little sister from beginning to end."

Betty rubbed Lina's back in circular motions as she continued the story.

"Betty." Jalissa's voice remained low, but urgent almost as if she could feel herself fading and needed to talk in order to remain in the here and now.

"I'm here, Jalissa."

"Please. Take. Care. Of Lina."

Betty shuddered as the tears flowed down her face.

"Oh my God. Oh my God. No. Noooo Don't. Jalissa, just hang on. You hear me? Stay with me, Jalissa. Stay here."

"Promise me," she breathed, weaker.

"You can get better. Don't leave, Jalissa. We can fix this."

Betty felt sick to her stomach. "Lord nooooo," she moaned. "Please no, Lord. Don't take her." But she could see in Jalissa's leaving in her eyes. Betty's punishment would be to witness her sister's very last breath.

She held on to the fingers of Jalissa's hand that connected to an intravenous tube. As a child, Jalissa used to be scared so of the dark she whined her way into bed with Betty in order to fall asleep. She wanted to crawl into the hospital bed beside Jalissa now. The darkness would come for Jalissa soon. She didn't want Jalissa to be afraid.

"Jalissa, don't be afraid."

"I'm not afraid."

"I'm here."

"I love you, Betty."

Betty summoned a smile. "I love you too, Jalissa. I always have. I never stopped loving you." She choked through the tears. "I'm so sorry, Jalissa. For all of this. I should have forgiven you in my heart. I do forgive you. I do. I love you and I love Lina as well."

At the mention of Lina's name, Jalissa struggled to remain alert. She opened her mouth to speak the words.

"Lina," Jalissa croaked harshly.

Betty leaned in closely.

"Linaaa…"

"Jalissa, what? Tell me about Lina."

Jalissa met Betty's eyes with her own sadly. "Promise."

"Jalissa… promise what?" Betty leaned closer.

"Pleassss…" Jalissa's voice ended in a fading whisper and hiss.

At last, Jalissa stopped fighting. The hospital room quieted as she relinquished her spirit back to the place from whence it came. Betty called for the nurse as she squeezed Jalissa's lifeless hand.

"I will! I will, Jalissa! I love you, Jalissa! And I love Lina. I will."

"I repeated it to myself so I would remember it for you. I thought it was important for you to know exactly what she said."

Lina cried anew and held on to Betty, the last living link to her mother. Unhappy at home, she realized only in her mid-twenties that her mother's temper didn't result from sheer crazed grouchiness. She was an alcoholic and suffered from depression aggravated by a volatile temper. Lina wondered for a split second what life would have been like if her mother had chosen another man to be her father. What if Aunt Betty and Kenzi had stayed a part of their lives? What if her mother had no reason to drown her loneliness and shame?

But thoughts like that did no good. The fantasy of *that* family differed from the reality of *this* family.

Betty spoke again.

"Lina, I made a mistake with Jalissa. Years ago, I told her that I forgave her, just because I thought that was the right thing to do. But, in my heart, I really hadn't. Seeing you and Jalissa brought back the pain of my failed marriage and so I left Dallas to try to forget by putting distance between us. I missed so much of both of your lives because of that. But your mother forgave me my part in this whole mess. Lina, it is important for you to know that you are not responsible for the decisions that Jalissa, Jonathan, or I made. We're responsible. Not you. Not Kenzi. I don't want you two girls to take this out on each other. I know this is hard. I know it is. It's almost too much to take and… it has worn me down. I can't even imagine how you must feel learning about all of this all at once. But, if you can, I hope you can forgive me too. Jalissa's last wish was that we always be a part of each other's lives. We're all that we Maltons have got now. Please just think about it."

Lina hugged Aunt Betty, her face red and swollen, and said, "It's so much all at once. All at one time… it's just so much."

Betty and Lina walked out of the bedroom with reddened, tear-stained faces.

Jonathan got up stiffly.

"I think it would be best for me to return to Rollins right now." As Betty glared at him, he added, "It may be too much to handle in one day." He chose not to see Betty's head shaking with disgust and instead focused his gaze on Lina.

"Lina, I do want to talk with you and Kenzi about… everything," brief pause, "once you've had a chance to rest and absorb the news. I'm very sorry about your mother. I'm sorry about," he cut himself off seeing Betty angrily draw a finger under her neck.

Lina didn't look up.

Jonathan turned to Franklin with a curt, "See you around, Franklin."

"Dr. Farrell."

Kenzi stared blankly at Jonathan, her… father, as he left the apartment. He nodded at her and said simply, "Mackenzie, I'll see you back in Rollins." She searched her mind for any indicator of remembrance, some familiarity, and found nothing at all. Just the usual emptiness that had always existed when she thought of her father. She filled the empty spaces from her imagination. But there he went. She didn't watch him walk away.

In his parked car, Jonathan sat still. A long time passed before he started the car and put it in gear for the drive back to Rollins.

Betty poked her head outside the front door and found Ray holding Kenzi in his arms.

"Kenzi, come back inside."

Franklin's true nature finally won the struggle against the unnatural mask of concern he'd worn the last couple of days. "Just what is going on here?"

Betty and Kenzi remained silent. Ray felt an impending sense of dread.

Lina sighed wearily. "Jonathan is my father and Kenzi's father."

Franklin visibly started. "You have got to be kidding me." Lina said nothing more but met his gaze steadily.

Comprehension set in as Franklin took a closer look at Lina's facial features. He glanced at Kenzi who looked away and reached for Ray.

"Jonathan. Dr. Jonathan Farrell is your father? You two are sisters... and cousins?"

Kenzi didn't reply as Franklin's gaze drifted to Betty who stiffened.

Franklin settled once again on Lina who still leaned against Betty.

"Oh my God. Anything else I need to know about, Lina?"

Lina flared up, "Shut up, Franklin! Shut up!"

Franklin chuckled. Lina and Franklin argued. Betty and Kenzi and Franklin argued. Kenzi cursed Franklin out.

"Man, just leave it alone." Ray finally took over the discussion that threatened to escalate past hysteria. "Just leave it," he finished in disgust.

Franklin looked at Ray who now dated his ex-girlfriend and seemed to take charge of the entire room. He never did like the boho motherfucker. They all watched as Franklin sized Ray up and mentally calculated the odds.

"I'll be in the car, Lina."

Outweighed and outnumbered, Franklin struck back in typical style by leaving Lina stranded in Dallas and driving off with her suitcases and belongings back to Rollins.

After a few more choice words, Kenzi quietly offered, "Lina, you can sleep on my futon until we can make plans and figure out the next move. You'll want to get your things from Franklin."

Lina nodded wearily.

Ray got a late start on the drive back. He wanted to assure himself that Betty would be okay in Dallas. No sound came from inside the car except a news program that no one really listened to. However, it covered the silence that screamed out and pressed down upon the three of them.

They listened to the monotonous muttering punctuated with occasional static. They listened to the sound of the tires turning. They watched road signs and gas stations get larger, larger, larger, then *whoosh* as they passed by. The dark curtain of night gave temporary relief from having to look into each other's eyes.

Kenzi leaned wearily against the car window with her eyes closed trying to decide whether the uncontrolled dreams of sleep or the waking nightmare of listening to Lina cry would be worse. *Shut. Up. Lina.* She felt too tired to say it aloud. And it wouldn't be right to say it anyway. *Let her cry. Let them all cry for this fucked up world full of its fucked up people.* Kenzi felt entirely too tired to move her head. She felt entirely too tired to close her eyes. Ray remained silent. What could he possibly say in this situation anyway? She didn't want to talk to him now either.

She eased herself into a trance staring into the blackness beyond the window. Neither here nor there. Neither asleep nor awake. Neither alive nor dead. Just nothing. Because *nothing* seemed easier to deal with than *something.* The blankness, the emptiness, the vacuum – all of it seemed so much easier. *Something?* No. That was just too much right now.

At last the exit sign for Rollins loomed over them. Blink and you missed it. Ray stopped in front of Kenzi's apartment.

Kenzi handed Lina her apartment key.

"Just make yourself comfortable. I'll follow inside in a few minutes."

She felt drained. Kenzi couldn't begin to imagine what Ray must think of her and her family and the crazy scene he'd witnessed. She didn't even know what to think of all of them herself. Was dysfunction an inherited characteristic? Did it lurk deep within her genes and taint her destiny? Maybe Betty's next surprise would be to show Kenzi her adoption papers. Would choices and decisions she made today cause pain to her own children years from now? *What was wrong with them all?*

Even as Ray held her hands between his, she didn't meet his eyes. He held her to him for a long time and kissed her goodnight, whispering, "It's all going to be okay, Kenzi. It will."

"No it won't."

Kenzi finally released the pent-up emotions of the day and broke down sobbing. She mourned Aunt Jalissa's violent death. She mourned the years in which she never really knew Jalissa and now never would. And she mourned the years of happiness each member of her family lost because of walls. She kissed him one last time before he returned to the pickup and drove off to where normal people lived.

"Kenzi... thanks for letting me stay here."

"Lina, don't. We're family. We both have a lot to talk over. But just get some sleep for now, okay?"

Kenzi entered the bathroom to wash her face and cried anew under the sound of the running tap.

Who are we anymore? Who am I? And where are we all supposed to go from here? What are we supposed to do with each other?

She remembered her and Lina's last telephone scream fight over Franklin and shook her head. Even Lina didn't deserve the pompous jerk. Kenzi realized that she also didn't deserve Franklin or any of the other losers she'd allowed into her life before meeting Ray. Ray, the man who made all other men disappear.

She patted her face dry and stared into the mirror at the tired, worn-out emotional wreck staring back at her. She went to bed dreading the moment when she and Lina would have to face the complex layers of baggage that lay between them.

Lina laid in the dark as she listened to her sister cry. She lay awake a long time, thinking.

Chapter 12

Lina and Dhan

For Ray, spring planting brought Aunt Tilly's passing back to him. He missed her and her wise sayings as well as her sassy comments on current events and his love life, whichever she thought in worst shape at the time. Now that Ray really thought about it, Aunt Tilly had backed off of him since he'd met Kenzi. No cackling remarks or ominous warnings about yellow rain and whistling girls. It seemed as if he'd known Kenzi all of his life and she had become a part of him and his family. Ray heard the phone ring from the garden.

"Ray, we need to get Lina's car. It's still parked at Franklin's since she left it there when he drove her up to Aunt Jalissa's funeral. I don't trust Franklin with her car, especially after he stranded her in Dallas."

"You think he might do something to the car?"

"It would be like him. I just hope he hasn't had time to do anything stupid like flatten the tires or scratch the paint with his keys. You know how he is."

"Childish bully. I still haven't forgotten his leaving you at the estate sale. Way on the edge of Rollins by yourself."

"He's vengeful. But you know, it wasn't all bad. That estate sale led me to my knight in shining armor."

"More like rusty armor. But my truck never lets me down."

"Or me." Kenzi laughed. "And of course, that rescue led to our first... you know." Thoughts of Ray always made Kenzi feel warm and fizzy inside.

"Oh, I do know." Ray's low baritone stroked over her.

"Ray, I really want to see you, but I can't let too much work to pile up at the bookstore. Even with all this happening."

"Yeah, I know how it is. Look, Kenzi, I'll try to take care of Lina's car from this end. Don't worry about it for right now."

"Thanks, honey."

Ray caught Dhan who'd just arrived to the homestead from Houston and was about to head into Rollins.

"Dhan, Kenzi's younger sister needs some help moving furniture."

Dhan was puzzled. "What sister?"

"Lina."

"I thought Lina was her cousin?"

"Long story bro. Family business. Yesterday, we all found out at the funeral they're cousins and sisters. Don't say anything though. Lot's of hurt there. Just help her, okay?"

"Yeah, okay. Help her what?"

Ray handed Dhan the keys to his flatbed which still held Jalissa's belongings. "Pick her up at Kenzi's. Take her to Franklin's to get her car and help her get her stuff out of his condo. You'll probably need to help her put her and her mother's stuff in storage."

Lina used her own key to open the door.

"Franklin teaches an early morning class."

Dhan warily followed her. "It takes just one loser like that to spoil things for the guys who actually know how to treat a woman."

Lina didn't answer.

He sensed fragileness in Lina. Even with Ray's warning, Dhan knew not to ask questions after expressing the one opinion. He silently lifted objects that weighed too much for Lina to handle on her own and helped her to pack them in her car and Ray's truck still holding her mother's belongings. She followed him to a storage space near Kenzi's apartment. Lina, usually so quick with the clever remark, withdrew into sadness. He wondered if she thought of Franklin.

Lina actually thought about her upside-down world, jerked off-kilter within the space of just a few days. She lost her mother to the crash of metal against metal with a scream of fear cut off by shattered glass and life leaking and dripping over the car seats. She found her father standing over her mother's grave. The boyfriend she'd paraded around Rollins and Dallas for the single girls to envy abandoned her in Dallas. And now, she depended on the cousin that she'd disliked most of her life for a place to stay. As of yesterday, that cousin became her older sister.

She felt glad that Dhan wasn't the high-maintenance type who required a constant stream of chatter about nothing in order to feel secure. She really didn't feel up to small talk. They piled her electronics and her summer clothing, extra shoes, and other miscellaneous items into the unit without saying much except for, "Excuse me," and, "Can you hold this?" At last they finished.

Lina exhaled, winded from the exercise. "Wow! I can't believe all that stuff fit."

"You know what you need, Lina?" Dhan grinned at her.

"What?" she asked suspiciously.

"Follow me and I'll show you."

Lina followed him to Organic Soul for a lunch of lentil soup filled with leeks, tomatoes, garlic, peppers, and herbs, then ladled over a steaming pile of curried rice with sides of warm sweet cornbread and butter, flavorful collard and turnip greens, shock-to-the-system sweet blackberry cobbler, and hot chamomile tea with honey and apple mint.

"This is such a nice place."

"You know Lina, Organic Soul is like my second home. I always feel at peace here. I worked summers here in high school and college. Dharma made sure I knew every position. I washed dishes, bussed tables, worked in the kitchen, did a little hosting. But then she figured out what I really liked to do was crunch numbers and order food and supplies. You know, take care of the financial and the administration of the budget. I paid the bills and made allocations for advertising. That's when I decided to do the MBA program."

"That is so cool that you came up that way. I'm still not sure what I want to do with myself." She sighed and shook her head.

"It'll find you."

Dharma served Lina and Dhan personally in a quiet corner and instinctively gave Lina a quick hug and backrub.

"Hey, Lina. I'm so sorry about your mother. I wish I'd been able to join you all in Dallas but I had to hold things down here."

"It's okay," Lina smiled slightly. "Thank you though."

"Well, it's a small thing, but I made something for you and Kenzi." Dharma set the pastry box on the table and opened it. "See? It's *bibbikan.*"

Lina peeked in. "What is it again?"

"I'm so glad you asked!" Dharma smiled as Dhan laughed in anticipation of Dharma's lecture. "Last night, I added sugar and honey to scraped coconut and cooked them together over a low flame. Then I added raisins, substituted pecans for cashews, lime peel, dates, ginger, and sultanas. That sat overnight. Then this morning, I added seminola, flour, vanilla, cinnamon, and rosewater and baked it all into this cake."

"It smells delicious."

"It is delicious!"

Lina laughed with Dharma and Dhan. Dharma slipped a sympathy card under the box and walked away quietly.

Dharma knew something of the conflicts within the Malton family through Ray, but felt no judgment towards Lina. People made mistakes. But that didn't mean that they didn't deserve love. In fact, they were the ones who needed love most of all. This quiet acceptance helped Lina unwind a little from the dark combination of guilt, shame, anger, and grief.

"Your family seems very close, Dhan."

"Oh most definitely! We grew up kind of tight since our parents died. I was fourteen and Ray had to fight to keep us together. That's when Aunt Tilly stepped in as our guardian. Now, we do argue once in a while, don't get me wrong."

He leaned in conspiratorially to Lina.

"You may have already noticed that Dharma can be a little on the bossy side," they laughed together, "but she has strong love. She holds us together. I told her she was a junior Aunt T. She hit me for that one." He rubbed his shoulder in memory. "Yeah, I love the fam. And the kids are great of course. I tease Santi and the twins, make 'em laugh, throw 'em around. I'm only twenty-five and still in school, so I'm not trying to have any of my own right now. Besides, I don't need children since I can visit with Ray's and Dharma's. I ruffle and rile them up and then leave when they get grouchy and sleepy. That's Ray and Dharma's payback from when they bossed me too much," he chuckled.

"You're so funny. And sneaky! I'm gonna stay on your good side now that I know what you do," Lina laughed.

"Don't get me wrong, I love my brother and I'll always look up to him. I don't think I ever told him this and it's funny that I'm telling you, but if it hadn't been for Ray's example of manhood, I might be running the streets of Houston or Dallas with a stable of women and their jealous ex-boyfriends on my trail. I could be caught up in gang warfare. I could have chosen the cheap and easy way to make money. You know the kind that doesn't get listed on tax forms. I could have died several times before I reached my twenty-first birthday. A few of my friends that got caught up in it are dead now. Or they're locked up."

Dhan stared Lina in the eyes, "My family gives me life." And then he smiled at her.

Lina smiled as she hesitatingly thanked Dhan for his help. "I can see why Kenzi is drawn to you all. This cake Dharma made smells delicious."

Dhan smiled back and assured Lina, "Well, you're practically part of the family as well, you know. Seriously. Once you're in, you're always in." He chuckled, "Ray will probably try to recruit you to help with the vegetable garden and the fruit trees this summer. Consider yourself both invited and warned."

They both paused briefly, remembering Aunt Tilly's passing just a few weeks ago. After a sympathetic silence, Lina took a deep breath and offered, "I'm sorry about your Aunt Tilly. I keep hearing from Kenzi what a wonderful woman she was."

Dharma walked up to hear the tail end of the conversation.

"I brought over some food for Kenzi. I saw her go into Kinfolk Books this morning so you can take this to her."

Dharma sat down.

"You know, there'd had been a run on Aunt T's quilts by the regular customers and even people I'd never seen right after she died."

Dhan looked around the restaurant. "I didn't even notice the walls were all bare."

Aunt Tilly carefully stitched her quilts by hand and infused them with the essence of her character. Kenzi came to the Grant homestead on a visit once to find Aunt Tilly and Miss Lydia stitching together. While Kenzi sat and watched, Aunt Tilly told them both about quilts produced during the days of slavery in America that contained secret codes to help guide slaves to freedom. Slaves sewed routes and stops on the Underground Railroad into the quilts. The spectacular designs mapped the way to freedom.

Quilts, by the nature of their creation, held a lot of history and tradition. Aunt Tilly would take the out-grown and cast-off clothing of the family and cut them into shapes so that their lives and memories lasted long after fashion trends of the day had come and gone. Ray, Dharma, and Dhan each had their own quilts made especially for them as did the children. Ray had shown his to Kenzi and pointed out certain squares that chronicled his long association with denim. He wore down his jeans until they softened and thinned at the knees and frayed at the cuffs. Then he handed them to Aunt Tilly. She cut them into squares and saved them into piles to sew his special denim quilt. Heavy and thick, the quilt kept him warm as toast in the winter. He loved it.

Dharma spoke to Lina. "Aunt T's quilts are easily identifiable, you know. She caught the business bug from me, I think, and so we offered her quilts on the walls of Organic Soul." Dharma looked at the bare walls.

"I rotated them and kept the extras folded in plastic bags until it was time for another unveiling. Then I would unfold the quilt to hang on the wall with Aunt T's business card that also had the name of the quilt written on it. They sold here and there, once in a while. But in the week following her death, twenty quilts sold to various members of the community. Everyone wanted a Miss Tilly original. But I held two in the back of the store and I'm going to put them up for permanent residence on the left and right walls of the restaurant as reminders."

Dhan picked up the narrative.

"And you know what we found out at the reading of Aunt T's will?" He glanced at Dharma briefly for permission. She nodded and he continued.

"We learned that Aunt T willed the proceeds of her quilt sales to be held in trust for the higher education of her grandchildren. We were all stunned."

"We had no idea the depth of her character. Her love and complete devotion to us was always unspoken, you know. Underneath all those wise-cracks, and the jokes, and the stories was an endless supply of love. So her legacy will live on. We'll see to it."

At the reading of the will, Dharma broke into tears while Ray and Dhan cleared their throats and blinked rapidly. Even the attorney paused now and then. Aunt Tilly got to him too.

Even now, Dhan paused and looked down at his plate, "So thanks, Lina. I mean it. I really appreciate you saying that. I do miss her. We all do." Dharma walked away, once again overcome with her own emotions.

He continued softly and carefully, "I'm sorry about your mother."

Lina smiled shakily through her tears and nodded, not able to speak yet. Dhan squeezed her hand for a moment in support and she knew he understood.

After taking a breath Lina curved her mouth into the shadow of a smile and answered, "Thank you. Thank you, too."

She gazed out the window wistfully. The pink-gold caress of the morning had changed while she'd packed up her old life. During lunch, the sun rose further in the sky. True, pure gold shone over every tree and flower growing and every man and woman walking. Every butterfly and ladybug living and flying flourished under its rays. Things seemed so much clearer now.

"You know, I can't remember the last time, or even the first time I picked fruit off a tree. Although a close-up view of nature is probably just what I need to clear my head. I don't know if you guys could stand me long enough though. I might get in the way thinking I was helping."

In her own way, Lina wanted to be considerate and offer Dhan a way to back track and withdraw the invitation if he regretted the impulse. Still hurt from Franklin and the absence of her own father while dealing with an alcoholic mother, Lina felt unsure of bonding and how it worked since she hadn't experienced it to a great extent in her own life. She waited anxiously and braced herself for a too-quickly spoken, "You know, you're probably right. Maybe you should stay home and rest."

Instead…

"Nope! No you don't! Too late now. Ray knows how to find you and so do I. I got you, Lina." Dhan laughed triumphantly and gave Lina a quick hug. "God, you're so easy!" Dharma waved them off as they left together and headed across the street, Dhan carrying Kenzi's lunch and Lina holding the cake.

Dhan gave Kenzi a hug. A real long one. Lina fidgeted nervously. In some ways, Dhan reminded her of Franklin. He wore his hair cut close to the skull in a conservative style. He groomed himself or paid someone to groom him perfectly. Lina sensed the dark, good looks characteristic of the entire Grant family combined with intelligence and humor likely attracted many women. But Dhan had some things Franklin did not have and never would – character, kindness, a sense of purpose and dedication. From Dhan's interaction with his sister, Dharma, and the way he spoke of his Aunt Tilly, he did not seem the type who enjoyed hurting women. She wondered if Dhan felt attracted to Kenzi even though Kenzi dated his older brother.

Meanwhile, Dhan decided Kenzi and Lina needed time alone.

"Well, folks, Ray's gonna send out an all points bulletin on me if I don't get back to help him out."

Lina quickly added "insightful and thoughtful" to her silent assessment. He gave Lina a quick hug on the way out and she thought to herself, "Damn, they sure like to hug. But it's nice."

Lina further realized what she'd missed out on behind her brittle, mocking facade. She missed loving shows of affection that cost not a dime, so invaluable to both the giver and receiver.

Turning to Dhan before he left, Lina said clearly, "Thanks for everything, Dhan. You and Dharma both are good people."

Dhan tried to deflect his embarrassment at Lina's compliment by reaching to tug the ponytail she'd hurriedly made that morning. "Lina volunteered to help us with the gardens this summer. Right, Li Li?" He'd nicknamed her already.

"Yeah right," Lina laughed. "I volunteered."

Li Li? Kenzi paused from wrecking destruction on the collards and turnip greens to register a new softness in Lina's demeanor and the fact that she'd reached out to another human in grateful acknowledgement.

"By the way, you'd better give fair warning to the fig trees that I'm coming for them." Lina teased Dhan back.

"Look out!"

The human reached back to Lina and she smiled. But then the last couple of days had been nothing if not unusual and tragic. Kenzi looked at Dhan with uncertainty but wisely held her tongue and chose to not show any notice. Dhan gave her a quick kiss on the cheek as Kenzi squeezed his hands in hers. "Thank you so much Dhan, thank you for being there for us today. And tell Dharma thanks as well for thinking of us."

Dhan stood up a little straighter at the praise to say, "Of course. Call me if you need anything else. You know the number."

Mission accomplished, Dhan drove back to the homestead. Helping women in distress made him feel good. Ladies Love Cool Dhan. Dhan, a known ladies man at Rice University, dealt with Ray's frequent precautionary reminders over and over.

He knew Ray didn't want what happened between him and Darlene to happen to Dhan. Darlene hurt them all when she left and again when she died so needlessly. Still, he had a duty to rebellion as the youngest child. He told Ray to back off with plenty of bass in his voice.

"I'm a grown-ass man, Ray. I got my life under control."

Their arguments over his lifestyle increased when he started college at Prairie View. Good-looking and well-spoken with a teasing, fun-loving manner underscored by a sense of responsibility and goals, the women went completely crazy for him.

Ray persisted. "Dhan, I'm telling you. You need to slow your roll, man."

Dhan went to offense. "So what is it really, Ray? You feeling some envy because I'm finishing my education and you didn't?"

Ray stared back at him in speechless anger. Like Dhan just sucker-punched him in the gut. Even Dhan looked surprised at what came out of his own mouth. Ray slowly shook his head and stared at Dhan as if he'd never met him. Dhan couldn't tell if Ray wanted to smash him to the ground or cry. Dhan got up and left the room knowing that he'd gone just one step too far. Today, Dhan winced and made a mental note to apologize for what he'd said. They squashed it years ago as brothers do. Still, he knew Ray still remembered that conversation because he never spoke on Dhan's personal life ever again.

Thinking of Lina and Kenzi's situation, he counted himself lucky that he had known his father. He knew how a man cared for his wife and family. He had memories of their father with his tall, proud military bearing always carrying his toolkit off to this job or that. All he had to do is look in the mirror to remember Reginald. But then his father died just as he reached fourteen. On the verge of making the difficult transition from young child to moody teen, he searched for his own identity as the youngest child.

Ray, Dharma, and Aunt T filled in the blanks for him and provided him with so much love he never had to wander the streets to find it. Besides, he knew from experience that Ray would come looking for him if he went a step too far beyond. He never endured gangs, turf wars, or criminal acts as an initiation into manhood. Instead, He, Ray, and Dharma grew up as a team. His brother and sister formed his gang. The Grant homestead served as his turf. Work at Organic Soul in various positions of responsibility and trust initiated him into the ways of the adult world. Each time he needed Ray, Ray showed.

"Lina, do you feel any different?"

"Not really. Do you?"

Kenzi shrugged silently.

Lina sighed and sat still a moment. "It's a relief to have some blanks filled in and a lot of my own questions answered. I feel sort of relieved that the truth is out."

"Me too."

"So, Lina, or should I say Li Li," Kenzi laughed, "Are we gonna call a truce and start fresh? What do you think?"

Lina laughed. "Dhan is silly." A small pause. "But yeah, let's do that."

"You know, we might still have tiffs now and then," Kenzi warned.

"Well, sisters do that."

"Look, Lina. You can stay with me for about a month until everything settles down and then we can see a little more clearly about what to do next." Kenzi squeezed Lina's shoulders.

"Thank, Kenzi."

"I'm gonna need some help at the shop though. Can you do that?"

"Definitely. What do you need done?"

That afternoon, Lina pitched in to help Kenzi prepare the store to reopen. She marked down books to move faster and filled display cases. She shelved the books Kenzi finished processing while she and Dhan stored her belongings. Kenzi took advantage of the extra help to catch up on bookkeeping and accounting. She piled the bills neatly in order and plotted the pay-off strategy. Listing the inventory online for the world to see had been a smart move. Both of them stayed pretty much lost in their own thoughts.

The next morning, Kenzi called Jonathan Farrell's office.

"Hello? I'd like to speak with Dr. Jonathan Farrell, please."

"He's out of the office at the moment. Would you like to leave a message?"

"This… is his… daughter. I'd like to arrange an appointment, if I could." Kenzi frowned. "Wait, is this the same graduate student who dropped off the book donations at the Kinfolk Books opening?"

"Oh yeah. That was so long ago. But yeah, that was me. I didn't even realize you were his daughter."

Neither did I.

Jonathan decorated his office in dark wood with brown and red tones, very masculine in nature.

"Have a seat, Mackenzie."

"Kenzi."

"I'm sorry. Kenzi."

She sat in the chair that faced his large desk and glanced around to learn a little more about the man who gave her life. A shelf filled with many books, many of them on African history, stood against one entire wall. He had a few carvings on the shelves and some paintings and masks. On his desk sat the expensive office ornamentation that large university budgets allowed.

She didn't speak. She didn't have anything to say. It was Jonathan who owed her an explanation of her life and his. Jonathan sat for a moment taking in his daughter's face and the golden eyes that reflected his own hazel irises obscured behind thick lenses. She stared back at him much calmer than when she jerked away from his touch a few days ago. He got up and leaned his stout figure against the frame of the window for a brief moment as if to gather his thoughts. Rather than returning to his desk, he sat in the chair beside Kenzi and turned to face her.

"When I last saw you, you were named Mackenzie Farrell. You wore two pigtails. And you were just learning to read a few words. Then I open the paper twenty-nine years later and I see a beautiful woman who looked very much like a woman I used to know. Or thought I knew. And when I see that this Kenzi Malton opened an independent bookstore in the very same town I lived in and that she'd stopped working at the same university a few days before I joined, I knew that the moment I'd waited for and thought about for years had finally come."

"I didn't know. I never knew any of that. I only remember myself as Mackenzie Malton. I didn't remember the name Farrell. No one said anything. Mama Dee never said. Grandaddy never said. Aunt Jalissa never spoke about it. At least not to me. There were no photographs. No cards or letters. Nothing. Nothing at all. All I knew was what Mother told me. That you left because you had more important things to do than be a father to me."

"Yes." Jonathan spoke carefully and deliberately. "That was what you were told."

Kenzi frowned. "What do you mean?"

"I mean, you know what you've been told."

"What?"

"I think… your mother should tell you the other part of that story."

A long pause stretched where each waited for the other to speak, to explain the disconnect and fill in the discrepancies. Again, Kenzi won the stand-off and listened quietly as Jonathan spoke of his activities during the lost years.

Kenzi then told him about her internships and travels and college years and what brought her to Rollins. By doing a comparison of notes, she discovered that she and Jonathan had come close to meeting during her wandering years when she'd decided to backpack from Seattle to San Francisco to Los Angeles to Mazatlan and back again. *What did she really search for back then?*

"What were you doing in San Francisco?" she asked him.

"I was delivering a paper at an academic conference. The usual."

"So the day before I arrived to that youth hostel near Chinatown, you checked out of a hotel a just few blocks away." Kenzi let out a breath. "Wow. Four years ago, we walked the same streets only a day apart." *Would he have recognized her and pretended not to?* Kenzi looked at him uncertainly. *What would they have said to each other then?*

They paused while the graduate student brought in coffee for Jonathan and tea for Kenzi.

"It took me some time to accept who you were, Kenzi, even after I saw your picture in the paper. In my heart, of course, I knew. But part of me thought it couldn't possibly be after all of these years. Once I did accept that you were that same little girl, I decided to try to be there for you when and where I could. It took me some time to work up the courage to meet you in person though. I thought you would hate me."

"Sometimes, I did hate you."

"I figured as much. I didn't know whether it would be worth it to introduce chaos into your life. Then, of course, once Jalissa died, it all came to a head and I knew something had to be done no matter the consequences."

Kenzi broke in. "At my own aunt's funeral though? That was rough, Jonathan."

"It had gone on long enough."

"Still…" Kenzi shook her head slightly then changed the subject. "At the opening, Kinfolk received a single donation of almost four hundred books. That was…"

"Guilty."

"And the art supplies and the financial gift?"

"Kenzi, I hope you understand where I'm coming from… all the time that I, that we lost… I truly hope you'll continue to allow me to somewhat be a father, or if not that, then at least a friend. To you. To Kinfolk Books. It would mean a lot to me. I want to see you succeed. This community needs the bookstore. *I* need the bookstore. After I donated the books and the art supplies, I didn't cringe as much as I used to when I looked in the mirror. I actually felt… I felt like a decent human being. It was nice."

Kenzi sat in silence.

"I'm not trying to buy you, Kenzi."

"Well, I'm not for sale."

"I know that. You just can't put a price on something like this. I know all of that will never substitute for actually being there as a father and supporting you as you grew up. I missed out on a lot and so did you. Kenzi, please believe me. I am so very sorry that our lives turned out the way they did. I would give up everything if I could go back in time and change how things turned out. There are so many things I would have done differently. I might have made better decisions. I hope you can forgive me someday for not trying hard enough to be who you needed me to be and who I should have been all along."

Kenzi finally lost control. Sure enough, here the tears came. She felt angry at herself, at him, and at the circumstances that arranged and shaped her life.

"Geez. Why did you do that? I'm so sick of crying! It's always one thing after another all the time!"

Jonathan sat quietly and anxiously. But, he didn't run or walk away this time. And neither did she. He handed her tissues off his desk and solemnly waited for her to decide what came next.

"There were times I needed you and you weren't there. You were nowhere!"

"I know."

He looked down at his hands folded on top of the desk.

"I missed you. Other people got the best years of your life."

"Now hold on a minute, Kenzi!" Jonathan mocked annoyance. "I'm old, not dead."

Kenzi sniffled and laughed, trying to pull herself together again.

"Jonathan, it doesn't seem as if you're quite the villain I thought you were."

He smiled at her cautiously.

To herself, Kenzi thought, "And my mother quite wasn't quite the saint I thought she was." Betty had some serious explaining to do. She took a deep breath.

"You know you have to talk to Lina too."

"Yes, I know," he replied quietly.

"She's staying with me now. I'll give you the number." She wrote her home number and address down on the back of her business card.

Jonathan's voice firmed. "I'll call her immediately."

Their meeting seemed to have wound down. Kenzi had to get back to the store and Jonathan had to get back to his research… and Lina. Still, Kenzi hesitated as she reached the door, looking at Jonathan uncertainly. A creeping sensation slithered through her mind. Vague memories floating at the edges. Something she should remember. But like smoke, it wafted away and disappeared. Jonathan, noticed her hesitation.

He spoke quietly.

"Kenzi. I'm not going anywhere. Now that we've found each other, I'm not going to leave *ever*. I will be here for you and Lina from now on for the rest of my life. I *will* be here. If you want to get in touch with me, after you've had time to think all this over, just call. This is my home address and phone number. I don't care how late or early it is. Please call. Or stop by. I mean it. Okay?"

She didn't hug him. He made no move to touch her. That would still take time.

"Okay."

By the time she returned home, Lina had already spoken to Jonathan by phone.

"He's taking me to dinner this evening."

"Oh right. *You* get dinner."

Lina shrugged. "I guess we're going to have the same conversation you did this morning."

Kenzi wondered how Lina would react. Their circumstances appeared similar in some ways, but very different in others – as different as their personalities. Grateful to have the little apartment to herself for a few hours, Kenzi called Ray while Lina showered and dressed. Ten minutes after Lina and Jonathan left, she heard his pickup come to a stop outside.

This time, Kenzi needed the comfort of Ray's touch. While the cicadas roared their songs of the night, Ray balanced her above him and allowed her to take everything his body had to offer her. As she swayed and shook looking down into his eyes, she felt in her heart that she never wanted this to be over. If she could hold him and feel him inside her for the rest of her life, she would give up everything in the world – the joy, the pain, the agony, the ecstacy, all that part of living. She lay sprawled across his body while he smoothed her down and talked gently to her like a restless pony.

He stepped outside just as Jonathan and Lina pulled up. Ray spoke to them briefly and continued on home.

Jonathan looked at her and said, "That's a fine fellow."

Kenzi replied quietly, "That's the man that I love."

Jonathan watched Ray's truck drive away.

He and Lina exchanged smiles as Kenzi stared vaguely in the distance.

"Yes," she said again.

Kenzi snapped out of her reverie to invite Jonathan in for coffee or tea. Jonathan accepted but said only for a minute.

"Jonathan, I forgot to ask before. Do Lina and I have relatives on your side of the family? Do we have a grandmother and grandfather, aunts and uncles, cousins?"

"I'm afraid not Kenzi," Jonathan smiled ruefully. "What you have before you, for better or worse, is the proud product of the foster care system. I never knew my parents."

Kenzi and Lina both stared at him and each other blankly as if wondering how to absorb that bit of information.

Lina said, "So it really is just us."

"Yes."

Kenzi looked at him with the dawning knowledge of what his life must have been like after Betty left him. "You were alone for a long time."

"Yes, I was, Kenzi. But part of it was my own doing. You and Lina are not responsible for how things happened. And I hope that you never would blame each other for the mistakes that other people made. You're both very good, very beautiful women. I'm proud to know you both. I'm so sorry that I wasn't in your lives when you were growing up. I've missed you. I've missed having a family."

All three of them cried by the time he finished. Somehow, Jonathan's words set them all free. Kenzi hugged him at last and Lina threw her arms around them both. They had a second chance to be the family they never were the first time around. She still could not bring herself to call Dr. Farrell, "Father" or "Dad." Though she was Jonathan's daughter, she had no real memory of being his child.

Kenzi knew within herself that her relationship with Ray enhanced the emotional recovery process. Loving him had opened up something new inside her that had not existed before. She felt safer. A year ago, she might have ordered Jonathan away from her door and slammed it loudly behind him in disgust and anger. Then. But now... she was still Kenzi, but something a little more. She'd made it through emotional trials without breaking. And she did love her sister. She loved her father, though she didn't know him well. Time would change that. She loved Ray. She did not know what she would ever do without him.

She was so proud of herself!

She could twist herself around the column on Mama Dee's front porch three times without stopping and without letting go. She could go very fast because she was small and quick. No one else could do this. She hadn't seen any one else do this. The Only One. She'd made up a new game all by herself. She wanted Big Afro to see.

He would pick her up and place her on his shoulders so the whole world could see her and wave to her while she gripped clumps of his hair for balance. Sometimes he would run fast and yell loudly. She would scream in delight and hold his hair tighter. He didn't seem to mind.

She called to Big Afro in her tiny little child's voice,

"Watch me do this! Are you watching? Watch me!"

She wound around the column. Her hand slipped.

"Oh no!"

She messed up her new trick in front of Big Afro. It had worked every other time when he had his back turned talking to Mama Dee. He turned too late. He wouldn't get to see her trick. She could see the teeny tiny little rocks frozen solid in concrete rush up close... closer... closer...

Now, Kenzi stroked the vertical marks under her nose. She'd forgotten how they got there. All these years, she thought the marks were a strange birthmark that no one else in the family seemed to have. Jonathan noticed her peering under his and Lina's noses while they spoke. The vertical notches came from stitches inserted after she'd blacked out, he told her.

The past would never change. Relationships ran both sides of a two-way street. She knew all too well that adults, especially her parents, existed as mere humans. They had moments of weakness. Petty thoughts. Sometimes they expressed anger and jealousy.

But they also loved and gathered together and supported each other when allowed.

Chapter 13

The Confrontations

"I don't want to talk about it!"

"Kenzi…"

"Lina, stop! Just stop. Please. I can't deal with this right now."

"When?"

"When I'm ready."

"When?"

"Lina!" Kenzi's voice escalated to a near scream.

"Okay!" Lina backed away a few steps. "I'll be in the back."

"Okay." Kenzi tried to smile an apology though she still felt a little shaky. "Thanks for the help today, Lina." Lina didn't answer.

So now, at Kinfolk Books, Kenzi frowned thinking about her life and her issues and personal short-comings. She woke up that morning feeling just a little off-center and it colored her mood while she worked on the Juneteenth display case. Lina's persistence in wanting to discuss their newly-discovered father's identity irritated her. And she still hadn't figured out the deal with Stacy. Whenever Kenzi broached the subject of the distant turn to their friendship, Stacy merely pasted on a smile and laughed the conversation away.

Instead, Dharma and Lina stepped in as confidants and sounding boards. "People come into our lives for a season, I guess. And then drift away when that season comes to an end." Kenzi told them with a sigh. But thanks to renewed interest and support, the art program continued and despite Stacy's aloofness, that was something to give thanks for.

Kenzi's thoughts wandered as she filled the display case. Texans proudly viewed themselves as independent spirits and rebels to authority, but the perception of what that rebellion really meant usually depended upon who you asked. Even the war with Mexico had several interpretations. To some, war with Mexico meant freedom from a tyrannical government. To others, the war with Mexico showed a rabid obsession to maintain the right to own other humans and steal their labor even after Mexico had declared it illegal. Texas fought for slavery once more during the Civil War. A race of people sacrificed centuries of labor, history, religion, families, education, and legacy to support the economic wherewithal of the southern power structure.

Yes, history meant many different things to many different people. Kenzi made the effort to represent every point of view in the display case. Deacon Waverly's Buffalo Soldier actors agreed to come to the shop the third Saturday of the month to discuss their often-forgotten roles in the Wild West during the days of cowboys, natives, outlaws, and gunmen. Also on Deacon Waverly's referral, she'd spoken to a storyteller from a retirement center to come give a history of the oldest celebration of the end of slavery in Texas. He gave her a preview:

"On June 19th in 1865, Union soldiers led by Major General Gordon Granger arrived at Galveston with news that the war had ended and all slaves were free. They had actually been freed two and a half years prior with the signing of the Emancipation Proclamation on January 1, 1863. However, it had taken that amount of time to overcome resistance by slave owners and Confederate troops."

The many wars for freedom in Texas and across the US meant different things to different people. Life was two sides of the same coin. Like rock and roll's separation from blues by the color line. A folk and blues guitarist would come later the same day to provide entertainment. She'd heard Big Red play in Austin before and couldn't wait to share his music with the store's customers. Like southern cuisine and soul food were separated only by who was in the kitchen. And Organic Soul would bring over snacks and beverages. At Dharma's Organic Soul, one found soul food. Food nourished the soul and spirit and reminded people of their culture and heritage. Who they used to be and from where they came. Africa met America. Soul food migrated North during Jim Crow and during both World Wars when the soul people fled the harsh apartheid system of the South. They left the South and brought soul up North with them.

Now *southern cuisine* was soul food done as a trend, a fine art, the place to be during Black History Month, a sound bite to sell cookbooks. It served as a substitute. Substitutions served as nostalgia for a tradition and culture that blinded one to the skeletons in the closet, the maggots that crawled beneath unturned stones. Sure southern cuisine and soul food seemed the same. But they weren't really.

Kenzi broke off her meditations and stood. She really needed to make up for screaming at Lina. She found her sister in the backroom creating shelf labels on the computer.

"Lina, I just wanted you to know I'm glad you're here to help me. I don't feel as tired and worn down lately. I look around and I can see that a lot has been accomplished the last few days."

"No problem, Kenzi. Really."

"Well, I've wanted to shift the books to include inventory backlog for a long time. Even better, we've been able to dust and vacuum and clean the windows. Much more bearable with two people than one."

"I had no idea books created so much dust, Kenzi. My God." Lina laughed.

"It's a constant battle." Kenzi leaned against the doorway. "I organized the store's records and made economic projections for the fall. Kinfolk Books may be all right. But just barely."

"Well, I know that must be a relief."

"Definitely. By the way, Stacy's due in later this morning to help plan the art discussion that's gonna follow the storytellers."

"Oh? Good."

"We're hoping to exhibit the children's artwork during the week leading up to the Juneteenth celebration at the store. The store's definitely on the rebound."

Aunt Tilly and Deacon Waverly finally broke through the suspicion of the surrounding community. But not just the endorsement of two influential community leaders assisted the break-through. The death of Kenzi's Aunt Jalissa followed so rapidly the death of their own beloved Matilda Grant that Kenzi received expressions of sympathy where previously she'd met only apathy. Death, the great equalizer laid claim to rich and poor, old and young, citified/siddity and country/rural, native and transplant. They responded with outpourings of support. Life was funny like that sometimes. But despite the changes in her business and personal affairs for good or bad, Kenzi would have given it all up in a heartbeat to have her Aunt Jalissa back.

The memories came more often lately.

The small, rusty, pea green car coughed as it tried to fight its way up the hill. She sat in the back seat terrified that today would be the day that the little car would stop running and they would all roll backwards down the hill where the car-eating monsters waited for them with gaped-open mouths full of teeth. The tailpipe made short noises like the guns she heard on last night's cop show. They strapped her into the back seat. Her legs didn't reach the floor. Her young hands couldn't find the skill to undo the seatbelt. She'd seen someone jump from a car on the cop show. But her slender arms felt too weak to open the car door to jump out. The car chugged and jerked back and forth. They jerked with the car.

The Lady said… "Hit the gas, Jon."

Big Afro's hair made him even taller with his frame folded up in the driver's seat. He was stronger and smarter than all of the real and the imaginary world. When he read her stories at night, the monsters in her closet and under her bed hid away. They knew to behave.

Big Afro tugged back and forth with his right hand. He shifted his feet pushing something on the floor and the car coughed then roared as it surged forward to climb to the part of the street that flattened. They made it! The Lady smiled at him. She smiled at Big Afro too from the back seat, though he didn't see her. No hills lay between here and Mama Dee's house. Later that afternoon, they would coast back down the hill on the way home and it would feel like one of the fun rides at the park. The hill didn't get them today.

But what about tomorrow?

Kenzi shook herself from the memories that crept and tiptoed around. She hadn't spoken to her mother since Aunt Jalissa's funeral. She still couldn't get past the lies that defined her childhood and her teen and adult years. She didn't trust Betty anymore. She'd held her mother on a pedestal of suffering and sacrifice. Now, after talking to Jonathan, she knew that her mother inflicted much of that martyrdom on herself. Angry as Betty had been with Jonathan for his betrayal, her mother had no right to make the choice to separate Kenzi from her father. Betty's spite went way too far. Kenzi had the right to make that choice for herself. *And what else has she lied about?*

The negative thoughts continued to roam around Kenzi's mind until she felt sick with it. She ran past Lina to vomit in the bathroom. *I hate this day and it hasn't even started yet.*

Lina walked in after her and held her hair back. After Kenzi finished, she handed her a dampened paper towel to clean up. "Kenzi, I think you're pregnant. How long has it been since…"

Kenzi's mind immediately shut down the thought. "Lina, I'm not pregnant."

Impossible. If she had a baby inside of her, she would know. Wouldn't she?

"Well, look I'll make you some tea. And you'd better eat some crackers to settle your stomach. I've got some in my purse."

Kenzi silently ate the crackers and sipped the steaming hot rosemary and marjoram concoction gifted to the shop by Dharma. Lina cleaned up the bathroom as Kenzi rested against the Juneteenth display case she filled.

"She's being awfully helpful," Kenzi grouched inside her head.

"I'm not pregnant!" she scoffed aloud to her book collection.

The bell on the door rang and Bobby Forrest walked into the bookstore looking around in scorn. "Your business will fail."

She noticed for the first time how small his eyes appeared and how close together they sat over the nose that wrinkled slightly as he sneered like a broke-down J.R. Ewing. His horrible disposition affected his appearance and he probably didn't realize it. She allowed him to keep talking to figure out the agenda. Fortunately, being a braggart, he soon revealed his motivation.

"Are you alone?

Where do you get your books?

Have you read any of these books? Do you know what this book is about? Do you speak Spanish? Can you translate this? I'm not going to buy it. I just wanted to see if you could read it. What other languages do you know? How did you learn all of that? You're not from here are you? Where are you from? Where did you go to school? What degrees do you have?"

Where do you get your books?

What is your mother's name? What does your father do for a living? How many exits are there here? Are you the sole owner? Who *really* owns the shop? Where did you get the money to start up?"

Kenzi deftly deflected his questions and gave vague answers. Other questions she completely ignored or pretended to not understand.

"Where did you get the books?

How much does the store make per month? I bet you make no more than two hundred dollars per month. How much does the store make per month? How much rent do you pay? Where do you live?

I bet you thought this would be fun. I bet you don't think that now. I bet you're going to close down. I bet you're struggling. You're over. This store is over."

Lina finished cleaning the bathroom. She overheard Bobby Forrest's verbal attack just as she moved to join Kenzi in front. Kenzi seemed even keel, but Lina decided if it got crazy out there, then so would she. You didn't get through the Dallas public school system without learning how to do all that was necessary to be done in order to survive the playground, the gym class, the bathroom, and the bus stop.

"Why aren't you open on Sundays? Why aren't you open more hours during the week? You need to sell. You need to sell to me. You need to sell to me for ten cents per volume. You need to sell to me for ten cents per volume and then come work for me.

My friends told me you were finished. They told me you couldn't make it.

You may as well give up and sell to me while you can. This store is done. It's dead. I offered you a good deal."

Lina had a sinking feeling as Forrest progressed that a regrettably nasty conversation she had with Franklin while they lived together had found its way to Bobby Forrest. She remembered sitting at the mall's food court.

"Kenzi doesn't know what she's doing. She's screwing up at the shop. You know she lost a book signing, right?"

"She should have stayed with the university. Figures. Kenzi never did know a good thing when she had it. But you can't tell her anything."

"The store's finances are a disaster. When her store fails, I'm sure she'll humble herself then. She better hope somebody offers her a job."

Lina cringed as she remembered her spiteful laugh. Franklin bought her a necklace from the jewelry store. She wore it now. She slipped it off. Partly from guilt and partly to protect Kenzi's new condition, Lina stepped around the bookcase and walked to Kenzi's side.

"Get the fuck out of here, jerk!"

With Forrest's attention diverted to Lina, Kenzi glanced down to grab her pepper spray and saw what she hadn't noticed before. Forrest held a cell phone in his hand turned towards her. She could see the open phone line that shared the violating conversation.

But she also remembered Aunt Tilly's very first lesson. She leveled her gaze at Forrest. Deliberately leaning towards the hand that held the cell phone, she spoke calmly and clearly, "You are not welcome here. Your attempts to harass and intimidate also are not welcome here. Not anymore."

The front door buzzed open.

"As of today, you are officially trespassing on my property. Leave now and don't ever return." The silent listener on the cell phone could consider themselves warned as well.

"Kenzi…"

Kenzi didn't turn to Miss Lydia.

She still gazed, unblinking, at Bobby Forrest, who now found himself outnumbered by three women who looked as if they would have no problem kicking him in the places where the sun never shined.

"Well? Git the hell on out, Bobby, like she said," Miss Lydia rasped in her cigarette voice.

He left.

Kenzi sank down on the chair, feeling queasy once again from the encounter. Lina got Kenzi another cup of tea and rubbed her back the same way Dharma had done for her the day after her mother died.

Lydia noticed Kenzi's queasy look. "Yeah that fool makes me sick too. My husband, may God rest his soul, never liked Bobby. Harold should have gone with his first instinct. I know I do now. If I sense something ain't right, I tell it to git the hell on out, just like Bobby. Bobby ain't even one bit right."

"How did you and your husband know that guy?" Kenzi asked.

After a small discussion, Lydia left ten minutes later. Kenzi leaned against Lina who put her arm around her. "Lina, I'm glad you were here today." She went on, curiously. "Why did you defend me? I didn't expect that."

"Are you kidding? Even though no one has a choice about family, blood is still thicker than water."

Kenzi felt a slight twinge of guilt because she'd had the same thought about not being able to pick one's family several times, usually after an encounter with Lina.

Lina exclaimed, "You stood up for me to Franklin, didn't you? When he tried to down me about my mother and stranded me in Dallas, you gave me a place to stay. I didn't even have to ask. You were there for me when I needed you. I want to be able to do the same. Forrest is a word that I won't speak right now since you're not feeling well, but I know you know exactly what word I could say. And so is Franklin."

Kenzi could just imagine Lina's rich and varied vocabulary. "Well, we're probably thinking the same word."

Lina continued on, "You're my sister and you're probably carrying either my niece or nephew. The creeps of the world get none here."

Kenzi started at the reminder of her possible pregnancy and sighed. "Lina, like Jonathan said, neither of us should take on the responsibility for the decisions and mistakes of our parents. It's not our fault that they screwed up. I missed out on getting to know my only aunt and she missed out on knowing me. No second chance on that. Her pain and my mother's anger and our father's shame kept us all divided. Now it's too late. I miss her. I really do."

Kenzi began crying. "I don't want my child to miss out on getting to know his or her Aunt Lina. I don't want that. Please Lina, we have to make it right between us. We do. Please!"

Lina's voice sounded funny as if holding back tears. "So, I guess we're gonna talk about it after all?"

Lina decided that now would be a good time to try out a trademarked Grant hug. Without the slightest hesitation, Kenzi hugged her back. Their relationship, at least, deserved a second chance.

"I don't think we've hugged in years!" Lina said in wonder.

"Or maybe ever. We have a lot to make up for, don't we?" Kenzi laughed tearily.

Lina laughed in response and then stopped abruptly thinking about her relationship with Kenzi since she'd moved down to Rollins. Kenzi caught her haunted look.

"You know, Lina. Ever since I opened Kinfolk, people have told me so many times how lucky I was to have this store. They even told me they were jealous of me for being my own boss. And I just don't think folks really get it. They see the glamour and romance. But what they don't see is the struggle to raise money, to come up with a workable business plan, to acquire supplies and equipment and inventory, and to operate everyday. It takes dedication and sacrifice and focus and perseverance and faith on an unbelievable scale. I gave up a lot to do this. A whole lot."

"You know what, Kenzi? From the outside looking in, it did seem to be all about you."

"If I came across like that, then I owe you an apology. I guess I haven't been there for you the times you needed me."

"You're here now."

"And you too. I need someone to talk to from time to time. Plus, you have a car!" Kenzi laughed, "I gave mine up to save money. And I may need to borrow some of your clothes once in a while. Mine are like five years old. We're about the same size, you know."

"Nope. You're about to get the big belly. Maybe after the baby comes we can get you into some hot pants. You're going to need a whole new wardrobe now though."

"Well, maybe. Speaking of that, I want to thank you for standing by me through all this craziness."

"You're my sister!"

There remained personality differences as well as differences in style, yes. But similarities existed in their high cheek-boned, almond-eyed appearance. Kenzi's eyes shone as the strange golden-brown gift from Jonathan. Also Jonathan's daughter, Lina's eyes flashed a darker brown. Her reddish hair hung long and relaxed to her shoulders while Kenzi's dark brown hair floated and soared high above and around her head.

They'd had their share of scream fights, sure. Especially after the Franklin episode. But neither of the two would allow themselves to be pushed around by persons outside the family.

"Lina," Kenzi finally sighed, "I may be pregnant."

"No kidding," Lina laughed.

Kenzi took the pregnancy test that Lina quietly purchased from Mr. Oliver's pharmacy. They whispered in the store's bathroom with Lina acting as look-out, counselor, hand-holder, and finger-crosser. After the craziness of the first hour, the rest of the morning crawled by. Mercifully, the store remained empty. The entire scenario resembled an after school special or a John Waters teen flick. Kenzi wanted to sneer at the silliness of it all. For now, she just leaned against the wall of the bathroom stall. Sitting on the lid. Feeling lousy.

"Who was at the counter when you bought the test?"

"Mr. Oliver. I'm probably the talk of the Sunday Afternoon Park Bench Bird-feeding Society. But hey, I'll take one for the team *this* time."

She tried to get Kenzi to laugh.

Panic circled over Kenzi's head, and then swooped closer.

They waited the required minutes for the test results. "Well?" Lina stuck her head back in the bathroom for the confirmation of what she already knew.

"Well, I'm pregnant."

Chapter 14

The Talks

Kenzi's machine clicked on at various times of the day. Betty's anxious voice pleaded with her to pick up the phone. "Kenzi, please talk to me. Don't shut me out. I'm sorry for everything. I am. I really am. I'm sorry for everything I did that hurt you. Please just give us a chance to talk this through."

Kenzi cried as she looked at the machine. She walked away. Her mother made her feel so tired.

They fought. Their voices rose. They were loud and angry. Big Afro yelled. The Lady screamed. They told her many times before that once they put her in bed, she better not get up until morning. Bed meant Go To Sleep. But he hadn't read her a story that night. So she didn't feel sleepy.

She lay afraid. What happened while she hid under the covers in the dark room? A monster came in the house! She'd seen monsters on television while she watched with Big Afro. They made horrible, loud noises and you had to shoot them with a laser and then escape by dissolving into crystal lights. She had to save Big Afro and The Lady. She had to help!

She threw back the covers and ran into the living room to help them fight the monster so they could dissolve into crystal light together. She broke the rules. They would understand when she saved them. They would sit and talk about the monster later.

She stopped in the doorway. Big Afro and The Lady shouted. Where did the monster go? They shouted at each other? Why did they do this? They said words she didn't understand. They hated each other. Their words would kill each other. She didn't want them to die.

Her tiny child's voice screamed out, "Stop it!"

Kenzi shuddered as the fear of that night came back to her. None of them could see the monster. But the monster still broke her family into pieces and made her father disappear. Their home disappeared into a tiny box with thin walls and loud neighbors. The monster made her mother leave early in the morning and return late at night. It made the shadows blacker and the sound of the wind louder.

Kenzi dialed Betty in Dallas.

"Hello?"

"Mother… tell me what happened. I want to know what really happened between you and Jonathan and how all of this came about. I already spoke with Jonathan. I want to know everything. And this time, don't lie to me."

"All right, Kenzi. I'll tell you." Betty took a deep breath. "Your… father and I were greatly in love once upon a time. We first met when I was an undergrad and he was just starting his doctoral program. We dated for a few years and got to know one another pretty well. Life was good during the first couple of years after we married. But as time went on, your father and I grew apart. Jonathan spent most of his time teaching and doing research. While he socialized with university faculty and other academic colleagues, I dropped out of school to stay at home to keep house and to take care of you. The plan was that I would go back to school to finish my degree after you were old enough for preschool. But that never really worked out.

After a while, Jonathan and I found that we really didn't have much to talk about. We lived in two different worlds and couldn't seem to come together on anything except general dissatisfaction with each another. I… found out that Jonathan had a brief affair with my," Betty struggled with the words, "with Jalissa when Jalissa told me she was pregnant and that Jonathan was the father. My own sister," Betty sighed. "That was… an awful time. After that, our marriage was beyond rescue and I filed for divorce."

"I remember the fighting."

"I know, Kenzi. We didn't mean to fight in front of you. But whenever we spoke about anything at all, it turned into an argument. We tried to wait until you were asleep."

"Sometimes I heard you."

"I'm sorry, child. I am. I don't think we realized the damage we caused. We thought you were too young to understand."

"I knew something was wrong. What happened when you filed for divorce?"

"Kenzi, you asked for the truth, and I'm going to tell you. Let me know if you want me to stop."

"Okay."

"You know, I felt betrayed on several levels: One issue was the fact that Jonathan looked for affection from another woman instead of his own wife and the mother of his child. The second issue was the fact that the woman was my own sister. Mine and Jalissa's relationship was never the same again. The final straw was when I realized that I'd put my own education and dreams on hold to support his and to take care of our home and family. I felt cheated by Jonathan on several levels. I felt he cheated me out of my life and my dreams. On top of that, I lost my sister. The divorce was the hardest period. Your father and I fought each other for custody of you."

Kenzi gripped the phone tighter and pressed it hard against her ear. She'd had no clue of the depth of the undercurrents in her family.

"Our relationship was already pretty sour, but the fight for custody made it bitter and hateful beyond all imagination. I mean, Jonathan and I couldn't even remain in the same room together for very long. That's how bad it was. Since we knew each other so well for so long, we basically tore each other to shreds in front of the judge. It was... it was ugly and I think even our lawyers were afraid of us. The judge finally awarded me custody." At this point, Betty sighed and fell silent. Kenzi waited her out wanting to hear the next part, and yet still afraid to hear the rest of the story.

Betty picked up the narrative again.

"I hated Jonathan so much. I... considered him an unfit father. I ordered him to stay out of both of our lives. He refused. In a way, I was still nervous that Jonathan would try to use his higher salary and his social contacts to take you away from me. I changed my name back to Malton, tied up loose ends, and then we... we left town. That's why we relocated so much, Kenzi."

"Oh my, God." Kenzi moaned and started crying. "Oh God!"

"I was trying to discourage Jonathan from finding us. That was easier back when there was no internet. I just thrust both Jalissa and Jonathan from my mind and poured all of my energy into raising you. But, Kenzi, even though I felt very devastated by the pain, it was my love for you that kept me motivated and moving forward. I knew I had to create a better life than the one we were living. After all those schools and jobs and apartments, I found my way back to Dallas. Mama Dee let me know that Jonathan had since relocated elsewhere. No one, including Jalissa, had his forwarding address. Lina never met him. And by then, I assumed that Jonathan had given up on finding you and me. I never heard from him until I saw him at Jalissa's funeral."

Kenzi wept openly at this. Betty paused to let her catch her breath.

"Oh God, Mother, what did you do? What did you do!"

"Do you want me to stop?"

"No," through clenched teeth. "I've waited all my life to hear this and I want to hear it all."

"Jalissa developed a drinking problem. Mama Dee told me it was an effort to numb the shame of what happened years ago. Jonathan rejected her. I rejected her. And she also experienced economic hardship due to the fact she never really developed marketable job skills. And then Jalissa had no one to turn to because Mama Dee passed away shortly after we came back to Dallas. You remember?"

"Yes. Mama Dee's funeral was the last time I remember seeing Aunt Jalissa. I barely saw Lina either after that."

"Lina, was at the center of a storm that erupted before she was even able to speak. She… absorbed a lot of Jalissa's anger and negative emotion. Basically, she lost her childhood to a mother who punished herself with alcohol, an aunt who kept her at a distance, and a father who she didn't know her and didn't seem to want to know her.

"I… have to go."

"Kenzi, wait."

"*Mother!* I have to go. I have to!"

Kenzi hung up the phone and sat queasy with her head in her hands as another memory surfaced.

The Siamese hated her. The Siamese loved her. He hated her because he loved her but he loved his freedom more and she wouldn't give him his freedom because she loved *him*. The unspoken dilemma of the beloved house pet completely missed the oblivious owner holding him hostage.

She held him in her arms and he yowled for release. She followed him and picked him up again and rubbed her face on his beige fur tinged with brown here and there. She loved him so. The Siamese hissed again and again to warn her. She loved all those funny sounds he made deep in his throat.

The Siamese waited for his opportunity. He knew that at bedtime, The Lady changed her from her spunky little corduroys into a nightgown. He would watch and wait. She would learn. Go To Bed. His ears pricked in recognition. The Lady didn't like it when she whined to stay up later to watch more television shows. Where did Big Afro go? Nine o'clock. Go To Bed.

The Siamese crouched motionless. His ears pointed forward. His tail flickered slightly with anticipation. Soon… Sure enough, she ran from the living room towards her bedroom in her little nightgown with the flower patterns. Now! The Siamese sprang and unsheathed his claws. His paws extended and spread out. He wanted to hug her? No. He hooked into her bare skin, and then deliberately moved his front paws downward. She screamed in pain and surprised anger. Why did he do this? Why? She should have loved him more?

The next day, the Siamese disappeared. The Lady told her that she had to give the Siamese to Aunt Jalissa because Aunt Jalissa seemed to need him more than they. She didn't see Aunt Jalissa for a long time afterwards. She never saw the Siamese again.

Kenzi cocked her head to the side thoughtfully. She pulled up the hem of her dress. There ran the four-inch scar, barely visible on her left leg. The years faded it away and she'd forgotten how it got there. They never spoke of the cat. She didn't ask. Why didn't she ask?

Aunt Jalissa never had a cat.

"But she lied to me!"

A week later, Ray and Kenzi enjoyed a picnic in Central Park to which Ray brought one of Dharma's special cakes. The spicy coconut loaf had a dense texture of coconut, ground rice, cardamom, cloves, cinnamon, nutmeg, orange flower water, and orange juice. The orange flower water, consisting of 4 drops pure oil of orange, 4 drops oil of bergamot, and 1 cup water, gave the cake its kick. The cake sat waiting.

Kenzi wanted to enjoy a rare afternoon away from the store. Lina ran the shop with two elderly volunteers for story time and a young man from one of the neighboring high schools who shelved books. Kenzi glanced around and spotted Deacon Waverly and Mr. Oliver concentrating on a chess match overseen by Miss Lydia who waved at them. Miss Lydia laughed about something and looked more alive than Kenzi had ever remembered seeing her.

"Kenzi…"

"She lied, Ray! All of my life was a lie. How could the woman who raised me look me straight in my face and make up something that wasn't even true?"

To Kenzi, it seemed liked she'd cried all summer. "It's too damn hot for this!"

Ray held her without speaking for a moment. Kenzi felt safe enough to lean against him for comfort. But then he jarred her out of her comfort zone.

"Kenzi. Betty called me last night. She said you spoke on what happened at the funeral and she thinks she made it worse, not better. She thinks you hate her."

Kenzi shook her head. "I don't hate her."

"You hate the lies."

"Well yeah. My mother was the one person who I could count on all of my life. And to know that she'd told me so many things that weren't true and had me believing it because I trusted her… It makes me wonder just what I *can* believe in. It makes me wonder what else isn't true. I'm just… so confused."

"What about your Aunt Jalissa?"

"My Aunt Jalissa's dead."

"I know. I know. But even though she betrayed your mother…"

"Yes."

"…your mother forgave her."

"I know."

"What about you?"

"What do you mean?"

"Are you still angry with your aunt?"

"No. No." Kenzi sat silent a moment. "I figure, I understand why she did what she did. She had low self-esteem and she looked up to my mother. She figured if she had what my mother had – Jonathan - it would make her life better. Only… it made things much worse… kind of like with me and Lina."

"Have you forgiven your Aunt?"

"Yes. Yes, I have. I always loved Aunt Jalissa. I still do. I miss her. I wish we could have spent more time together. I wish she had come to the opening. And I wish she could see what I'm doing now. And how Lina has turned out for the better."

"You know what? Jalissa probably does know. When she left this world, her family came together for the first time in a long time."

"What is it about funerals?"

"Funerals remind us that we don't have forever." He paused. "So… what about Lina?"

"She's my sister. I love her. There were times when I didn't understand her or even like her when she was being a real brat. But I'm not trippin' about Franklin. He's not worth it. She's more important to me. I really didn't know that her life had been so hard. We didn't spend a lot of time together. And I had no idea that that Aunt Jalissa was an alcoholic." Kenzi teared up again. "I didn't know *anything*."

"Something about family togetherness makes people stronger. Life is too hard to face alone. It's a cruel world sometimes. I don't know what I would have done without Dharma and Dhan standing with me."

"Well, Lina and I talked. We've sort of drawn a truce, you know? We're letting things settle down. Trying to sort out our lives. There's still some hurt left, but we may eventually get to the place where things are better. Someday soon, I hope."

"And Jonathan?"

Kenzi laughed ruefully, shook her head, and stared across the park.

"I have no idea what this family must look like to you."

"It's not your fault, Kenzi."

"I know. I keep telling myself that. So does Jonathan. I talked to him the other day. He let me know his side of the story. I could understand, somewhat. He deceived my mother. Then my mother deceived him… and me. They couldn't stand the sight of each other back then." She sighed and shook her head. "It was probably better that they stayed apart. But I wish I'd known him. I won't ever get those years back. They're gone for good."

"Are you angry with him?"

"No. I mean I used to be. But it was so long ago. I can't hold it that long. I mean, I still haven't come to the place where I can call him Dad or anything, because he hasn't been my dad for a long time. But, I can acknowledge he is my father. It's not like I have a whole lot of other choices. They don't grow on trees."

Ray laughed, relieved to hear her joke about it.

"It's just going to take some time."

Ray looked out across the park.

"So… you've forgiven your aunt, and your sister, and now your father…"

"Basically. Yeah."

"So why are you still punishing Miss Betty?"

"Because she lied."

"But she wasn't the only one."

"Who's side are you on?" Kenzi's voice rose. "Don't you get it? She was the one person who I could always count on in my life. We were so close. And she showed me that the person I counted on never even existed. It's like a rug was jerked out from under me and everything I knew changed."

"But that's just it! Don't you see?"

"See what, Ray?"

"You counted on her all of your life. All of your life Betty has been there for you. How were you able to rise from where you started and go through school?"

"My mother helped me."

"What about your bookstore? Who supported you and helped you?"

"She did. She was there when no one else believed it was possible or even should be done."

"Kenzi. Don't you see? The answer is there if you just listen to what you're saying?"

"What? What am I saying, Ray?"

"You're saying that... all of your life, your mother did what she thought was best for you to the best of her ability. She took what life handed her, what other people did, and tried to make sure that you were okay despite it all. That you didn't experience the same pain that she did. It may not have been the best way, but her intentions were good."

Kenzi shook her head in denial.

"What she told you, she probably told you to protect you. Jonathan had proven himself unreliable and untrustworthy to her in the past. She didn't want to give him a chance to do the same thing to you. Especially as a child. As a father myself, I can understand that."

"But Ray, she just kept going with it, even when I was older."

"Well, that's the thing with lying. Once you start, it's hard to stop. It gets even more tangled so it's better not to in the first place."

"Are you thinking of Darlene?"

"As a matter of fact... yes."

"What about her? I mean, have you been able to forgive her?"

Ray sat a moment then sighed.

"Yeah. I've forgiven her. She was tormented inside. She wasn't an emotionally complete person. But she gave me Santi. And because of Santi, I'm forever grateful."

"That's good."

"Yes, especially for Santi's sake. I don't want her to grow up under a cloud. Maybe when she's older, I'll let her know more. I've tried to protect Santi from her mother's family for years. But sometimes I do wonder if that's been the right thing to do."

"What about them?"

"Kenzi, they are damaged people. Just bent. I rarely speak of the things that I've seen on several occasions. But what broke the camel's back was the time I went to pick Santi up from her grandmother's. I got there about an hour and a half earlier because I happened to be on that side of town. Maya had some sort of party I didn't know about going on. A room full of people loud talking, cursing, drinking, likely drugs, playing cards and dominoes. I didn't even know most of the people there and this is a small town, you know. Santi was in a back room by herself, unsupervised. Actually, she was underneath the bed with a blanket. She told me she was hiding. Not the hide-and-seek kind of hiding. She was afraid. I don't even like to think about who or what she was hiding from. But it was enough to know that my daughter was terrified of something or someone in a house full of strangers. I picked her up and didn't say goodbye. Didn't look back. Just filed the papers. Santi doesn't ask about them as much anymore."

He changed the subject back to the original topic.

"So… back to your mother. Kenzi, somehow, someway, you're gonna have to get past the pain in order to understand her side of things."

"I know she didn't intentionally hurt me, Ray."

"No. She didn't. Betty loves you. I see her swelling up with pride. Even that first day at Kinfolk I knew who she was before she even said. She was the woman who not only looked like you but also looked like your number one fan. If you were a rock star, she probably would have been in the first row center leading the mosh pit."

He laughed heartily and Kenzi joined him.

"She told me once…" Then he looked at Kenzi and said, "Nah… I don't want to give you the big head."

Kenzi punched him in the arm.

"You better tell me!"

Ray hugged her to him and spoke softly in her ear.

"She said, anything she's ever gone through in life was all worth it just to see you happy. Whenever she calls the store and you answer 'Kinfolk Books' she wants to do a cartwheel."

They both laughed at the idea of Betty's legs flying through the air.

"She told me that she didn't have much in life. But she had a daughter who she could look at and tell the world and the universe and the Martians and whoever listened that you made her glad to be who she was."

Kenzi silently put her head in her hands. "You really like to hit under the belt, don't you?"

"Whatever it takes."

She didn't cry. All those nosy phone calls, the long lectures, the extreme sacrifice so she could get through school… all of it for her and only her.

Ray's mouth nuzzled her ear gently as he spoke quietly. "Kenzi, if you and I are to have a future, we are both going to have to know the value of forgiveness. It isn't easy. I know this myself." She felt his warm breath flow over her as his chest rumbled underneath her. "Pain and anger and guilt – these emotions – they devour happiness only if you let them. The next move is yours, you know."

Kenzi tensed into stillness in his arms. "You mean…"

"I mean my daughter means the world to me, Kenzi. And Santi has been through a lot. Even before Darlene died, Santi never had a real relationship with her. Do you see what I'm saying?"

Kenzi watched Ray's mouth say the words.

"I need to know your heart, Kenzi. I need to know that you can love me, love *us*, actually. And that you'll stand with me even when times are tough between us. That's what a family is. I cannot risk my daughter's well-being on someone who's so caught up in years of blame," here Kenzi flinched, "and pain, that there's nothing left to offer but heartache. I've been through that already and I'm not going back. Neither is Santi," he finished firmly.

"Ray!"

She understood the implication of Ray's warning. She would have to make a change and grow beyond who she was. For himself and Santi, he needed a woman who could function as a family member.

"Kenzi, I can't let this go."

Kenzi looked across the park unseeingly through tears she wouldn't allow to fall. He asked for a lot. But for the life inside her that needed him, and for her very soul that had tied itself to his very essence, she would give everything she had to offer.

"I see that. I just want to tell you…"

Ray stopped her from going further.

"Kenzi, one other thing." He swallowed. "When she died, Darlene was seven months pregnant."

Kenzi instinctively felt her stomach with her right hand as he gripped her left hand.

"I don't know whether... it was my child or... the other guy's. They wouldn't tell me anything. Maya's mind was completely blown back then. She didn't even know if it was a boy or a girl. But... when Darlene overdosed, she took the baby with her."

Kenzi bowed her head and looked away.

"Kenzi, I need to know and you have to tell me. You and me depend on it. Are you woman enough to be a wife and mother?"

"Think hard about it, Kenzi. Think very hard." He squeezed her hand hard. "Because I'm going to hold you to your answer for the rest of your life."

That was the moment. That was her cue. All she had to do was open her mouth and say, "Ray, I'm pregnant with your child." She could feel him looking at her. The silence filled the air between them. She parted her mouth to speak, but nothing came out. The silence lengthened.

Suddenly, Ray growled and roared like a bear as he attacked an ear of corn gnawing at it while Kenzi laughed.

"Too much talking. I'm starved. Let's eat!"

The lighter turn to the conversation relieved her but she still said in a low, stiff voice that Ray could barely hear, "I'm not Darlene, Ray."

He didn't answer her.

After Ray brought her home from the park, Kenzi sat alone in the dark and felt the guilt and confusion roll through her.

"Ray, I'm going to have your baby."

"I'm going to be the mother of your child."

Fragments of the conversations with Jonathan and Lina, Ray, and her mother swirled through her mind. She never knew about her father's affair with her mother's sister. She only knew what her mother told her - that her father didn't care about her. And then she stopped asking questions and stopped trying to find out more. If he didn't care about her, then she didn't care about him. But he had cared. He did try. Her mother protected her behind a wall of make-believe. Her life read like a cheap, tattered paperback novel.

And poor Lina!

Their parents did both of them wrong. Very wrong. Still, despite Lina's pettiness and Kenzi's fantasies of shaking her stupid, neither of them had had problems severe enough that required hospitalization, detoxification, or bail. However, they both made grievous errors in men.

She considered the case of Ray's mother leaving her entire family and her homeland to marry. She considered Darlene, Santi's mother, who had left Ray and one child, then destroyed another child and herself.

She called Betty again.

"Kenzi?"

"Mom, I just have a few questions that I wanted to ask you and I need for you to be truthful and answer honestly. It's very important that you tell me the truth."

"I will, Kenzi."

"Did Jonathan hit you?"

"No. There wasn't anything like that. He never raised a hand to me."

"Did he… did he hit me or abuse me?"

"Absolutely not, Kenzi. Never. Jonathan loved you and you loved him. You watched television together and he read to you at night."

"I remember a little. We watched *Star Trek* together didn't we?"

"That was your favorite show. Both of you would run to the sofa right before it came on and I never heard a peep from either of you until the show was over. You were a *trekkie* even before you started kindergarten."

"At any time did it ever occur to you to tell me the truth?"

"Yes. When… you got older. When I didn't think he would be able to take you from me. When you turned eighteen, I thought that would be the time. But it had gone on so long that I didn't know how to begin. And I didn't even know whether Jonathan was dead or alive by then. You seemed to be headed the right direction with school and I didn't want to do anything that might shock you or upset you. And after a while, just too much time had passed."

"Mom, our family's dysfunction could not possibly be addressed in a one-hour talk show."

"I know. I know."

"Mom, I don't hate you."

Betty sucked in her breath. "Okay."

"I also know that forgiveness is in order if we're to move on with our lives. And if me and Ray are to have any future together, I have to make peace with the past. Life is short. I just... still can't believe you lied to me for over twenty-five years about my own father."

"It was wrong of me. It was very, very wrong. I thought it was the right thing at the time. But I definitely wasn't thinking straight then. Despite my own issues with Jonathan, it wasn't fair to you. Someday, after you've thought it over and we've talked some more..."

Kenzi shook her head in the dark. Not yet.

"Just... Mom, now that I've gotten some answers, and I can understand a little bit more, I've got something to tell you as well."

"Okay."

"I'm pregnant."

"Is it Ray's baby?"

"*Mother!* Of course! Who'd you think? Geez."

Betty laughed at Kenzi with her *Mothers*! Their voices lightened somewhat.

"I'm sorry, honey. I was really teasing you. Lina called me about two hours ago and let the cat out of the bag."

Kenzi groaned and shook her head and sighed. "She's such a squealer."

"Yes, she is. Sooo..." *Pause.* "What have you and Ray decided to do?"

Kenzi gripped the phone anxiously and took a deep breath. "Ray doesn't know yet. He... I'm definitely having the baby. But, I don't... I don't know if I'm getting married. I don't think we... I don't think I am."

Betty considered a cool, calm, and collected routine to set Kenzi at ease and to let her know whatever decision she made was fine. No. *Screw that.*

"I see."

"Neither of us is ready."

"Right."

"With all that's happened recently, I'm just so unsure. I don't want my baby to grow up in a family where people hate each other. I know I love Ray. I love him like I've never loved anyone before. And he is a wonderful father to Santi. So it's not that. It's just. I don't even know about me. I don't know what I bring to the table, you know? Ray's been hurt before by Santi's mother. He's cautious and suspicious and... it's hurting us. And again, I don't know about me. If I'm ready. If I have what it takes to be a good wife and mother. There's just this cloud of darkness hanging over us and I don't want my marriage to be like that. I don't want my child to wander the world lost and confused or filled with bitterness because of wrong decisions I made."

And just like that, Betty learned the circular nature of the universe. Call it karma. Call it the golden rule. Whatever. Life held everyone accountable for every little thing. If Kenzi yelled or screamed at her, she could have handled it. If Kenzi withdrew, she could have eventually coaxed and teased her back out of hiding. But now, Betty realized the long-lasting damage of denial and half-truths and bitterness. Her sister was dead. Her niece wobbled along a tightrope. Her daughter couldn't commit to the one decent man who came into her life. Unseen, Betty covered her mouth with her hand and to hold back the guilt and horror she felt.

"Kenzi, you are not responsible for decisions me or Jonathan made. I need for you to know that what happened back then wasn't your fault. None of it. But I'm not going to press you right now. You've already been through a lot. We can talk about it later." She switched gears. "Have you been to the doctor yet? Did he you give you pre-natal advice?"

"I saw a doctor and I promise to schedule another appointment immediately, Mom. By the way, you might be glad to know, Lina and I are communicating better now."

"I'm glad, Kenzi. I did tell Lina that Jalissa's last wish was that Lina always be part of the family."

Betty didn't dare to demand forgiveness for herself. At least her daughter trusted Betty enough to give her the news about the baby.

We may be okay.

Chapter 15

The Panthers

"Besides the fact that she's pregnant, his whole manner towards her was threatening and pretty aggressive. Lucky thing me and Miss Lydia jumped in to back her up. He had her shook although she set him straight and told him to leave the store. I can't believe she didn't tell you about it." After a long pause, Lina tapped the phone with her long fingernail. "Ray. Ray?"

Silence.

"Ray! Are you there?"

"I'm here," Ray ground out in a low voice.

"Don't tell Kenzi I told you, okay? I was just concerned and I thought you should know because of the baby."

"Right. Because of the baby." Ray felt hurt and hollow that he learned Kenzi would have his child from her sister. He'd just seen Kenzi and opened his heart to her. She said nothing about it. Not a damn thing. "Anything else, Lina?"

"No. Just that." Lina paused uncertainly. "Ray? Don't be mad at Kenzi, please. She needs your help."

"I'm not mad." *Just furious.* "Thanks, Lina. I'll take care of it. Don't worry." His hand tightened on the phone. If Bobby Forrest stood in front of him at that moment, Ray would have throttled him on the spot.

"Look, let me go," he managed. "But thanks, okay?"

"Good luck. Whatever happens."

Ray looked out the window of the Grant family home towards the orchard and waited for the red mist of fury to clear from his eyes and head. He felt almost sick with the need to throw something hard against something breakable. Or something breakable against something hard. The fact that the love of his life carried his youngest child and didn't bother to mention it didn't help. She didn't trust him. Even after the long heart-to-heart they had in the park about trust and forgiveness, she didn't trust him. Should he trust her? Was it his baby? Was she planning an abortion? What the hell was she thinking about?

Fifteen minutes later, Ray called Dhan at his apartment near Rice University.

"Dhan, when you get here, just make sure to jump in if it looks like I completely lose control. Right now, everything in me says to pound him into the dirt. I can't stand aggressive motherfuckers and bullies like that."

"I got your back, bro."

Ray continued. "You need to be lookout in case anyone gets too interested. The only thing is I don't think he'll open the door to two big black men."

"We need to catch him off-guard… decoy him."

"Let me think a minute."

Ray thought about it.

"You know, Lina mentioned that Miss Lydia walked in on the whole thing and told them about how Bobby did her husband wrong years ago. You remember that, right? He swindled them out of their retirement money and her husband died of a heart attack from the stress."

"Oh yeah! I do remember that! What was so messed up was she couldn't even touch him legally after that went down. She lost her husband and almost all her money. That jerk got away with everything."

"She's good people. She's been across the street from our restaurant since we opened. Her and Aunt Tilly used to do quilting together. I always wondered who it was who swindled her."

"She probably couldn't talk about it if it was part of the legal settlement."

"But now we know."

"Calling it business, not personal."

"Fucking parasite. Know what Dhan? He messed up bad this time. 'Cause I'm not gonna use a lawyer."

Instead, Ray called Lydia.

Bobby Forrest padded to his door at eleven o'clock at night carrying a baseball bat in answer to the doorbell that yelled him awake in the upstairs bedroom. You never knew what kind of street punks would be out in the middle-class neighborhoods these days. Punks and meth heads.

He looked through the peephole and saw, not tattoos and earrings and slouching shoulders. Instead he saw graying hair and glasses and a scowl.

Lydia.

Not this again. He tired of this old, dumb woman and her wild accusations. It was business, not personal. And all of it was legal. The rest wasn't his fault. He was sorry that the old man had died, but that's what you paid attorneys for – the fine print.

He should have guessed she'd come stalking him after their last encounter at the bookstore. What exactly did she think she would do, throw her walker at him? He smiled grimly.

Loud, foul-mouthed bitch. She'd tried to slander him about her husband's death and their savings. He used his lawyer to set her straight. One phone call followed by a couple of certified letters shut her up.

But she was alone now. She didn't have her *kinfolk* to back her up now. *Hysterical bitches.* He formed his features into the intimidating scowl he practiced now and then in front of the mirror. He tossed the baseball bat on the sofa. No need to have her try to slander him again about trying to beat to death a helpless old grandma with glasses.

He popped open two deadbolts and two chain locks and stood behind the screen door with his arms folded.

"What, Lydia?" Intimidating scowl.

She didn't look intimidated.

"Bobby, you too cowardly to come out here and talk to me like a man? Course you cain't come out cause you *ain't* a man. You're a snake. I wanna address the things that you done to me and mine. You think you got away with it, but you are an illness on this here community. I know it and you know it."

Forrest snorted. *Sounded like the old bitch practiced in front of the mirror too. Whatever. This'll be short.*

He opened the screen door and stepped out, arms crossed, taking up space like he'd learned to do from the self-defense video.

"Lydia, you need to let it go. That was business and it was finished years ago. You're not even supposed to be here. You been drinking? You need to get off my porch and off that hooch because my lawyer said…"

Suddenly, he sensed movement in the shadows. From either side of the doorway, two quiet figures swiftly moved to join Lydia. Two men he hadn't seen because their dark skin blended with the shadows wore black clothes from head to toe. They moved too quickly for his attempted retreat back inside for his baseball bat. And his gun lay upstairs in the end table next to the bed.

Damn her. Furious and afraid, he turned on Lydia.

"You set me up, bitch!"

Lydia calmly smiled, spat on the step where he stood, and deliberately turned her back to him as she walked several feet away. By the time she turned around to watch the rest of the confrontation, the calm smile rearranged itself to a look of triumphant glee. She didn't bother to hide it. She'd accomplished her part without a hitch.

The larger of the two grabbed the front of Forrest's robe with both hands and stood close to him while the slimmer figure stood guard, glancing from the larger man holding Forrest, to Lydia, to a quick sweep of the neighborhood for any signs of interest from the neighbors. Not a peep. No passing cars. No barking or howling dogs mourning their containment when they'd rather be hunting. No howling alley cats frustrated by the inability to access the lovely silky Persian next door. No cicadas, singing their endless song louder then softer then louder then softer.

"Lydia! Lydia!" Forrest desperately croaked for help.

"Lydia who?" Miss Lydia rasped quietly. "I ain't even supposed to be here. And even if I were, too bad 'cause then I musta been drinking and I won't remember nothing."

Together, Dhan and Lydia blocked Ray's chest-hair-pulling grip on Forrest from view. Dhan stood close enough to Miss Lydia to hold her back if she decided to take the opportunity she missed in the bookstore to "kick him where the good Lord split him." He wondered uneasily if she carried a gun but decided not to ask. If he didn't know, he wouldn't have to testify to it in a courtroom.

"I know a place you can hide something won't ever be found," she said to Dhan conversationally. "Just mentioning."

No, he wasn't quite sure about Miss Lydia.

He barely heard Ray's low conversation with Forrest, just the occasional word or phrase.

"...I promise you... over at Kinfolk... tell you what... Organic Soul or Kinfolk Books... and don't think... fuckin' consequences... more than what you can deal with... I know you now, Forrest. I know you..."

Ray finally released Forrest and stared him back into his house.

"He loves her," Dhan decided as all three walked silently from Forrest's yard, business concluded.

When they reached her car parked a few blocks away in a dark alley, Miss Lydia turned to them and Dhan realized that he really didn't know her. She cried.

"Thank ya'll both for taking up for me. I hated that man for so many years I swear I wanted to run him over with my car. If ya'll had beat him up, I wouldn't have said nothin' but 'Let me get my licks in too.'"

Ray hugged her. "It's all over now, Miss Lydia. If he even looks your way or says your name, come get either me or Dhan. You aren't alone anymore."

Dhan hugged her as well. Just as she slammed her car door shut, she shook her head and told them, "I'm glad I left my shotgun in the trunk."

Dhan laughed. "You sure like to joke, Miss Lydia."

"Who's joking?"

"You are."

She made as if to speak but Dhan cut her off. "You are. We'll follow you home. Okay?"

Along the way, Miss Lydia fantasized how it might have gone if Forrest had decided to fight back or argue. His cowardice took most of the fun out of it. Still, she felt peace that she'd done her part to prevent what happened to her from happening to anyone else she cared about in Rollins.

"That was all for you, Harold." He did not die in vain. She smiled with satisfaction and waved back to Ray and Dhan sitting in the truck watching as she went in the front door.

Like inky black panthers roaming the night, the Grant men had nothing to prove to the world. They would not initiate a fight, but would definitely finish a fight and take any questions for clarification after the lesson concluded. Ray and Dhan rode silently on the drive back home, but now stood outside the house talking in the dark.

"Dhan, I wanna thank you for helping me handle this."

"Man, you don't have to say that. You know I'll always be down. I'm just glad I didn't have to help ya'll bury a body tonight though. Miss Lydia is off the hook."

"I know," Ray laughed. "But I just want you to know I'm glad you had my back."

"Look, Ray…"

"What?"

"Ray, uh… I been meaning to talk to you bout something.

"What?"

"This ain't easy for me to say…"

"God, what is it? Talk to me, Dhan."

"Imma say this because it needs to be said. I been meaning to say it for a while."

"Just say it!"

Dhan looked up at the sky.

"Ray… I miss *Amma* and *Appa* sometimes."

"I know. I miss them too. I think about them from time to time."

Dhan gave Ray a sidelong glance. "I probably wouldn't have seen twenty-one or even eighteen if you hadn't been there."

Ray cleared his throat and looked into the night. He couldn't speak. Dhan continued.

"If you hadn't been for you, man… I mean, if I hadn't been able to see you handle life and different situations… You know what I'm saying, man. Don't you?"

"Yeah, I think so."

"Well, I just wanted to say... Having you to look up to, that gave me something to strive for. It let me know what a real man was about. Taking care of business, taking care of home, taking care of family. Nothing to do with money or degrees or prestige or how many women you can get. It's all about how you handle yourself."

Ray, nodded, still not wanting to interrupt what Dhan had to say. Dhan, the joker and show-boater, pretty much liked to keep things light and easy. So whenever Dhan came with the real, it had to be something serious.

"That time when I said what I said about you not finishing school... well... I was wrong for that. I was out of order and I shouldn't have said that. I don't even know what I was thinking."

Ray nodded as he spoke. "You thought I was giving you a hard time just to give you a hard time."

"Something like that. Ray, sometimes, you can be kind of hard on people, you know? Put people through the wringer to measure up to your vision of morality."

"But you know why."

"Yeah, I know. But what I don't know is if you could handle the same thing you dish out."

"What are you talking about?"

"Like Michael Jackson said, 'I'm talking 'bout the man in the mirror.'"

Ray sighed and shifted remembering past conversations with Dharma and Kenzi. "Look," he said, at last. "Something else you didn't know is when you speak, I do listen bro. I may not always agree, but I do hear you."

Ray looked directly into Dhan's eyes and told him, "I'm about to get real on you, Dhan. I hope you can handle it." He put his hands on Dhan's shoulders and faced him.

"If *Amma* and *Appa* could see you now, they would be so proud of who you've become. All they ever wanted was for us to be the best we were meant to be. I know for a fact that I am proud to call you my brother. You and Dharma gave me a purpose for my life, you know. Looking after you helped me to be a better person than I had been before."

Dhan looked at Ray sharply.

Ray laughed at him triumphantly. "See there? You didn't know all that, did ya? Serious. I wouldn't be who I am today if it hadn't been for you two."

Dhan remained silent.

"See, that's what you get for stepping to me, son." Ray punched him in the left shoulder. Dhan punched him back.

They mostly just did brother things together when he drove up from Houston. They took care of the house and gardens. They picked up supplies. They watched sports or news together. They worked at the restaurant under Dharma's bossy supervision.

Dhan stopped the back and forth jostling. "Okay, obviously, we missed out on a few conversations we should've had a long time ago. We could really stand to take the communication up a notch. But now we know what it is."

"All that comes in time. You, me, and Dharma are a team. We're still relatively young, but think about it. We're the elders in the family now. We're gonna need each other to share the load."

"Ray, you better *not* say a word about that garden."

"I was talking about you washing my truck."

"Okay now. You need to tell Santa Claus about that."

Ray laughed. "Imma tell Santa Claus I want you to wash my truck."

Dhan laughed with him.

"Serious, though," Ray said.

"Imma be there, Ray."

They hugged each other and then Dhan lightened the intense moment with a laugh. "Okay, okay man. We don't have to get all crazy with it. We know the deal."

The night finally over, they went inside.

Forrest's description and hostile attitude quietly circulated amongst the other small business owners in the area. They knew and loved Lydia. They got to know Kenzi. The entire block and several streets over kept a wary eye out for Forrest and decided to let him know he had no welcome. They looked through him and reserved the right to refuse service. They also began a call tree and a neighborhood watch association in case another store owner came under threat.

Mr. Oliver spoke anxiously with Kenzi and Lydia over a cup of tea at Kinfolk Books.

"You can always count on me. I'm just next door and I have a baseball bat."

Miss Lydia teased. "I didn't know you played baseball, Oliver."

"I don't." Mr. Oliver shrugged. "Unless someone invites me to the game." He glanced over and smiled at Kenzi's startled eyes.

A certain late-night visit melted away purposefully disregarded. The bully made the classic mistake of taking on more than he could handle. He'd offended too many people. One by one and in groups, various people trooped in to buy books, greeting cards, and school supplies anxiously assuring Kenzi that her store would be all right.

"*Betty* filled me in, Ray."

Jonathan felt put out that Ray hadn't called for him to participate in the vaguely-worded late night "handling" of Kenzi's difficult visitor. For so many years, he'd thought about the little girl with her bright eyes and big ponytails and French braids. For so many years he wondered where she lived, whether she hated him, whether she was okay.

Jonathan assured Ray firmly, "I wasn't always this buttoned-down conservative with bifocals, you know. I've done a little something in my lifetime so don't be fooled. I may be old, but I can still take care of business when I need to."

"Well, Jonathan, keep in mind your position at the university. Plausible deniability works both for politicians and university professors, if you know what I mean."

"I do."

Despite the desire to get down and dirty, sometimes, various means resolved various situations. It took Jonathan only a split-second to agree.

"Well, I'm glad to know my daughter found a man with common sense. I'm also glad to know you care enough to stand up and defend her from the assholes of the world."

"But you're not entirely off the hook, Jonathan." Ray laughed without humor. "There's still part two. Franklin Bellaire. I think you can reach him more easily than I can since you move in the same circles. Personally, I'd be tempted to beat him into the ground just as soon as look at him."

Jonathan chuckled and nodded while squaring his jaw with satisfaction, "Uh *hunh*. Well, this time I'm way ahead of you, Ray. That also has been *handled*, as you say. We won't be hearing much from Franklin in the future."

Jonathan responded swiftly to the news of Franklin's treachery and Bobby Forrest's intimidation of Kenzi. Jonathan also knew that Franklin stranded Lina in Dallas after her mother's funeral. He loved both of his daughters and had no sympathy for the man who hurt them both. Franklin or himself. None. He also did not like the knowing smirk that Franklin flashed him once in a while as if to remind Jonathan of the more disastrous portion of Jonathan's personal life.

Three decades of academic maneuvering that began when he arrived as a student, then as a teacher's assistant, on to junior faculty and then jaded, world weary, and heavily-published tenured faculty taught Jonathan something important about the careers and reputations of people who tore hunks out of the hands that fed them, gasoline-torched bridges, and assumed every shut eye under a snowy, silvered, salt and pepper covering of hair was asleep.

He'd wanted to believe in Franklin who reminded him of himself at the same age. In fact, if not for the inner turmoil and guilt over his mistakes as a younger, more foolish man, he would be Franklin. But that knowledge did not temper Jonathan's anger. Rather, it fueled his anger, because he understood exactly the type of person Franklin hid underneath the smirking charm.

So he destroyed Franklin with the tools life afforded him. A mere twitching of strings here and vaguely worded calling in of favors there denied Franklin the tenure and promotion he so vainly and undeservedly coveted without Franklin's even knowing where to look for answers. With denial of tenure, a tenure-track faculty member may as well not exist as far as respect on campus goes. Everyone from the dean who approved the promotions to the janitors who cleaned the classrooms knew there was no way to save face and no way to overcome the bureaucratic system. Immediately leaving the vicinity of a wrecked career to do salvage elsewhere remained the best option. But elsewhere did not exist for Franklin.

Jonathan had a long reach.

By August, both the university campus and the town decreased in size. Franklin encountered cold glances and brief monosyllabic conversations. This distancing proved especially hard to endure since his personality demanded a certain amount of public adulation to justify his own ego.

The promise of intended violence in Ray's eyes when they pulled into the same gas station together pretty much let Franklin know that he'd worn out his welcome regarding Kenzi and Lina. Franklin drove off with a squeal of tires to find gas elsewhere. Both families pulled together to protect their own from outside threat.

Betty called Jonathan from Dallas for news.

"Jonathan, what's going on down there?"

"It's handled, Betty."

Betty knew first-hand how purposeful Jonathan could be when crossed. She accepted as a given that if Jonathan said a thing was handled, then that's exactly what the thing was. Handled.

"Thank you, Jonathan. Thank you for looking out for our little girl."

"Yeah. I do all right sometimes, Betty."

"Sometimes you do."

Jonathan blinked his surprise at her agreement while Betty hung up the phone lost in thought.

Chapter 16

The Gatherings

"Why not, Daddy? Why?"

"Santi."

"Why? Why won't you let me see her? Why? Daddy. Daddy?"

"Santi, did she try to contact you? Did she try to see you?"

"Nooooo."

"Then why do you want to see her all of a sudden?"

"Reggie and Davey have a grandmother and I don't! Why do they get to see their grandmother and I don't. Why? Why? Daddy, you're not being fair. You're not being fair!"

Jackson whined and cried from underneath Santi's bed then fled the room as Santi's sobbing rose to a screeching, "Whyeee!" Her little face was streaked with tears. She'd exhausted herself finally and lay crying on her bed with her back to her father.

Ray stood for a moment wondering what Cliff Huxtable would have done in a moment like this. But this episode never aired on *The Cosby Show*. The grandmother on that show didn't pay the rent on her back. But how do you explain that to a little girl in the real world? Ray left and went to the kitchen. He slammed his huge fists on the edge of the sink and looked out the kitchen window into the garden. *It's so beautiful here. But it's still not enough. It was always about the people. Aunt Tilly knew that. Reginald and Vasanti knew that.* He got himself a glass of water and filled another for Santi leaving it on her bedside table since she'd fallen asleep.

At Kinfolk, Santi's artwork reflected the pain in her eyes. Drawing after drawing of Aunt Tilly with Jackson, Aunt Tilly with Dharma, Aunt Tilly in the garden, and Aunt Tilly holding Santi's hand filled her drawing pad in colorful crayon. In a rare moment, Kenzi talked it over with Stacy.

"We should do something, Stacy. Don't you think?"

"Well, I helped her to sew the left page edges together. So now, it's sort of a book."

"Yeah it's definitely a book." Kenzi flipped through the pages carefully. "I think I have an idea. Stacy, can you create about… twenty invitations? I think we should hold a reading and a signing."

A few days later, minutes after the store closed to the public, Kenzi, Ray, Dharma, David, Reggie, Davey, Lina, Jonathan, Betty, Stacy, Lydia, and Mr. Oliver gathered together for Santi's reading in the children's section.

Dharma crumbled leftover catfish and blended it together with whipped potatoes, rice flour, onions and garlic, pepper, a bit of salt, and an egg. This she patted into little round cakes and covered them with an extra layer of seasoned rice flour and fried them in olive oil. She served this with slices of lime and sauce. She also sliced plenty of fruits and vegetables. Miss Lydia brought a box of ginger snaps from the local bakery. They had a choice of either hot rosemary tea or limeade, both sweetened with honey. Santi waited quietly as she sat next to her father while Kenzi gave the introduction.

"Wearing her favorite pretty, bright, buttery yellow sundress which is a Matilda Grant original, sits our guest of honor, Santi Grant." Santi smiled and tugged on one of her two giant ponytails that Ray carefully created a few hours earlier and decorated with yellow ribbons. "Santi Grant is an artist with promise and we at Kinfolk Books are pleased that she agreed to debut at our store. Miss Santi Grant, everyone!" Kenzi signaled Santi to begin after the polite applause.

Santi's sweet voiced piped out, "This is how Aunt T keeps the chickens safe from Jackson. She flipped through the pages awkwardly so Kenzi helped to hold the book upright.

"Me, Daddy, Dharma, Dhan, Reggie, Davey, Uncle David and everyone else ate dinner." Kenzi heard a few coughs in the audience.

"We ate outside in the backyard because it was a clear day. Aunt T said the air was good for us." Santi pointed out her illustrations and scrapbook-like inserts and photographs. "This is us picking up pecans for Aunt T's pie. Aunt T always put extra pecans in hers."

They all had a hard time holding back the tears, including Miss Lydia and Mr. Oliver. Kenzi quickly started off the applause concerned that Santi might not understand the reason for all the tears. "What a beautiful book. So truthful in its message. Santi, Stacy tells me that this is your best work ever! We're all so proud of you!"

Mr. Oliver gave Santi a bunch of flowers. Ray hugged Santi tight on his lap.

"I'm so proud of you, sweetheart. This book is wonderful. That's exactly how I remember Miss Tilly too." She sat safely in his arms while they took another look through Santi's book. Kenzi gazed at them wistfully.

"Smile, you two!" Kenzi snapped a photo then another of Ray sitting with Santi so Santi would always remember and never have any doubt about the love in her life. She printed them out on the computer and saw…

She stared at the first photo that showed Ray's shadowed expression… almost angry. Then the other photo, a split-second later, showed him smiling down at Santi. "Here you go, Santi." She handed Santi the second photo and dropped the first one in her pocket.

"You can paste these in your book as well. How about here?" Kenzi turned to the page that said simply, "THE END."

She gave Ray an uncertain glance then turned to everyone chatting quietly in the children's area. "Normally, authors sign books for their readers. But this is special. Earlier, Santi asked me to ask you all to sign her book." Even Reggie and David scrawled something across the page. Then Santi, in return, signed their invitations she and Stacy made together.

During a quiet moment, while everyone else chatted, Kenzi moved next to Stacy. Maybe the moment for a small talk had arrived.

"Hey Stacy. Funny, isn't it how the best art is born out of great pain?"

"Right. It's often like that."

"Well, fortunately she had you to help her channel it positively." They both looked at Santi laughing with Dharma.

Stacy smiled. "She looks like a sunflower with those ribbons."

"That little girl's a heart-breaker." Kenzi tried to gauge Stacy's mood. "Stacy, you did great work with Santi."

"She's definitely talented. It just takes someone to bring out the best of what she has to offer."

"Yeah, I think so. Look, Stacy. I was wondering if there…"

Stacy cut in, "Goodnight, Kenzi."

Kenzi stood open-mouthed and stunned as she stared at Stacy saying quick good-nights to everyone else on her way out of the shop. *Well, that was pretty abrupt.* Stacy halted a moment, looking to the right and said something to someone standing outside. Kenzi frowned and craned her head. She could see the shadow of someone against the store's front window. *What was Stacy doing now? Oh, wait! It had to be…* She saw Stacy move away as the shadow shifted. Catching David's eye, under the cover of the activity inside the store, Kenzi took care of the one errand she didn't want to forget.

Later, she moved to talk to Dhan who helped himself to generous portions at the refreshment table. "Don't be shy now!"

"Well," Dhan pretended to think it over, "Okay, if you insist."

"Oh, I definitely command you."

"Your command is my wish!" Dhan piled on more of Dharma's fish cakes while Kenzi laughed.

One afternoon few days later, Lina joined Santi in the children's area and took another look at Santi's book while Santi explained it's creation to her. Santi quickly adopted Dhan's nickname for her. So Lina became "Li Li" to Santi and Reggie and Davey, as well.

"Thank you, Santi." Lina hugged Santi and thanked her for sharing it with her. "You know what, I think your book was a wonderful idea. And you know what?"

"What, Li Li?"

"I'm going to make a book for my mother."

Santi smiled in approval as Lina flipped through the pages slowly. Lina caught Kenzi alone at the cash register.

"Because of all these secrets in our family and my mother's alcoholism, I just feel like there's so much else I never knew about her.

Things I missed. I want to remember the happier times of our lives, Kenzi."

Kenzi waited a beat before she answered. "The best person to ask is probably my mom, you know."

"I know." Lina leaned forward with her elbows on the counter. Kenzi leaned forward as well. "I'm gonna talk to Aunt Betty and Jonathan. See if I can get some materials together."

Kenzi sighed thoughtfully. The pretty little sunflower had produced seeds.

Sentiment and nostalgia didn't strike just Santi and Lina. Dharma revealed that she wanted to remember both her mother and Aunt Tilly by publishing an official cookbook for Organic Soul full of the recipes they'd taught her.

"It'll be a way for the Southern and the Eastern world to meet. Like a spicy blend of rice, onions, peppers, spices and… soul, of course."

"Of course!"

"I'm trying to transcribe a lot of what they taught me from memory – all the explanations and traditions."

"Sounds good to me. Do you need help?"

"Nope. Not really. It's almost like I have to go through the motions of cooking to remember it all. I don't want any of the recipes to be lost or forgotten. Tell you what, you can help us eat what I cook."

"I'm so there for you, Dharma," Kenzi solemnly assured. And they laughed together.

"By the way, we're taking Dhan out to dinner to celebrate his MBA. The graduation's not until the spring, but we decided we couldn't wait that long."

Kenzi nodded. Then Dharma laughed.

"Actually, it was Dhan who couldn't wait that long!"

Dharma openly cried at "Little Dani" being a man now as Reggie and Davey fought each other on the seats between her and her husband. Kenzi chuckled at Dhan's reaction to hearing himself called Little Dani. Ray, Dhan, and Dharma's voices rose and fell with the musical, lilting quality that showed itself whenever they spoke to each other.

Ray, let out an audible sigh of relief and turned to find Kenzi's smile radiating across his face.

"Looks like Little Bro is well on his way, hunh?" she whispered under her breath.

"Dhan's gonna be just fine... for the most part," Ray laughed quietly.

"It's almost like I can see the weight of the world lifting from your shoulders, Ray."

"Yeah."

"You've been a good brother," she told him while stroking his back.

He kissed her cheek.

She loved this family. So much that she'd allowed herself to be drawn into its inner workings. So far, Ray didn't suspect what she and David had done together. It took Kenzi only a moment to slip to Kinfolk's front door during Santi's signing.

But they finally discussed her pregnancy. After studying Ray's photo, she figured out he already knew. And though she got the classic "Ray" look, Ray let it go. Just, "Don't ever do it again," he said. And because he let her off so easy, she felt somewhat uneasy about her and David's secret maneuvering.

Ray laughed aloud now, "To Little Dani!"

"To Little Dani!"

"To the MVP with the MBA!"

"Happy MBA!"

Lina, Santi, Betty lifted their glasses for Dhan. Jonathan sat quietly next to Betty, and whispered in a low voice, "Betty, it's good to see what sort of family our grandchild is being born into."

Betty flinched at "our grandchild." Then she smiled. "Yes, Jonathan. It's very good."

Jonathan stared back at her startled a moment. Betty broke eye contact first and continued to toast Dhan. Jonathan followed suit.

Later that evening, Dhan and Ray spoke matter-of-factly.

"Kenzi was just the person you needed, and you were the person she needed."

"Think so?" Ray replied guardedly.

"Cut it out, Ray. This is Dhan you're talking to."

"Stay in a child's place."

Dhan snorted, "Make me."

After Dhan finally called "Uncle," Ray released him from the headlock.

"I know that something happened."

"You won't have to worry about it again."

"What did you do, Jonathan?"

"I just told you not to worry."

"You know what? Every time I'm here, someone from the community walks in and makes sure to tell me everything's gonna be all right. It's funny."

"They care."

"Yeah, and it feels good but... well, okay. Obviously, you're not gonna talk."

"We're talking right now, Kenzi," Jonathan chuckled.

"Fine, Jonathan. I'll leave it alone." Kenzi shook her head. "Fortunately, Lina's taking on more of the day-to-day operations here. I spent most of the morning at home and Ray's picking me up to visit at the homestead this afternoon. It's nice to rest."

"Good man."

"Jonathan... I'm not sure what Ray intends for us."

Jonathan grew instantly serious.

"I know that I do love him. I know that he loves me and the baby."

"Of course he does."

"I think we both have some more thinking to do."

"About what?" Jonathan asked gravely.

"About me. About him. Us. Me." Kenzi fiddled with a stack of postcards with the Kinfolk logo. "I know that I absolutely do not want this baby to grow up without a father." Jonathan winced but nodded his head.

"I mean, it's taken me a while, but I've forgiven most of it, you know. Still, those years are just... gone."

"I know. I know."

She still didn't call Jonathan "Father" or "Dad" yet. Kenzi hoped Ray wouldn't take too long to reach a decision. Sometimes families were weird, going around in circles with each other, whispering, trying to solve problems.

Back from a visit to the homestead, she spoke with Betty on the phone.

"I've shown Ray who I am. He knows me. He knows us. He's seen my strong side and things I'm still working on. Places where I'm still growing. I've seen things he needs to work on too. He's staying with me. I'm staying with him. We're together. I do love him. And he knows that too."

"So what's the hold up?"

"Well, he's not the type who'll be pushed, for one. I think he's waiting for me... I don't know. But we're hanging tough. All the hurt and the pain and the baggage. The issues from past relationships. All that's kind of dragging slowing things down."

"Life is short, Kenzi."

Kenzi had no answer for that.

She sat eating a meal with Dharma at Organic Soul while Dharma fussed at her to eat more and more and more.

"He's going to have to come to me, Dharma. I have to know that it's a choice he's making freely, not just because of the baby. When he decides the time is right, then the time will be right."

"What about you?"

"Dharma, I wouldn't have the will to ever leave Ray as long as I drew breath into my body. Wherever he went, I would follow." Dharma sat stunned into silence, which didn't happen often, or ever really.

"I have it bad, I know. But that's just the way it is."

"Does he know that?"

"I've been trying to show him."

"Kenzi." Dharma hesitated as if making up her mind. "You know about Darlene."

"Yes."

"You know…"

"I know. Ray told me."

"I'm not going to say any more than that. We don't… we don't really talk about it."

"I know."

Dharma switched the subject.

"Ladies and gentlemen, before we begin Dr. Jonathan Farrell's book signing, I just wanted to announce that this very day last September, Kinfolk Books opened its doors for the first time. In honor of that, we went the extra mile for tonight's refreshment table. Please help us celebrate by not leaving a single bite!"

Under the cover of a round of applause, most of the attendees rose once again to demolish the piles of food. Kenzi continued while they returned to their seats.

"Texas has a unique history with many textures and layers that form this state's identity. Dr. Jonathan Farrell, associate professor of sociology has written a book," Kenzi held it up, "that uncovers many of those layers. My father, Dr. Jonathan Farrell."

Jonathan looked surprised even as he sat up straighter in his chair. A few surprised looks radiated from a few of the university big wigs who took Jonathan's book signing and short lecture as an opportunity to visit the newest independent bookstore for the first time. Kenzi covered the awkward pause with applause. They quickly joined in.

Jonathan reached the podium and stalled a few moments straightening out his notes. "Thank you to my daughter, Ms. Kenzi Malton, owner and operator of the best bookstore in Rollins, Texas. Actually, all of Texas," he smiled as the crowd applauded Kenzi's bookstore. She smiled back at him as he found his place.

"This is an uncomfortable lecture. To be reminded of past human failings and offenses we've committed against various people is a hard thing to handle." He glanced briefly at Kenzi.

"However, I ask not one person, but an entire state to remember the prosperous Negro business communities in Texas burned and destroyed from existence and from history by neighboring white populations during the days of Reconstruction and Jim Crow. While North America participated in wars against foreign powers…"

As Jonathan spoke, Kenzi reflected on the defiant pride and quiet shame of Texas and how past events shaped present attitudes. Because of the ethnic diversity in Texas with Native American, Mexican, African American, Asian, and ethnic European immigration, the state remained volatile on many issues – criminal justice, immigration, education, welfare, etc. Kenzi shook herself as she realized Jonathan's lecture finished. He began to field questions.

"From oral histories, we've seen that a very real geographic and philosophical division continues to exist, as with most university towns, between locals (or natives) and transplants (faculty and their spouses and children, along with students). The respondents had difficulty describing the division with words. Much of the differences involved class, culture, and community ties that were not spoken overtly. When I interviewed her, a certain Ms. Matilda Grant told me the community would consider such a thing impolite."

Jonathan winked at Kenzi's exclamation of surprise.

"Who belonged and who just visited, they ascertained by speech, dress, demeanor, outlook, and social circles. The native residents quickly identified outsiders and excluded them from ancient conflicts and familial gatherings. From what I've seen on the university campus, the native Rollins population provides the university daily services, and then returns home to real lives lived away from the so-called tourists – faculty and students."

By this time, Kenzi positioned herself to moderate the audience who continued a stream of questions.

"Well, yes, Anglo cowboy nostalgia, often romanticized by movie and television programs seemed to forget the presence and participation of the darker-skinned peoples of the Wild West. They descended from the ethnic immigrants from the days of the European explorers, the native members of tribes older than memory or the written word, the workers from the Far East, and the slaves who fought to escape their forced contributions to the American Dream. They blended and settled in communities, still clinging to various aspects of the culture of their mothers and fathers. So when someone orders them to 'go back where you came from,' they simply look around and say, 'We are where we came from. Just as you are. Or maybe even more so.'"

"Related to the invisible wall you encountered while accumulating oral histories how were you able to put your subjects at ease during the interviews?"

"It took a certain amount of skill to navigate the various perspectives on history, language, culture, and pride. Often, it took more than one interview. Just asking the questions: Who was a real Texan? What did a Texan look like? How does a Texan speak? What does a Texan eat? Who made Texas great? These usually encouraged responses. And any answer given could jumpstart yet another discussion."

Jonathan grinned. "Kind of like this discussion. I'm sure we could go on all night. Texas is completely fascinating."

Kenzi took the hint, ended the lecture, and got the lines assembled for the book signing. While Lina totaled the purchases, Jonathan signed each copy and held conversations with well-wishers. Betty handled the line while Kenzi circulated and shook hands. A few people asked her to request Jonathan to speak to their church groups and community organizations.

Several of the university professors took her aside to consult on various research materials she might be able to obtain. Two of them mentioned the same university grant program she'd tried for the previous year.

"I actually sit on the committee now. A spot came vacant when Franklin Bellaire left." The professor eyed her curiously. Kenzi simply nodded her head thoughtfully.

"You know, we have a meeting room available here if you have a class or group that needs to meet once in a while. And, of course, you're always welcome to hold a book signing here for when you published."

"Here's my card. I have a book coming out this spring. Kind of on the dry side."

"I'm sure it's very relevant to the world today. And, of course, there'll be refreshments." Kenzi didn't miss the interested gleam in the professor's eyes.

Ray silently watched Kenzi work the room. *What kind of fool am I?* He knew Kenzi picked carefully through the merchandise at Lydia's baby shop. And just this morning, Mr. Oliver beamed at him proudly when he went into the drugstore, "Kenzi is taking all of her vitamins. She is a good mother. She wants the baby to be strong!"

A few days later, Betty drove down to Rollins again for a brief visit during which Jonathan met her at the Grant homestead to help pick up the pecans that rained down in late autumn. Long ago, Reginald had shown his children how to nail an old tin can to the end of a stick to pick up the pecans.

"They still use the same sticks even as adults, Mom. Aunt Tilly used one last year so she didn't have to bend over."

"This is what I've been missing in the big city. It's actually kind of fun."

"Well, when you pick pecans up alone, it seems such a chore because there's so many. But in a group, it goes much faster."

Betty interrupted to yell to Jonathan in the distance as he swung a full bag into the back of Ray's pickup.

"Jonathan, that's too heavy. You'll hurt your back!"

He waved her off and muttered under his breath. Ray told Kenzi later that they reminded him of an old married couple. Kenzi replied, "I hope to God not."

Betty and Jonathan wandered off together picking up a pecan here and there while they spoke. Eventually, they dropped the pretense and turned to face one another. Betty leaned against a tree.

"It's so quiet and peaceful here."

"Yeah. It's a nice change of pace from the university campus. I'm very happy for Kenzi. The Grants are good people."

"Yes."

"Betty," Jonathan's voice lowered, "Sometimes, do you wonder if Jalissa's car crash really was an accident?"

"What are you talking about, Jonathan? The coroner didn't say anything."

"No, I don't mean that."

Betty stared back at him uncomprehendingly. Slowly, Jonathan's real meaning dawned upon her. She covered her mouth in horror and closed her eyes. "Oh God." She shuddered and shook with silent sobs. Brief snatches of memory from that last visit at the hospital came to her. Jalissa smiling, finally at peace. Jonathan handed her a handkerchief.

"Betty, I'm sorry. I didn't mean to make you cry. Seems like I've done that too much already."

"No. It's okay. I think at the back of my mind, I wondered the same thing. I pushed it back down though. I didn't want to dwell on it. I didn't want to think that my turning my back on Jalissa might have had something to do with her giving up on life. I know she was alone and unhappy. And maybe she saw Lina's move to Rollins as yet another person drifting away and abandoning her."

Jonathan stared at the ground, his jaw clenched. Just as he unclenched to admit to cutting off Jalissa's hush money, Betty continued. "I sometimes wondered if that was the reason why Lina volunteered to help Kenzi at the shop – to escape from Dallas and Jalissa's alcoholism. It's for Lina's sake that I'm choosing to look forward and not back. Jalissa's gone. We can't bring her back, Jonathan. We can't change anything at all. I can't. You can't."

Jonathan blinked.

"Jalissa can't. We can only go forward and focus on the living." Betty faced Jonathan and looked directly into his eyes. "Jonathan, whatever happened back then, just leave it there. Let it just die and go far, far away. Please, I can't take any more. We have two children and now a grandchild to guide through life. They need us. Both of us. It's a cold, cold world out there. But you know that."

"Yeah, I know."

"But family helps us get through the rough times. We're going to have to work it out together."

Jonathan stared at Betty as if he'd just met her. "I think... that's best as well. To look forward, I mean. Family is important. I have to say, all the things I accomplished... it just seemed... empty. Vain. With no one to bring it home to."

Betty smiled lightly. "So what happened to that cold, cold heart, Jonathan? Where did it go?"

Jonathan winced, sighed, turned, and began walking slowly without any real direction. Betty quietly matched his stride. Jonathan slowed and then stopped under a tree.

"You know, I'd attend a conference and read a paper. Then go home. I'd write an article or win an award. Then go home. I missed having someone there to share it with. And now I've just had a book signing of what might be my most important work at my own daughter's bookstore with everyone there…" Jonathan stopped abruptly and Betty halted next to him. He turned and looked at Betty intently and gripped her by the shoulders.

"Betty, I'm so…" he choked out the words, "So very sorry. So sorry. I'm sorry for everything that I did to hurt you and Kenzi and Jalissa and Lina."

"Jonathan…"

"No, Betty. I need to be able to hold my head up. I have to face it. I told Kenzi that I could never replace the missing years. But from that day forward, whenever she needed me… I would be there for her. She could count on me. I told Lina the same thing. And now I'm telling you." Betty's eyes widened. "Yes, Betty. It's important to me. It's all that I have left that really means anything. Betty, you understand?"

"Yes. I understand. I do, Jonathan. I just wanted to say that I'm sorry as well. What I did to you and Kenzi was wrong in so many ways. I look in the mirror and I wonder what kind of woman would do what I did to her own daughter and the father of her child. She didn't speak to me for days. When she finally did, she told me Ray helped her understand that she needed me to be her mother even as much as I needed her to be my daughter."

"He's a good guy."

"He is." Betty stared at Jonathan. "I just wanted you to know…" She began to sob again and Jonathan drew her close.

"I know." He stroked her back. "I know." It had been so long since he held Betty other than the brief encounter at the funeral where he'd threatened her. The familiar feelings stirred within him and grew.

The compulsion came over him suddenly and he touched her cheek that jutted in sharp reflection of the angular plane of her jaw and strong, proud nose. Betty's face had always fascinated him. Her full mouth and beautiful dark brown eyes softened the sharp lines and warmed him with their depth. Kenzi inherited Betty's every feature save the eyes. Betty had grown more beautiful. Only the man who'd memorized her every feature years ago would notice the tiniest lines at the corners of her eyes. She'd mellowed into a mature calmness and a new vulnerability that allowed her to reach out to the man she'd sworn first to love and then to hate for the rest of her life.

Jonathan kissed her smooth dark brow and Betty lifted her head in surprise. The same surprise held her still as Jonathan kissed the hollow of her cheek, her chin, behind her ear, her neck, and the corner of her mouth. It had been so long. She responded and opened her mouth to him hungrily. Jonathan tightened his hold on her. Her body molded itself to his body in remembrance. When they separated at last, they stared at each other in puzzled amusement. Jonathan looked at her beautiful mouth.

"We should get back to the others."

"Yes, we should."

But neither of them moved.

Chapter 17

The Proposition

Ray stared at the open page in Santi's book in shocked bewilderment. For days, he said nothing, trying to figure it out. After his last confrontation with Santi where she drove herself into near hysteria, he didn't want to have it out with her again over the shaky, near illiterate signature in her book next to a recent photograph of Maya. He reflected over his options about enforcing the court order and knew deep inside, that he didn't have the heart to do it. It would hurt too many people. But somehow, she'd made contact without him knowing and he didn't like that. He didn't like that at all.

He phoned Dharma and figured out through her stalling that she was trying to cover for David. With a little more big brother bullying, he got an even clearer understanding of Kenzi's role. *Kenzi!*

"Ray, don't go off half-cocked, the way did with me just now."

"Dharma, this is my daughter you people are messing with!"

"We people? She's my niece and she's unhappy with what you're doing!"

"Dharma, I'm only going to tell you this once. Back the hell off. Back off me. And back off Santi. You keep your mind on Reggie and Davey and stay in your lane. I'm telling you. Are you listening to me?"

"I heard you."

"I didn't ask you if you heard, I asked you if you were listening."

"Ray, don't pull that daddy crap with me. It worked when we were younger and we needed that from you, but it's not working anymore. You need to stay in *your* lane."

Ray exhaled loudly.

"Dharma, look. Just please don't pull this shit any more."

"Ray, I didn't pull anything."

"Well, tell your husband…"

"You tell him."

"No, *you* tell him. You brought him into the family, you need to check him and let him know what it is. Because right now, my first instinct, before I even called you was to ask him 'What did the fist say to the face.'"

"Ray. Ray."

"Dharma, I'm fucking furious. Check your man. I'm not having this behind-the-back shit again. *Ever.* Not with my daughter."

"Well, then you need to check Kenzi since she's the one who had the idea in the first place."

"Don't worry, that's next on the agenda."

"Ray, don't you find it funny, though?"

"Funny?"

"I mean, it was someone who married into the family and your girlfriend who tried to fix this up, not one of us. Maybe we all need to take a step back and really think it over."

"I don't like it."

"Well, it's done now."

Ray threw himself into work around the homestead. He knew he was too upset to have an extreme discussion with Kenzi in her condition. And like Dhan said, sometimes he could be kind of hard. As a matter of fact, both Dharma and Dhan had gotten on him about that lately. David in his own way. And Kenzi too. He needed to pull back and think this through.

"Star, you and Jackson understand it, don't you?" Ray spoke to the horse and dog as he saddled up in the barn. Star galloped around the perimeter helping to check on the fences that surrounded their land with Jackson bounding close behind. He dismounted for a closer look at a couple of sections and thought back to when he saw Kenzi for the first time as she bounced across the street with the sunlight lighting her eyes to gold.

"I knew even then something would happen, you know." Star snorted in response. *Sure you did.* Jackson seemed to believe him though.

After learning of her hesitation to talk about the baby from Lina, he knew serious fear. So many options for a single woman existed. He remembered real terror of the possibility that she'd consider aborting or giving the baby up for adoption. And he'd already lost one child with Darlene's death. Even though he wasn't sure of the baby's paternity, it rocked him.

"She wants the baby and I want the baby. She knows I want the baby." Star chewed on the grass.

He turned to Jackson. "She's not Darlene, Jackson." Jackson looked up when he heard his name. "You hear that, boy?" Jackson barked. "Alright! Calm down."

"Darlene doesn't hurt me anymore. It's the past, you guys. We have to let the past go." Ray walked along the fence and examined the parts that crumbled from rot. He'd have to replace the posts. This entire section, as a matter of fact.

"I've forgiven Darlene. In my heart, I've truly forgiven Darlene. I don't excuse her, but I forgive her. Despite what Maya said, the decisions Darlene made were Darlene's decisions. But the most important decision out of all of them was to give birth to Santi. And that's the most important result of our time together. That wasn't a mistake. That was the most beautiful thing."

Star walked over and bumped his shoulder.

"You know what, Star? Kenzi really likes it out here. She doesn't mind what I do everyday. She understands how it is out here in the country."

Ray stopped speaking for a time, lost in thought while he stroked Star's mane. This land sheltered him. Star bumped him again and woke him from his trance.

"But she's been messing shit up lately. I just don't know. She said she didn't want to repeat the mistakes of her own parents. I think that's why she dropped the bug in David's ear and why he did the same for Maya. Kenzi just can't bear to see a broken family. Betty and Jonathan are good people though. They like me okay, I think. But Star, she said she wanted a marriage that would last or no marriage at all." Ray swallowed. "She drives a pretty hard bargain, you guys."

Ray mounted Star again and they finished their rounds. Finally, he galloped over to the catfish pond for a rest and drink. He swung off Star who shrugged and dropped her head to the water. Jackson joined her and then ran to the other side to bark at the fish frantically swimming away from his shadow.

"So what's the problem?" Star ignored him. "You're no help." Ray struggled to remember. A beautiful woman he that he loved, loved him in return. His daughter loved her. His family loved and accepted her. Her family loved and accepted him. She carried his child in her body. Except... he had to hear about it from other people. She was smart, kind, generous. She respected and helped to continue family traditions. Except... for the Maya episode. Their sexual chemistry together escalated to phenomenal heights. Now that was all right. *What kind of fool am I?*

Ray laughed aloud. Star scorned his rude interruption of the peace all around them and walked off a ways. Ray grew serious again and sat down on the grass.

"I challenged her commitment, but she hasn't said a word. I can't even tell what's on her mind," he complained with a sigh of impatience.

"I could stare at this pond all day." And Ray seriously considered doing just that. He stretched out on his back. Instead... Jackson ran up to him and licked his face and barked for him to get up.

"I know. You're right. You're right, boy. I'm gonna have to be a man about it and make a man's decision."

Ray sighed as he sat up, found a rock and threw it into the water as the cane whispered and creaked a reprimand. Star came back to reprimand him as well.

"I do love you, Kenzi," he whispered.

They drove out to the homestead for an afternoon picnic under the shade of the tall pecan trees. A bump pushed out Kenzi's middle. She glowed radiant and so happy. He loved to look at her. Her eyes had a serene, dreamy quality lately, liquid and golden brown in the sun.

Ray's spoke quietly looking over the gardens and orchards.

"You know, Kenzi, until you came into my life, I'd made up my mind to never get seriously involved with another woman. I... loved Santi's mother very much. I gave her everything I could give. When she left me and Santi, I thought it was because I wasn't enough of a man to keep her. That hurt. It really did. She threw the love I gave her and that Santi gave her right back in our faces."

Kenzi closed her eyes. *What did he tell her — that he could never love again, trust again?* She trembled from the hurtful possibility.

Ray continued, "I finally figured out that Darlene's abandonment wasn't because she was a bad person. Or because I was a bad person. I know this now. Darlene just couldn't handle the reality of a loving relationship as a wife or a mother. She... didn't know how. So she removed herself from the equation."

Kenzi remained silent, listening.

"You know, I should have seen it. When I met Darlene's relatives, especially her mother, I never sensed any kind of family closeness. When I met her mother and some other relatives, I saw it all right in front of me. There was this spirit of hopelessness and despair. A lot of anger. Almost all of them lived in self-sabotage, addiction, violence, and... poverty. I saw it, but I didn't focus on it. It was always about Darlene. She came across as exciting and vivacious. I thought to myself... she's too good for all this. I'll take her away from it. But there was more under the surface that I didn't see. Aunt Tilly tried to tell me, but I didn't listen until it was too late."

He smiled at Kenzi. "I know you're wondering where this is going. I have a point. But I wanted to make sure you understood where I am, right now. What it's all about."

"No, it's okay Ray. Speak your truth, *brother*," she laughed lightly. "Tell your story. I'm just enjoying this fresh air. These trees." Her mouth curved. "You."

Ray smiled back at Kenzi and continued.

"I don't excuse her actions or diminish the pain she caused. She hurt all of us. But at least... I understand now. I'm... going to allow her spirit to rest. And now I know that I don't have to avoid talking about her to Santi. I can speak to Santi about Darlene with love in my heart instead of... everything else."

"That's the most important thing."

"Well... that and... something else."

Kenzi raised her eyebrows in inquiry.

"I know what you did with David and Maya."

Kenzi stiffened and looked down, bracing for the blast of outrage, the condemnation. "Ray, I'm..."

Instead, he squeezed her closer. "Thank you."

Kenzi glanced at him, shocked. Ray laughed.

"If you could only see your face, Kenzi."

"That was the very last thing I expected to hear you say."

"That's the only thing I can say. It was only a matter of time. We spoke earlier on some of this in the park.

"Yes," Kenzi remembered his challenge to her and wondered where he would go with this.

"I'm going to work something out with the court. Anyway... there's a reason I've been able to forgive Darlene... and Maya." Ray faced Kenzi now, anxiously.

Kenzi really wondered.

"Life has changed so much, Kenzi. I can barely remember what happened to me before you walked into our restaurant. We've both been hurt. And... I know neither of us is perfect. But," Ray swallowed, "I think we're perfect for each other." Ray held her hand. "Kenzi, I love you. I love you so much. You've brought so much to my life. I love you."

"Oh Ray," Kenzi began to cry as Ray held her and rocked her gently. "I love you too. I've been waiting for so long to hear you say it. I've loved you for so long. You helped me to learn to forgive as well. Since we met, I've gained a father, a sister, and Dhan and Dharma who are like a brother and sister to me too. And I love Santi so much and now I seem to have two children – and a dog."

They both laughed at crazy Jackson who'd ambled up between them and flopped down.

"I love your beautiful heart, Ray. I love you so much."

"You know I'm not a rich man. Or a highly educated man. What you see is what you're gonna get, Kenzi."

"Ray," Kenzi said sternly, "You know that your education has never come up as an issue between us. Only that time when you brought it up. Remember? And you know how we resolved that. Don't you?"

Ray chuckled in remembrance of that night. "I do remember that night. You were so beautiful in all that silk. I couldn't keep my hands off you. I still..."

Kenzi laughed. "Let me finish before you go on that tangent, okay, baby?" But she leaned heavily against Ray's side.

"Ray, you are one of the most intelligent men I've ever known. Just looking around at what it took to build this land and help raise Dharma and Dhan tells me that. And Santi is as smart as a whip. It *has* to be in the genes. And as for being rich, I hear it's over-rated, but then I wouldn't know anything about that. Ray, between the two of us, we'll build a wonderful life together. If I eat beans and rice for the rest of my life, then I want you across the table from me passing the salt and pepper. You are everything I always wanted in a man and father to our child."

"Kenzi. What about…"

"Let's definitely talk about that."

"Okay." Ray waited.

"Please know that I'm going to be what you need me to be and so much more. Now, the past cannot be changed. Yours or mine. You know all about where I came from and all those skeletons. Like you, I'm ready to move on."

Kenzi stared into Ray's eyes.

"I'm not going to leave you, Ray. You or Santi. Ever. As long as I have breath in my body I will never leave your side. I told Dharma that…"

Ray frowned. "Dharma? Dharma never said anything. And she loves to get in my business."

Kenzi smiled. "Good for her. She probably knew you wanted to hear it from me."

"Well… yeah."

"I have what it takes. I'm woman enough and more for you, Ray."

"Kenzi."

"I mean every single word."

"You won't feel tied down?

"Not unless you tie me down. Will you?"

"Will I what?"

"Tie me down. We haven't tried that yet, have we?"

Ray threw his head back and laughed. Kenzi felt her heart leap to her throat. The man's sex appeal took her breath away when he smiled.

"I want you to marry me, Kenzi. I want you to be my wife and mother to our children. You know who I am and what I'm about. I know who you are and what you're about. I love you and I want you to be by my side always."

Kenzi's head began to whirl. Oh my God. Oh my God!

"Ray, yes! Oh yes! As long as I have breath in my body I will love you. I never want to leave your side. I love you and your family so much. I love you."

He kissed her fervently.

"She said yeah."

Ray casually broke the news to Dharma and Dhan while they cleaned up after hours at Organic Soul. Santi was spending the night with her cousins, Reggie and Davey, and Uncle David. He loved the shocked look on both of their faces as they came to realize what he referred to.

"It's about time! Sheez! I knew it was going to happen. I knew it! Raman, you never could hide from me. I knew you were in love whether you liked it or not. And I knew Kenzi was completely strung out."

"Yeah, she told me you guys talked. Why didn't you say anything?"

"Because you wouldn't have listened. You always tell me to stay out of your business and stay in my lane, so I did," Dharma ended piously.

"Yeah *right*."

"Yeah, right!" Dhan finally overcame his surprise to hug Ray. "Congratulations, man. You finally manned up and did it, hunh?"

Dharma giggled as she teased her older brother. "Now you'll have a house full of women while I raise my own house full of men."

She ordered, "Dhan, you'll have to split the difference and have a boy and a girl to balance everything out."

Dhan, long-experienced at diverting Dharma's attention, quickly laughed her off and changed the subject. "So, when's the big day, old man?"

"He is the right man for you and I knew it the first day. You remember how I cut out of the store real quick on opening night?"

"Yes, I do remember that, Mom. I thought that was so strange too."

"Well, now you know!"

"Mother, what am I gonna do with you?"

"You're going to take me along when we pick out your dress and cake and flowers and everything else."

Kenzi laughed.

"Oh Mom, Lina just walked in. Let me call you back."

"No, wait I want to hear you tell her."

"Lina, guess what?" Kenzi waved her over closer to the phone. "I…"

"He asked you, didn't he?"

"Lina!" Kenzi screeched excitedly. "I was gonna tell *you*!"

"Oh. Oops! I'm sorry."

"Mom, did you hear what she just did?" Kenzi shouted into the phone. "You always do that, Lina!"

"Hey, Aunt Betty!"

"Hey, Lina!" They could hear Kenzi's mother shout back.

"Okay, Kenzi. Tell me again."

Kenzi pouted a moment but couldn't contain herself.

"Hey, Lina. Guess what?"

"Chicken butt!"

"Stop it," Kenzi laughed and pushed her.

"Okay!" Lina hugged her. "What?"

"He asked me to marry him!"

Lina laughed and shrieked, "Congratulations!" They jumped around with Betty laughing over the receiver.

Lina stopped jumping. "Wait a minute. Wait a minute!" She looked stern.

"What?" Kenzi looked at her, puzzled.

"What did you say when he asked? Did you accept?"

Kenzi picked up the phone receiver. "Mom, did you hear that? She wants to know if I accepted."

They both heard Betty ask, "Well, did you?"

Kenzi paused to shrug, nonchalant, particularly to punish Lina. Then she giggled.

"I said, 'Raaaaaay Graaaaant! Come on down!'"

They all laughed a while longer until Kenzi finally hung up the phone. Lina hugged Kenzi around her growing middle and told her, "I'm truly happy for you, Sis. I love you and I love my niece or nephew already. Ray is a good man and Santi is a beautiful, sweet child."

Betty called back later that night.

"Kenzi, I've been thinking about this for a while."

"Thinking about what?"

"I'm ready to leave Dallas. I'm making plans right now."

"Where are you going?"

"Well, probably Rollins."

"Rollins!" Kenzi laughed, "You want to come to this hick town? Not Houston or Austin?"

"Well, I may as well move to Rollins since I've been spending so much time down there anyway. Seems like I drive down almost every two weeks. Don't get me wrong. I enjoy being down there. All the action – you, Lina, the baby, and even Jonathan - is in Rollins. To tell the truth, I still avoid that part of Central Expressway. You know... where Jalissa crashed. I just can't do it. There are so many bad memories here. Your Mama Dee and Grandaddy are gone. There's just nothing left for me here."

"Is this about Jonathan?"

"It's about me thinking you may need help with my grandchild or Kinfolk Books. You'll probably want to take it easy for the next two years."

"Of course, Mom. You're right. I'm so excited that Ray and I are getting married and for the baby, of course. But there's been so many changes, I've been feeling overwhelmed lately."

"Kenzi, I just want to reassure you that I am dedicated to being your mother. Even though I've made mistakes in judgment, I'm going to be there for you."

"Mom, we've been through that, and I told you I forgive you. I do. I'm just ready to be a mother to my child. That's all I'm thinking about now. I want my baby to grow up in love. That's it."

"All right, Kenzi. I... also intend to keep my last promise to Jalissa. I'm going to be there for Lina as well. She's changed somewhat in the last few months. She's losing that hard edge. But still, we all need safety nets. I think... we need each other."

"Right. So when do you plan to make the move?"

"In about two weeks. I've been tying up loose ends here. I waited to tell you until I was sure."

"Do you need help packing?"

"Not with packing, but with lifting."

"Okay, I'll make some calls, okay? Mom, don't lift anything."

"Yes ma'am. And Kenzi?"

"Ma'am?"

"Congratulations, sweetheart. You deserve the very best, and I think you have it in Ray."

"I do. I DO!"

Chapter 18

Family Bonds

The first postcard arrived a week ago addressed to Kenzi's attention at Kinfolk Books. The Rollins, Texas postmark was dated the previous day. The handwritten words, "DO YOU TRUST HER? WHY? LIKE MOTHER LIKE DAUGHTER," marched across the back. A pair of leather cowboy boots occupied the front.

Though startled, Kenzi knew exactly what it meant. Someone wanted to either warn her or to hurt her. Someone close who knew the Malton family history. Who would do such a thing? And why? She stuck the card in a drawer uneasily.

And today, she looked at the second card as it lay on the counter. The front featured a gigantic rabbit fit with a harness – a 'jackalope' found in almost every Texas gas station.

"GAME RECOGNIZE GAME," the card read in the same block letters.

"Someone hates me," Kenzi muttered. Someone wanted her unhappy and unsure. She loved Ray. He loved her. She wanted to marry him. Nothing anyone could say would ever change that. She loved her sister, Lina, as well. But then… hadn't her mother loved Aunt Jalissa? *Who would do this?*

The sender of the postcards delivered a warning… from her mother? Betty said she wanted to move to Rollins. Would her mother send her this if she felt she couldn't come to Kenzi and speak on her fears? But Betty told her to not blame Lina. Besides her mother very distinct handwriting – not like this.

Would Jonathan send this? Apart for so many years, she still didn't know her father that well. The writer wanted to instill distrust of Lina and Ray in her. The writer knew her and the store.

Stacy. Stacy knew the whole story. Had Stacy seen something, heard something? It didn't seem right. Stacy used to come across as very upfront and usually had no problem saying what lay on her mind. What happened to the Stacy she used to know? Stacy had been pretty chill for a while now. Some kind of disconnect like the night of Santi's book signing lay between them. Afterward, she hadn't seen Stacy much lately being so preoccupied with Ray and preparing for the baby. But if it was a family issue, maybe Stacy wouldn't want to interfere directly. Or maybe she would. Hence, the postcards. Someone knew her family and its interesting dynamic. Someone had a problem. Did Stacy hold some anger against her? What kind of issue lay between Stacy and Lina or Ray?

"Or me?" Kenzi thought.

How do you confront someone unknown and unseen? Someone probably watched and waited to see what she would do. Who would do this? Maybe someone in Darlene's family who felt Kenzi was going to have something with Ray that Darlene never did. Maya? But why would Maya do this after Kenzi helped her at Santi's book signing? Now her head hurt. It was just too much. She didn't want this problem. Someone wanted her to have it though. Kenzi felt faint stirrings in her middle. The baby.

"WHAT HAPPENS WHEN THEY'RE ALL ALONE TOGETHER?" was on the back of the third card featuring the Guadalupe Mountains. *What the fuck?*

She saw Lina almost everyday at the shop and their apartment. Kenzi listened carefully to each word out of Lina's mouth. She watched Lina for any sign at all, any indication of something left unsaid. Lina seemed her usual self – helpful, joking, homegirl, sister-cousin-girlfriend-like.

"Lina, anything going on?"

"Nothin' but that big belly, girl." Lina happily patted Kenzi's expanding middle.

To keep her mind off things, Kenzi rented a condominium for her mother's relocation from Dallas and arranged for utilities. Her mother planned to give a lot away to churches and missions in a sort of purge. Still, that left a lot of belongings to handle. She arranged for Ray and Dhan to drive Ray's flatbed up to Dallas to load up Betty's household and to deliver the donations. Jonathan would follow Ray and Dhan in his car, then he and his ex-wife would ride three hours down to Rollins together. Kenzi prayed her mother and father would be able to handle that amount of time alone in a small space.

Betty's relocation went without a hitch. And then Betty invited her niece, Lina, to move into the extra bedroom. Kenzi's tiny apartment exhaled. Lina decided she liked Betty's donation idea. She donated most of Jalissa's furniture to a homeless shelter retaining only personal knick-knacks and important papers. After they moved all the heavy furniture into place, Ray and Dhan left. Soon, only Kenzi, Betty, Jonathan, and Lina sat together.

Kenzi held the fourth postcard with the message, "HOW DID HE KNOW THE STORE WAS IN TROUBLE?" and a dollar sign with a big X slashed through it. This postcard featured cacti on the front. She didn't even know who the "he" referred to. Maybe Bobby Forrest, the non-customer who harassed her at the store. If Forrest sent this, then she would go to the police. But how would Forrest know about her family's past? He always focused his interest strictly on the business. It just didn't make sense.

So she sat here now with all the postcards waiting for an opening. Or maybe she would just have to speak up. They sat at the dining room table surrounded by boxes haphazardly stacked in the rooms they belonged to.

"Lina, lets unpack everything tomorrow. It's been a long day."

"Right, Aunt Betty. This stuff isn't going anywhere."

Kenzi took a breath.

"We haven't really had a family discussion. Maybe it's time although, I wish it could be under different circumstances." Kenzi slowly pulled the postcards out of her purse and laid them one by one on the table. The giant rabbit, the cowboy boots, the Guadalupe Mountains, and the cacti lay face-up. Kenzi waited.

Betty spoke. "What are these, Kenzi?"

Kenzi didn't look at anyone. She looked at the postcards. "Someone's been sending me these the past few days but not including their name." She turned the cards over. "They have messages on the back that have been somewhat upsetting and I think that's what the sender intended. I wanted you all to read them."

They read the cards silently. Then aloud.

"Do you trust her? Why? Like mother like daughter."

"Game recognize game."

"What happens when they're all alone together?"

"How did he know the store was in trouble?"

Kenzi waited. They flipped the cards from back to front and checked the postmarks. Now they knew what she knew.

Her father spoke first, "What do you think is happening?"

"I don't know, Jonathan. That's why I'm asking you all. I don't have any answers and this is strange enough that I don't want to speculate or try to handle it on my own. I'm not sure why someone would do this or... or what the motivation is."

Betty asked her, "Why didn't you say anything before now?"

"I thought, at first, it was just nothing. I thought the first one would be the only one. But then they kept arriving one after the other. Mom, I... I just... don't know." Kenzi turned to look at her sister.

"You know what the cards mean?"

Lina stared at the cards in consternation. "Yes, I think so." She bit her lip. "It means, someone thinks I'm shady and out to make trouble."

"Are you?"

"No. No." Lina shook her head and her face scrunched in a grimace. "No!"

Kenzi knew the keening wail would hit in about two seconds if she didn't head Lina off at the pass. "Who would do this?" Kenzi looked carefully and questioningly at Betty and Jonathan.

"Kenzi... *no*." Betty shook her head firmly. "I didn't send those. I would never send those. If I had any concern at all, and I don't, I would come to you and voice it to you. You are my daughter. I love you. I love you, and Lina, and Ray. I see nothing but the best in you all."

Kenzi looked at Jonathan who stared back and slowly shook his head. "No, Kenzi. Not me either." Kenzi held his gaze. After so many years of separation, she only recently got to know her father.

"What are you thinking, Jonathan?"

Jonathan moved closer to the table and looked at the back of the cards. Something stirred his memory. "I'm thinking... that someone who cared about you, really cared about you," he paused, "Would do as

Betty said. They would voice their concerns to you and not throw rocks then hide their hand. So, I'm thinking the cards come from someone who doesn't care about you or Lina or Ray."

Kenzi bit her lip. "It doesn't seem like something Dhan or Dharma would do. I thought maybe Stacy. It doesn't seem like her though. But then again, Stacy really hasn't been speaking to me much lately. Or Santi's grandmother, Maya. I just don't know." Kenzi shook her head in frustration.

Jonathan spoke again, "Kenzi, it may not come to you right away. Now that we all know what's been going on, we can put our heads together. You don't have to carry this alone."

Betty interjected, "Yes Kenzi. Don't wear yourself out dwelling on this. We're a family. We're all here and we're in this together. We'll figure it out."

Jonathan stacked the postcards together. "Do you mind if I hang on to these? Something may come to me." He frowned.

"Go ahead. I'm tired of looking at them and thinking about them." Kenzi pushed her awkward shape off the sofa tiredly. "Can one of you drop me off back to my place? I need to lie down."

"Sure honey, I'll take you. You worked so hard today helping me and Lina get settled in."

"Thanks Mom."

Betty and Kenzi left Lina and Jonathan alone.

Jonathan and Lina still sat on the sofa. "Lina, you are my daughter and I love you."

Silence. Jonathan stood up to move around the room as he spoke.

"I worry about you and Kenzi sometimes. There are people in this world who are unhappy with themselves. They go out of their way to bring that unhappiness to others so they can feel justified in their own negativity." He glanced at Lina who still sat frozen in misery.

"I know," she whispered.

Kenzi glanced at Betty as Betty drove them from Jonathan's well-to-do neighborhood towards her side of town. "Mom, do you think Lina's gone back to her old ways?"

Betty shook her head. "Not at all."

"Those postcards were freaky... and creepy." Kenzi looked out the car window. "Do you think that ever since Ray proposed to me, she might be jealous?"

Betty looked at Kenzi's profile. "What you think is more important than what I think."

"I've rolled it over and looked at it from several different directions. I didn't want to think Lina would do something strange like this. But who else? It's someone in Rollins who has a problem with me."

"Different people have different problems," Betty replied quietly.

Lina began to sob as Jonathan held her.

"Lina, its okay. Talk to me. Just talk to me. Tell me what's going on. Do you know something about the postcards?"

Lina didn't speak.

"You didn't send them."

Lina shook her head.

"But you have an idea of who did."

"The last one. It was the last one that said 'How did he know?' It was the last one."

"I think I understand." Jonathan looked grim.

"Mom, I love Ray so much. I can't believe it took this long for him to come into my life. And I love our baby. I think I understand more how you must have felt about me and Jonathan once upon a time. I refuse to allow anyone, anyone at all, to interfere with our family. I've seen, obviously, what can happen."

"Don't jump to conclusions. Wait, Kenzi. Just wait. I think Jonathan's talking with Lina. Your father... and I always respected this about him if nothing else... Your father is an extremely smart and very intelligent man. He'll likely get to the bottom of things and find a solution very soon."

"I hope so."

"Kenzi, you did the right thing in bringing those postcards to us. Don't try to handle this on your own. Think about the baby."

"The baby is exactly why I brought it up to you all. I'm a different person than I was a year ago. I feel so much stronger. I'm not afraid to confront my fear or stand up for what I know to be right and good. This baby is right and good. I'm willing to fight." She rested her hands on her stomach. "I'm not afraid."

"Do you have any doubts about Ray?"

"No. None. Ray did lay down the law on some issues. That's why it took us so long to get to the point where he asked me to marry him. We cleared everything up. Once he makes up his mind, it's made up. He will never settle for anything less than what he really wants – from anyone. And I know that he wants me. I have no doubt about that." Kenzi's voice tightened. "Someone wants to break us up."

"Do you have any doubts about Lina?"

Kenzi sighed. She didn't know about anything or anyone other than she lived to love Ray and their baby.

Lina pulled away from Jonathan.

"Jonathan, why is it always about Kenzi?"

He frowned. "What do you mean?"

"All those years. You searched for Aunt Betty and Kenzi. My mother and I were *right there*. All that time! You knew where to find us. At the very least, where to find me."

Jonathan sat down on the sofa heavily, clasping his hands in front of him.

"Yes, I knew."

"Jonathan?"

Jonathan looked up to find his daughter staring at him piteously.

"How do you think it feels to be thrown away? What is it that you think I see when I look in the mirror? A glamour girl? A beautician who's her own best customer? Some fly girl? A dime? Well, I don't." She shook her head sadly. "I see a woman whose own father didn't want her. That's what I see. Everyday, that's what I see!"

Lina collapsed on the opposite end of the sofa in angry tears. Jonathan stared back at the floor a long moment until Lina's sobs died down. He spoke quietly.

"Lina, don't blame Betty or Kenzi for this. And don't blame your mother. Blame me."

"I am blaming you!"

"And I accept that. I accept all that. I will say this, however." Jonathan turned to look at her. "I do know what it feels like to be thrown away. Any kid who goes through foster care knows. But... that's a story for another time. Just think about this for a moment. Not only did you lose your mother, Lina, your Aunt Betty lost her sister. Kenzi lost an aunt. Somehow, Lina, you're gonna have to do something extraordinary. You're gonna have to do something that an ordinary person could never do. Please try, Lina."

Lina eyed Jonathan cautiously.

"I am your father. Whether you like it or not, whether you like me or not, for better or worse, I am the father you were given. You also have a sister and an aunt. Soon, you'll have either a niece or nephew. You've been done very wrong by us – me, Betty, and Jalissa. It's true. But how long can this go on? When... do we... let it rest and call it over?" Jonathan paused a moment. "What will it be, Lina?"

Jonathan stepped out of the room to get something to drink from the kitchen allowing Lina time to consider.

"Mom, Ray's confrontation saved us. It saved our relationship. Because Ray stood up to me, I finally learned the meaning of family, trust, commitment, friendship and teamwork. If he hadn't... I don't even like to think..." Kenzi broke off a moment and stared through the car window as she and Betty sat parked in front of her apartment.

"Someone's testing me. Someone wants to kill the love I have for both Lina and for Ray. Who would do that?"

"Kenzi, no one can do that if you stay strong."

"It's hard."

"That's the way love is. If it came easy, no one would take it seriously. Kenzi, I have a lot of confidence in Jonathan. And you know coming from me that means a lot considering our history. Just... hold on. Don't give in to it."

That night, after Betty returned to her new condo, Kenzi's memory finally gave her what she'd sought for so long.

Big Afro came to see her at Mama Dee's House. Grandaddy lived there as well, but they always called it Mama Dee's. Mama Dee took care of her when The Lady dropped her off in the morning and then collected her in the evening. She loved breakfast with Mama Dee and Grandaddy. Mama Dee made grits with eggs in the mornings. Sometimes they had rice with fish or chicken leftover from the night before - a nice switch from cold cereal. It was an atmosphere of routine where she knew exactly what to expect.

Like clockwork, Mama Dee and Grandaddy argued during the meals served exactly at 8:00am and 12:00pm. One such argument launched with spectacular effect because Grandaddy couldn't decide whether he wanted tea or coffee with his breakfast. Mama Dee held the kettle of hot water dangerously close to his head while he sat placidly weighing the pros and cons out loud. Coffee? Or tea? Or coffee? Or... tea? Mama Dee shrieked her frustration at him as Kenzi stared wide-eyed. She wasn't sure if the steam clouding Mama Dee's glasses rose from the pot or Mama Dee herself. Mama Dee's face turned red. They argued over which of their friends were dead or alive. They argued over Grandaddy's not-so-hidden supply of candy and potato chips. Their arguments made her laugh. She wasn't supposed to laugh. That would be disrespectful. So she hid under the table and giggled. She wondered if they argued for the evening meal too.

They watched game shows and soap operas. Cartoons always seemed too few and too far between. When daytime television got boring, as it eventually always did, she explored the backyard and the garage and the front yard and the basement. She found old clothes to try on. She ate dirt. She looked at bugs. She practiced rolling forwards and backwards. She dug a hole. She picked up acorns and scraped them on both sides to make acorn rings. She could also make acorn earrings and pretend to be The Lady. She wasn't allowed to leave the yard.

Did The Lady know Big Afro came here? They sat side-by-side on Mama Dee's sofa in the sitting room. Big Afro looked sad. He held her hand. She showed him the acorn ring she made earlier that day. He looked at her tiny little nails. He said they needed to be cut. She'd already scratched her face once with them. He cut them for her. He cut slowly, very slowly. He talked while he cut her nails. He talked very slowly. He sounded tired and worn and sad. Mama Dee silently left the room. He told her… He said… What did he say? He said… to not forget. To not forget what? Then he left. The Lady would pick her up soon. He didn't like to see The Lady. And then she forgot. She forgot that he loved her. He told her so.

While Kenzi dreamed, Jonathan called Betty.

"Dallas Independent School District," he told her triumphantly.

"That's all I needed to know." He heard the edge of menace in Betty's voice.

"What are you going to do?" Jonathan asked curiously.

"I'll call you back." Betty hung up.

Betty called Jonathan back the next morning.

"Write this down."

About the same time Betty and Jonathan spoke that morning, Kenzi received the fifth postcard. "SURVEY SAYS SHE WANTS WHAT YOU HAVE." The foul message desecrated the Rio Grande. She called Jonathan who arrived to pick it up from her that afternoon.

"Kenzi, you can trust that we're getting closer to resolving this. I don't want you to worry." Jonathan actually sounded like father.

Kenzi replied matter-of-factly, "I'm not worried. Whoever sent these cards is desperately unhappy. That isn't my problem. Although they're trying to make it my problem, I'm not buying into it."

Jonathan cautioned her, "Also, Kenzi… don't lose faith in your sister. She's made her mistakes. She owns up to them. She loves you and the baby and she doesn't want to see either of you hurt."

Kenzi snapped her head up sharply. "She told you this?"

"We talked about it last night."

She frowned. "What did she say?"

"She confirmed what I already knew." Jonathan stopped.

"What?" Kenzi's eyes narrowed.

"I can tell you for sure tomorrow after I find out a few other things. Your mother is helping me. Can you hold out that long?"

"I'm fine, Jonathan. I just want this over." Rather, she wanted to kick someone's butt. As soon as she found out who. Jonathan had better hurry.

"If I'm right, it will be over tonight." He squeezed her hand and she squeezed his.

Lina walked down the stairs of her and Betty's condo.

"Need any help?"

Betty laughed. "You have no idea."

"Actually, I do."

As they worked from room to room, they kept up a steady stream of conversation, as if to make up for so many years of hostile silence and miscommunication. Betty made up her mind not to broach the discussion she knew Jonathan and Lina must have had while she drove Kenzi home.

Instead, "Lina, do you believe in second chances?"

"I guess." Lina slowed her unwrapping of the glassware and set the bowl down carefully on the floor next to her. "I mean, yes. I didn't before, but I do now."

"I was hoping you'd say that." Betty paused. "Does that mean," she choked a little, "that you can give me a second chance?" She steadied her voice. "I mean a second chance to be the aunt I should have been to you long ago?"

Lina's voice clutched on itself so she couldn't answer. Betty waited hopefully. Lina nodded at last and they embraced.

Kenzi worked it out in her head. Maya barely knew her. And surely, Maya understood that if she hurt Kenzi, Ray would completely close the door to Santi. He had the legal means and the moral authority. And he would do it too.

The obvious choice fell on Lina. Not Dharma. She and Dharma always talked square biz. And not Dhan. It didn't fit his personality. So that left... But even as annoying Lina could be sometimes, the notes were too stupidly obvious. Despite her promise to Jonathan, she needed to get things out in the open. She dialed the number she'd stopped dialing months ago.

"Stacy, this is Kenzi. I don't know what the deal is between us, but we used to be friends. Or so I thought. If there is something you want to tell me or think I need to know, you have my number at home and here at the shop. Use either one." She hung up. Nice and abrupt because that was the way Stacy liked it.

At six o'clock that evening, four men dressed in dark clothing drove three hours to Dallas from Rollins in a luxury car. They circled a certain block – checking for occupancy, for neighborly activity, layout – finalizing the plan. The men parked behind an abandoned building three blocks away. Their errand would take no more than twenty or thirty minutes.

Earlier that day, a certain teacher received an anonymous letter, typewritten and folded, in an office mailbox with no envelope. No outside visitors came to the school that day, the teacher checked. Someone from inside sent it. Someone who knew things the teacher had done. Someone who watched. At least that's what the letter said.

"GAME RECOGNIZE GAME. BUT TURNABOUT IS FAIR PLAY."

He looked at the letter now as he drank a second glass of wine to calm his nerves. He hadn't been in Dallas long enough to make a discreet connection so wine would have to do.

The knock at the door made him jump. The wine ran over his hand. He turned on the porch light and looked through the peep hole at a stocky, light-skinned brother in glasses with a dark suit and gold bow-tie. *You have got to be kidding. Since when did The Nation make house calls?* Cutting into Jehovah's Witness territory. He considered turning off the porch light, but the brother stared at the door with calm expectation like he planned to be there all night. Better get this over with. He would ask to be removed from the list.

He opened his door.

"Why are they sending you all out after dark?"

"We find that people are most receptive to our message at night."

"But that doesn't make any…"

The man removed the bow tie and glasses and put them in his pocket. Franklin frowned. They never took those bow ties off. Three dark shadows materialized. Franklin hadn't even glanced around to see if anyone else stood out there while he talked.

Game.

Franklin moved back to close the door. The dreadlock bastard balled up his fist in Franklin's shirt and yanked him from the doorway. Jonathan smiled, calmly reached inside the door, flicked the porch light off, then shut the door. Four men surrounded him. Franklin didn't recognize the third guy who looked like Ray – probably his brother or a cousin. The fake Muslim shifted to the back and looked out into the night blocking the figures behind him from neighborhood view.

Ray moved to hold Franklin's left arm. The brother or cousin moved to hold Franklin's right arm.

"You guys are fucked. The cops see you here all I have to say is…"

Jonathan gripped Franklin by the throat. He spoke of various things that could befall a man in the dark of night when people chose to not hear him scream. He spoke of things that could be accomplished when you know people and people owe you favors and when people had their own axes to grind anyway. Jonathan spoke of no place to run and no place to hide. Ray and the other guy tightened their grip each time Franklin struggled.

"So, that's pretty clear, isn't it, Franklin? Need a visual aid?"

Franklin frantically tried to say, "no."

"What was that?" Jonathan tightened his grip on Franklin's throat. "You do need a visual aid?"

Franklin managed to shake his head slightly within the tight confines of Jonathan's fingers.

"Good," Jonathan nodded approvingly at him and loosened his grip then rewarded Franklin with another pleasant smile and polite nod. The four made movements to turn and walk away.

Unfortunately, Franklin, for all his education, still lacked common sense enough to know when to shut up.

"Jonathan, you're fucking crazy, man. You know that? Fucking psycho with a fucked up, inbred psycho family!"

Jonathan lost patience and socked Franklin in the gut then chuckled as Franklin crumpled to the ground.

"Jonathan?" Ray asked and pinned the side of Franklin's face to the porch with a large foot. "*Jonathan* was never here. Listen good, motherfucker. If Jonathan ever is here, so will the rest of us. Feel that?"

Ray pressed his foot down harder.

"Yeah, you feel that. I got a large family, little girl. If it's not us, then it will be others like us. You have no idea. You. Just. Don't. Know." He bent closer. "Forget you ever knew Kenzi. And Lina. Focus on the future, man. And don't you *ever*... step foot... in Rollins again." Ray's voice dropped lower. "Don't come back, motherfucker."

Jonathan, still laughing, tugged at Ray. He and the other guy joined the fourth who alternately watched the encounter and the neighborhood with his arms crossed. The four men slowly strolled the three blocks back to the car, unmolested in its hiding place.

"Ah. Now, that's the Jonathan I remember," Betty smiled into the cell phone. "By the way, how did you know it was him?"

"That's right. I didn't tell you. Wait a minute! Betty, you fell in line with this whole thing and you had no idea?"

Betty sighed. "How, Jonathan?"

"At a certain faculty meeting, a certain pompous, loud-mouthed idiot doodled an even more idiotic bit of wishful thinking on a pad of paper."

"And you remembered."

"Took me a while."

"Don't make me say it."

"Say it."

"No."

"There's no one to hear but me and you."

"You already know, Jonathan."

"Betty, don't start something you won't finish."

"I won't." Betty ended the call leaving Jonathan to wonder what exactly she meant.

Kenzi and Lina also spoke on the phone.

"I'm so glad this is over. I suspected Stacy. Lina, I'm glad you came clean on everything. Since it happened earlier, I can understand it was a different person who said all that about me and the store. I just need to know that the games are over for once and for all."

"They are, Kenzi. They are. I promise you. I would never cause harm to you or the baby. I'm sorry for what happened before. I am. I really am. I feel very different about myself and other things now. I would never go there on you or Ray or the baby, ever. I wouldn't."

Kenzi spoke quietly. "I will hold you to that."

"Look, Kenzi, why don't you take a little break from the store. You know, just get some rest. Me and Aunt Betty are almost all the way unpacked. We can run the store for the next few days. How's that?"

"Are you kidding? Please do!" Kenzi laughed. "Thanks Lina. Thanks for standing up for what's real."

"Yeah, sis. Speaking of that, have you noticed that we make better sisters than cousins?"

"Mmm, yeah."

"So let's ride this sister-thing then. See where it takes us."

"Okay," Kenzi laughed. "Let's."

Chapter 19

The Revelations

Together, Dharma and Lina threw an intimate, low-key bridal and baby shower for Kenzi. Betty, Lydia, Santi, and a few of Dharma's female cousins attended.

Betty raised her glass for a toast.

"Kenzi, I love you. You are my wonderful daughter and I am so proud of you. You are the best thing that ever happened in my life. You are a beautiful woman and I admire you so much. Mama Dee and Grandaddy and Jalissa, I know, are smiling down on you. I am so happy to have Ray as my son and I cannot wait to see my grandchild. Then you'll understand what all those phone calls were about!"

Kenzi, couldn't fight the tears as the toasts continued.

"Kenzi, you've taught me how to believe in myself and to follow my dreams. You've been a good role model to me and you've inspired me to do the work to meet my own goals in life. I love you and I want to congratulate you on finding true happiness in life. You're a good sister to me." Kenzi crossed the room to hug Lina tightly. Santi hugged them both.

"I hope you're always my mommy, Kenzi! And you're always Aunt Li Li!"

Kenzi sobbed openly now and someone handed her a tissue and stroked her back. She couldn't even see for the tears in her eyes.

Dharma spoke up next. "Kenzi, Ray is my older brother and I love him. I've seen him hurt and in pain. I want to tell you that I've prayed for his happiness for a long time. When you walked into my restaurant a year ago and I saw the way he looked at you, I knew there was going to be a change in all our lives. I love you like a sister already. Even Aunt T told me you seemed ready-made for the Grants."

Kenzi closed her eyes. She missed the Grant family's matriarch.

Dharma continued, "I love you, Kenzi. I love you for being the person you are and for loving my brother the way he deserves to be loved."

The emotion overtook them all. Not a dry eye remained in the room by the time Miss Lydia added her own words.

"I want to thank all of you for including me in on the family and for being good neighbors. Since Harold died, it's been a long row to hoe, but I don't feel so alone anymore. Kenzi, your work with Kinfolk Books has been a blessing to the community. You brought so many people together. More than you may realize. I want to congratulate you on your engagement to Ray. He's a good man and you're a good woman. You'll make an excellent mama. So congratulations and I wish you continued success with everything!"

Another round of hugs and conversation followed. Kenzi felt a momentary pang when she thought of Stacy's absence. Her former friend met Dharma and Lina's invitation with silence. She also wondered whether Maya, Santi's grandmother should have been invited. But that was out of her hands. She and David had more than pushed their luck with the Grants, but any further outreach had to come from either Ray or Dharma. But even Dharma knew the limits to Ray's understanding and patience.

Dharma handed Kenzi a large bag. "Kenzi, this is from me and Miss Betty. The vitamins and special teas are to keep you healthy and I even included some foods for you to eat."

Betty chimed in, "And there's also coconut oil and shea butter that you can rub into her skin to prevent stretch marks."

Kenzi grimaced, remembering her weight-on, weight-off college years. "Thanks Mom, and thank you too, Dharma."

Betty added, "Tell Ray plenty of rest and a lot of massage will make your pregnancy go smoothly."

Dharma found the top layer of the last quilt Aunt Tilly started but had grown too sick to finish. Apparently, Aunt Tilly methodically collected a piece of old clothing from Dhan, Ray, Dharma, Reginald, Vasanti, Santi, Reggie, Davey, David, and herself. They noticed a strange fabric that no one recognized. A strange sort of yellow-green rayon fabric turned bluish in spots with swirls of purple-red paisley here and there. Dharma finished the quilt and showed it to her now. It would hang in the living room of the Grant homestead as a wedding present from Aunt Tilly. Kenzi recognized the pieces from her shirt.

Dharma laughed. "Good ole Jackson! He wasn't about to let you get away from us."

"Dharma, do you think Miss Tilly knew even then that Ray and me would be together?"

"Maybe. Aunt Tilly always had her own way of getting things done."

Under the cover of light jazz and more talking, Lina and Kenzi drifted towards Dharma's kitchen.

"Lina that was beautiful what you said in there."

"I'm glad that I was able to say it. Life has definitely taken a change for the better."

"The whole Franklin thing, it's all over. He doesn't deserve any more of our time or energy."

"No he doesn't. Thank God we both came to our senses!"

Lina ran her hands across her hair. "Kenzi, I wanted ask you about going natural. I'm going to stop perming my hair. I already started. See?" She lifted her bangs and Kenzi leaned close to see tight, reddish brown curls hiding below the straightened orange mass.

"Good! Welcome to the club, girl. Why pay someone for the privilege of putting battery acid and drain cleaner on your scalp and hair? Me and Miss Tilly had a long conversation about that about a year ago. A lot of billion dollar corporations would go under if black women ever recovered their self-esteem."

"Shut 'em down!"

"I know, right? Dharma gave me some tips on conditioning using natural products." Kenzi smiled to herself remembering how that lazy winter afternoon of beauty treatments led to her and Ray's first night together.

Lina's hand traveled again to her hair. "I used to love that my hair was long and straight, but it feels kind of thin and brittle now."

Thin and brittle like her old self. Time for new beginnings and new mindsets. Time to look further within herself.

"I'd like for the roots of my hair to see sunlight without being punished for being curly."

"Go for it."

"You know what? A few days ago, I stopped in the beauty supply store to pick up some hair products. It's Korean-owned. And it's the only one in town that carries a large inventory of products for black hair."

"Mmm. I don't think I've ever been in there. I find almost everything I need at the organic foods store or from Dharma."

"Well, I also wanted to tape a flyer advertising my services as a hairdresser in their door. I see a lot of other beauty salons advertising themselves there. So I opened the door to walk in and when I did, I saw something so crazy and strange."

"Purple glitter?" Kenzi laughed.

"Stranger than that. The owner or manager, whoever, was behind the counter. And about fifteen women stood in front of the counter kind of bunched up. All along the back wall were rows and rows of weaves and wigs and falls and ponytails - silky, wavy, and curly. And then when I looked at the women, really looked at them, I saw why they were bunched at the counter. All of them, every single one, wore weaves of various colors and textures that didn't match their own. Middle class, low-income, old and young, they were all wearing other people's hair. But that's not the worst part. The owner of the store was dangling a straight fall of yellow hair, in front of the group. Like he was Santa Clause or something. He held the hair just out of their reach and kept repeating, 'thirty dollars.' The women were jumping up and down trying to clutch the hair almost as if they were desperate. My stomach turned."

"Mine would have too. I wonder if I walked in there with my big afro what would he think."

"No sale."

"Exactly."

"I talked to the owner after the excitement over the ponytail died down. I asked him could I put up my flyer and he said 'Yes.' Then, to be fair, I offered to put up a flyer from his store at the salon. He told me that he didn't advertise. He never had to. Once they put up the pictures of black women with straight perms in the window, the customers flocked in and never stopped, which was pretty evident from what I saw."

"That sounds about right, unfortunately."

"It's past time for me to be who I really am."

"You have beautiful hair."

Dhan threw Ray an equally low-key bachelor party, inviting Jonathan, David, a few of their male cousins and neighbors, and Mr. Oliver. Reggie and Davey romped in another room with Jackson. The older men sipped blackberry wine and peach wine, played cards and dominoes, ate the pizzas Dhan picked up from town, and told stories that ended in uproarious laughter. All to a classic soul and blues soundtrack. While the other men talked about fast women and girlfriends and wives and ex-wives, Ray and Dhan talked about Maya.

"She told me that Santi has a cousin a year younger attending the same school. Santi probably knows him. She just doesn't know he's her cousin."

"Serious?"

"His name is Quintavion."

"Damn!" Dhan laughed aloud and shot Ray a sidelong look. "That boy is gonna need all the help he can get!"

"His father is Darlene's younger brother. He's in jail now. I only met him once. I barely remember him. But he was a pretty low character back then and it seems like it went downhill from there. Maya wants Santi to meet, you know, like *really* meet, her cousin so they can know each other on that level."

"So what did you say?"

But just then, Jonathan pulled Ray aside for a heart-to-heart conversation that Ray sort of expected would be coming. They both stared into the night from the back door of the kitchen that opened to Aunt Tilly's herb garden.

"Well, Ray, looks like you're going to get yourself a whole new family soon."

"Looking forward to it, sir."

"You strike me as the sort of man who takes family seriously."

Ray smiled briefly. "Without my family, I wouldn't be who I am today."

"You make a good point. Sometimes, a man won't realize that until it's too late." Jonathan thought about his daughters. "But it seems like you learned that early on."

Ray leaned against the door frame. "My father taught me that. He told me a lot about life and how to live it before he died. I never forgot."

"Military man, hunh?"

"Yeah. He paid his dues. Settled down." Ray reminisced. "He was stern and wasn't the kind of guy who smiled a lot. But he took care of business. I always respected that about him. He made sure we knew what was what and who was who. I miss him. I wish he could see how we all turned out."

"That must have been a job for you being the oldest."

"Yeah." Ray nodded. "It was. It is," he finished with a laugh.

"Well, I think he would be proud and so should you. You, Dharma, and Dhan have done very well for yourselves. I was just thinking that if Kenzi married, it would be good for her to marry into a family that had a sensible mindset towards life. I know you're a man who'll give her the love and care she needs and deserves." Jonathan sighed. "And I know our new grandchild won't experience what she did."

Ray understood that Jonathan stated both a confession and a question. He turned a steady gaze to the older man.

"Kenzi is the only woman I ever would marry in my life. If she hadn't walked into Organic Soul, I would be alone the rest of my days. I love her. I don't even want to think about life without her. It took us a while to get past some things in life that hurt us both. But we made it. My daughter loves Kenzi. And Kenzi loves Santi. I don't know if Santi needed a mother more than Kenzi needed a daughter or if it was the other way around. But we fit together. All of us. And I'm so happy about the baby. I think Kenzi will be happy with me. I know that I'm happy with her." Ray chuckled. "She told me she was woman-enough and a whole lot more for me. And I believe her. She said she had what it takes to be a wife to me and mother to our children."

"She is." Jonathan agreed. "She does."

Jonathan continued ruefully, "I haven't been the best father to Kenzi, you know. Years go by and time slips away. I don't know who missed out more, me or Kenzi, during the time we were apart. Regardless, I'm here now. I've been given a second chance and I'm determined to see that Kenzi gets what she deserves – the very best that life has to offer. Despite all of what happened within our family, Kenzi turned out well. Her mother… did a fine job. It seems as though life has given us all a second chance to do things the right way this time around."

Ray casually gazed out into the night.

"Maybe a second chance for you and Miss Betty too?"

The cicadas dramatically paused their symphony of screams. Breathless, they waited for Jonathan to confess what happened under the pecan trees that day…

"Betty, it's still there. It's always going to be there between us. You feel it too, don't you?"

Betty tried to laugh and gave up the charade.

"I feel… something." She pulled away from her ex-husband. "But, you have to agree, we're better as friends than husband and wife, Jonathan. No matter how much we feel… that we belong together or even how much people keep saying we look right standing next to one another, there's just… too much water under the bridge."

"I know. I know." Too much pain. Too many words spoken in anger. Too many ghosts and shadows from the past. Jonathan tightened his jaw. "We ruined it, Betty."

Like the sun and the moon criss-crossing the skies above the Earth, they each remained committed to their prospective paths. Bound by the rules of Mother Nature to provide life and sustenance, but never allowed to come too close to one another. That disaster would destroy them and anyone caught within the gravitational pull.

Jonathan shook his head. "We really beat each other into the dirt, didn't we?"

"We did… just that. And Kenzi and Lina are only just now recovering from it. Which is more a credit to them than us."

"Right."

"Well. It's like this. History keeps us apart, but it also draws us together. Like you said, it's always going to be there. We're forever a part of each other's lives, Jonathan. We'll just have to accept it."

"Can't we... repair the damage we did - to each other and Kenzi and Lina?"

"We owe that much to Jalissa. Her death... shouldn't be the end of the story. Kenzi's child and Lina's future children have the right to grow up happily and healthily. We'll do what we can."

"Ray... I think... Betty and my time has come and gone," Jonathan replied with a sad smile. The two men silently looked out into the night as the cicadas struck up the cue and continued their humming.

Kenzi and Betty had a mother-to-daughter chat the morning of the wedding.

"Jonathan started a trust fund for Santi and Matilda. He wanted to make sure they had a chance for higher education."

"Really? Oh my God, Mom! Ray and I are both so heavily invested in the bookstore and the restaurant and the homestead. We kind of wondered if we would be able to save enough. I'll have to thank Jonathan."

"Well, actually, you're not supposed to know. He doesn't want you to feel obligated. Kenzi... he's... doing his best to make up for... all those years. I told him, we all need to move on. We both made some bad decisions. But it's time to look forward."

Betty and Kenzi looked at each other in the mirror as Betty fiddled with Kenzi's hair.

"Still, you know, he's proud as some men are. He wants to do right. It means a lot to him. He's... hoping to have a place in the family."

"Mom, he doesn't have to buy his way in. I told him that."

"Maybe you should show him." Betty swiftly changed the subject as she smoothed down Kenzi's hair. "Let me get this part over here."

"Changing the subject." Kenzi smiled mischievously. "So, I guess I shouldn't ask what happened when you and Jonathan disappeared that afternoon we were picking pecans."

"Well, Kenzi, when you get to be my and your father's age, you won't need to ask."

Kenzi laughed. "That's your way of telling me to stay out of grown folks business."

"Pretty much."

"But I *am* grown."

"Not *that* grown."

"*Mother!*"

They both laughed.

They held the small wedding at Kinfolk Books one Sunday afternoon. Golden light streamed through the glass front and bathed them all in its soft glow. Just the immediate family witnessed the ceremony. Dharma and her twins, Reggie and Davey, and her husband David sat together. Dhan and Lina sat together. Betty and Jonathan completed the party on either side of Santi.

After many tears shed by the women and shoulder claps by the men, they took photographs of each other and headed across the street. Many in the community attended the reception held at Organic Soul. Bookstore customers, authors, and artists along with Aunt Tilly's church colleagues mixed and mingled with the various social and political and religious groups in the community as well as the enormous Grant extended family.

Dhan laughed it up with Lina at the refreshment table. "I'm glad to see Lina's turned over a new leaf," Ray observed

Kenzi smiled as they danced. "She's reaching out more. I think Dhan brings out her good side."

"Well, that's why family's so important. She deserves a second chance."

"Guess what? She said she's been inspired by my example. She's working on a business plan to open a booth in a corner of the bookstore to sell natural soaps, oils, candles, and hair care products. Incense and things like that. I'm so glad. I'm gonna discuss the possibility of buying the building with her. I'll have to speak with Tex about drawing up the papers…" She shook herself. "Wait a minute. What am I doing?"

"That's just what I was just wondering. No talking shop at our wedding. Or the honeymoon!"

"Right. That's for Betty and Lina to worry about until we get back," Kenzi laughed.

"And Dhan and David are gonna hold it down for me at the restaurant."

Kenzi murmured bemusedly, "I did ask Lina what she would name a baby if she had one."

"Kenzi," Ray warned. Then, "So what did she say?"

"Daynelle if it's a girl and Daniel if it's a boy."

Kenzi looked again at her sister smiling and laughing with Ray's brother. She raised her eyebrows. She'd wondered a few times whether any spark existed between Lina and Dhan – her younger sister and new brother-in-law.

Ray and Kenzi couldn't overhear Dhan's whispered declaration, "I'm going to relocate to Houston permanently and open my own consulting business.

And Lina's excited, "Oh Dhan! That's wonderful!"

Dhan leaned in close, "It means selling my part of Organic Soul and pulling out. I don't know how Ray and Dharma will take it."

Lina leaned in as well as their whispers continued.

"Not a word, Kenzi. Not one word," laughed Ray twirling her away. "Tonight is for us!" He gripped her closer and she caught her breath. "Now that's better."

Still Kenzi couldn't help noticing her mother sitting with Jonathan Farrell while they chatted about, *what* she wondered.

"So Jonathan, what have you learned from that big, bad world out there?"

"Maybe I'll show you."

"Something I don't already know? You silly man."

"Snow on the roof, fire down below. You know how it is."

"I know how it used to be."

"Still is."

"Well, if I don't know, you might actually get me drunk enough to want to find out."

"Ah, now that's the sweet, darling Betty I've been dreaming about."

The laughed and dirty-talked as he finally persuaded her to get up and boogie on the dance floor with him.

Kenzi smiled at them. Betty and Jonathan stepped so easily into their new roles as matriarch and patriarch of both the Grant and Malton families.

Dharma danced with David and waved to Kenzi across the room.

"Are you and Ray cool?"

"He told me I paid for my, ah, cutting in his lane."

"Ray and Kenzi have completely exhausted me."

"Another job well done, Dharma. Which just leaves me, babe."

"And what do you need done?"

"Oh Dharma," David kissed his wife passionately. "Dharma…"

"Oh David, I love you." Dharma teared up. Later that evening, when they were alone she would finally announce another addition to the Gardner family. But this day belonged to Kenzi and Ray.

A radiant Miss Lydia and genial Mr. Oliver sat together and sipped blackberry wine.

"Oliver. You ever gonna tell me who sent that letter to the paper?"

"It was anonymous, Miss Lydia. Who knows?"

"I almost feel sorry for the dirty bastard. Almost, but not quite."

"Well, you can only buy so much cold medicine before you're suspected. He could have burned his house down and taken out a whole block. And God help him if he was his own customer."

"So after he ran through Harold's money, he tried to finance his comic book business with crystal meth."

Kenzi watched as Deacon Waverly walked up to their table. Miss Lydia had two beaus!

"The newspaper said allegedly, Miss Lydia" Deacon Waverly corrected.

"Deacon, you could see the nasty in his eyes a hundred feet away. But it explains why he was so interested in her bookstore."

Mr. Oliver shrugged. "They found a customer list leading to Dallas. Allegedly."

Lydia didn't really feel sorry. "Well, he dirtied himself up somethin' awful this time. Let's see his lawyer get him out of that."

When Stacy walked into the restaurant alone, Kenzi noticed her entrance immediately and gave a cautious nod. Stacy never returned her last phone message and ignored the bridal shower invitation. Kenzi decided that pretty much told her all she needed to know about their friendship. However, Stacy spotted her and headed over.

Ray hugged her.

"Hi Stacy. Good to see you again."

"Congratulations Ray, Kenzi."

Kenzi silently nodded.

Ray spoke up again. "Thank you, Stacy. But you know what? It's a party here tonight. Make sure you enjoy yourself, okay?"

They looked at Santi dancing with her twin cousins and then Dhan who grabbed her by the hands and whirled her around until her feet left the floor while she screamed and giggled.

Ray turned to his new wife. "Kenzi, I owe Santi a dance. Something to do with a combination of skipping and the hand jive. I don't know. Maya can help me out, I'm sure."

They all laughed as Ray ran over to his daughter who jumped around with Maya and Quintavion. While not invited to the bridal shower or the wedding itself, Ray decided, after much discussion, that the wedding reception would be ideal for Santi to meet her grandmother again after so many years. After seeing how this first meeting went, supervised visits with Ray present might follow. Maya seemed to be making the most of Ray's thawing. Kenzi, still smiling, turned back to Stacy.

"So. It's been a while."

"I'm relocating to New York after the New Year." Stacy went on to say something involving her longed-for art gallery and a gentleman with deep pockets. Kenzi never did completely understand, but that didn't matter.

"I'm happy for you Stacy. It sounds like your dreams are coming true." Kenzi paused. "Stacy, even though now's maybe not the right time, I'd like to know why things got so chill between us all of a sudden. No explanation or anything. I mean, it's like there's this wall or something and you couldn't or wouldn't hear me."

"I know, Kenzi. I can't argue with you on that." Stacy waved to Ray who waved back as he danced with Santi.

"No, you can't," Kenzi agreed matter-of-factly. "What happened, Stacy?" She persisted, "I mean, tell me *something*."

Stacy raised her eyebrows in surprise. The old Kenzi would have said, "Don't worry about it," and smoothed it over.

Stacy sighed. "Something just crept up in me. Earlier when the classes were scrapped, I felt so... just... betrayed. Like something that I truly loved was snatched from me. It was unsettling and I felt maybe you just..." Stacy paused.

"I just what?"

"Maybe you just weren't serious enough or capable enough to handle the program. I think I didn't trust you."

"I see." Kenzi thought that over for a moment. "But we got back on our feet. Not even very long after. You saw that yourself. You were there." Kenzi waited a beat then persisted again. "So what was it really?"

"I know. I still felt unsettled about it. And kind of resentful. And then I felt guilty about that too. You called all the shots. I just wasn't where I thought I should be. Not getting to the places I wanted to go."

Kenzi frowned.

"I almost can't believe what I'm hearing."

"Look around you, Kenzi." Stacy gestured to the room full of excited chatter and laughter. "You have everything. A growing business, friends, family, a baby. And best of all, a complete hunk of a man to slay dragons for you. You can't believe what you're hearing. I can't believe you don't realize what you have."

"That's where you're wrong, Stacy." Kenzi faced her squarely. "I do realize. I realize more than anyone else what I have because I worked hard to achieve it and maintain it and keep it. There's nothing saying you can't do the same, you know."

"Kenzi, I wish you only the best."

"Thank you, Stacy. And I wish you well in New York. I will never forget what you've done for the bookstore. Look, stay in touch with us down here, okay? There are people here in Rollins who support you and want to know that you're doing well in the glamorous life."

"I will, Kenzi. I promise."

They hugged and Stacy moved away to circulate. Kenzi wondered if she would ever hear from Stacy again. But then, it didn't matter. Where once she drifted alone, the love of the family and community she could count on surrounded her today.

Later that evening she did it. She held Jonathan's hands in her own and called him... 'Daddy' the way she did when they watched their television shows together. His hazel eyes widened. Her own eyes, so like his, filled with tears. He hugged her tightly to him as she cried.

Chapter 20

Sri Lanka

"Are you ready to see them?"

"May as well. Tickets to Sri Lanka don't come cheap." Ray tried to joke. "I wonder what they'll think of me, of us?"

The day after their arrival to the island nation, Ray and Kenzi enjoyed the excitement of the bazaars. They visited museums and strolled through gardens. They took many pictures of the tree-lined streets with elegant houses in one of Colombo's most fashionable neighborhoods. Tomorrow, they planned to visit the city's mosques, temples, shrines, and holy places that represented the different religions in Sri Lanka. They would also tour the University of Colombo campus. They planned to return to Texas in one week – just in time to spend the December holidays with the family. But first, they would have to get through tonight.

"My mother never said much about her family. They stopped communicating after she married my father. She pretty much focused on us. I remember only one time she talked about the tea plantation. She said she worked there with her brothers and sisters. But I never could get her to talk about it again. She became an American and that's how she raised us, for the most part. I don't know what we're gonna find here, Kenzi."

"Well, so far, I'm delighted with your mother's homeland."

"That was good of Jonathan to pay for the trip."

"He's really enjoying the Big Daddy role. I guess I am too."

"Well, I like being Big Daddy too." He patted Kenzi's stomach making her laugh. Ray took her hand and they continued their slow walk back through the bazaar.

"Too bad my mother's parents already passed on. But at least we'll see my aunts and uncles and cousins here. Pretty clever of Dhan to track down the ones studying in the States."

"At least we know from them that most of your relatives moved to Colombo. And we'll see them tonight at the restaurant."

"They want to hear all about my mother's life in Texas before she died. I guess with this generation, or the passage of time, the hostility's died down. I wonder if I'll recognize any of them from my mother's photos. They didn't send any new ones. Look, Kenzi," he squeezed her hand, "if any of them act crazy, we're just going to leave, okay? We'll step out and enjoy the rest of Colombo and feed you all this food and..."

Kenzi stopped to look at him.

"Ray, regardless of what anyone thinks, you have a wife and family that loves you and will always love you until the end of time," she declared, rubbing her belly full of the soon-to-arrive Matilda. "Think of Santi. She's already planning to twist and braid her little sister's hair like mine and Dharma's. She's drawing the little outfits Matilda will wear. Do you know what? I saw her practicing on her dolls picking out books to read. We love you and each other no matter what."

Tonight they would email Santi the pictures they took with the digital camera they received as a wedding gift from Dhan.

"You're right." Ray kissed her and they continued walking.

Ray leaned over.

"Hey there, Matilda!"

"I think Matilda's excited."

So much happened the last year and a half. Two funerals. A graduation. A wedding. Various birthdays had come and gone. Dharma's pregnancy. And now, the birth of her own child approached. All marked the passage of time and a common humanity.

"Well, how could Matilda not be excited? She has the greatest mother in the world." Ray kisses Kenzi. "And I have the greatest wife. I love you, Kenzi."

"And the world's greatest father. I love you too, Ray. You mean so much to me."

Her eyes held that eerie glow in the early afternoon sun. At those moments, Ray wanted to stop the world so he could marvel at her beauty forever. He took the tiger's eye and hyacinth jewelry from the box of memories and wrapped them in a leather pouch he kept in his overnight bag. He watched it carefully make its way across the conveyor belts of various security checkpoints along with the letters and photos that served as his mother's only link to her past life in Sri Lanka.

The humidity stirred by Sri Lanka's northeast trade winds encouraged Kenzi to wear her beautiful, wild mane of soft, cottony hair in coiled rope twists that hung several inches past her shoulders matching his locs that had grown towards his waist. The sheeny ropes framed her face beautifully. Sheba, the African queen with brown skin and golden eyes that glowed like jewels. She mentioned in passing that she was thinking about allowing her hair to loc after Matilda's birth.

He would put each piece of jewelry on her himself, slowly, lovingly. He still remembered that night of fantasy after he met Kenzi for the first time. He remembered the night of orange silk love. But fantasies did not compare to the alive woman standing by his side with love in her eyes.

Kenzi felt so right in his life. Certainly neither of them suffered from perfection. But they were the right man and the right woman at the right place. And finally, the right time.

Do you Raman Grant take this woman…

Do you Mackenzie Malton take this man…

They both answered "yes" fervently and held each others hands tightly. If they would be together, then they would be together forever. Nothing less would do.

"Well, I'm going to finally greet the people who gave us that "other" look. Find some answers, fill in the blanks of my mother's early life, and discover all of who I am."

"I'll be by right by your side."

"You and Matilda."

"Me and Matilda."

He kissed Kenzi and she leaned against him.

"Well, as for me, Ray, I've finally found my place in the world, the place I really belong. I've searched for it all my life."

"And?"

"I'm an entrepreneur and businesswoman. I'm a member of my community. Best of all, I'm a mother, a daughter, a sister, a friend."

"And?" Ray growled.

"And what?" she asked innocently.

"Kenzi..." He tugged her hair.

"And your woman and your wife forever."

Calm flowed through her as she stood with Ray while their baby moved inside her. She threw her shoulders back, lifted her head high, and smiled for another kiss.

"Bring it home to mama, babe."

His large arms enveloped her.

Acknowledgements

Kenzi developed from a desire to tell a relatively realistic romance. Relatively realistic because it is, after all, a complete fiction. But realistic all the same because it includes friends, family, work, race, ethnicity, morality, loyalty, disloyalty, jealousy, courage, fear, varying images of inner and outter beauty, hope, love, and tenderness. In addition, it includes social and cultural commentary. What I didn't see in many of the popular mass-market romance lines concerning the complex world and complex people of African ancestry, I wanted to include in *Kenzi*. Coming from a large family myself, it was important to me to show that no one is perfectly good or perfectly bad. Even "good" people have bad thoughts. And sometimes "bad" people come through when they are needed most of all. Though we all have our strengths and weaknesses, what keeps us bonded is love. For this reason, I wish to acknowledge the four people who were the strongest symbols of family in my life. And though I miss Queen, Theodore, Mamie, and Quaker, they are with me always. Grandparents are special people. I consider myself very blessed to have known and loved all four of my grandparents into adulthood. I spent time talking and listening and learning and growing with them as a child, a teen, and a young adult. They taught me so much about the world and where I belong in that world. I couldn't possibly write all that wisdom down, but I feel it guiding me even now. And for this reason, I'm grateful for the time I was allowed with them.

Reach Just A Little Further

I see you glance away and I drop my eyes
Chance again, you're watching me
But now I'm not surprised

Because then I feel you fall to me
A little hesitant when you take my hand
I feel my heart opening when I hear you speak

I want to hear the vibrating sound
I wonder if it could be what
I've been listening to all my life

When will you get to where I am?
Reach out you're almost there
We have the day before tomorrow

www.ingramcontent.com/pod-product-compliance
Lightning Source LLC
Chambersburg PA
CBHW050016180626
46810CB00002B/451